I0612889

©2025 Kat Drennan All rights reserved.

No part of this publication may be reproduced, distributed, or transmitted in any form or by any means, including photocopying, recording, or other electronic or mechanical methods, without the prior written permission of the publisher, except in the case of brief quotations embodied in critical reviews and certain other noncommercial uses permitted by copyright law.

This is a work of fiction. Names, characters, places and incidents are either products of the author's imagination or are used fictitiously. Any resemblance to actual events or locales or persons living or dead is entirely coincidental.

ISBN: 979-8-9994527-3-3
Publisher: KC Publications, Ojai, California

MONARCH
The First Migration

Kat Drennan

contents

Map of Dannais Valley

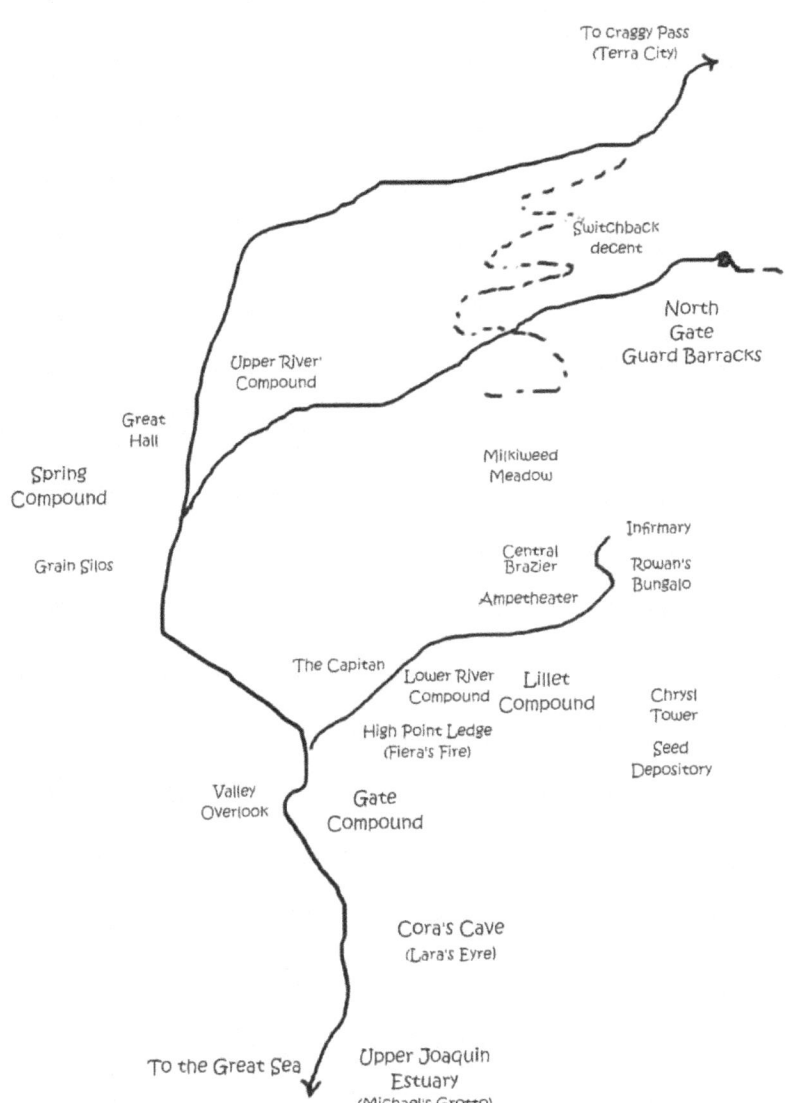

To Craggy Pass
(Terra City)

Switchback
decent

North
Gate
Guard Barracks

Upper River
Compound

Great
Hall

Spring
Compound

Milkweed
Meadow

Infirmary

Grain Silos

Central
Brazier

Rowan's
Bungalo

Ampetheater

The Capitan

Lower River
Compound

Lillet
Compound

Chrysl
Tower

High Point Ledge
(Fiera's Fire)

Seed
Depository

Valley
Overlook

Gate
Compound

Cora's Cave
(Lara's Eyre)

To the Great Sea

Upper Joaquin
Estuary
(Michael's Grotto)

part one

LARA

When my great grandmother first looked out on our world, she had only her benevolent spirit and unselfish will to guide her. She knew nothing of our origins and very little of her own. With every fragment of her being,
she refused to believe the legends.
Yet when Lara de Nyphalaidae Homo Sapiens first stepped out onto the rocky precipice that would become her new home and felt the beacon call, she began a journey that would ultimately lead around the world and back to this very spot. Without her, the first true migration would never have taken place, and I would not be able to tell you this story from such a mighty stronghold of Monarch spirit as
I do today.

--Lara de Nyphalaidae III, Opening address to the nymphlings at Lara's Eyre, 100th anniversary of the First Migration to Rubicon

CHAPTER 1 - THE HOMECOMING
Northern California Coast – Present Day

Lara lifted the glider canopy, balanced it over her head, and adjusted her angle of attack—nose down and slightly to the right—a move that went against all reason and would launch her directly into the cliff. She pulled in a breath between clenched teeth. A prickle of uncertainty zipped up her spine, every cell shrieking against an act logic told her would surely end in disaster.

Okay. Okay.

No sense going off halfcocked. She'd made this jump a hundred times and should be used to it. So, she'd had a bit of nausea this morning. She felt fine now. And who was to say with her schedule when she'd have a chance to fly again in good weather?

She shook out her shoulders. *Relax. Give it a minute, then go.*

She reset her footing, let out her breath, and cast her gaze once again around her near space. Fragrant eucalyptus trees flanked the precipice, their sickle-shaped leaves quivered with visiting Monarchs. Wings overlapping like petals on tropical blooms, the black and gold butterflies would soon break away to follow their instincts for thousands more miles—generation after generation—to preserve the species.

She only needed to lift off this ledge and fly a half an hour to shake off the woes of the world. "If they can do it, you can, girl. So, let's do this."

Setting her sights on the distant seam between the blue green of the Pacific Ocean and storm clouds crouching on the horizon, Lara huffed in two, three more breaths, and with a last look over her shoulder at the gathering monarchs, dove headfirst over the edge.

The giant glider dipped and speared toward the cliff for several heartbeats before its wings predictably snapped taut in the updraft, pulled her clear of the rock face, and spiraled her out over the waves in a wide, breathtaking arc. Her lighthouse home grew smaller and smaller as she circled higher. Pushing out on the hand bar, she shifted her body to leverage wind currents ancient as the first vertebrates that crawled out of the sea on wobbly legs.

Lara merged into a different reality. She was the pivot point, stationary, an anchor in the sky on which everything else turned. Stabilized in the updraft, she slipped first one foot and then the other into the nylon boot and pushed into prone position. In her fabric cocoon, she glided effortlessly, surveying her world, leaving rational thought behind, if only for a little while. Euphoria surged within her—a shift of the body, a change in angle, and she was free, like the Monarchs, answering only to the wind. Gliding fed her fantasy, nourished her soul. She was a free-flying gull—circling, diving, alert.

On her next pass over the lighthouse, a movement caught her eye. Someone waved from the brass railing at the top of the tower.

Michael. Home two days early?

His hands cupped around a shout. She couldn't hear over the wind, the distance, and the squeaks and bumps of the canopy, but it didn't matter. Just the sight of him warmed her to the core. A welcome surprise. She was dreading his upcoming trip to Australia, would miss him terribly. Now his early arrival from Hawaii said he was thinking about her, too. She couldn't wait to get her arms around him and... *whoops!*

A sharp shift in the wind sent her into a wobbly dip, forcing her attention back to soaring. *Focus, Lara. No need to rush.* He would know she'd complete her pattern before coming down.

She widened the arc, gliding on the updraft, and passed once again over the edge of the cliff, higher this time, the great crescent of Wing Bay stretched before her, the crashing waves hushed by distance, the landscape caught in a generous watercolor stroke.

Again, a sudden movement caught her attention, this time close to the shoreline. A dusty cloud of orange rose steadily from the sand. She fought the urge to tip away, curiosity taking over. As the edges of the cloud drew near, the mass broke up into distinct individuals, and she was suddenly enveloped by fluttering wings. Thousands of them, flickering, gliding, reflecting the sun. *Ahhhh...*

The monarchs. *Danaus Plexippus.* After the Greek goddess Danaë who came to Zeus as a shower of gold. A native of the California coast, Lara had studied the monarchs in school, had them perch on her fingertips, watched their chrysalises form on stalks of milkweed.

She had watched them rise from the beach many times, but she'd never met them in their own element. Now they shimmered about her, their tawny wings laced in black filigree, their undersides dusty, opalescent white. Hundreds of them landed on her now, on the canopy, and all along its riggings, hitching a free ride. A thousand tiny wings under one giant one, and for a blink in time, she was part of their migration. And then, as if by one command, they lifted away and continued on their own, a mass of individuals reformed as a living cloud, driven by instinct programmed in their DNA.

She adjusted her angle for her last high pass, skin still tingling with the essence of fluttering wings. What would a little undeniable instinct do for humans? What if we only lived one or two seasons? Would life feel more precious? Would we take less for granted? Would we seek less fortune and more light?

Humans? Not likely. Which was why she escaped to the sky as often as she could.

She stayed aloft, watching the monarchs waft out of sight, then circled back low. If she didn't return soon, the wind would be too strong for a safe landing on the cliffs. And, then there was Michael.

How, of all the women in San Francisco—in the world, for that matter—did she have the luck to end up with the man of her dreams? She was serious. Practical. Realistic. And he was… a waterman. A carpenter— good with his hands—but foremost a waterman.

One of surfing's elite.

Lara was skittery near the water, more at home in the sky. Michael lived day-to-day; she had a career. He was at home anyplace on earth; she was grounded at this northern California lighthouse, the only true home she had ever known.

Other men had waltzed through her life with eyes that haunted and lips that warmed, but none had taken her heart and set her thinking about the long term. It was the first time since she'd been a dream-struck teenager she longed for someone who would be there for all the dances, even the last one.

A few feet off the ground, she turned her head toward the lighthouse in anticipation of seeing him. Her feet hit hard, knocking her off balance. The big wing dragged her along for twenty feet or so until she got control of it and laid it down. If there was one thing she knew about landing in a strong head wind, it was that landing should be the *only* thing on your mind when you did it. She got up and brushed herself off, removed the cross bar, stowed the glider on its dolly, and dragged it toward the base of the tower.

Michael bolted from the door at a run and caught up with her near the garage. "Rough landing!"

Lara laughed and threw her arms around his neck. "I was a little distracted. When'd you get in?"

He scooped her up, twirled her around, and slipped his arm around her waist as they walked toward the lighthouse. "Called from the airport. Your voicemail was full."

"Again?" They swept through the split Dutch doors into the main room. "I'm afraid I encourage the shelter girls to leave 'detailed' messages. They're teenagers, what can I say?"

Lara eyed a package loosely wrapped in tissue paper on the mariner's trunk that served as her coffee table. An anthurium was taped on the top, its florid, crinkled red flower framed an irresistibly suggestive "stalk" in the center. Smiling at his sense of fun, she unfastened and removed her gloves.

"What's 'sis?'"

Michael snapped up his carry-on bag and headed for the spiral stairway that led to the bedroom landing. "Just a little *somethin'* from Haleiwa for my badass hang gliding woman," he said over his shoulder, then hopped up the stairs two at a time.

Lara stepped into the kitchen alcove and pumped a bottle of water from the cooler. The shower came on upstairs.

Michael. She knew why he was home early. She'd be taking off for Washington DC in the morning and home only a day before he left again. It was why she loved him and why it all worked.

The water felt cool and crisp on her throat, dry after nearly an hour's flight. Back in the center of the round living space at the bottom floor, she slipped the flower off her package and opened it to find a silky wrap sarong; soft pink plumeria on a field of black.

She slipped out of her jeans and windbreaker, pulled her T-shirt over her head, and tossed them on the couch.

"So, they decided to interview Jerry Lopez instead of you, huh?" she asked, shouting to be heard above the shower.

"Age before beauty." The shower water slowed and then stopped.

"Ha! Better not let him hear you say that." She wiggled out of her panties and wrapped the silky fabric around her, tied the corners low across her breasts, and slipped the anthurium in her cleavage.

"You decent?" She headed up the stairs.

"Never."

When she stepped up to the bedroom level, Michael was drying his hair in front of the tall mirror in the frame he'd made her for her birthday. She grinned at his reflection. A wet shock of dark, sandy blond sifted over his forehead as his eyes took her in, coming to rest on the flower between her breasts.

"Just as I imagined." He pulled her to him, covering her mouth with his own.

She slipped the anthurium from its warm cleft and pressed it behind his ear. He loosened the wrap, slipped it off and draped it over the mirror, all without taking his eyes from hers. Eyes, ice blue clear, that always took her by surprise. Now they welcomed her in like an old friend. Funny how that felt—like new lovers and old friends at the same time.

He slid strong hands over her hips, up to her neck, and into her loosened hair, caressing, guiding, until his mouth met hers once again, pulling her down on the plush area rug. On their knees, reflected in the mirror, his deeply tanned body contrasted with her fairer skin. She ran her hands over the familiar contours of his shoulders, hardened by years of pumping through massive, pounding surf.

Her fingers poured love into healing scars, gnarly reminders that he was in fact human, and not impervious to the sun. Her breasts pressed against his plated chest. His hand slipped down, cupped the warmth between her thighs, teasing, dipping, until she rocked back on the thick rug and pulled him down with her.

Ah, the sex part.

Lara gave him her full attention as they let loose a week's worth of pent-up longing. When it was over, she trailed her fingers over his back and let him slip into a nap. She couldn't blame him. He'd been traveling for hours just to spend a day with her and then he would travel again. She slipped away to let him sleep awhile, donning a loose-knit cotton sweater, and a fresh pair of raggedy, relaxed jeans, looking forward to shower, dinner, and then...a more relaxed, lingering, round two.

The doors above Lara's kitchen swung out wide to let in the sea breeze, an idea of hers Michael had brought to life. She tidied up the kitchen sink, then shucked the shells off jumbo shrimp, tossed them into a stainless-steel bowl, and put some water on to boil for the pasta.

"Those are gorgeous," he said, slipping up behind her. He kissed the back of her neck and caressed her breasts through the sweater.

"H-m-m. I picked them up at the embarcadero on the way home from *Alternatives*."

"Really?" He teased her nipples with the palms of his hands.

"Really." She sighed and turned in his arms then pressed him away with her hands on his chest. "How 'bout making yourself useful and deglazing that pan." She kissed him deeply then pushed him again.

He moved reluctantly to his assignment, splashing white wine into a pan already sizzling with mushrooms and garlic, and stirred them around. "How's good ol' Aleta, anyway?"

Michael didn't much care for her business partner. *Too stuffy and fake*, he insisted. Lara would give him stuffy. That was fair. But Aleta was accomplished, good at what she did, and Lara respected her business know-how.

"She wants me to meet some doctor at the conference. A genetic expert guru type."

"Still playing the matchmaker?"

Lara laughed. Aleta did have a hard time buying 'surfer boy' as a proper mate for her business partner.

"Fundraiser. His wife's Felicia McCormick. The McCormick Foundation?"

Michael shrugged and kept stirring. "I'm afraid I don't' follow the Bay Area society columns."

Something about the set of his shoulders put her on alert. She ran cold water over the colander of peeled shrimp then stepped behind him, circling her arms around his waist. She leaned her head into her favorite place between his shoulder blades.

"You saw the doc in Hawaii." It was a statement, not a question.

"Um hum." More stirring.

"And?"

Big sigh.

"And, the spot on my cheek's another melanoma." He stopped stirring, turned the heat down. "He says I need to stay out of the sun."

"Ha! Like that's going to happen." Her heart thudded against her ribs as she stirred a handful of cherry tomatoes into the simmering liquid. "That's got to feel pretty scary. I'm sorry." It was more than scary. It literally confirmed what they'd both feared.

"I could wear a mask like those Mexican wrestlers," he teased. He waved the spoon like a microphone and announced "Michael Chance, aka, *La Lucha Libre*." The wrestler.

The image brought a fleeting smile to her lips, but there was no humor in his tone. The words hit her in the gut, swift and hard. So far, his surgeries had been successful, but they were no laughing matter, especially because his father had had basal cell, then melanoma, then Merkel Cell that metastasized. He had died only last year. Michael carried those scars in his heart. There was no point in stating the obvious. They both knew the statistics.

She swigged from her water bottle again. "So that's your plan? *La Lucha Libre?*"

He cupped her head into his chest. "I'll have the surgery here, at UCSF Medical Center. *After* Australia."

Lara turned the water off over the shrimp and let them drain. "I mean, long term. You can't ignore the fact that this could—"

"Yes. I can." He pulled her back to him, lifted her chin with his fingertips and looked into her eyes. "There's a better chance I'll starve to death if you don't get those shrimps going, and I don't mean of hunger for food."

He turned her back to the stove and she squeezed her eyes closed on the first sting of tears.

A bittersweet melancholy settled into her heart as they ate the meal they'd prepared together. It was wonderful to have him there with her, but his news, though not entirely unexpected, had put a damper on his homecoming. They sat holding hands out at the cliff in Michael's version of Adirondack chairs, the tops sculpted like breaking waves. The afternoon wind had blown in a rack of slate blue clouds and left them overhead, flat and still, threatening to steal the blaze out of the coming sunset. Except for the soft crackling of a fire Michael had started in the fire pit, the shore, the cliff, and her lighthouse home were bathed in a rare stillness. Even the gulls had settled down on the beach, quietly picking through rocks and sea grass exposed by the low tide.

Lara closed her eyes, wishing she could spend the next two weeks alone here with Michael. Just ignore her responsibilities at *Alternatives*. Aleta could take care of the girls at the center. Lainie and Steffie weren't due until next month, there were no fundraisers on the schedule. And unless there was some emergency—

"Lara?" Michael's voice pulled her up out of her funk.

"Hum?"

He squeezed her hand and lolled his head toward hers, fixed her with those clear blue eyes. He was wearing his old Pendleton shirt, the gray and blue, and the St. Christopher's medal she'd had engraved for him in Santa Cruz. He was also wearing that same sly, one-sided grin she loved so well. "I took care of some other business while I was in Oahu."

He eased a small black-velvet box out of his shirt pocket. Lara's jaw dropped and her throat tingled. She swallowed hard. *Oh. My gosh.* He placed the box on the wide arm of the chair between them and pushed it toward her with the tip of his finger, then waited expectantly, his smile broadening to light up his whole face.

One hand went to the base of her throat; she took the box in the other.

Before she could open it, he rolled out of the chair and knelt before her, his sun-bleached hair unruly, just the way she liked it, silhouetted against a violet glow that had managed at just that moment to slip under the clouds.

"Lara, I… " He took both her hands in his and cleared his throat. Oh my god! He was really going to propose? A sharp bubble expanded in her throat…

"Lara… "

She let herself fall into those amazing, unforgettable eyes relishing the moment, no matter how long it took.

"I want us to be together for the rest of our lives. You know I love the water, the wild waves. But wherever I am, I'm only half there unless you're there with me. I want us to be married. Right here, on this spot. When I get back from the tour. I've loved you from the first moment I saw you. I see you on the face of every wave, in every flower—"

"Oh, that's good enough," she cried, and lunged, laughing into his arms, the velvet box tight in her grip as they rolled over into the ice plant at their feet. She nipped at his lips at first, then kissed him slow and deep. "I will. I do. You are so amazingly my wonderful hero."

She straddled him, poised to open the little box, then leaned down and kissed him again. She knew he was unconventional and trusted him completely. Whatever was inside the box, it would be just like him. She took a deep breath and cracked it open. The stone inside took her breath away, a harlequin cut aquamarine, the color of his eyes, caught the fading light. The pale blue gemstone nestled in a swirl of golden sea foam, studded here and there with diamonds, small but fiery, like stars glinting on the Pacific.

Michael sat up and took the box from her. "You like it? I designed it myself."

He took the ring out and slipped it on her finger.

"It's perfect." And it was so him.

"I asked your grandad earlier, while you were up there." He gestured toward the sky with a flip of his head.

"You didn't."

"Guess I'm old school that way. My dad was afraid I'd never settle down. Get married, I mean. Wish he could be here to see it."

His words fisted a tight lump in her throat. That was the rub, then wasn't it? Michael was likely to suffer the same fate as his father. Not now. Not yet, but probably sooner than either of them cared to think about. He was here now, pledging his life to her, however long that could be. She would take it. Take all she could get. Her eyes watered as she swallowed the lump, lay down on his chest then rolled over and fit her head into the crook of his arm, savoring the moment. "He'll be here, Michael."

She held her hand up again to admire the ring, the gold warming to her skin. The diamonds glinted in the firelight. Whatever happened to them—whatever the future brought—the gold, the diamonds, and the pure beauty of the aquamarine would endure in some form long after their time on earth was up. Life was fleeting after all and no one was exempt from the inevitable. "He'll be here," she said again, as if repeating it would make it so.

She snuggled against him soaking in every beat of his heart against hers and wished to hell she didn't have to leave for DC in the morning.

Chapter 2 – Our Nation's Capital
Washington DC – Present Day

Lara arrived late at Georgetown University for the President's Symposium on Bioethics, an assignment she was not looking forward to. Aleta had signed her on to a discussion panel later in the week. Lara figured Michael had it pegged. This would be a major beg-a-thon.

Flight delayed out of San Francisco International, she didn't have time to drop her bags off at the hotel and had to bring them straight to the conference room. Arriving ten minutes late and accidentally slipping into the wrong conference room by mistake before she discovered the right one, she was obliged to take a seat at a table at the back of the hall. The podium was as yet, dark and empty. She had made it before the speaker started at least. A low buzz of conversation hung over the room. At the arrival of another latecomer, she toed her roller bag against the wall to be out of his way and collapsed the handle.

"Bioethics Symposium?" His stage whisper drew the attention of another woman who was already sitting at the table. Dark hair slicked back over his head, he looked like he had just rushed out of a shower; a stray strand escaped and fell over his high forehead. His white dress shirt, open at the neck with crisp folds down each front panel looked like it had just been pulled out of a shopping bag.

Surprised at first, the other woman's visage changed as though she had detected a foul odor. "Well." She looked him up and down. "Look who decided to show up. Late as usual."

"Marion." Late Man nodded with a pleasant smile. His tone ignored her rude remark. He pulled out a chair for Lara. "Quite an interesting discussion across the hall," he said quietly near Lara's ear, as if they were old friends. "Global warming, hot topic… "

Lara suppressed a grin, sat in the chair he offered, and scooted in. "Thank you. I made the same mistake."

Marion's eyes, set too close together in a long face, flashed back and forth between the two of them like a fish coming at them straight on, a prim smile turning down at the corners. "And who's your friend?" she asked after a telling pause.

"I'm Dr. Lara Paine, Director of The Alternatives Center in San Francisco." Lara stood up again and extended her hand across the table. The woman simply nodded.

"Marion Sturgeon, Committee on Economics in Healthcare for the National Institute of Health, and… " she said, nodding at the portly gentleman sitting beside her. "This is Dr. Albert Saito, Director of Genetic Research, the Nagawa Institute." Saito rattled his fingers halfway into a bag of Cheetos, blinked at them once slowly, and returned his attention to the front of the room without comment.

"Pleased to have you among us, Ms. Paine," Sturgeon said, through her expression looked anything but pleased. "I believe I've read about *Alternatives* in a recent issue of *New Challenge*. Something about a demonstration by Right-to-Life advocates?" The woman annoyingly looked somewhere near Lara's hairline as she spoke. Her tone was rude at best and put Lara on the defensive.

Alternatives had been picketed by representatives on both sides of the abortion issue and took all the press coverage in stride. "They don't understand what we're doing," Lara began. "If they'd researched the center, they'd have learned that we don't advocate—"

Sturgeon turned to Saito, speaking over Lara's words. "Ms. Paine runs an abortion clinic in San Francisco."

Saito raised his eyebrows lifting three folds of skin across his round, shiny forehead. He paused to lick orangey powder off his fingers.

Lara lost her smile. Determined not to let them get away with the smear, she began again, "*Alternatives* is a home, Ms. Sturgeon, the young women who come to us have already made their choice."

Late Man cleared his throat, deflecting the attention his way. "I don't believe we've met," he said, extending his hand to Saito, and a sincere smile. "Patrick Allen— Genetic Research—U.C. Davis."

Saito snorted, and very obviously adjusted himself under the table.

Lara took Allen's hand briefly. "We're practically neighbors, then. I live just north of The City, when I'm not at the Center."

Sturgeon interrupted. "Dr. Allen works *strictly* on grants from the McCormick Foundation—" She shot him an evil glance. "—that's Allen as in Felicia McCormick-Allen."

Allen sat down, fumbled a pen and small tablet out of his pocket.

Well, isn't that convenient. Aleta sends me here to meet Allen and he practically drops into my lap. Lara ignored

Sturgeon's tone. Obviously, she was a person to be avoided in the future. "Good to meet you Dr. Allen. I've heard a lot of good things about you."

Sturgeon visibly ruffled her feathers as someone clinked a water glass at the front of the hall and their eyes shifted in unison in that direction. A tall, white-haired gentleman stepped up on the raised platform. Lara recognized him immediately. Dr. James Rosenthal, Assistant to the Surgeon General for Genetic Issues. She had heard him speak only the month before at Berkeley. Lara prepared herself for the same *schtick*. Long on rhetoric, short on content.

Rosenthal began as if giving an invocation. "The more we study and experiment," he pontificated, "the more we learn about DNA and genetic code, the more we discover about ourselves—"

Blah, blah, blah. Lara had heard it all before. The Genome and stem cell research, once strictly academic, had steadily progressed into the political arena. She had hoped a symposium on bioethics would hold new promise for an old agenda.

Rosenthal droned on, "…among the list to be considered is more robust funding for stem cell research…"

Allen leaned into Lara, "They'll have a hard time promoting that one, considering the current administration."

"As if it matters to you," Saito hissed, cutting his glance over to Lara. "Our friend, Mr. Allen, has pretty much a free hand while he enjoys exclusive funding through his wife; god *knows* what he's up to out there in California." He said *California* around a mouthful of puffs as if it were some foreign territory where immoral and illegal activity could be conducted on any street corner. At least Aleta had *her* facts straight.

Her own feathers starting to ruffle, Lara rested her chin in the crook of her hand, deliberately covering her lips with her fingers.

Sturgeon had no problem joining in. "At least a *federally* funded program can be adequately *controlled.*"

Allen fell silent, scribbling on his notepad. Lara had never met Felicia McCormick-Allen, only seen her picture in the society pages of the *San Francisco Chronicle*. That was her mission as she understood it. Make friendly with the husband, get an introduction to the wife. Funny, she had a hard time putting the down-to-earth, literally-wet-behind-the ears Allen anywhere in the same stratosphere with Felicia.

Rosenthal held the floor. "…Our panelists comprise representatives from the bioethics committees of four universities. Dr. Roberta Pritchfield, Fetal Stem Cell Research, University of Illinois …"

Patrick perked up and leaned into Lara's shoulder. "Bioethics my ass," he said under his breath. "Talk about a fox in the henhouse."

Saito bristled. "Well, if we don't get the material we need by legal means, we'll have to resort to getting it from places like the alley behind Ms. Paine's clinic."

Patrick held up his hand as if to fend off an intruder. "I think that debate is scheduled for later this afternoon. Miss Paine isn't—"

Lara cut him off. She'd had enough of strangers assuming they knew her position. "Dr. Saito, that is far and away the most offensive comment I've ever heard any professional—" Her voice came out louder than she intended.

"Shhh." People at an adjacent table glared at her. Lara's face flushed heat. It was all she could do to keep herself in her chair.

Why did she feel the need to defend herself? Who were these people, anyway? They obviously could care less about bioethics, they just want to make sure they get their piece of the pie. Michael had been right. This was the mother-of-all beg-a-thons. She looked around, hoping to find an empty seat at a different table. Surely there were people here who were sincerely interested in the subject.

She spotted a couple of vacancies nearer the front door and got up but couldn't resist having the last word. She leaned into Saito's ear and said out loud, "You are a disgusting toad!"

Two people from the table in front of them turned and scowled their disapproval.

Someone in the front of the room banged vigorously on a water glass. Rosenthal cleared his throat. "Excuse me, can we please have it quiet in the back of the room."

Suddenly all eyes were on Lara. "Hell with it," she mumbled, grabbing her shoulder pack and roller bag. She yanked the nearest door open and burst out into the hall. The door bounced once on its air shock and then banged closed behind her with righteous finality.

She followed the signs to the nearest ladies' room, zig-zagged through the offset barrier walls and stalked straight to the sink. She waved her hands and punched buttons uselessly on the paper towel machine, finally pulling a handful of towels from a pile on the sink. The water cooled her temper as she wiped it over her forehead and around the back of her neck. She glanced up to see herself in the mirror.

"You idiot," she said out loud. "You are a complete nincompoop!"

Her head hurt. She pulled the clip out of her hair, shook it free, and let out a deep purging sigh, then made a face at herself in the mirror. "To hell with the bioethics symposium," she grumbled under her breath. "If there were any real ethics to be had, we wouldn't need the symposium, would we? No."

She gathered her bags, set her shoulders, and headed out of the bathroom. She was in Washington DC for heaven's sake, and she'd never been here before. There were much better things to do than listen to a bunch of self-important—

"I don't think you're a nincompoop, Ms. Paine."

Lara nearly jumped out of her skin. Patrick Allen leaned against the wall next to the ladies' room door. *Listening to her in the bathroom? Would there be no end to this nightmare?* She could find no words for him. She just stood, mouth agape.

"Are you alright? You seem a little... upset." His fingertips lightly touched her elbow as he waited for an answer.

She hadn't noticed anyone had followed her out of the lecture hall. Apparently, Patrick had. And, he'd been lurking outside the ladies' room door.

"Oh, I'm just *fine*, thank you." She pushed past him, avoiding eye contact, and headed down the corridor at a fast pace, as if she knew where she was going.

Patrick caught up to her with long strides, turned and shuffled backward ahead of her. "I know how you feel; that was pretty rude. Sturgeon obviously misjudged you and your—*enterprise.*"

She stopped and stared at him. He did the same, letting the air around them hang empty and unthreatening.

"I don't encourage abortions and we don't make any profit off the home. We mostly give the girls a place to stay until they..." She let out a deep sigh. "I only try to help girls avoid making the mistakes I—"

Patrick put up his hands to interrupt her before she revealed herself further. "No need to explain. It's obvious where you were coming from. We scientists need people like you in the world to keep us in tow. Otherwise, we'd develop who knows what monstrosities. Look at *The Fly...* "

"The Fly?" Lara stopped and glared at him. She wanted to scream like she had screamed in the conference room. The last thing she wanted was a conversation with this guy. Red flags she couldn't explain shot up all around her brain. Every cell in her body wanted to push past him and run. But what would that accomplish, really, other than prove her professional ineptitude. Best to be civil, at least. For Aleta's sake. He was her target, after all.

She dropped her shoulders and surrendered to the inevitable. "You give me more credit than I deserve. I have no great desire to save the world from science." She started forward again, more slowly this time. "I left responsibilities at home. I'm the one who misjudged. I trusted I was being asked to the conference for something valuable. Instead, I made a complete fool out of myself. I'm afraid I'm out of my league."

"Lara?--it's all right if I call you Lara, isn't it?"

What she wanted was to check into her room, unpack her things, and cool off. As a conference attendee, she'd surely see him later. This was all starting up too fast. "Look, I, ah…"

Patrick slipped his arm through hers, guided her to sit on a quad bench. "I'm not in with them, you know. In fact, they don't have much of an opinion of me either, as you might have guessed."

She looked into his eyes. His smile was genuine, his expression sincere. Perhaps he would be an ally. At least, Aleta would be happy to hear she had actually had a conversation with him. "So, what were you doing here?"

"Information. You know. I do have to keep abreast of things. And there's always the expense-paid trip to… *wherever.*" He waved his hand limp wristed, as if to include the entire country in his *wherever.*

"I felt like any moment they might ask me to hand over any quality fetuses I might run across. Like I might have a couple of extras laying around in the back room or something. Damn them." Her shoulders drooped, and she let her head fall forward into her hands. "I didn't come here for this."

Allen relaxed on the bench, crossed his ankle loosely over his knee. He wasn't your classic nerd; he had culture. And style. She wouldn't have picked him out of a crowd to be a genetic researcher.

He rested a strong chin on his fist and pursed his lips a moment. "I wouldn't think Saito would be involved in anything that sinister either, but I wouldn't put it past that Sturgeon woman. I've seen them at work. Wherever there's a government buck. Saito's been known to work in some pretty gray areas, and Sturgeon's been investigated twice, though nothing's ever come of it."

Lara studied his dark eyes. There was something hidden, something veiled. She couldn't put her finger on it. "And you? Have you ever been investigated?"

"Didn't you hear? Strictly grants from the McCormick Foundation." He stretched out his long legs and leaned back on the bench, flashing a wide, tight smile. "Where are we headed, anyway?"

Lara stared at him. *We?* She sighed, pushed her hair away from her face, and looked back at him, laughing at herself. "I have no idea where I'm going. I've got a reservation at the Watergate, of all places." Phantom shapes, crept around her memory, flashlights sweeping the walls, peeking out windows of high-floor-numbered rooms.

She let her body fall heavily against the back of the bench. "I really lost it back there. My temper, my direction, probably my career."

"Now you're giving *them* too much credit. I never have; they don't deserve it. If they don't stir things up once in a while, people will forget who they are when it's time for appointments and commissions." Patrick relaxed his arm across the back of the bench and leaned closer to include her in his physical sphere of influence. "I'll admit I don't know a lot about *Alternatives*, but what I have heard is admirable."

If he had let his eyes stray one centimeter below her nose, she would have kneed him in the groin. Instead, she sighed and looked away. She missed Michael right now more than air.

"Let's get you to your room, you can freshen up, and then I'll take you to dinner. We Californian's have to stick together out here in Foggy Bottoms." He smiled and brushed a stray wisp of hair out of her eyes.

Lara drew back from the too familiar gesture. Something about that smile caught her off guard, held her in check. "You know, maybe you've got the wrong idea about me. I'm not looking for…"

Patrick assumed a hand's off pose. "Sorry. I didn't mean to seem… forward." Only then did he flick his eyes to her ring. He sat back a less imposing distance from her on the bench.

Didn't' mean or wasn't successful at. Well, now that the boundaries had been set, she could at least be polite, if not professional. "I could use something to eat, preferably not in a plastic cup or molded into a tiny serving tray-sized block."

24

He grinned at her. "You came straight off the plane."

"Yeah." She laughed, tipping the relief valve. "And I could use a drink. I guess I have the right to drown myself for what I did today." He got up and offered his hand to pull her off the bench.

"Always go drowning with a buddy, those are my rules."

He guided her back toward the main entrance to the campus with a light touch at her elbow. "There's a cab waiting. Watergate's only a few blocks from here." He helped her put her bags in the backseat. "Here, take this and call me when you're ready." He scribbled his hotel name and room number on a handout from the Climate Change lecture and stuffed it into her bag as he waved at the cab driver.

At last, in the solitude of her room, Lara sank into steaming bath water. Adding a few drops of eucalyptus oil to remind her of home, she slipped low into the water. Tension eased from her shoulders and floated away on the steam. The sharp fragrance of the oil cleared her head and started her thinking rationally.

What louts! What asses! Not behavior she expected from professionals, especially in the academic community. Besides, what had *Alternatives* to do with anything? It was none of their business. And she was expected to attend two days of this crap? No way. Tonight, it was a quiet dinner alone in her room, bed, and back to the Bay tomorrow. Okay, a nice trip to the Natural History museum, and then back to the Bay. And, The Met. They could carry on their little outrage without her. Besides, how could you really use the terms bioethics and genetic experimentation in the same sentence?

Then she remembered Aleta. She had met the genetics guru, but she hadn't really befriended him. She unwrapped a little bar of soap and set it on its side on the edge of the tub. *He had been polite.* She unwrapped another one, lined it up behind the first, a little square white cow following the leader. *Relatively harmless. And they were two Californians, after all, in a strange city.* Another little bar went up in line. She was pretty hungry, and room service was always so cold by the time they got it up to you. She was fresh out of soap bars and the water was getting cold. And, she hadn't eaten anything but a mouthful of pureed sweet potato and a couple of Biscoff since she'd boarded the redeye at SFA. She would call him for dinner. She was a big girl. She could certainly hold him at arm's length long enough to make an impression. And then bed. Alone.

"Sorry I was so rude to you back at the university. I was really angry at *myself.*" She sat back in the upholstered chair and put her napkin on the table. Patrick had chosen a wonderful restaurant—much more expensive than she would have allowed herself, and far better than room service. The food and wine were delicious and satisfying. A true rescue.

"You agonize over every one of them, don't you?"

"What? Oh. An unwanted pregnancy?" *More like the same one, over and over.* "It's something you tell yourself you'll get over, but you never really do, no matter what you do about it."

"Well, they had no right to go after you like that. They're just evil people. I think it was worth it to see the look on Saito's face when you called him a toad. Served him right. I don't think he's seen the inside of a research lab in years—and Sturgeon may be on a committee of economics in genetics studies, but the only economics she's interested in are the ones that affect her own bank account. Believe me, the ethical people in the genetics field are the ones in the trenches, not the ones holding the purse strings." He cocked his head to one side and looked up at her mischievously, as if they had actually been conspirators. He gave himself another pour of the expensive wine he'd ordered. "More?"

Lara nodded her approval. It was likely the nicest Primitivo she'd ever tasted. "Regardless, I lost control. I just can't stand it when they talk about fetuses in terms like "material, as if they, or their mothers weren't human."

"Maybe. We scientist types do tend to think of life on the molecular level too often." He smiled into her eyes. "We need your point of view. Keeps us human. In Sturgeon's case though--" He grinned, sat back in his chair again, and shook his head like it was hopeless.

Lara tapped a fancy matchbook embossed with the name of the restaurant silently on the white tablecloth. "She doesn't seem too fond of you."

"More like extremely jealous. To her, the McCormick Foundation is my built-in meal ticket— *You don't have to go out and scratch for grant money—you get it from your wife*," he mimicked.

Lara sensed Aleta tapping her on the shoulder. *Here's your chance.* She put down her glass and cleared her throat. "My partner and I spend half our time writing grants, with no guarantees. Lots of competition. And we're a full-service women's shelter, so it gets expensive, especially in Bay Area."

Patrick lifted his cell phone and wallet from his inside coat pocket, swiped his thumb across its face. "I suppose," he said, his eyes scanning the screen.

Conversation over. O-kay then.

The waiter brought the bill in a leather folder on a silver tray. Allen snatched it up, pulled a credit card out of his wallet.

Lara caught a flash of *McCormick Foundation* on the name before he slipped the card inside the folder. She let out an involuntary sigh, recalling a photo of Allen's wife, Felicia, from a recent story in the paper. A dark-haired, handsome woman of high fashion and cultured good taste. One of the largest charity benefactors in the state. Couldn't hurt to have the McCormick husband in Alternative's back pocket. *Go get him, girl.* Aleta grinned at her in her mind. Lara straightened at the thought. *Talk about lack of ethics.*

"What's the matter?" he asked. He slipped his wallet back inside his jacket.

"Oh," she said, looking down at her hands. "Life's so complicated these days. Sometimes I wish I'd lived in earlier times—maybe in the old west—or with the Anasazi--"

"When the Earth was *without form and void?*" he said, dramatically, setting his phone on the table. He raised his eyebrows in jest, but his features softened. He wasn't mocking her, simply embroidering on her fantasy.

"Yeah, well, maybe not that far back." She dug her own wallet out of her purse, slipped her credit card into the folder with his. "Let's split this."

She smiled at him broadly and gestured to the waiter who appeared instantly and slipped the silver tray silently away before Allen could protest.

"Things aren't actually all *that* complicated," he said, visibly disappointed. "My wife and I haven't actually lived together for many years." His voice was still playful, but his half-smile hinted at an emptiness he tried to ignore. "I don't normally take women to dinner. My work keeps me too busy."

"That's not what I meant." She had read his mind perfectly, and they both knew it.

Patrick raised an eyebrow. "I know, but I felt the evening coming to an end, and I didn't want it to."

Okay, Aleta, I know. Don't shut him down. Just hold him at arm's length and make nice. "Lecture number three in my curriculum for young girls trying to make it on their own. 'Don't get involved with married men, no matter *what* they tell you'."

"I don't know, you look like a full-grown woman to me."

God, he was not giving up. She sipped her wine, with her left hand this time, her new sparkly ring in full view. "That would be a full-grown, *engaged* woman."

Patrick gave her a rueful grin. His eyes drifted thoughtfully from her eyes, to his wine glass, to the ring on her finger. "So. Who's the lucky guy?"

"Michael Chance. Made it official last night, in fact." Just saying the words set a warm flush in her cheeks. He was actually the first person she'd told. A perfect stranger. But then who would she tell? Accept for Aleta, the young girls she helped support, and her grandfather, of course, who already knew, there wasn't anyone. Heat spread to her neck and probably her ears.

Patrick relaxed into his chair as if an uncomfortable burden had been lifted. He gave her a genuine smile and held up his glass. "Well. Congratulations are in order in that case."

They clinked and sipped together. "Thank you."

"Wait." Patrick put his glass down thoughtfully. "Michael Chance? *The* Michael Chance? The surfer?"

Lara laughed. "He prefers waterman, but yes, the same."

"I heard he had some trouble lately. Skin cancer?" Patrick sat forward, a look of concern tightening his brows. "It was in the paper."

"Yeah. And, his father died of Merkle Cell last year."

"I'm so sorry to hear that. That's rare. Directly related to heavy sun exposure," he said, waited a beat. "But, you know, that can also be--"

"Hereditary? Yes. The doctors have told Michael to stay out of the sun, like that's going to happen."

"I'm assuming he uses a good sunscreen."

"Nothing he's used has ever made a difference."

Patrick sat back in his chair. She could almost see gears spinning in his brain. "What?"

"Nothing, it's just... that's my field, you know. I've done some successful work in skin cancer prevention. My patients are showing good signs and no recurrences with my formula."

She sat back and waved his words away in front of her. "Super sunscreen? Really. He's tried them all."

"No. This is... different. Works at the genetic level."

"Genetic level?" Now he had her attention. The waiter returned the receipts. Lara added a tip, signed for her half of the bill, stuffed her credit card and the receipt into her wallet, and sat forward again. *A coincidence? Of course. What else could it be?*

Patrick smiled warmly at her. "I have a sample of the serum with me, well, back at my hotel. I could bring it by your room later." His grin spread wide and teasing.

Lara got up. "You don't give up easily, do you?"

"Don't give up at all." He got up and helped her with her coat, respectfully keeping his distance. No accidental boob skims or knee bumps.

Lara laughed. He was a harmless flirt, and a gentleman after all. "Tell you what. Why don't you meet me at the Watergate for breakfast in the morning. I've decided to ditch the conference for a day at the Met."

Patrick started to respond but was interrupted by his cell phone again. His eyes gave away concern as he checked the sender's name. With an expression Lara couldn't define as agreeable, he nodded and signaled the waiter. "Would you call Ms. Paine a cab, she'll be returning to the Watergate."

CHAPTER 3 - THE SCIENTIST
Washington DC – Present Day

The dining room was crowded for ten a.m. People got up late in Washington DC. At least the ones in suits and ties. Sitting alone near the entrance, Lara pretended to read a *Wall Street Journal* someone had left on the table next to her. It was late for her, too. In fact, Michael's promised call at 6 a.m., his time, had pulled her from a deep sleep. She had never been good at jet lag. Still, she needed to hear his voice. The nation's capital was a foreign land, even if they did serve Sonoma wine. She told him about her change of plans. If she left a day early, they would have two nights to celebrate their engagement before he left for Australia.

The server refilled her coffee. "Ready to order?"

"Thanks, but no. I'll just wait a few more minutes. I'm supposed to meet someone." He nodded and moved on to the next table. What had happened to Patrick Allen? For a person who never gave up, she would be surprised if he turned out to be a complete *no show*. She sipped her coffee and vacantly watched the Weather Channel on the flat screen at the end of the room. *H-m-m-m-m.* High surf warnings for the California coast. She would have some competition for Michael's attention when she got home.

"Excuse me. Ms. Paine?" The server had returned to her table holding a message pad. "I believe this message is for you." He tore off the top sheet and handed it to her.

Handwritten. Patrick must have come by earlier. The writing was happily legible, for a doctor:

> *Had to leave town unexpectedly.*
> *See you back in The Republic.*
> *P.A.*

He'd left a number with a San Francisco prefix. Fine. She would enjoy the Met a lot more without having to fend off his *innocent* passes.

The server stood by--waiting.

Lara folded the paper and slipped it into her purse. "I'll have the Eggs Benedict."

Whispers of the incoming tide rose up the cliffs, stole through the lighthouse window, and pulled her gently from sleep. Lara wasn't surprised to find that she had slept until noon.

Radio blaring and windows down, she had arrived home from SFO just before dawn, numb with cold and exhaustion, only vaguely aware that she had been at the wheel. Now she knew why they called the late-night flights "red eyes". She was grateful that her grandfather kept an oak fire alive in her woodstove most winter nights whether she was there or not.

She was glad to be home. More than glad. Ecstatic. The late hour, the particular curve of light across her bedroom walls, and the elegant, luxurious absence of stuffed shirts soothed her and brought her alive as she stretched out in bed.

The woolen sailor's blanket with its bold colored stripes had been a fixture in her room for as long as she could remember. Today it was warm and comforting around her shoulders as she sat near the window at the head of her bed and watched the rising tide lazily wash away last night's low watermark. Like the returning tide, her thoughts strayed to Michael. Neither his truck nor the trailer with his quiver of surfboards and Skidoo's were in the driveway. No point in calling his cell 'til midafternoon. And not expecting her early arrival, he'd be down in the swell, lost in a watery world of his own.

On the way to the shower, she noticed there was a voicemail on her phone, a number she didn't recognize. Curious, she touched the message button.

Patrick's voice came over the speaker. "Sorry I had to cut it short in DC. One of my patients needed me. But, I've got the serum cream I told you about and I was in the area, so I thought I'd bring it by. Should be there by ten."

She checked the time: two minutes till. *H-m-m-m.* Got my number, got my address. Doesn't waste any time. But in the neighborhood? Not hardly. The lighthouse road wasn't exactly in the city. There was no neighborhood. Not anywhere near.

She laughed away the little alarms going off in her head. He had proven to be persistent, but harmless. Still, she went back to the window to make sure her granddad's old Chevy was in the cottage's garage. A thin smoke ribbon spiraled out of the chimney on the little house. There if she needed him. Always had been.

"I'm up here," she shouted, waiving from the tower window when she heard gravel crunch on the driveway. Patrick had mistakenly parked nearer the old house.

He looked up over his shoulder, waved, pulled a leather case out of the van, and strolled toward the door. A sensible minivan. Not the sort of car Lara expected of a man with a PhD at the end of his name and McCormick at the end of his purse strings. She greeted him at the door and led him to the small French stove in the center of the room, still radiating heat from the night before, watching him survey the circular space that was her living room, dining room, and kitchen.

"Would you like something to drink? Coffee? OJ?" She poured herself a cup of coffee and stirred in some cream as she waited for his answer.

"Yes. Thank you. Coffee. Black." He unloaded his coat and the black leather bag on the seaman's trunk. "So, Michael's into hang gliding, too?"

She poured another cup and brought it to the table. "Nope. That would be my glider you saw out there. Ever tired it?"

Patrick made a show of shivering. "Not me. I'm a little squeamish about heights."

"It's not as scary as it looks. Anybody can learn. But I wouldn't dream of teaching you out here. Too dangerous."

"You're an expert?"

"Ten years. These cliffs belong to me. And then there's El Capitan in Yosemite when the conditions are right. Keeps me grounded." Lara laughed at herself. "Guess that's sort of a *paradoxical.*"

Patrick didn't seem to get it. In fact, he looked distracted. Nothing like the cocky, self-assured doctor she'd met in DC. She hoped she'd hadn't just made a grave mistake about his character.

"Something wrong?"

"Ah, no... I... " He shook his head and at last settled at one end of the well-worn leather sofa. "It's not an easy drive, coming here."

He seemed to calm down. But there was that something again. Something behind the surface of those intelligent, dark eyes.

She raised an eyebrow and let him squirm. "That's the point. Privacy, quiet."

"So, 'In the neighborhood' didn't exactly work for you."

Lara folded her arms, working not to appear annoyed. "Not if you want me to believe anything else you have to say."

Patrick glanced away briefly, then sat forward, picked up the coffee mug in both hands, and sipped. "I just wanted to get the serum... the cream, to you," he stammered. "You mentioned Michael was headed to Australia soon?"

Lara continued her steady gaze. She pursed her lips, waiting for the rest of it. He squirmed like an inch worm looking for his next grasp. Finally, he pulled the black satchel into his lap and thumbed open the latches. "Might be good for him to have the serum on his trip."

Curious, Lara sat beside him, sipped her coffee, and watched.

After a moment's digging, he produced a folded plastic pouch. Inside were two containers; one round and flat like a jar of shea butter, and one smaller, threaded with a plastic cord, like a tube of ChapStik® on a rope.

"He's got to use this every day." He handed her the larger container. "I feel like the Avon lady," he confided. "And this," he held up the stick, "is a regular lip balm with the ointment added."

Lara turned the containers over. No labels. No instructions. Lewis Carroll waved a warning finger in the back of her mind.

"Private label. I just call it UV. Builds up in the system. Takes about a week to be fully active... *depending.*"

"Depending?" She raised an eyebrow at him.

"Some people respond more quickly than others, and then there's the possibility ingredient quantities vary. We're not in full clinical trials yet."

Were the tips of his ears that red when he came in? She wasn't sure. She opened the larger jar and sniffed. "I don't understand. How does one get from gene splicing to..." she asked, leaving the question out there.

"The Avon lady?" Patrick leaned back against the couch and pressed his lips together for a moment. "It's not simple, but it's not that complicated, either. You cut one part of the DNA and replace it with new DNA that contains the trait you're looking for. In this case, an enzyme developed from the Pupa of Dannus Plexippus for its UV resistant qualities."

"The... pupa."

"Inside the chrysalis. Of the Monarch Butterfly." He closed the briefcase and set it down next to the sofa like there was nothing unusual about this at all. "Once the new DNA settles in, it starts producing its special type of enzyme. When you're satisfied with the result, you use the new DNA for your application."

"You make it sound easy." An image of clumsy fingers and blades cutting tiny sprigs of colored fusilli fleeted across her mind. "But the genes are so small, how do you cut..."

"Oh," Patrick gestured in the air as if gene splicing was something anyone could do at home on their kitchen counter. "It's a chemical process, using a very specific set of enzyme 'cutters'."

"And the FDA, what do they say about this creme? I'm not sure we should try something that's not approved."

Patrick snorted. "FDA. Slows everything down." His eyes flicked away for a second while he cleared his throat. "We're still in small scale trials, but so far, we've been amazingly successful. We'll be scaling up soon." He turned and took her hands. "You'll see. Michael will be the poster boy for one of the greatest medical breakthroughs in the twenty-first century. No more worries about over exposure to the sun. No more deadly skin lesions. Done deal."

Lara pulled away gently and set the containers on the coffee table, putting her natural skepticism on hold. It was only sunscreen, after all, not some woo-woo, *Kevin Trudeauian* snake oil. Patrick had been kind enough to bring it to her; it was up to Michael whether he wanted to use it. "Thanks. I'll let Michael know."

Patrick sighed, relaxing at last into the back of the couch. He looked around and then up into the tower. "Now this… is not what I expected."

She followed his gaze upward. "Lived here most of my life, except when I was at UC Santa Cruz."

"Mind if I look? It's fascinating." He inclined his head toward the winding stairway at the edge of the room.

"Be my guest." Lara led him over. It was the standard reaction whenever she invited someone new to her home. They couldn't resist wanting to climb the tower.

He put his hand on the carved wooden railing. "Spectacular."

"My grandfather renovated most of it himself, after the war. He named it *Rubicon*, after the point further north."

His gaze lingered on her face a beat. "Point of no return." He put his foot on the first step, rubbed his hand approvingly over the curving wood banister. "Nice. He do this too?"

"No. That was Michael. He's helped with a lot of the details, sculpturing, extra windows. When he's not surfing, he's a master wood craftsman—we can go up if you like. It's a great view from up there."

Patrick looked up and took a deep breath, then back to her. "We'll see how far I get. Looks pretty high." Nevertheless, he began to climb. "This where you sleep?"

He stopped at the landing off the wide loft, taking in the obviously hand-made sleigh bed, the tall mirror, and the bath area enclosed in glass brick. "Impressive."

With eyes widening, he concentrated on placing one foot carefully on each step. They continued up the stairway. The tower narrowed as they neared the top, continuing their steep climb. Lara stepped in front of him and climbed the steeper ladder of polished brass pipe that led up through a small opening into the beacon room. Sunlight shone intensely now as they stood inside the glass-bound chamber. The rocky California coastline stretched miles northward before it vanished into haze, and straight ahead, the Pacific glinted in the late morning sun, only a hint of a breeze ruffled the surface.

She unfastened a windowpane and flung it outward on its hinges. "You can go out there, if you like, on the catwalk. It's pretty scary if you're not used to it though."

Patrick held firmly to the inner brass railing and only peeked out of the window as the briny ocean air filled the little beacon room.

"My great-grandfather operated this lighthouse until the end of World War I. He owned the land, some cattle, and the little house down there."

They watched her grandfather shuffle a bag of garbage out to his side porch, raise his hand to his eyes and look out to sea from the little stoop like a tiny figure in a coo-coo clockwork.

"He used to bring me up here when I was a little girl. By then, they'd built the lighthouse at Point Reyes, and later new technology took over completely." She rested her hand on the beveled glass cylinder that housed the gas-burning light. "This beacon hasn't operated in more than sixty years." The thought never failed to hit a sad note inside her, like the tower was missing a piece of its soul.

Patrick studied her a moment before he white-knuckled the railing and craned his neck to look below. Once again, they watched the coo-coo clock man turn, scrape his feet, and shuffle back inside his little house.

An unfamiliar cell phone jangled its tune. "Must be yours," she said, patting her cell phone in her back pocket.

Patrick risked a look down briefly, then straightened. "Run down and get that for me, will you?"

Lara laughed. She reached behind him, closed and fastened the window. "Best to go down backwards to the second landing. You'll be okay after that."

Once on the ground floor, Lara busied herself in the kitchen, taking inventory of supplies for the evening's meal while Patrick checked his messages. A moment later he stood beside her at the sink and idly picked out an oyster knife from a set on the counter. A curious expression clouded his features.

"Something wrong?"

He let go a slow sigh. "Just a message on my answering machine. Probably nothing." But he stared out the window, holding the knife poised as if he were about to drop it and run. She took it easily from his hands and placed it on the counter.

"*Probably* nothing?"

Patrick cleared his throat. "An older subj--*patient*. She's had a reaction to a, uh, medication I gave her. Nothing serious, I'm sure, but—" He waved his hand, dismissively.

"I didn't realize you were that kind of doctor."

"I'm not, at the moment, but I—some of my people are old, alone, you know. They don't have anyone else."

"*Your* people?" Lara folded her arms across her chest and leveled her gaze at him.

"They come to me, I help them." Patrick held up his hands as if to ward off her accusing gaze. "I have access to your standard drugs. I dispense them."

"But… isn't… that—"

"Illegal? Huh. Prescribing hundred-dollar-a-pill drugs to old people on social security should be illegal. I'm helping in my own way." He twisted away from the counter.

Lara began to question why she had been so cavalier about letting a near stranger into her house, the conversation at the Ethics conference taking on a whole new meaning. "There is Medicare—"

"It's more than that." He shoved his hands in his pockets. "They depend on me. I couldn't stop now, no matter what. They're like wild birds. You feed them and pretty soon, they forget how to make it on their own."

Lara knew the feeling very well. The young women at Alternatives were a great responsibility. But she would release her little birds, stronger for their stay; healthy, contributing citizens. *His* people were at the wrong end of life for that. "Will she be all right? This woman?"

"I'll have her stop using the meds till I see her on Monday." He studied Lara's face a moment, as if to see if she believed him, then headed back to the warmth of the wood stove.

Heat crawled uncomfortably up her neck as her gut issued a warning. Better to end this little encounter here and now. She picked up his coat and took a couple of steps toward the door.

Thankfully, he took the hint. "Sure, well. Of course. I interrupted your day." He picked up the black case. "Sorry I missed Michael. I was hoping to meet him."

Lara rested her hand on the door handle. "He's easy to miss. Winter's his busy season. He's here till tomorrow, then gone a month." *Darn. Why did I tell him that?*

Patrick headed reluctantly to the door, then slowed to a stop and turned around. "Listen. I was thinking about your center. Alternatives? Felicia's having a benefit luncheon on our estate Friday. Why don't you come along? I can introduce you to her."

There was that look again. The one that sent up little red flags of warning in her psyche. But there was also Aleta, waving double green flags. *This is it. Go for it.*

"Of course," she said at last, dismissing the flutter in her gut. "I would love to meet Felicia."

Patrick smiled and stepped to the doorway. "I'll see that you get emailed an invitation, at Alternatives something?"

"Lara at Alternatives2live.com."

"Got it."

She closed the bottom half of the Dutch door and stayed there watching as his van pulled out of sight, a knot of anxious pressure building in her chest.

CHaPTer 4 - THe BeNeFIT

Michael and Lara's two days together flew by faster than any she had ever known. They had consummated their promise many times over, covering most of her property, including the back seat of her granddad's old Chevy stored in the garage. Still, it seemed that almost before he arrived home, cold and exhilarated after a full day of tow-ins at the world-famous surf spot, Maverick's, Michael was packing to leave. Lara had sent him off with his love tanks emptied, already missing him but anticipating his return, fully recharged.

She sat now in front of her computer, a cup of jasmine tea steaming in her favorite mug. She had a month to plan their wedding on the cliffs. If her mother had been alive, she'd have held out for more time. But granddad didn't need much time to prepare to walk her to the altar, and heaven knew, Michael wouldn't need much time to… well, better not to think about that now.

She had already found an independent chaplain to perform the ceremony and was applying for their marriage license online when the email popped in with a perky "doink."

Attached is an invitation to the benefit. You'll need it to get access to parking on the grounds. I'll find you there, but I could be late. Please don't leave until you see me. I need your help. — PA

Her help? Lara clicked the attachment icon. A formal invitation to the McCormick Foundation Benefit opened before her, complete with a map and dress code.

Gosh. She had nearly forgotten. She'd briefly thought of it when she'd packed the skin cream Patrick had given her in Michael's go bag, but then, with everything else that was going on...

The *soiree* started at two. And it was Black Tie. She knew the road in Marin, had passed by it many times. Lara checked the desktop clock. If she skipped washing her hair, she could just make it.

She hit the print button on the invitation and headed for the shower. It was impossible not to think of Michael in there with her, only hours before--bodies slipping and sliding and gliding—and the last time on the bed, of all places. A chorus of Beyonce's *Drunk in Love* rolled in her brain like sweet *Gran Marnier*. She had to force herself to think: dress, shoes, jewelry. She whirled out of the shower, shook her hair out of a big clip and began pulling an outfit together. There was that swanky little BCBG sweater dress... Michael had loved it. He'd be well out over the Pacific by now she mused, holding the dress against her body.

But she was meeting Patrick. Better play it safe. A conservative suit, neckline up to here... No. Too *businessey*. Finally, she chose a black, high-necked halter with a just-above-the-knee skirt. Elegant, yet...

"Hey, Lara," her grandfather called from downstairs.

"Up here, Papa." She poked her head over the balcony railing, sticking a black pearl earring post through the pierced hole in her ear.

Her granddad dumped a pile of wood near the woodstove. "Where're you off to? I thought surfer boy had left already."

Lara laughed. "Left before you stopped snoring this morning." Her grandfather could call Michael surfer boy all day long because she knew, he already loved him like a son. "I've got a benefit in The City."

She grabbed the invitation off the printer, scooped up her shoes and purse, and hurried down the stairs. "There's ribs and potato salad from last night in the fridge if you want them," she said, pointing with the shoes. "Sorry I can't stay and eat them with you."

She grabbed her cashmere sweater-coat from a hook near the door, then slipped back to her grandfather and gave him a shoulder nudge. "That will be Mrs. Surfer Boy to you in a month." She smack-kissed him on the cheek, then stepped back to the door. "See you later this evening."

She heard him say "Love you," as she slipped on her shoes and ran across the driveway to her little red car.

"Exactly what is your relationship with my husband?" Felicia managed to smile as she crooned the unexpected words.

Heat seared up Lara's neck to her cheeks. Felicia's scathing tone held an unwarranted accusation, but unused to dealing with people like her, it was enough to trigger Lara's guilt. The words in Patrick's email played back in her head: *I need your help.*

Lara had hoped to avoid Mrs. Felicia McCormick-Allen until her husband showed up. But she had already been there an hour, with no Patrick in sight. It had been easy to lose herself among the guests at this lavish, fundraiser's dream. She had never seen so many gloriously wrapped silent auction items set up on twenty or so tables distributed throughout the wide grassy lawn.

Attendees gathered around high top seating, flutes of champagne aloft. Diamond bracelets glinted on wrists, gleaming white teeth smiled inside professionally made-up faces, air kisses floated past proffered cheeks in the late afternoon breeze.

From a podium on the mansion's generous veranda, Felicia had eventually introduced her guests of honor, announced the recipients of various public service awards, and thanked big name donors to the foundation with a champagne toast. Then she systematically worked her way across the lawn, facilitated by an assistant who shadowed the hostess through the crowd, no doubt whispering people's names in her ear as she dropped in on small groups, until she finally made it to the *hors d'oeuvres* station where Lara had been hiding out.

She gripped Lara none too gently by the elbow, laid her sheer-gloved hand across her forearm, and guided her to a reserved table across the wide expanse of manicured lawn, nodding and smiling at her as if they were old friends. She invited her to sit in one of the two high-backed rattan chairs at the table.

Now, her question hung in the air like expensive perfume, identifiable, but way too strong for Lara's taste. She fought to recover herself. She had nothing to be nervous about, because nothing had happened between she and Patrick McCormick-Allen.

"Well, actually, we just met, I--"

Felicia smiled a she-dragon smile. "I haven't stopped sleeping with him, you know. And then there's *Sloan*."

Wow. For a woman who often headlined San Francisco society pages, she was that insecure? Lara relaxed a little into the deep-cushioned chair. Maybe she wasn't outclassed here after all. She'd been to benefits before, but nothing on this level. Felicia's unsolicited candor was like someone had lifted the skirt on the dark underbelly of an entirely foreign world.

"Sloan?" she asked, ignoring the more obvious accusation. Again.

Felicia jingled with malicious laughter. "He didn't tell you about his son? Well, I suppose I wouldn't either if I was him. Doesn't bode well for future action if you know what I mean." She leaned in and lifted her gloved hand to Lara's ear. "The boy isn't even his." She leaned back in her chair and folded her arms over obviously enhanced breasts. "I'm saving that little bit of information for a time when I might need it."

Lara was completely fascinated by the woman's capacity to read into something that didn't exist. She was angry at first, being accused of something she hadn't done, but the deeper Felicia dug herself into the hole, the more Lara felt sorry for her. Her polished appearance tarnished a little right before Lara's eyes. Felicia had obviously been imbibing in the champagne long before her guests had arrived.

At Lara's continued speechless stare, she straightened in the rattan chair. Lara caught a hint of regret in Felicia's nervous movement. Perhaps her vindictive nature had gotten the better of her; she'd said more than she intended. Lara let her squirm in her own mistake and waited to see what she would reveal next. She didn't have to wait long.

"He dotes on the boy. Pampers him. As if it would do any good." Felicia's gaze strayed to the great lawn that glimmered in the waning light. "He pays him almost as much attention as he does his precious projects." Felicia laughed. The sound of it played flat notes on Lara's heart. She had assumed the couple's uneasy relationship over the boy stemmed from the usual jealousy and selfishness, hurting no one as badly as the boy himself. But Felicia's reaction indicated a deeper resentment, a bitterness rooted in more than a superficial jealousy of the man's affection for the boy. Perhaps one born of guilt. The flick of her hair and the straightness of her back presented a picture of a woman wronged, but something in her eye betrayed the presence of a dark secret, one that she now wished she hadn't revealed.

As if sent from above, two ladies approached wearing identical white tailored jackets, names neatly written on benefit name tags. They diverted Felicia's attention with questions about the day's proceedings.

Lara exhaled, taking the opportunity to observe the famous Felicia in action. She was even more handsome in person than when she appeared in the pages of the *Chronicle*. Her elegantly cut, auburn hair was lustrous under the care of a private hairdresser, her creamy skin needed little make up to create the radiant glow that out shown most of the women Lara knew. In fact, if she could find any flaw at all, it was that all that perfection appeared untouchable—a porcelain façade. Lara couldn't help but wonder what was hiding behind it.

She had learned to ignore words spoken in public behind gloved hands. Regardless of her intent, Alternatives did occasionally support therapeutic abortions when the medical situation warranted it. So, Lara expected to be whispered about. What she did not expect was to be accused of having an affair with Felicia's husband.

The women still listened as Felicia reviewed the list of final events. Lara grew restless under fish-eyed glances in her direction. She accepted a tall glass of iced tea from a tuxedoed waiter and sipped it as she considered an answer worthy of Felicia's tone. *Screwing him, what did you think?* It would have given her great satisfaction to say it. For all she knew, Patrick deserved to have his balls hung out to dry. He had certainly given his best shot at the chance of playing with her.

Guests pressed around them, women called to one another; some strolled arm-in-arm among the rhododendron-shaded trails while others took up positions at the tables arranged under lacy Japanese Maple trees that arched around the edges of the lawn.

Maybe Lara could just slip away silently. Get into her car and drive back up the coast to the lighthouse at Wing Bay, forget all about grants, genetic research, and Patrick Allen's wife.

If only she had not gone to the conference in DC. If only she had majored in accounting instead of sociology. If only she had let Kimberly Harper be the one to make love to that handsome jock that got her pregnant. If only she could get back to ground zero. *Oh, Lara grow up. There is no ground zero, and there never will be again...*

And suddenly he was there, across the lawn. Thank *gawd*. She'd find out what he had to say that was so important he needed her help and get the hell out of here.

He appeared uncomfortable in his white dinner jacket and black tie. Even from this distance, he looked like a traveler suffering from jet lag and too many tiny bottles of cheap vodka. He craned his neck and made eye contact with her, then visibly winced when he saw Felicia sitting at the same table.

Lara had gone against her better judgment coming here, but she could hardly decline an appearance at a benefit that could bring funding to Alternatives if she played it right. She forced a smile and turned attention back to Felicia, refusing to stay on the defensive. At last, the women left, and Felicia's eyes again fell upon her, the sweet, fake smile spreading on her perfectly glossed lips. "Where were we, my dear?"

Thankfully, Patrick slipped up to the table just in time. "Hello darling." He gave Felicia a perfunctory peck on the cheek. "I see you've already met Ms. Paine."

Felicia reprised her dragon-woman smile. "Why, yes, but we haven't had a chance to talk." Felicia made a show of presenting her gloved hand as if they hadn't spoken at all. "Marion Sturgeon's told me so much about you."

Sturgeon? Oh, for *chrissake.* Lara took the offered hand briefly then put her own back in her lap. That explained a lot.

"Oh, yes. We all sat at the same table during the opening remarks at the conference in DC." Lara wondered what tale Sturgeon had conjured up out of thin air and repeated. Perhaps she had seen them leave together, seen them at dinner. Perhaps Patrick had a history of…

"So, I understand." Felicia flicked her hair and started to get up. Patrick put his hand on her arm. "Actually, I invited her here. I thought Alternatives— the Alternatives Women's Center, here in San Francisco? —I thought you might be interested in…"

Felicia snapped her fingers in the air, her diamond and emerald tennis bracelet glinted in the last slanting rays of sunlight. A server appeared instantly. She raised her empty champagne glass over her head without looking up. "Keep it coming."

The server nodded and disappeared in a rush as she turned her fiery eyes on Patrick. "What makes you think I would associate the McCormick Foundation with an abortion clinic?"

Patrick raised a brow. "A little defensive, aren't we?"

Felicia glared back at him. The server returned with a tray of champagne. Felicia took one glass and drained it, then took another.

Lara tried not to wince. She felt like a pawn in a checkmate battle between warring spouses. Her stomach did a little flip-flop. What had she gotten herself into?

The waiter offered the tray to Lara. "Just more iced tea will do, thanks."

She would be driving.

Soon.

"I don't give a damn what center she runs, you have certainly got the nerve to bring her here, right under my nose!" Lara feared the delicate champagne flute would shatter under Felicia's tightening grip.

Now Patrick looked uncomfortable. Whatever his plan was, it was backfiring, big time. And it wasn't doing Lara's cause any good either.

"More than one person has told me you were having an affair."

Apparently, Marion Sturgeon got around. Fast. Lara started to get up. Felicia turned on her. "I suppose in your simple little mind you think you'll marry him one day," she hissed.

Without batting an eye, she nodded and smiled a hello to passing guest, then turned back on Lara without missing a beat. "Well, it doesn't matter darling.

I just wanted you to know that." She continued to smile as if they were enjoying pleasant conversation. "Screw your lovely brains out. There's no live sperm there." She tilted her glass and emptied it, then placed it back on the table, a little too hard. "You'll never see a penny of the McCormick fortune from me or anyone else."

A waiter approached the table and refreshed Lara's tea, then slid another flute in front of Felicia.

The interruption gave Lara a moment to study the two of them thoughtfully. If this was what inherited money did to a person, then she was glad to come from more modest roots. She stood. "Alternatives will survive," she said, soothing her dry mouth with a sip of tea.

A perverse smile stretched the corners of Felicia's perfectly painted mouth. She tipped the flute to her lips and drained half of it. "Not in this town."

CHAPTER 5 - MRS. KELLY

Lara resisted the urge to gulp her tea. A shrill voice behind them gave her a start.

"Felicia, darling!" A heavy-set woman in a flowing caftan waved as she approached. "You must meet my nephew. He's come all the way from Manhattan to get a taste of the West Coast for a change."

Felicia rolled her eyes, then turned and gushed a greeting. "Naomi, how wonderful to see you." She got up and floated away.

Lara closed her eyes and waited until the two women were well out of earshot, then grabbed Patrick's champagne and gulped it down. "Some introduction."

"Never mind that. I need to talk to you."

"Never mind? Your wife accuses us of having an affair and threatens to ruin Alternatives and you say 'never mind'?"

She grabbed her purse from the chair back.

"I don't care what Felicia thinks."

"Maybe you don't, but I was here on behalf of *Alternatives*."

Patrick's pinched expression said he had no empathy for her predicament whatsoever. He reached for her wrist. "Look, Lara. I need your help."

She held up her hand. "*Oh* no. I've had about enough of this party, and I've definitely had enough of you. Don't call me, don't email me, and don't ever consider—"

"Remember that phone call I got at the Watergate? My patient?"

Lara turned, a shot of cold fear tingled in her fingertips, stopping her in her tracks. Her jaw tightened, she swallowed hard on a twinge of fearful intuition. "What about her?"

"There's been a… development. You're the only one I can trust."

Don't listen to him, he doesn't even know you. She looked into those bottomless dark eyes. "Why me? Surely you've got someone, your wife, an assistant, one of your… your… romantic alliances—"

Patrick stood now, moved closer, "You have heart, Lara, and a conscience, and you have… " He urged her forward, leaving the rest of his statement hanging in the air. "I'm afraid time is, as they say, of the essence."

Why was it that the most important choices in life had to be made in an instant? She dragged in a deep breath and squeezed her eyes closed. She realized now, this development was no longer about Sturgeon or Felicia or Patrick or herself. It was about one of his little wild birds.

It was about heart and conscience. The two things about which her grandfather said he was the most proud and also feared.

I love that about you, he often said, *but you can't expect to rescue every bird that falls out of the nest.*

Heart and conscience were the reason she continued to work for too little pay at Alternatives, an activity that consumed nearly all of her time. She glanced at Patrick, weighing the situation. Considering how the "introduction" to Felicia had gone, this was probably one of those times she should walk away.

But the desperate look on Patrick's face disintegrated her resolve. What if she *was* the only one who could help? He was a brilliant scientist, run amuck, maybe, but brilliant just the same. Maybe she could help him recover his right mind while she was at it, an item he seemed to have misplaced.

"Come with me." His eyes pleaded. "I'll bring you back for your car when we're done. I'll explain more on the way."

Dust billowed around the van as Patrick gunned out of overflow parking area adjacent to the estate. They wound their way to Highway 101, past Sausalito. Lara studied his profile as they skirted San Pablo Bay and merged onto the Highway toward Sacramento. He was handsome in a dark sort of way, the exact opposite of Michael. Blue-black hair, slicked and long enough to be caught at the nape of his neck in a tight pig tail; straight nose, deep-set eyes so dark it was hard to tell exactly what color they were. His hands gripped the wheel, his fingers lean and long and well-manicured. Compelling. She could see how a wealthy debutante would be captivated by him, though he definitely wasn't her type. But those eyes, their intensity, their depth. She simply could not say no.

They took the first turn off Highway 80 to Davis, wound through an old neighborhood and finally turned into a small trailer park. Patrick stopped in front of a tiny single-wide mobile home, turned off the engine, and sat staring at his hands. Lara waited. She could almost see his brain circling for a place to start.

"Mrs. Kelly," he said at last. "She called me Friday?" Those eyes met hers and the cold gripped her again. "Remember I told you about her?"

Lara nodded, slowly.

"I tried to get her this morning. No answer."

"So?"

"So, she never goes out. I always see her here. She has no relatives, only the manager here, and... " His voice trailed off and his gaze drew to the front door of the trailer. "She has had... she's been ill. I've been giving her... medication." He met her gaze again. "—a new formulation. It's been very effective." A strange lilt of enthusiasm crept into his voice.

"You *experimented* on her?" Deep in her consciousness, the little alarms clanged louder. The hairs on her arms rose and tingled.

"I know you don't approve, but I hope you will help me rather than stand in my way right now. Regardless of how or what has happened, or who is to blame, Mrs. Kelley needs our help."

Our help. Guilty by passive participation was still guilty. But, if the old woman is in some kind of trouble, how could she turn away? And, if he was in fact practicing medicine illegally, maybe she was the only one in a position to stop him. He angled away from her as if sensing her distrust and started to get out of the car. She stopped him with a hand on his elbow. "All right. I'll help you this time. But you have to promise me, no more of this... experimenting. Whatever the outcome. You have to promise me. This goes against everything I—"

"I know it does. I know. I just... I don't know what we're going to find in here. Please... just... help me help her."

"Okay. I'm here." Against all her better judgment. She swallowed hard on a dry lump in her throat. He'd ducked that promise, hadn't he? But those eyes, those dark, troubled eyes. How could she not respond? Lara covered his hand with hers. Regardless of the cause, she sensed a true concern for Mrs. Kelley. His intentions were good, if his methods had been less than ethical.

She was reminded of the time her best high school friend had called her in the middle of the night bleeding profusely from a miscarriage. Lara hadn't even known she was pregnant. Her friend had let her in through a bedroom window, begged her not to tell her mother, refused to let her call 911. But there was just too much blood. Lara had assured her she wouldn't tell, then went into the bathroom and called 911 anyway. The emergency-room doctor told the girl's mother she would have died if Lara hadn't made the call. Her friend was angry. Never spoke to her again. But she was alive.

Lara let out a resigned groan. "All right. I'll go in with you and take a look." But if she saw anything off, anything at all, she was calling 911.

Patrick's eyes searched hers a moment longer, as if he could read her mind, then he straightened, pulling himself back, and slowly stepped out of the van. She was glad Michael was traveling. It would be hard to explain how she ended up in Davis alone with Patrick Allen in a tumbled-down trailer park. Something told her the consequences could run deeper than a little hanky-panky. Much deeper. But she kept going. At this point, her conscience gave her no choice.

"Mrs. Kelley?" he called, turning the knob on the side door of an aluminum screen porch. "She never locks this door; I keep telling her... "

"Mrs. Kelley," Lara echoed, looking around. Though neatly kept, the tiny house trailer was filled with garage-sale quality bric-a-brac, stacks of Women's Day magazines, and rows of pictures in a collection of ornate frames. Patrick went through the narrow hall to the bedroom while Lara stood near the doorway and idly picked up one of the frames. In it was a faded photo of a chorus line of young women in tap shorts, their legs kicked high. Someone had stuck a little gold star next to the first girl in line. Mrs. Kelly no doubt. She had been beautiful in her blonde pompadour hair style and ankle-strap dancing shoes. A thump in the other room pulled her from the thought. "Patrick?"

No answer.

She stepped through the hallway to the bedroom door and peeked in, then caught her breath, immediately wishing she hadn't looked. Patrick knelt motionless next to an oddly shaped—*what?*

"*God.* What *is* it?" Her knees weakened a moment, but her feet were riveted to the floor.

Patrick slowly shook his head, as if denying what he saw. Shocks of black hair had escaped his pigtail and draped haphazardly across his face. He ran shaky fingers through it.

"The crust that was forming on her arm—seems to have covered her entire body—not just covered—encapsulated. It's like a... " He shook his head slowly. "A chrysalis." His voice was almost a whisper, the words were slow and labored, as if he did not believe himself. When he turned to look at Lara, his forehead was beaded with sweat.

Lara covered her mouth with her hand to stop her chin quivering, her lips suddenly cold. *Don't faint, don't faint, don't faint.* "But, surely it's not Mrs. Kelly—How could it possibly be?" This was the stuff horror movies were made of. This sort of thing didn't happen in real life.

Patrick stared, motionless. "I thought I'd gotten it right this time," he said softly to himself.

Lara took a step back, bracing herself against the wall before she toppled over. *This time?* How many lost birds were there?

He rose, wiping his brow in the crook of his arm, his face pale as boiled fish. He swallowed on what was obviously a throat gone dry, then babbled on. "It's possible that the cell's DNA has mutated in a way I never dreamed—"

Lara couldn't make any sense of what he was saying. She wrapped her arms around her waist and pulled herself into a tight space, her teeth chattering. Surely she would wake and find herself shivering in a horrible nightmare. But the wall behind her was solid. The chrysalis was real, looking much like the delicate seashell shapes she used to find attached under the lighthouse window frames. So fragile, yet secure in the wind and the rain until one day a beautiful creature emerged.

But this chrysalis, a translucent red amber instead of green, held a thin, aging woman, curled like child in slumber. Lara could see every detail, her silvered hair, a mole near the corner of her mouth, arms folded over a stilled chest, a small, emerald-shaped amulet resting in the dip of her neck where her frail collar bones met. Lara closed her eyes, knowing she would never be able to erase the image from her mind.

"This is, this is… j-just not right. We have to r-report this—"

"*No!*" Patrick flung himself into action. "We *can't!*"

He seized Lara by both arms, making her shriek. Startled by his own action, he let her go. She slipped to her knees.

"—at least, not yet," he relented. He stepped over the hideous form and knelt beside it. "Help me get it into the van. I know a place we can keep it until it hatches."

"Hatches! You mean you think she's—*it's* alive?"

"I can't make out a pulse, but maybe with my instruments--Pupa aren't dead while they're in chrysalis—I just don't know," he said, backing away. "I never expected anything like this to happen. I'm not sure what *this* is."

"How will we get her out of the trailer without someone seeing?" Like that was the most important question. How in bloody hell had she let herself get involved with this guy?

Patrick lifted her by the elbow and guided her back down the hall. "Give me a minute." He rubbed his hand over the top of his head and gripped the back of his neck, staring toward the bedroom.

Lara crouched near the doorway, as far away from the thing as she could get.

Her intuition had tried to warn her, way back on the day they'd met. She hadn't listened. And now she'd linked herself to a madman. A genius, caring madman, but a madman nonetheless. She bit her bottom lip, unable to move a muscle.

"I need to pick up some things from my lab. Want to wait here, or--"

Did he have no sense of the horror he had created? "Y-you want to me stay here alone with that--that--*thing*? You don't need me. Just take it to your lab, get some student to help you."

"I can't risk anyone else seeing. They wouldn't understand."

Oh, they would understand all right. Dr. Patrick Allen, husband of the trustee of the royal McCormick dynasty was a full-blown lunatic. The thought must have been written all over Lara's face. Patrick gave her a look of genuine apology. His voice cracked and he slumped against the door jam, hiding his face with his hands.

After a moment, he dragged in a shaky breath and straightened. "No. I can't take her there. But I need some of my equipment. My lab's not very far from here. We can get what need, then come back and get… her."

When he let go of his neck, his hands were shaking.

"Christ," Lara said, her mind made up, God help her. She could never unsee what she had seen, or forgive herself if there was any chance of help the old woman. She pushed past him. "Better let me drive."

She snatched the keys from his hand before he had a chance to object. He followed her to the car and got into the passenger seat without argument. She swallowed hard on a surge of sour that came up her throat. What would happen when the old woman failed to pay her rent and they finally realized she was gone? Somebody will say *Last I saw, there was that doctor who always took care of her. And the woman with him.* The thought that someone might actually already have seen them made her want to wretch. She was in it now, like it or not.

She white-knuckled the steering wheel, steeling herself against the urge to run. "I'll help you do this thing and then I don't want to see or hear any more from you, do you understand? This is *your* problem, *not* mine."

Her voice sounded cool, even. The voice of someone else, devoid of emotion, numb with denial. She didn't want to talk about it anymore. It would make it seem more real. A person, rubbed with a serum derived from a butterfly, had actually gone into chrysalis state. And Patrick acted as though they had just put a cocoon in a mayonnaise jar with holes in the lid. Now he was about to take it somewhere and—and––what? Wait for it to open? And what would emerge?

Lara shivered at the thought. She had never met Mrs. Kelley and wished her no ill, but she sincerely hoped that she was dead and long beyond knowledge of what had happened to her.

"Bring that recorder, would you?" Patrick gathered apparatus from shelves and cupboards, gaining momentum as he worked. Lara stood in the lab doorway, her arms crossed obstinately over her chest, her discomfort building as she watched his demeanor ramp from efficiency to perverse excitement.

He slipped past her again, arms loaded with equipment, made another trip to the car, and back to the lab. "You never can tell what will be useful. If I can get ultrasonic images on file, I could bring them back here for analysis."

She couldn't believe what was taking place before her eyes. A rational human being would be stricken with remorse, would be terrified, would be shaking all over as she was, if not in fear of the thing, then of the consequences they might suffer through his part in this hideous mess.

Instead, Patrick was growing more animated by the moment. Getting off on it. She should slow him down. *Do something!* "Patrick—"

"—'Course it won't be real time," he mumbled, passing her by again. "But it should detect any differences, day-to-day--*Oh!* We'll need the generator and some propane, and--"

She swiped at his arm and missed as he hurried across the lab. "Patrick—" He stopped, looked through her, fingertips tripping across his forehead. "What else--*what else?*"

Lara blinked slowly. It was clear she wasn't getting through to him. Maybe the quickest way to get on the crazy train with him and get this over with. "Video camera. I really think you should get this whole thing on video, I mean, maybe you can make some money on the side with the movie rights."

"Right. Good idea," he said, without blinking an eye. He rummaged through a lower cabinet. Forget cell phone video, he was going for the full setup. Pulling out a camera case, he tossed it at her as he bumbled out the door with a portable generator. "Make sure the car charger's in there—"

"Champagne, caviar, straitjacket--"

"What was that?

"Nothing." She shouldered the camera bag and followed him to the van, her eyes darting this way and that, hoping no one saw them together. It was near midnight when they reached the trailer park again. Nearly all the trailers were dark. Together they rolled the chrysalis into an old, braided rug from the bedroom floor and dragged it down the narrow hallway.

Patrick poked his head out the front door, looked around. "All clear. Go."

They each picked up one end of the rug and carried it to the van. Patrick scrambled into the back, pulled the hatch closed, and secured the cargo in place with a couple of bungee cords.

Lara could still feel the weight of the load in her arms. It made her feel sick to her stomach. She didn't wait for him to join her in the front seat before she gunned the engine and roared out of the trailer park. "Where are we going anyway?"

"Head down Interstate 5 toward Fresno, then take the 41. There are some caves I know of where she won't be disturbed."

"Caves?"

"Yeah. It'll take us a couple of hours but it will still be dark when we get there. We'll sleep in the van and move her as soon as there's enough light. I'll check her over more thoroughly then and we'll be back in time for lunch."

"I'm not sleeping in this van with that *thing*, or you, for that matter."

Patrick crawled into the passenger seat from the back of the van and stared at her for a long moment as if he actually heard what she'd said for the first time since this all went off the rails. "The cave is near the south entrance to Yosemite. We can get a hotel room there."

Lara made a swift lane change, prompting him to give her a disturbed look. "Make that *two* rooms."

"Of course," he returned excitedly, looking over his shoulder to the back of the van. "Two rooms."

An hour before dawn, they left the motel and were zig-zagging their way up a single-track, unimproved switchback road that got impossibly steep, the van engine straining at every turn. Holy crap, would the van even make it up another level? But just then it topped a turn and they were looking at a dead end at the face of a steep, rocky wall. The headlight beams shown on a makeshift trail marker nearly hidden by a drooping buckeye:

Steep climb
Stay on trail

Patrick shut down the engine. Lara leaned her head against the window and rolled her eyes to look up. She couldn't see the top of the wall.

Climb? Trail? How on earth would a person know how to get to this place? In broad daylight, you would have trouble spotting the sign. In the pale, pre-dawn mist you would have to have been here before to find it. The thought made her shudder.

He thumped the door handle, pushed the door open and got out, then leaned in and said, "Help me unload the equipment." His voice was animated with an enthusiastic pitch like they were off on a weekend hike in the wilderness to escape The City.

Lara leaned forward, biting the inside of her cheek as he stalked around the outside of the van and opened up the tailgate. She steadied herself with a hand on the dash and studied the trailhead through the windshield. He actually wanted her to get out of the van. Her strappy sandals were going to be absolutely useless. The prospect of hiking up that trail in her bare feet wasn't tantalizing either.

"What are you waiting for?"

She flinched at his words, her shoulders had hiked up almost to her ears, her rear rooted to the seat.

"You can start with the camera," he ordered. "And the tripod over there." Hands full of equipment, he nodded toward a plastic milk crate against the wall opposite the chrysalis.

Lara blinked at him a moment longer. So, this was really happening.

Now.

She could barely breathe in the truth of it, let alone move a muscle toward helping. She bit her bottom lip and met his gaze. His shoulders slumped.

"Look," he said. "I know this is unusual. But the sooner we get it done, the sooner we can get back to The City and move ahead." He cocked his head as if to elicit her agreement.

Finally, his words hit a nerve. She pushed out of the front seat, stepped over the console, and faced him.

"Unusual?" She braced herself against the back of the seat. "No, *Doctor* Allen, this isn't *unusual*. This is insane! You know that, don't you?" *How could he not know that?*

He stared at her, and for a fleeting moment, she thought she'd gotten through to him. Thought she saw a tiny grain of remorse. It was time to call the authorities. Time to get help.

But the moment passed. "It is what it is," he said finally, shrugging. "I can't put this genie back in the bottle. So, we have to do what we can." He wrapped his arm through a coil of rope and stepped out the back. He pointed up the side of the cliff. "That's the safest place for her right now. And then we'll see what happens."

See what happens? What? She'll turn into a butterfly and we'll all live happily ever after? Panic scrambled up her throat; she glanced over her shoulder to the driver's seat. What was to keep her from waiting till he was up the cliff then driving off without him? Nothing. But a soft jangle of metal had her turning her gaze back. He dangled the minivan keys in his fingers.

Right. Of course. A Ph. D. and the end of a name had never been a sign of common sense. And right now, neither one of them was showing any.

Defeated, she regained her balance, pulled the camera and tripod out of the crate, and passed them out to Patrick, then watched him slip his arms through the handles of the duffle, slide them up to his shoulders, and shift the weight up to carry it like a backpack.

When he was done, he fixed her with an expression that looked more like excitement than remorse. "It won't take long. I promise. I'm going to rig a hoist from the top to help us get the chrysalis up there, and then I'll get you back to the Bay."

Lara wiped a shaking hand over her lips at the prospect of touching the chrysalis. *Hoist it to the top and leave it there? Sure. Why not?* What else was she going to do at this point? Walk out of here in the dark by herself in her strappy sandals?

She stepped past the ominous shape bungeed to the opposite wall and sat down at the back of the van, her feet dangling over the side. A familiar numbness crept over her. A safe, insulating numbness that gave her a false sense of calm. It was better than no sense at all, right?

Nothing about the scene felt real. Not the fragrant trees reaching to the brilliant starry sky, not even the feet at the ends of her legs, and definitely not the man making his way up the trail illuminated by the van's headlights. She pulled her coat around her shoulders and waited while a dim purple glow began to light the cliffs on the horizon with Venus looking down on them from her place in the morning sky. If she wasn't so damn cold, tired, and angry at the situation and herself for agreeing to go along with this lunacy in the first place, she would have said it was one of the most beautiful sunrises she'd ever witnessed. One she hoped she could forget.

By the time she heard him coming back down the trail, purple light had brightened to a clear golden glow on the granite mountains in the distance. At least, she hoped it was him, because if it wasn't, there was a very large, heavy-breathing something else coming in her direction. She braced herself, ready to scurry deeper inside the van. She would almost welcome sasquatch rather than face what Patrick had described was next on his agenda.

"Okay," he said, handing her a loop of rope, like this was something he did every day of the week. "Slip this around your waist so I can assist if you lose your footing." His brow was covered in sweat.

"Wait. Stop. I don't understand." She was stalling but she couldn't help herself. She did *not* want to do this.

He bent over a moment, catching his breath, then explained as he wiped perspiration off his forehead. "I set up a tripod at the top of that ledge up there, added a double pulley, and dragged two ropes down with me. Here's a harness for the chrysalis," he said, tossing her a tangle of ropes. "I'll stay at the bottom and leverage the weight while you guide the chrysalis straight up the side of the cliff."

Oh. No. Just. No.

This wasn't happening.

"The sign says to stay on the trail." As if that would change his mind. It was a futile attempt.

"You can do this, Paine. You're an athlete. I saw the pictures in your living room, remember? You know how to repel."

True that. She'd done her share of climbing, with a glider strapped to her back no less, so she grasped the intent. It was just that…

"Okay, let's do this, I don't want anyone seeing us out here," Patrick encouraged, looping the ropes around his body and setting some tension.

"Sweet Jesus on the dashboard," she mumbled, kicking off her useless sandals. She moved toward the base of the cliff next to the chrysalis, slipped the harness around the bulk of it, trying to ignore the scratchy rasp of its surface. The rope tension tightened behind her.

"Okay, on three, lift it up over your head."

Right. Like she was strong enough to lift Mrs. Kelly over her head. But surprisingly with Patrick's assistance, she was able to guide the weight above her shoulders, then took a first step up.

"I'll tie off the ropes when you get to the top," he went on as she found the next footing with her toe. "There's a ledge you can sling your leg up to, then scoot over the top. When I get there we can swing the load onto the ledge and haul it into the cave. I'll bring up the rest of the equipment, we'll set up the cameras, and we'll be back home in time for lunch."

Great, she thought, choosing her next foothold. Like she would ever have an appetite again. She glanced over her shoulder to see his concentrated expression about twenty feet below and ridiculously regretted not wearing leggings under her dress. It was better to worry about him seeing up her dress than thinking about what she was actually doing.

The sun was bright in the rearview mirror as she drove the van down the interstate, trying unsuccessfully to erase the images of the last few hours from her mind. Her shoulders ached and her hands, feet, and shins burned where she had scraped the skin off them on granite at least a dozen times while lending her weight to help Patrick hoist the horrific load up the side of the cliff. Now, Patrick's head lolled to one side; he was actually sleeping. The fact that he could sleep like a baby after what they'd just done gave her new insight into who and what he was.

She drove like a zombie, her eyes fixed open, as they left the mountain passes behind and headed into the tule fog on the straight, empty highway toward the bay. Her pulse was racing as fast as the engine. She willed herself to think about something sane, something good. Something that didn't feel like a horror show playing in her head.

Michael.

In four weeks they'd be married. She moved her pinkie to straighten the aquamarine stone on her ring finger. The memory of the afternoon he gave it to her filled her with a sense of warmth and stability. And then suddenly, reality struck her like a landslide. The UV serum cream. The lip balm. Were they the same creams that had put Mrs. Kelly into a chrysalis state? Why had she not thought of that sooner? A burning blob of bile rose up her throat and into her mouth. She screeched over to the righthand lane, jammed on the brakes, and managed to get the door open and lean away from her lap a second before she puked. Patrick never moved a muscle.

She dug in her purse, pulled out her phone, and frantically pressed the Favorites button. Michael would still be in the air on his first leg of the journey to Australia, but she could at least leave a message. The call went to voicemail as she expected. "Michael. Don't use the cream I gave you. I'm serious. Do NOT use the sunscreen. I'll explain later."

There. It could be nothing, but she couldn't take that chance. She sat a moment to make sure she was through being sick, then sipped from a bottle of water she'd brought from the motel, guided the van back onto the highway, and headed for the McCormick Estate where they'd left her car.

Standing next to her car, her hand on the door handle, she watched Patrick's van disappear into the fog. Aleta would have to drum up funding from some other sector, because as far as Lara was concerned, the McCormick ship had sailed over the horizon and completely off the planet.

Fumbling for her key fob in the bottom of her purse with fingers numb to the cold, she pressed the unlock button, opened the door, slid into the driver's seat, and took her first full breath in what felt like days. What were the chances the last eight hours had been nothing but a macabre *Bodysnatchers* nightmare? Too much champagne at the fundraiser? She closed her eyes, dropped her head onto the steering wheel, and let herself sit with that possibility for a moment. Nope. She hadn't drunk that much champagne. She could never drink enough champagne to imagine that scenario.

She let out a long, slow breath and opened her eyes. The scrapes on her hands held the raw, burning truth she would never be able to erase from her memory: Mrs. Kelly's frail body curled inside golden amber, the weight of the chrysalis as she guided it up the face of the granite wall, the manic charge in Patrick's eyes as he set up his cameras inside the secluded granite cave, and more dark shapes in the shadows she dared not ask about. At least she had left the message for Michael. Hopefully he would pick it up before he went charging off to some epic break the moment he got picked up at the airport.

She dug her phone out of her purse, and left another message, just to make sure he'd noticed her calls. "I repeat: DO NOT USE the sunscreen. Call me when you get this message." But she feared it still wasn't enough. The crazy fool had once left his motor running, the keys in the ignition, and his wallet on the seat of his pickup truck when he pulled up to his favorite surf spot to find perfect barrels peeling off of a point break.

Where was he staying? She could call ahead and leave a message at the hotel. He'd left her a folder with his itinerary. She closed her eyes and tried to see the logo of the hotel on the brochure with no luck. Her mind was too crowded with things she could never unsee. The call would have to wait another hour until she reached home.

Of more urgency now was stopping Patrick Allen from further endangering unsuspecting people. If she didn't stop him, who would? She could call the authorities. But which ones? Food and Drug? The university? The FBI? And what would she say? That a madman injected some bug serum into an old lady and she hardened into a chrysalis? They would think she was nuts.

And they would be right.

Even if she told the authorities here, could she actually lead anyone to the place where she and Patrick had hidden the evidence away? She wasn't sure. And what if, as Patrick had assured her, he was the only one who could save them? He wouldn't be able to do that from prison.

On that thought she lapsed back into a mental fog as thick as the one outside her car. Better not to think about any of it. Just get home, call the resort in Australia, then sleep.

One step at a time. You can do this.

She straightened in her seat, started the engine, and slowly let out the clutch, then crept out the driveway, her heart heavy with fear and dread, driving by pure muscle memory. She skirted the bay, past Sausalito, then headed for the coast and followed the two-lane road back toward the lighthouse. Carefully matching her speed to curves she knew by heart, she felt like a tiny ant, crawling along the edge of the continent. So tiny that any business of hers could have absolutely no consequence whatever in the bigger picture. It was a remedy she often resorted to when problems loomed out of proportion. The Earth would certainly not turn on its axis any differently if one ant strayed from its path. Nothing out of balance. No seconds lost.

But it wasn't working. Not this time. Each time the image of the old woman inside the chrysalis rose up in her mind, it triggered her gag reflex. Each time she pushed it down, she knew it would spring back up again. She would never forget, never. But she could go on living, let Patrick take care of his atrocities. She only hoped he was right. He couldn't help Mrs. Kelley from a jail cell. Lara would have to trust him that far. And she could definitely do without the complication of Felicia McCormick-Allen in her life. Nope. She wouldn't turn him in. She would put as much distance between her and Patrick Allen as she could and then get herself back on track.

She would spend more time at the clinic. She would try to set up another scholarship program at Mills College. She would start planning her wedding, for goddsakes. She had warned Michael off the sunscreen, they would get married in a month, and all this craziness would be firmly in the rearview mirror.

The thoughts went round and round in her head, always winding up at the same magical, self-soothing, hopeful conclusion: everything was going to be alright. By the time her tires crunched into her own gravel driveway, she had almost convinced herself it was true.

A moment later her headlight beams shown on someone sitting on the lighthouse steps, a hoodie pulled over his head against the damp cold air. She'd know that posture, those shoulders, that muscular frame anywhere.

"Oh, my God, Michael," she croaked, swallowing back tears of relief. He was still here! Everything was truly going to be all right.

He stood up and dusted himself off as she shut down the engine. She bailed out of the car at a run and nearly knocked him over on the stoop.

"Lara," he croaked, wrapping his arms tight around her and pulling her close.

Lara leaned in, tried to catch his gaze, but he glanced away. "What is it? You're supposed to be—"

"Lara," he said again, his voice tight and anguished.

Oh, that wasn't right. She pushed back on his shoulders, "What's happened? Is it Gramps?" She shot a glance toward her grandfather's little house. "I don't understand. What's going on?"

The hood slid off his head; pale daylight shone fully on his features.

"Oh my god!" Lara gasped. That just can't... It can't be. His face was coated in a clear, honey-colored slime from the corner of his brow across his jaw, down his neck, and disappeared under his jacket collar.

Her insides turned to warm liquid as though they would melt and run right out the bottom of her feet.

Michael recognized her panic. He swallowed hard, his eyes wide with fear and that struck her to the core.

The man voluntarily barreled down faces of fifty-foot waves for a living; she had never known anyone as fearless. Yet he stood before her now like a child, terrified, looking to her for comfort.

"You used the sunscreen," she rasped. It wasn't a question.

Michael wrinkled his brows. "Thought I'd get in a quick surf session… before I'd be stuck on an eighteen-hour flight… and… then, at the airport, this shit shows up on my face and hands, I felt dizzy and… and they wouldn't let me through security, and…"

He slumped against her. *No. No, no, no…* She lifted his arm over her shoulder to help support his weight.

The image of Mrs. Kelly fully encased in amber invaded her mind along with a flashback of Patrick setting up his cameras inside that cave. Michael looked at her again now, semi-conscious but still on his feet.

No! She pushed the images away. That wasn't going to happen to Michael. *Not. Going. To happen.*

"Let's get you inside. You're going to be okay," she told herself as much as she tried to assure him. She staggered a bit under the extra weight, but made it to her steps, jammed her keys into the lock, and pushed open the Dutch door.

A few more heavy steps took them to the couch where she lowered him to sit, then dropped down beside him and covered her mouth to stop her chin from quivering. She gathered him back into her arms and held him close, hot tears spilled down her cheeks.

He sank deeply into the couch, those ice blue eyes losing focus. "Maybe we should… call 911," he said weakly, unsuccessfully trying to unzip his hoodie. "I don't feel so good…"

Lara's pulse beat somewhere around her ears, pumping harder by the second. Call 911 and then what?

How would she explain what was happening to him? And could they actually help? She pushed off the couch, paced the room, pushed her hair off her forehead.

What if Patrick *was* the only one who could help? He could certainly have made it back to his lab in Davis by now. If that's where he would have gone. "No, Michael, this is… I… I'm going to call Dr. Allen. I'm sure he'll have something for you. Just relax." She rummaged in her purse for her phone and the note he'd given her back in DC.

"Dr. who?" Michael mouthed, barely audible.

"Don't worry. I'll explain later. Just rest, okay? I'll take care of everything. Just hold on." No way was she going to worry him more by telling him what she'd been through that night.

Michael closed his eyes and slowly lay over on his side. The shiny golden stuff covered his forearms now. Lara paced across the room to the kitchen as she dialed the number. Patrick's phone rang four times before voicemail answered. She waited through the short message, which to her surprise, referred problems to *her* number. And how many problems did he expect? Anger sliced through her panic, and when she heard the beep, she dumped it onto the recording through clenched teeth. Michael shouldn't hear what she had to say. "Another one of your *mistakes* has just arrived on my doorstep. This time, it's Michael. Should I tell him our lives are over or do you have some kind of antidote back in your lab?"

The sunlight shown intermittently through the kitchen window through a shredding fog. Gasping for air, she splashed water on her face and blotted it dry on a hand towel.

Get your shit together, Lara. For Michael's sake. She glanced over at him now, growing stiffer and shinier by the moment. A sharp aching pressure built around her heart, like it was ready to shatter into a thousand little pieces. If only she'd ignored Patrick at the conference. If only she'd told him to get lost when he offered the UV cream. But really, how could she have known? It was only sunscreen. She would have done anything to save Michael from the disease his father had suffered.

Feeling closed in and panicked, she opened the back door and stood on the stoop for a few moments as the sun broke out into a suddenly open sky. She focused on its brightness, willing her arms to stop shaking, until once again, the damp wetness engulfed the lighthouse in heavy silence.

"Please," she pleaded to the universe. "I don't know what to do."

The release came like a dam crumbling under a flood, building to convulsive sobs more consuming than when she'd learned of her parent's accident as a young girl. And, like he was there next to her, her grandfather's words soothed her soul. *Just let it come, little one. Let it all out so you can breathe again.* And she let go. Let her heart shatter. She sobbed for a good ten minutes until there was nothing left to do but breathe.

The emotional purge made her feel a little better, but she was still afraid. What would she see when she went back inside? Swallowing her panic, she put her hand on the swinging door. She could barely breathe let alone make her feet move.

Go, you coward. If Michael was going to be sealed up in a chrysalis, at least she could have the courage to be there for him. He was awake again, looking at his hands, turning them over and back when she sat down beside him.

His eyes met hers, liquid brimming. "What's happening to me? Is the doctor coming?"

Lara couldn't believe how fast it was moving. The original places had hardened to a shiny coating; but the edges oozed, consuming the flesh up his arms and hardening like crack candy right before her eyes.

"You said it would keep me from getting another cancer—I tried to peel it off—it's—it's—what *is* it?" He scratched at his stiffening arms.

"No, *stop*," she said, capturing his hands in hers. "You might hurt the skin underneath," she gasped, not really sure what would calm him. "The doctor will be here soon," she lied, impending doom erasing all reason and hope.

Michael shivered. The goo was moving up the left side of his neck. Lara gasped in a ragged breath. "Did you have a good session? I heard the swell was building." If she could keep him talking, anything, not to focus on what might happen, what she knew *was* happening.

"Australia will be awesome... " he croaked, and broke off. The crust had spread to cover more of his face, and now oozed across his clavicles, sealing in the gold St. Christopher's medal hanging around his neck. Then it glossed over his chest, fusing his body in a fast-hardening shell. And then, just before the goo sealed over his mouth, he smiled at her, like a silly drunk in love. She stroked his hair and smiled back, hoping that someday, somewhere, he might... But then, his smile widened to a grimace and forced out a shaky word. "Cold."

She pulled the afghan off the back of the sofa and covered his body, even as his eyes glazed over.

"There, is that better?" Could he hear her? She'd heard somewhere that hearing was the last sense to go before someone died. It took every ounce of her resolve not to scream from her innermost depths. Instead, she simply said, "I love you," and in the next moment, she could see that he was beyond her reach.

She had often pushed down fears of losing him, but they were all tied to his passion, surfing. He would be devoured by a shark off the coast of South Africa, caught on a reef at *Mavericks*, crushed under a mountain of water at *Jaws*. But this? This was beyond anything imaginable in the real world. Michael, the love of her life, the man she had chosen to give her babies and grow old with had slipped away, and there was not a goddamn thing she could do about it. Nothing! Her breath came shallow now, as if her lungs had collapsed. How would she live through this? Why would she even try?

CHaPTer 6 - Inoculation

Lara burst through her Dutch doors and out into the afternoon. There was still no response from Patrick Allen. The sun was struggling to make a showing, overwhelmed by a relentless fog. Not unusual this time of year, or any time on the coast for that matter. It was familiar like the tower, the old house, and the gravel drive, each in its place. Familiar, like the lines in her own palm, yet distorted by the unspeakable events of the last two days. By her involvement with Patrick Allen. A mistake that could never be mended, with consequences so surreal she hysterically clung to a shred of hope that this was an incredibly long nightmare launched in an unfathomably deep sleep by some disgustingly terrible food.

She stood in the center of the gravel courtyard, one hand on her hip, the other knotted in her bangs, gulping air. There just wasn't enough of it, not enough to breathe. The air must be cold and damp, but she couldn't feel it, the surf must be crashing against the foot of the cliffs below, but she couldn't hear it. All she could hear was the storm inside her head and she knew there would be no clear sunrise in a new morning. Sleep, maybe—exhaustion, merciful and empty—but upon waking, the storm would still be there, drowning her screams, holding her under until her mind burned for release.

This was no nightmare, and every second she spent in denial was a second wasted.

If Patrick had an antidote, it would be in his lab. If she could get Michael in the car, she might be able to get him to Patrick's lab before his condition advanced to what happened to Mrs. Kelley. Maybe it was already too late, but she wasn't going to give up. She couldn't wait any longer to hear from Dr. Allen.

She started to run to her car, then stopped in her tracks, skidding on gravel. No. In Michael's stiff condition he would never fit in the passenger seat of her little convertible, and even if he did, his horrific condition would be on full display to every other driver on the road. No. That wouldn't work.

She would have to take the Chevy.

She ran across to the old house and pounded on the door. "Grandpa! Gramps!" She cupped her hands around her eyes and peered through the trio of windows in the front door. She saw him moving through the kitchen, then past the front room windows. Hearing the deadbolt's brassy clack, she stepped back as the door opened.

"Good morning, Sunshine." He laughed at his mistake. "Or, I guess it's afternoon, even though the sky makes it feel like morning." His wide smile fell as he registered the fear on her face she couldn't disguise, and he took a step toward her.

It was good to see another human being, a steadfastly sane one. Oh, how she wished she could charge into his arms and let him help her as she knew he would. But she couldn't involve him. She had failed to protect herself and Michael, at least she could protect him.

"I need your car. The Chevy. And if the tank's not full, dump in all the gas you've got." She couldn't afford to risk anyone seeing her cargo in a gas station.

"What the hell? It's foggier than a boatswain's head on Saturday night. I won't allow—" And she'd understood his worry. If it weren't for the damned fog, she might still have parents in her life.

"Look, Gramps, I'm not going far," she lied. "I've got..." What? A medical emergency she couldn't tell him about? That would send his nosey worry machine into high gear. No. It had to be something he'd let her handle on her own. "Ah... one of my clients needs to get herself and her stuff to a safe place. Right now." She gave him the best smile she could manage under the circumstances.

He stood for another beat, cocked his head, and looked her in the eye. He had always been able to read her thoughts. This time, whatever he surmised would be wrong. She turned and started back toward the lighthouse.

"Sure you don't need any help? I could get dressed, and--"

"No, no. It's not that much." She waved his attention away. "I just need extra space, that's all. My car's just not big enough."

She chanced a last look over her shoulder as he ambled to his kitchen and came back with a set of keys. "Just be careful, honey. Promise me."

"I will," she said heading for the garage.

The old Chevy turned over like a dream. She pulled it up as close to her front door as she could, left the motor running, and opened the door to the backseat. Inside, she stumbled, caught off guard by the sight of the chrysalis sticking out from beneath the rug like a chunk of ancient amber, a foot wearing a leather Reef sandal visible inside.

Lara turned away and sank to her knees. "Michael," she whispered. The words stung her throat. "Michael, I can't do this."

But you must, she told herself, *You absolutely must.*

She worked down a hard, spit-less swallow. What else could she do? Leave the thing on her sofa? Roll it off the cliff into the ocean? She rocked back on her heels, considering. How could she live here knowing what she had done? How could she live knowing she had even thought it? That thought got her off her feet.

She dragged the seaman's trunk off the area rug in front of the sofa and with her eyes clenched shut so she couldn't see any detail through the horrifying, hardening shell, she slowly lowered it to the edge of the rug, rolled it like a burrito, and dragged the heavy weight inch-by-inch across the room to the Dutch doors, bumping it over the threshold. Michael's chrysalis was nearly twice as heavy as Mrs. Kelly's. It took every ounce of her strength to move it just a foot at a time. It bumped hard down the two steps leading out of her house.

"I'm sorry, Michael. I'm so sorry." *Can you ever forgive me?*

"Sure you don't need any help?" Her grandfather called out from his doorstep. Thankfully, the car was between him and her "project" so no matter how hard he cranked his neck to see what she was doing, he couldn't, as long as he stayed over there.

"I'm fine. Thanks, I'll be fine now." She tried to make her voice sound cheerful. "You go on inside. You'll catch a cold out here."

He hitched up his khaki pants, then pulled his sweater close around him, shaking his head. She could have used his help getting the load into the car, but she couldn't risk it. She stood, hand frozen on the door handle, watching him go.

"G'bye, Gramps, thanks," she called as cheerfully as she could fake as he ambled back inside. Her cheer fell muted under the fog and onto the damp gravel drive, and she wondered for a moment if she would ever feel joy again.

The moment the door clicked closed behind him, Lara hauled the rug and its cargo as close to the wide back seat of the Chevy as she could. Despite her best efforts, the blanket fell free, revealing Michael's completely encased face. A ghostly image of his mother, keening her lost son flashed before Lara's mind. *His mother! Jesus, don't think of her. Just get him into the car.*

With more strength than she had ever demanded of herself, she lifted the widest end of the load as far up onto the floorboard as she could. Her ears pounded, she had to fight for every breath, her throat burned from the effort. Half the load still angled out of the door. A quick look toward the house assured her that her grandfather had gone back to whatever he'd been doing. She crawled over the seat and slid gingerly past the bulky form. With the last of her strength, she braced her back against the load and pushed with her legs until it inched safely inside.

"God!" She hoped Patrick would show up at the lab. She hoped she was doing the right thing, and, she hoped she could live with herself after she did it. Carefully, she rearranged the covering to conceal the horror that lay beneath.

It took a good deal of concentration to clutch and shift the Chevy's old three-on-the-column transmission around the curves and back up over the highway to Sausalito. All along the way, she forced herself to listen to the pounding pistons of the old straight six instead of the pounding of her heart. Her grandfather had always gotten a kick out of driving the old car. Now the sheer mechanics of it was keeping her somewhat sane.

"A real workhorse," he'd always say, patting his hand on the dash like she was a favorite horse. It wasn't that he was old fashioned, far from it. But he was practical. Down to earth. Cherished the fine old things he had managed to keep in his life, the old Chevrolet and the aging lighthouse itself.

What would he do if he knew what she was into? In her mind she saw him, standing in the lighthouse tower, windows flung wide, clear blue eyes pressed to a pair of binocs, watching the sea as if every sailor on it was still his responsibility.

She could almost hear him say it. "Turn that son-of-a-bitch in, that's what I'd do." For him, things were always black and white. As true as the table of tides. No deviations. A man lived and a man died, and when he was gone, another one took his place. So, he explained it to her at her parents' funeral. "And women too," he'd told her. "Your ma's flaxen hair and her sassy talk. You'll carry those on, and lots of other things passed down. She lives on inside you, Lara. And inside your children, and theirs. That's the way of it. It's not to mourn, it's to rejoice. The unfolding of God's plan."

Unless someone like me fucks it up. Lara wasn't so sure about there being a god somewhere with a plan. The way things were in the world right then, it seemed like he would have had a better one. But she'd let her grandpa have his notions. It made him happy and well, and that's all that mattered.

She couldn't help thinking of all those chain letters she'd never mailed. That her girlfriends insisted would have her struck by lightning if she didn't mail out every stinking one. Funny how the mind pulls up trivia when what you need are real answers. The brain was just a stupid piece of electrified meat after all.

On-coming fog lights along the San Rafael backwater speared her consciousness, but never really broke through. She carried on the conversation out loud, as if her grandfather was sitting right next to her, his blue eyes full of knowing, spurring her into action.

"Yeah. Turn the son-of-a bitch in. That's just what I *should* do. Don't know what I've been thinking." But she did know. Patrick could be Michael's only hope. And Patrick was sincerely concerned for Mrs. Kelly, despite his manic reaction. If Lara turned him in, who would care for Mrs. Kelly's chrysalis? And, she was forced to admit, now Michael's? She certainly didn't know what to do for him. If there was anything anyone could do, she knew, Patrick would do it. And Patrick's son, Sloan. What would happen to Sloan if Patrick was locked up? And that's what the authorities would do. Lock him up and throw away the key… "

And blah, blah, blah, blah, blah. The thoughts chased themselves around her brain, eventually returning to the obscenity of it all. By the time she found herself at the UC Davis turn off, her fear had cycled back to outrage.

She'd paid little attention to the details before, when they'd come to collect gear before driving Mrs. Kelly's chrysalis to the cave. Had it only been twelve hours ago? She didn't know street names, but she thought she recognized landmarks—left turn and right, she drove past the laboratory twice, passing it on the wrong side of the street. Yes. There were the stone steps leading up to a small landing, and there was the clay pot of white impatiens on the windowsill. That had to be it.

She flipped a U-turn at the end of the street, forgetting the age of the lumbering Chevy's suspension. Her tail end swung around on squealing tires. So much for secrecy. It was late afternoon, and she expected there to be more activity near the college, but right now, the only thing moving was a cat who skittered down the sidewalk and out of sight. She didn't see the van, or any evidence of activity inside the building.

"Son-of-a bitch." Where does a mad scientist go after he's hidden away the evidence of his madness?

She threw the car into park, pulled the hand brake, and slid across the prickly old plaid plastic seat covers to the passenger side. She flung open the door, jumped out, scurried up the steps, and tried the door without knocking. Locked, of course. "Damn!"

The ground floor window was tightly shut. Inside, a landline was ringing. She pounded the door with both fists. The phone rang again. She looked back over her shoulder at the car door. She'd left it open wide. A piece of the rug had unfolded and flipped a triangle of color in the door jam. The sight of it made her cringe. The phone rang again. Maybe Patrick had picked up his messages and was trying to call *her* at his lab. She had to get inside.

Desperate, she picked up the clay flower pot, heavier than she'd expected, and dropped rather than threw it through the window. Not like in the movies, but effective. Another ring. She took off her shoe and knocked away enough of the broken glass to crawl through without shredding her knees, then scrambled in and grabbed the telephone on the laboratory workbench.

The dial tone beeped its electronic straight line. "Damn!" Tears welled in her eyes, she squeezed them away. No time for emotion now.

The phone message light blinked. She pressed the button and listened impatiently to her own words. "…one of your mistakes has just shown up on my doorstep." That was all.

Lara slammed the receiver down on its cradle. "Damn, damn, *damn!*"

If he had gotten the message, he'd be on his way to the lighthouse, not here. *Stupid. Stupid. Stupid!*

Her chest contracted, forcing more tears down her face. "No!" Not yet. *You don't get to break down until… Until you've done every single thing you can.*

So, Patrick wasn't here. She would have to go it alone. She had got Michael--the thing--into the car, she could get it out again. She unlocked the laboratory door from the inside, poked her head out, and checked the street again. No one around, no sign of any activity. She might be able to drag the carpet into the lab without anyone seeing her if no one drove by. Besides, who would report a woman dragging a body-sized something out of a car and into a laboratory in a rolled-up rug? Nothing suspicious there.

Exterior, day, she thought, trying to distract herself from the horror of what she was doing. *Wide camera angle. No one visible in street.*

"Unah!"

Woman struggles body wrapped in carpet out of old Chevrolet. No one sees.

The steps were the kicker, but her body seemed almost numb to the pain.

With superhuman strength, the woman drags the last foot of the load over the threshold…

She closed the door and leaned against it until she caught her breath.

After a few moments, she was able to open her hands and pull herself erect. Now what? Make a last try for Patrick? She grabbed his phone again, punched up her own number and waited through her own message. "Hi. I can't answer the phone. If you leave a message though, we can play phone tag. Here's the beep." She looked at her watch. If he came to the lighthouse, he might listen to her messages; it was worth a shot. "Patrick, It's four thirty. I'm at your lab. Get your ass back here. Now."

Then she punched up his cell number. *"The party you are trying to reach is unavailable at this time. Please try again later."*

She slammed the phone back in its cradle. Such convenience. Cell phones, messages out the wazoo and you still can't get a hold of anybody. She stared at the bundled rug just inside the doorway, pressed past it, and turned on the overhead lights. The first time she'd been here, she'd spent most of the time standing outside the door. Inside wasn't what she expected.

Shelves lining the walls opposite the windows contained more books than vials and vessels. All of the laboratory glassware was inverted and neatly stacked next to a deep sink as if the janitor had just tidied up and left for the day. She glanced around the room, her eyes deftly skipping over the lump on the rug by the door. She tried the door into the laboratory. She remembered Patrick telling her he kept it locked against thieves because of the extremely expensive equipment owned by the college. The slate countertop on the back wall held various small instruments—an oven, a scanning electron microscope, a centrifuge, an autoclave, a metal grille fastened to the wall, a gas chromatography column, several large glass reactors, and an exhaust hood stretching like a big box store appliance display over the whole thing.

Next to the counter stood a white cabinet with glass doors. Chemical storage, she presumed, giving the various bottles a cursory read. Combinations of letters and words she could not pronounce, let alone recognize or begin to know what they were for. She was about to turn away when two letters caught her attention. On the top shelf, pushed away from the others, stood a pint-sized brown bottle labeled simply "UV." Her eyes fastened on the label and her ears began to ring. The UV serum. It had to be.

Drink me, her over-stimulated mind crooned.

She tried the cabinet door. Locked, of course. There must be a key. She pulled open Patrick's desk drawer, drawers under the slate bench, cupboards above the sink, scattering the contents haphazardly as she rummaged. She dumped the contents of a shoe box out on the counter, scratched through various rubber and glass stoppers, scattering them on the floor.

Nothing.

The serum. That goddamned serum! So, what if it prevented sunburn. You could buy sunscreen at the drug store. You could drink the damn stuff and all it would do was give you a belly ache. But this stuff...

She bent down now, both hands pressed against the glass. This stuff was something else. She thought of Mrs. Kelly, turning to a hardened shell all alone in her trailer, not knowing what was happening to her. Innocent, unsuspecting, an aging guinea pig, willing to do anything Patrick said. Trusting the hand that fed her.

And Michael, world-class athlete, would do anything to keep himself in the green room inside a wave. *Like, dude, put it on once and you're set for life.* She could almost see him passing it out to his friends. God, what if he had shared the stuff? That thought sent her pulse racing a marathon.

She rattled the glass doors, picked up a glass bottle stopper she banged against the glass. A little harder and she could probably break it. He could make more. She struck the glass again. But how long would it take? Long enough for me to talk him out of it? Long enough for Mrs. Kelly and Michael to break out of their shells and scare the living daylights out of him?

She rocked back on her heels now, thinking about what she was doing.

Breaking and entering.

Vandalism.

What difference did it make? She had already broken the front window. And how do a broken window and some smashed chemicals stack up against murder? Yes, that's what it was. Murder. She looked toward the hulking shape rolled up in the rug by the door. Michael. Young, prime, silent.

The feeling came welling up inside her like the hot lava, burning its way through all her inhibitions. If she couldn't get an antidote to help Michael, at least she could stop Patrick. Maybe not forever, but for now, and for a long time to come.

She gripped the large glass stopper in her fist, shielded her eyes against possible flying glass, and swung at the cabinet as hard as she could. "Ai-ee-ah," she screamed at the tearing pain as her hand, her wrist, and then her forearm followed the heavy stopper through glass, smashing into the bottles on the shelf.

The stopper fell from her grip as she winced and pulled away. The worst of the pain centered inside her palm. She opened it slowly. A large piece of brown glass lodged in the crease along her lifeline, another piece hanging from its pasted label with the hand-written letters, UV.

Okay, well, at least you broke the right bottle.

She clamped her jaws hard together and pulled the glass out. A lemony ooze ran down her fingers, filled in the open wound, then spread into open cuts on her arm.

She gasped, looking frantically about for a towel, a rag, anything to wipe it away, but there was nothing. She cried out her desperation as a wave of searing cold swept through her body, the instant-cold of an on-coming faint. Only she didn't lose consciousness. She blinked once in slow motion and then watched as the lemon-colored gel coagulated over the gash in her palm and stopped the flow of blood. The other cuts had been sealed off as well, in a strawberry and lemon Jello glaze. Her blood and the UV serum.

Lara leaned back against the slate counter. Suddenly unable to support her own weight, she slid down to sit on the floor.

Her blood and the UV serum, mixed on the floor, mixed in her bloodstream.

She had effectively given herself an injection of pure chrysalis-forming UV serum. She turned her hands over slowly, inspecting them for any sign of crustiness, but there was nothing. At least not yet. Only the gel dried on her skin, a hardened, clear orange candy coating.

"O-o-o-o, she sang, floating, a silly old melody rolling through her head, *"Ain't it good for you?"* She grinned, giving into lightheadedness, and let her head fall back against the lower cupboards. Her hands drifted to lotus position, palms up, resting open on her knees. *"Good ol' fashion' medicated goo-ooo."*

The room tilted and swam, making her giggle. She shifted her eyes to the mute shape near the front door. Michael had been incased in the chrysalis in twelve hours, start to finish. She grinned again, thought to inspect her hands, but no matter how hard she tried to lift them from her knees, they would not obey.

The room darkened, theater slow. Then, a face appeared, though she watched it for a time before she realized it was really there. Patrick. His lips moved, but she could hear nothing over a shrill, circadian churr in her ears. He reached for her, then his image faded until there was nothing left but the bright, white, empty screen which shrank to the tiniest pinpoint of light, she was overtaken by an all-consuming, searing, cold, and then… nothing at all.

CHAPTER 7 - EMERGENCE

Bright light tinted the insides of her eyelids red. She squeezed her eyes tighter against the intrusion and tried to turn away, her neck muscles stiff and resistant. She tried to move her arms, but they were numb and unresponsive like she had slept on them funny, cutting off the circulation. Trying again, she felt constrained. Maybe she wasn't awake after all. What time was it anyway?

She rolled on her side, slitting her eyes open, trying to see her nightstand clock, but the glare was too much. Where was it coming from? And why couldn't she move, dammit? The mere act of turning within her confinement left her weak, struggling for breath, overwhelmed by the sensation she wasn't in her bed. She wasn't home. She wasn't anywhere she recognized. Her heart fluttered against her ribs as if it were ready to give up altogether.

Her cell phone. If she could just get to her cell, she needed to call…

Call? Thought unraveled and dribbled away, replaced by a shrill emptiness, and the overwhelming urge to break free of her bonds.

She jiggled her shoulders and flexed her knees a little. Her arms and legs were returning to life with a tingle. She dug her heels into the hard surface beneath her and lifted her head up into the shaft of light enough to see the source of her problem: She was wrapped in an onion-skin-dry, half-translucent material.

Plastic?

"Now that's not funny. Not funny at all," she mumbled out loud, her voice scratchy and dry.

Borderline angry, she worked harder, jabbing at the crackling substance with her elbows until at last she broke one arm free, then the other. The effort left her weak, her heart racing painfully in her chest, until in a dizzying spin, she slipped back into the void.

On her next waking, the light shaft had slanted away from her. Her heart beat stronger, but still out of sync. Nothing else had changed.

Gingerly touching the brittle substance with just the tips of her fingers, she peeled away the remains of the shell from her torso and hips and held it up to the light. The yellowed material preserved the shape of her body like a snakeskin shrugged off and abandoned under a dry bush--a fragile, transparent sculpture of her breasts, her shoulders.

What the holy hell? Goose bumps rose and marched down her back. Nausea threatened. She swallowed hard, tossed the torn fragments into the unknown darkness behind her.

This had to be a dream. No way is this really happening.

Her thought spun inward, seeking any shred of memory among blowing threads of consciousness. She had been on some kind of mission, compelling and frantic, that much she felt in her bones, but the where, the when, and the purpose eluded her, flirted with her psyche, and flitted away. Just moments ago, she must have had a name, seen a familiar face, performed some ordinary act. Now she was alone in a strange place peeling off layers of herself. It just could not be right.

She eased herself down, let her head fall back. *Yeah. This is a dream.* She snorted, relieved. She would wake up soon, laughing.

Just breathe. Breathe. Breathe.

She lay quietly and waited, drifting off, until, once again, the light demanded her attention. Slicing into the darkness, a honeyed shaft caught her skin in brilliant light, reflecting luminous blues and violets, iridescent greens and yellows. She traced her fingertips over her arm, surprised to find the surface dry and velvet smooth. Her palms and the insides of her slender arms were silvered, beginning at the hairline in a barely perceptible mail of scales like those of a fish; but, no, she thought as she stroked her arm, they were dry, feathery, more like—like the tiny scales of a butterfly wing.

Oh, you'll have to remember to write this down when you wake up.

She lay quietly now, watching the thin light shaft tick across the space like the second hand on a clock, until, eventually it exposed a wall of smooth stone, not more than an arm's reach behind her.

A cave. Right. Even more absurd. She let out a soft giggle. She couldn't wait to tell… to tell… but the *who* escaped her as she drifted off once more.

After what seemed like only a few moments, she woke again. This time she was able with some effort to push up to a sitting position, roll out of the enclosure that contained her body, and scoot like a mermaid to lean her back against the wall, the cool, hard stone a soothing reality against her back, the light shaft warming her lower extremities. She closed her eyes and took a moment to regain her breath, then pulled her legs free of the remaining skin, and kicked it away with distaste. Her chest still ached from her first painful breaths, but it rose and fell more steadily now. Her pulse throbbed at her temples, her neck, the backs of her knees, pumping life into her legs and feet. At last, she could stretch her toes into the warmth of it and she rested against the stone while her eyes grew accustomed to the dim light of the enclosure. Still, she was little able to discern any features other than what the light revealed in its thin projections: a stone floor, scattered rocks, unidentifiable shapes deeper into the dark.

She smoothed quivering hands over her breasts, nipples spreading supple and fearless, surrounded by an opalescent, downy coat that shimmered under her touch. She raised her hands tentatively to her head and found the same smooth, silky covering, except for two tender bumps at either side of the crown that sent a prickly, electric sensation all the way to her toes when she touched them.

"Oh." She pulled her hands back and clasped them quickly into her lap, the exclamation coming out of her throat in a dry croak. "Oh," she tried again. A hint of saliva rose under her tongue. She ran it over her lips and gasped air. Her mouth was dry and her head hurt like she had drunk too much tequila the night before. The fear that this wasn't a dream crept firmly into her thoughts.

Just be calm and wait. Just wait.

But calm wouldn't come. If anything, her fear intensified. The heartbeat that fluttered in her chest when she first opened her eyes on this crazy scene pounded now, rushing like a flood. She squeezed her eyelids closed and covered her ears, but the sound wouldn't go away. If this wasn't a dream—and she still held out a thin thread of hope that it was—where was she? What on earth could have happened? The last thing she remembered was—was—. She shook her head. She couldn't remember the last thing she remembered.

And then, as the light shaft traced away from her, leaving her in shadow, a chill stiffened her limbs, stung her struggling lungs, and pulled her nipples tight. The sudden cold carried with it a terrifying reality. She cast her gaze hopelessly about, found nothing of comfort, only walls of stone.

The need to warm herself pushed ahead of her fear, channeled energy to her legs, and pushed her forward until she was standing upright in full sunlight at the opening of a cave that overlooked a gleaming granite canyon.

As sharp and real as the cold had been, the bright sun shone with crystal clarity. She stepped farther out onto a high ledge and stretched the stiffness from her back and limbs, forgetting for the moment she was covered in strangeness. The comforting warmth spread through her being like—like—again thought disorganized.

The sun's embrace became her entire universe, spreading warmth from the top of her head to the tips of her toes. She closed her eyes and spread her arms wide, bathing herself in liquid light. When she opened her eyes again, she was surprised to see the sun had lowered nearly to the horizon. To her right, a range of sharply carved mountains gave way to rolling green hills at their base. The valley directly below her ran north and south as far as she could see and was blanketed in fog. She blinked as the image tweaked a shred of memory. North and south? By the position of the sun and some inner felt rather than remembered reckoning, she knew.

It wasn't until one of the last rays of sun struck her hand that she noticed the ring on her finger. It cradled a blue stone in a nest of gold along with a sprinkling of diamonds the color of distant starlight. She twisted it back and forth across her finger, watching it sparkle.

Memories trickled in—strong hands slipping the ring on her finger—a tawny-haired man with a beaming smile. She waited, longed for what came next, but nothing more came. *Patience, girl,* an older man's voice prompted in her head. *Gramps?*

Tears stung her eyes. She let go a long sigh. How long would this torture continue?

She turned her hands over. *Her* hands. Prints still swirled on her fingertips, and her love and lifelines still cut across her palms, but there was an alarming feature that had *never* been there before. On her right hand, across her lifeline, lay a two-inch-long, ropy scar. She folded her palm and opened it again. It wasn't a wrinkle or a trick of light. It was definitely there. A scar she knew deep in her gut was never there before.

Intrigued, she began to trace it with the tip of her finger, and with a pulse of pain in the heart of it, jagged images flashed. Memories laced with dread—a body rolled up in an old braided rug, glass exploding, her blood-soaked hand...

And then, piece by piece, the images tumbled in, like playing a movie in reverse: Her world narrowing before her eyes, then going dark... A man's face floating before her, Patrick; her mad dash to his lab, her desperate attempt to destroy what was left of the UV serum; the love of her life, covered in a sticky gel hardening faster than she could scrape it away; helping

Patrick drag what was left of Mrs. Kelly into a cave in the Sierra…

The cave. *Oh my god!* She was in… *the* cave.

Her breath caught in her throat. She spun around, the cave's dark maw gaping before her. Were the others there too? She staggered to the entrance.

"Michael!" Her voice reverberated in an echo. "Mrs. Kelly!" She listened a long time hearing nothing but the wind outside. She took a few more steps inside to the wall where she had rested. "Michael!" she called again. Nothing but the echo of her desperation returned. Hollowed out and alone, she could not make herself take another step into the dark. It was a bad idea anyway, right? There could be predators. She was basically defenseless. Okay, she was a coward.

She turned to trace her steps back toward the light at the entrance, and stumbled into a long container with smooth, uniform ridges sitting just outside the rim of light, letting out an involuntary yelp.

When her heart stopped thrashing against her ribs, she nudged it with her toe. Though it was heavy, it moved a little. "Well now, that's interesting." She sat, wedged herself between the thing and the stone wall, and pushed her feet against it until she moved it more into the path of light. It was a sealed container; dusty, unmarked. About as long as she was tall. Rubbing a place clean with her hand, she traced a criss-cross, woven pattern over its surface. Carbon fiber? Two half cylinders, about two-foot diameter, bound together lengthwise and held together by stainless steel latches that ratcheted open when she levered them up. Running her fingers along the seam, she sought and found an opening to split the pieces apart.

Poised to lift the top half of the canister away from its mate, she hesitated, a cold fear shadowing her curiosity. What the hell was she doing? Opening a thing that looked like some new age sarcophagus? She thought briefly of Howard Carter and Tutankhamen's Curse and had to laugh at herself. She had just awakened in a cave, bald, naked, and covered in iridescent down, with some kind of super-sensitive nodules on her head and she was worried about an ancient curse? Really? What's the worst that could happen?

Open the sarcophagus, find the Bogeyman, and wake up screaming. Dream over, right? Right. Don't be a wussy.

She took a last breath in through her nose, set her shoulders, slipped her fingertips under the lip of the seal, and lifted.

The container released a soft vacuum, *pish*, no bogeyman, not even a stray moth. Instead, inside was a gold-foil-lined interior, and many smaller containers, also sealed, some marked and some not. She moved a folded metallic solar blanket aside to find a nest of foil bags. Riffling through them, she read the labels: dried fruit, M&Ms, beef jerky. Freeze dried mac and cheese? *Ewe.* It was a good thing she had no sense of hunger because none of those things sounded the least bit appetizing. Another pile contained flares, matches, a first aid kit, and thank god, several containers labeled H_2O.

She worked at the lid of one until she got it loose, poured water into the lid and took a tiny taste. Yes! She lifted the heavy container and drank from it, spilling water over the side of her mouth and down her chest before she'd drunk her fill.

A blanket of woven material folded into one end of the container appeared to be covered in dust. But when she attempted to brush it off, the particles flickered and dispersed like smoke through the waning shafts of light until nothing solid was left. She watched the dust particles fall, bits of her courage falling with them.

She rocked back on her heels, cast a tired gaze about her. This didn't feel like a dream anymore. She really was alone in a cave in the wilderness poking through a canister filled with—okay—survival gear. Never mind that her body was covered in some kind of fairy down. That was definitely unreal. But the rest.... She was alone in a cave with packets of food, blankets, makings for a fire. Someone had planned this very well.

Patrick.

Effing Patrick you're-the-only-one-who-can-help-me McCormick-Allen had cleaned up and hidden his messy mistakes in this cave. She sat upright and peered deeper into the cave, as much as the dim light allowed. If there were others stored in the cave, was Patrick coming back to get them? If so, when? Without more light, and a plan, she had no way to find out.

She dropped her head to the crook of her arm and rested over the open canister like a widow keening over a casket. The shaft of light trained across her arm now, she touched it, still disbelieving. The surface left a powdered sheen on her fingertips. She pulled back her hand and clenched her fingers into a fist. Even if the bastard showed up, what was he going to do? She couldn't go anywhere in this condition, least of all, home.

Her heart shrank to a tiny cold fist in her chest. From the back of her neck, a needling fear spread to her ears, and finally to the two sensitive spots on the top of her head. She was careful not to touch them as she pulled herself into fetal position and willed her mind empty of the frightening facts.

Don't think. Just breathe. That's all she had to do right now. Just breathe and live for the next breath, because thinking too much might lead to a place she wasn't ready to face. At least, not yet. She focused inward, concentrating on each breath—in—out—in—out—until at last she found some comfort in the simple, life-giving process.

When she opened her eyes again, she stared without moving for a long time. The light had changed again, traced away from the canister, leaving her partly in shadow, chilled. Stiffly, she rose and dragged the canister further out onto the ledge, into what was left of the day's sunlight and began to take a halfhearted inventory. If she were really going to spend the night here, and it looked for all the world like that's exactly what she was going to have to do, then she'd better get ready.

She sorted the items into piles: usable things in her "good" pile, useless things in another. She tossed more metallic packets of food into the good pile, maybe enough for a week, if she was careful. A week? What was she thinking? No way was this abomination going to last a week.

She tossed the unmarked containers aside. Some surplus store must have run a sale on canisters, they all looked like Army issue.

The temperature changed the moment the sun dipped behind the western saddle of the mountains across the valley, cooling first the top of her head, then spreading to her limbs. There was much more to prepare, but her energy was gone. She pulled the solar blanket around herself and leaned back against the big canister, drained, lethargic.

As the sky darkened, the atmosphere around her grew eerily quiet. A solitary cricket, not far away, began a rhythmic creaking. Soon, it was joined by another and another until the night was filled with song. She closed her eyes and listened to the oddly syncopated rhythms. In her drifting consciousness, she lay in a soft bed, in a room with graceful, curving walls, in the arms of her lover, listening to the crickets and distant surf breaking along a half-forgotten shore…

Drifting up through a pleasant dream, she awoke with a start, stiff and chilled, once again in unfamiliar territory. The other dream had checked back in.

The metallic blanket crackled as she fashioned a sarong out of it. It kept away some of the cold but gave no comfort. She wished she could return to the dream she'd been having—a dream within a dream—where she spiraled through the sky over a sea-cliff home. A wedge-shaped, Monarch patterned canopy wing foiled the air, carried her out over the edge of a cliff and down in a wide circle that replayed over and over, as dreams will, but never quite reached a conclusion.

She sat now, wrapped in metallic silver plastic, peering out at this strange place. She had made it through a day, a night, and now her first dawn. She was confused, but she was alive and for the most part, well. As well as could be expected. Patrick Allen was going to pay, big time, when he came back for her, that was for sure.

If he came back.

The sky was tinged with pink behind the mountains to the east, but the light had yet to touch the nearest treetops. Soft murmurings that reminded her of the ocean were louder now. That was curious. She hobbled, stiff-jointed to the edge of the cliff. Below, where yesterday there had been fog, a brightening sky was reflected in a polished mirror of water, as far as she could see down the valley, the shoreline nearer than she had imagined. What was it? A huge lake?

The questions triggered a memory. She had been on a long-awaited trip with her grandfather after her parents' accident. They lived near the ocean, but grandpa had always wanted to show her the Sierra Nevada, take her on hikes through the granite canyons of Yosemite, feel the heat of geothermal hot springs in Mammoth, and stare up the tallest trees on the planet in Sequoia. The unexpected loss of her parents in her sophomore year in high school seemed like a good reason to break out of the familiar and do something extraordinary. And it had been.

Now his words on that trip came back to her with profound impact. They'd been heading in a straight, flat line for what seemed like hours on a highway divided by an endless line of pepper trees when he'd announced, "Someday, if the Earth continues to heat at the rate it's going, this could all be under water."

A lot of people said, "It'll turn around. It always has before. Surely man has no power to make or break climate on Earth."

But Grandpa had always agreed with the scientists. The climate was changing faster than anyone could have predicted. One of her last memories before this— whatever it was—happened, was the lecture in DC about climate change and how it could affect one of America's largest agricultural assets: the San Joaquin Valley.

How long? Lara wondered, a painful bubble forming in the middle of her chest. She looked out over the vast body of water before her. How long would it take polar ice melts to raise sea level enough fill up the San Joaquin? A hundred years? A thousand? Her mouth went dry. Just the thought of it was like trying to count the stars. No matter how many you counted, a stronger telescope revealed a billion more. No matter how hard you try to get your mind around it, the idea is too big to consider without your whole world going on tilt.

There was no denying something familiar about the configurations of granite rock around her, the lay of the land, the flatness of the vast valley below.

But even more than the physical nature around her, the changes in her own senses set her mind ablaze with questions.

She shielded her eyes as just at that moment, the sun peeked over the top of the ridge, spilling a timid yellow light across the scene in a way she had never experienced before. While the largest slice of the light was yellow, the edges expanded to green and blue at one end and red to ultraviolet at the other. In the next moment, the sun broke full over the mountain, releasing a rush of bright fuchsia across the sky and mirrored in the water below. The vibrant color was overwhelming, flooding her senses, her psyche, her soul, so penetrating and rich she could almost hear it shrieking in her ears.

She held her breath, taking it all in until a searing pain pierced the center of her palm, and her mind suddenly filled with an image of blood coursing down her arm from a fresh gash. The image was so vivid, her mind recoiled, and her body responded with a set of chills.

She stepped back away from the edge, opened her hands and turned them over and back to convince herself. There was no blood there, just the ropy scar across her palm. A fragment of her past life she could literally hold in her hand. She stared at it a long moment as the shattering truth broke over her. She had been in that chrysalis a very, very long time. And more importantly, there was no reason to believe anyone was coming to save her.

She sat a moment, letting that thought sink in. Whatever she had been, whatever had happened in the past, was over now and there was nothing she could do about it. The silence around her confirmed the thought.

She had never been given to depression. Or delusion. The people she knew, those who knew her— her partner Aleta, the girls in the home, her grandfather, even Michael—always expected her to be the one to act from reason, clarity, and positivity. Which is why, she supposed, she wasn't bawling her eyes out right now. Though every cell in her body wanted to let loose and scream, she held on to herself. Her composure. Her sanity.

Instead of letting herself implode, she fished a packet of nuts and raisins out of one of the canisters and nibbled a moment, her eyes staring into the darkened cave interior for a long moment. Then, like an automaton, she set herself in motion.

She organized the items from the large canister against the wall. She tucked the mylar blanket around her torso once again, then set about exploring the confines of her ledge, careful to stay away from the edges as she remembered it ended abruptly in a sheer, rocky drop.

To the right, a narrow passage between two head-high boulders opened to a widening path overarched by pine. It promised a way down from the ledge. Lara studied the boulders. They stood like granite trolls blocking her way. Tolkein-esque entrance guards, maybe. She chose the latter and carefully passed between them, half expecting one to put out a sword and bar her passage, but, of course, nothing happened. She laughed out loud.

Tall woman in a feather body suit captured by trolls at sword point in the foothills outside...

That thought stopped her again. Outside where? Because if that really was the San Joaquin Valley down there completely under water, she had a lot more to worry about than why her vision was suddenly psychedelic and her skin iridescent.

"Best not to think too much," she said out loud, and spent the rest of the day collecting kindling and small pine branches to warm her through the night. She allowed her practical mind to take the lead, overriding every doubt and fear. "Keep to the basics, Lara. One day at a time. Don't borrow trouble. Food, water, shelter, sleep."

The moment the sun dropped behind the ridge, the temperature dropped, and a cool breeze swirled leaves and pine needles around the ledge. Time to go back into the cave.

Inside, out of the wind, she assembled the makings of a fire inside a ring of rocks obviously used for that purpose in some faraway past. Striking a wooden match to the dry pine needles, she watched them trip their way to the twigs, and finally to the larger branches, carrying with them a building warmth. Then, gathering the metallic blanket around her, she climbed inside what she thought of as her sarcophagus, and let the glowing flames mesmerize her as she settled in, her arms folded neatly across her chest. Someday in a faraway future, an explorer would discover her remains here in this sarcophagus, nothing left of her but an aquamarine stone in a nest of gold, surrounded by shining diamond stars.

CHAPTER 8 - LEAP OF FAITH

Lara awoke to a chilly dawn. Wrapping the mylar blanket around her shoulders, she climbed out of her make-shift bed. With a quick stir to the remaining embers in the fire ring, she added a few more branches and brought the flames back to life. She stood near the growing heat, rubbing a thumb over the jagged scar in her right palm where chris-crossed stitches knit their way through her lifeline, effectively cutting it into two distinct sections. On one side was the life she had known—the young girls at Alternatives, the lighthouse, her grandfather, and Michael. On the other side, was what? A Kafka-esque freakshow version of herself stuck alone in this barren cave until she ran out of food and water? It certainly wasn't the life she had dreamed of.

She poked at the fire a moment before desperate loneliness drew her once again to the cliff's edge, searching for a thread of motivation. Of hope. There had to be something out there. Something to hold on to. Her stomach growled. At least Patrick, or someone, had thought to leave her some food. Nuts and raisins weren't all that bad, right?

She gazed out over the precipice. The ledge was so much higher than she remembered, as though the road she and Patrick had climbed to get here had been washed away by time, or, more likely, sheared off in a massive quake. Heart pounding faster, she took another step forward, close enough to steal a glance over the edge.

Wide granite shelves waited like ancient altars ready to receive a gift to the gods. She shook her head. It would be silent and quick. Over in one breathless step. Like the young British girl in the Last of the Mohicans film, she would just drop silently away.

The top of her head tingled like she was receiving a message from the universe. *Really? You'd just give up?* It was her grandfather's voice inside her head. *That's not the girl I raised.*

That was the question, wasn't it. Was this creature with iridescent skin and probing antennae on her head still that girl? Or was she something entirely different? She lifted her gaze once more to the soaring granite canyon walls surrounding her. Walls forged in fire. Solid, timeless, unyielding. The same granite stone that was cold and solid beneath her feet. The ground may have shifted a bit, and the earth's waters risen, but it was still the basic elements.

The feeling started there. Right there under her feet. The strong, organic pull of gravity grounding her on the stone. She closed her eyes and breathed in, feeling the flow from the top of her head, down through her spine and into her heels, pinning her down, down, into the speckled stone. She would have to jump twenty-five thousand miles an hour to escape it. A sobering thought. She may be alone. She may appear strange and different on the outside, but she was still Lara Paine. Grounded one the earth. Alive. And as long as he lived, she would be that girl her grandfather raised her to be. In her next breath, the taunting *l'appel du vide* released its grip on her soul. No. She wasn't ready to answer *the*

Call of the Void. Not today. Not as long as she had any control over her actions. She let out the breath and turned to the fire, taking in the heat until the growing firelight revealed another container resting along the back wall of the cave.

"Hum." How had she missed *that?*

She picked her way carefully across the stone-strewn floor and crouched next to it. It was nearly twelve feet long and a foot in diameter. A solid cylinder, domed at one end and sealed at the other. More supplies? Water? Why was it so long? There was only one way to find out. She worked at the heat-formed plastic seal with a sharp rock until the fire grew low and she no longer needed its warmth.

At last, she broke through the seal and loosened the domed end. Working it off with her fingertips, she reached inside and pulled out a long metal pole, several smaller ones, and some rusty-orange fabric she was afraid to touch at first, after her experience with the blanket. To her relief, she was able to pull it out intact along with a packet of tools. She blinked a moment before the pieces fit together in her mind. Her glider? *Oh my god.*

A familiar tingle crept up her spine, the one she always felt just before takeoff. Now this was something to look forward to. A way down off this cliff that didn't end with her body smashed on the rocks below. Hopefully.

Excitement bubbled inside her chest, and for the first time since she awoke in this barren cave, she felt the emptiness of her stomach. She scooped a handful of nuts and raisins into her mouth and returned to the glider canister. Maybe life here was going to be worth living after all.

Driven by a new surge of hope coming from deep within, she unscrewed the lid of a water container, took a long pull, then set to work. Once she had begun the task, the glider seemed to assemble itself. Resting on nose and wing tip, it nearly filled the mouth of the cave. She stood back and studied it from between the twin monoliths at the edge of the cliff, her heart rate cranking up again. She knew nothing of the terrain here, the wind, the updrafts. Taking off from this cliff in the glider could be suicide just as easily as jumping off without wings. Or, it could save her life.

The scar throbbed inside her clenched fist, the gravity of what she was about to do sinking heavily into her gut. Better to die trying than just give up, right?

Wind whipped about her, gently challenging her position.

A sound, a rustle from behind her made her scalp prickle, contract, then relax. What the hell was that? She turned, cocked her head. The prickling again. And then the wind whining around her like a chorus of ghostlike voices: *Come, we have been waiting.*

She whirled back to look again out across the valley. There was no sign of human life. Anywhere. Not obvious roads, lights, electrical towers. Nothing. And then from the farthest end of the valley, a tiny pinpoint of light grew to a slim swath, then a strong beacon of light sweeping across the water. *"Come..."* it called to her, accompanied by a gentle tingle in the nodules on top of her head. The sensation made her flinch, then chill.

Then, once again, an unmistakable scraping of movement behind her. She spun around just as the wind whipped beneath the glider and lifted its nose off the ground. It half floated toward the edge of the cliff.

"No!" Lara leapt to grab the wing. It zipped from her grasp and flipped up and out of reach. A rush of dried leaves swirled around her feet, swept beneath the glider, and lifted it closer still to the edge of the cliff...

"Wait! No!" Without another thought, she leaped again, this time catching the pilot's bar, her body fully extended like a trapeze flyer, just before the glider lifted clear of the ledge and pulled her over with it.

"Ohhhh, shiiiiiit!" she cried as they plummeted together, diving crazily along the face of the cliff. Precious seconds were lost before her instincts kicked in. The only thing to do, even though it seemed like the wrong thing, was to dive. With luck, she could build up enough speed to generate lift before she hit bottom.

When the moment came, she was ready. With one tremendous effort, she hunched up on the bar, forcing the nose down into a sweeping turn that caught a draft at the cliff's edge. She slipped her foot into the nylon boot and pushed forward, forcing the nose up out of the dive. Only then did the terror of the uncontrolled dive overcome her. How could she have been so foolish? A moment before, she had actually thought about jumping over the edge and ending this nightmare. Maybe she would have, but for the prickling on her head.

"Thank you," she said aloud. She would decide later who she thought she was addressing. For now, it was enough to feel the wind on her skin and see the vastness of the water, the curve of the horizon, and her hands gripping the control bar, tight and strong.

The canopy lifted and soared at her command. The ground circled below her as the lift carried her higher, her fear replaced by the pure joy of flight. The little meadow below circled into view; spreading gently down the mountainside. The sun had traveled high enough in the sky to light the trees in the valley and send a flicker over the sea.

She circled again in a wide arc, surveying the land immediately surrounding her new ledge home. Her intellect had not, could not, yet face the facts of her new existence, for now the pain of her situation was too sharp to accept in concrete terms. She forgot about it for minutes at a time, and when the facts drew near again, she pushed them out of the way, for now, believing only in flight. Gliding had always been, and could be again, the strongest sense of joy in her life, if she could expect to claim one here in this new place. Whatever hardships she faced on the ground, at least there was this. The thought delighted her, took her away, dispelled some of her fear. From here the thought of Fresno underwater was not a long-feared environmental disaster, but an absurd joke.

Imagine some future Argonauts searching for Atlantis and discovering Fresno instead. Ha!

Spirits lifting, she was elated that a large hawk joined her on the updraft. His wings arched as he leveled into her pattern, his gold eye fixed straight upon her, as if asking himself *What the hell kind of bird are you?* Lara smiled, the euphoria building. She could do this, whatever this was.

Below, dogwood trees mimicked miniature rose bushes, white flowers dotting green puffs like a child's drawing. On the gentle side of the mountain, a grove of trees spread in haphazard rows. From this height, they looked like broccoli heads, but they reminded her of citrus; dark, shiny leaves drooping to the ground. They also looked like they might have been cultivated at some point, though the land around them now seemed abandoned; no apparent roads, pump houses, or buildings one might expect in a working grove.

Close inspection would mean a sea-level landing, and without a source of food or water, she doubted she would have the strength to climb back up the mountain to the relative safety of her makeshift bed and store of supplies. Better not risk it.

"Now those are the thoughts of a survivor," she said aloud. The sound of her own laughter lifted her spirits as much as the wind had lifted her body.

Outside of the suggestion of grove trees below, there were no other signs of order. No housing developments, no recognizable signs of civilization. Surely, if this were truly the San Joaquin Valley, she would at least see Highway 99 somewhere below. But there was nothing. Whatever civilization had been here in the past had been completely reclaimed by nature. What she did see were silver ribbons of water winding their way to the valley, there joined by other rivulets as they widened on their way to the sea. In the distance, foothill trees like Sycamore and Buckeye gave way to pine and cedar, with a few redwoods here and there towering like sentinels over the rest of the canopy. Beyond that, the tree line ended in snow-capped peaks. At least there was some sign of normalcy. As she soared closer to her ledge, there were lush greens and a mossy carpet of wet grasses in the nearby meadow, a sure sign of water close to her cave.

She circled toward the cliff, seeking the up draft "elevator" to the top. Two, three full circles brought her back to the highest meadow. From there, hopefully, she could find a way back to her ledge and her supplies. Shelter.

A soft landing both surprised and pleased her. She hadn't lost her touch. She slipped out from under the glider's wing, stepped back and admired it, taking a moment to catch her breath. Patrick Allen may have been one crazy mad scientist, but he had gotten one thing right.

Her bare feet sank into the spongy wet moss as she dragged the glider to a sheltered area near the rock-lined path that could lead back to the ledge. From there she followed a profusion of pink and yellow Gilly flowers to a shaded alcove dripping with black-stemmed maiden hair fern and sparkling, crystal water. A bubbling spring it wasn't, but dammed with a few mossy rocks, the water leaking from the side of the alcove wall would soon build enough to scoop a handful. And if she brought some canisters from the cave, she could catch enough water for at least a few days' supply.

She scooped a drink. The water tasted sweet and cold, definitely tastier than the water in the containers up in the cave.

Leaving the glider in the meadow, she slowly made her way up a sketchy trail back to her ledge. It was hard work, but worth the effort for the chance to soar and discover a fresh source of water.

Each time she went back to the cave to get more canisters, she felt stronger than the last. With each trip, she felt a new purpose. Something to hold on to. Something to keep her thoughts invested in living, one minute at a time. If Mrs. Kelly and Michael had been in the cave, they certainly weren't there anymore. But maybe, just maybe, they had been here, and if they had been here, there was always a chance they might return. It was a tiny shred of hope, but hope nevertheless. And that was enough to keep her going.

Tonight, she would be ready for sundown and the lethargy she knew would set in. She spent most of the day in preparation, filling half her sarcophagus with pine duff and leaves, adding twigs to last night's coals until she coaxed a small flame to return. Now she lay on her side in her makeshift bed, poking at the embers. She watched a small ant as it dragged a particle of nut more than twice its size across the dirt. An enormous task for such a small creature. It filled her with humility. The past was gone, and everything and everyone with it. For all she knew, she may be the only human to survive on the entire planet. If you could call what she was, human.

The sun had climbed well into the sky and was already warming her rock ledge before she unfolded herself from her bed and stretched her stiff limbs. She was about to spread herself out on the rock to soak up its warmth when she noticed with shock there was an object out on the ledge that wasn't there before.

Wait.

How could that be?

Disbelieving and wanting to believe at the same time, she crept forward, afraid to touch it for fear it would disappear. But the warm, rich colors and the scent of nectar compelled her forward. At last, she reached out a trembling finger to touch a very real, hand-woven basket of fresh fruit with lilies and fern tucked in all around.

part two

Jenera

CHAPTER 9 – THE VALLEY OF LIGHT

Jenera sniffed back a shiver of doubt and gazed up at the glassy, blue dome of an empty sky. The message would come. All her being vibrated with certainty. She would receive the sign, there was no other way it could be. Never mind that she was tired, that her knapsack had worried sore spots on her shoulders. Never mind that it was nearing the end of the three days the elders had given her to once and for all verify the prophesy. She had kept her grandmother's teachings well. She would hold to the Truth: that Wisdom resided in every cell of her body in the same way it lived in the plants and the trees all around her.

The answer would come. She just needed to listen.

But time was running out. Jenera slumped against a giant granite slab tipped up on end, taking advantage of the cool shade under a brake of tall, forest fern. It was already noon on the third day. Even if she did receive a message, a sign, she'd be a day late getting back to Rowan with it, and the doubters would carry their message to the rest of her people that she had failed.

Maybe they would be right.

You're not going to get any messages hiding under this rock.

Jenera straightened as sure as her grandmother had grabbed her by the collar of her tunic all the way from Rowan's fire. She stepped out from under the rock and shaded her eyes from the vibrant yellow sun. To her right, the valley floor ended abruptly where great granite giants shouldered through the clouds. Ahead, the foothills rolled, dappled in deep green patches where sweet trees gave their nectar to the bees and their summer fruit to her people. To her left, and stretching out of sight, was the great salt sea, calm today, as if to lure the unsuspecting out across its lazy surface. But Jenera knew better. One never went against the legends.

The Dannais had flourished in their perfect valley, but soon, their population would exceed what their land could support and some of them would need to find a new place to begin.

The message will come on the third day.

Jenera fought a battle with herself. It seemed so foolish to believe in a prophesy when realities of life were so clear. The sun had just reached its highest point in the sky, but shadows fell quickly in the high valley. If she left soon, she could make it home before the last of the night braziers burned out in the village, but she could miss the message if she did not wait until the last possible moment before sundown.

Determined to stay, she lifted her gaze to the north. A great hawk circled in the distance, his solitude adding to the overwhelming sense of loneliness and doubt building in her own breast. Three days she had been out here alone, and for what? Some story her grandmother had told her? What if she was wrong? What if her grandmother had been no more than a dreamer? A gypsy like some said, telling stories around the braziers, while others toiled on her behalf. What if *they* were right? Most of them had already tried to turn the councils against Jenera and the crysls.

Except her best friend, Bryn. He was full human, but that had never stopped him from siding with her even when some of his friends made fun of her antenna starting to protrude. The hawk circled closer now, reminding her of Bryn's calm, determined presence.

"Bryn." She said his name aloud and it made her feel good inside. She'd been promised to Esteban , the son of Rowan's best friend, a fate that would be sealed in two years' time. There was nothing she could do about that. But, here, away from all the tradition and snoopy ears, she could let herself dream. It was Bryn who made her skin sing whenever he was near. No matter what was going on with her, despite the fact that he bore no *Dannais* blood, he always seemed to sense what would make her happy, calm her soul.

Bryn would tell her to listen to her gut. "So what if there is no message?" she could almost hear him say. "So what if there's no proof of the prophecy? Would you abandon the *crysls*? Of course not!"

And he would be right. The beacon light thrummed within her, as it had in all Spirit Leaders. That much she knew was real. It had been a daily message in her life, and it was here with her now in this lonely place, a constant reminder of her destiny. Message or no message, the time of the migration would find her people ready, even if it meant she had to preserve the *crysls* all by herself.

She scuffed at decomposed granite at her feet, then squatted and drew spirals with her fingertips as the answer seeped into her mind. She would stay until the sun had traveled halfway to the horizon, and then she would leave, regardless. That would get her back into her valley at least by midnight when the full moon would cast its light. She felt herself settle into her decision and lifted her gaze to the sea.

At that moment a remarkable image circled and dipped upon the water's polished surface, then morphed into a shadow and slipped up the side of the nearby cliffs. Jenera gasped and dove for the ferns. The shadow circled and disappeared again before she dared to look up into the sky. She crept out slowly, then crouched in the branches of a pine, the silver needles shivering under her shaking hands.

What creature could cast such a large shadow over the Earth? And then she saw it again. A giant bird. The underside of it bore a black and white lacy pattern like a butterfly, but its body was unlike anything she had ever seen. She watched it without daring even to breathe. It was impossible to tell exactly how large it was, until, no doubt drawn by the same curiosity that stopped her in her tracks, the great red-tailed hawk rose to the heights and flew next to it.

"Dear Mother!" she cried aloud. Its wingspan was nearly ten times the size of the hawk, and like him, it soared effortlessly, gliding in the wind.

Pushing down her initial fear, Jenera stepped out into the open to get a better look. The bird's shimmery white forebody tapered back smoothly to a darker, thick tail and hung from under the wings in a way distinctly different from any bird she had ever seen. Could its body really hang from its enormous wings by narrow threads? She gasped, fearing she was about to witness a terrible fall, but the creature circled freely, confidently, until, reaching a height nearly equal to the highest level of the nearby cliffs, it angled away and out of sight, the hawk trailing at a safe distance.

Jenera was stunned. She had been out for two days, and nothing had shown itself. Now, on the third day, this, this… giant butterfly creature. Could this be the message? If not, what was it? The prophecy was of grave importance to her people, the Messenger's coming could be the sign that they had kept the legends well, in spite of the doubters. But what if it wasn't part of the prophecy? What if this great creature was something entirely new and had nothing to do with them or anyone else? She had to be sure.

Her grandmother's words echoed in her mind: "I make this solemn promise, if you have lived well, and kept the legends, our kind will multiply and migrate to the ends of the Earth. Never doubt that you have been chosen as Spirit Leader for a reason. Fill your heart with love and you will receive a sign."

So she had waited for revelation. Her blood flowed with it, her mind coursed with it, her heart pounded with it. She had fought many battles of will with her people to preserve the *crysls*. And now her heartbeat rushed with the possibility those battles would not go unrewarded.

Jenera searched the sky again, but it seemed the creature had landed up in the heights. If it really was the prophecy, she had only to wait patiently, with love, and this creature—The Messenger—would return. She remembered how large the creature had been in relation to the hawk with a quiver of fear. No matter, she must go forward for the good of her people. She was only sixteen years old, the youngest of any Spirit Leader before her, but with her mother gone, she was the only one of the direct bloodline left to carry on with the responsibility. The people depended upon her, at least the *crysls* did, and those who didn't, especially Rowan, would need proof beyond question, especially if she were a day late returning. They had long tired of sharing their resources for something that appeared useless.

She stepped further out into the open and filled her heart with love for the creature. Surely no harm would come to her from such a beautiful one. It would feel her presence and come to her. She would speak to it. Know its spirit, learn its purpose and to what legend it belonged. She stood silent and focused, waiting, the cooling breeze lifting her hair gently as it passed.

But the shadows lengthened, and the would-be messenger did not return. Jenera considered her options. There were worse dangers for a young woman alone in the heights after dark than being wrong about a prophesy. Most of them had teeth, claws, and a feral hunger for meat. As the moon put on its full coat and began its watch in the heavens, Jenera retreated under the granite slab and spent her third night on the mountain dreaming of a future where she soared the sky on wings of a giant Monarch.

Morning brought with it a new resolve. If the Messenger would not come to her, she would go to the messenger. Now that the three-day deadline had passed, she wasn't that excited about going home. At least she would have a story to tell, even if it wasn't the one they wanted to hear.

She scanned the sky. A thin, gray wheel of clouds circled in from the north. For now, only a whisper of wind, but soon, a shower, and then a downpour. She had better get started.

With a knobby branch from the pine, Jenera drew a triangle in the dirt, the sharpest angle pointing west, as her grandmother had taught her.

She pulled her chrism jars from the knapsack and carefully applied the colors of meditation to her face. Then she stepped solemnly into the triangle.

Chin held high, she lifted her gaze to the farthest Western horizon. "Not for me, but for the true Dannais, show me the Messenger one more time."

She waited, straining with all her youthful intensity, fighting back worried thoughts that the sky was only the sky and not the Breath of God, and that the sun was nothing more than a bright star. The doubts of the elders had crept into her being and robbed her of a piece of her spirit. At each meditation, their words invaded her prayers, contaminated her power.

No, she insisted. Their loss of hope cannot be my own. She shook off Esteban's words, that she was the last of a fading dream. "We don't need the dreams of spirit women to guide our fortunes," he had complained loud and often. "Your blood mixes well with humans, this we know. This is how we will continue."

"Your blood will be strengthened by mixing with mine," she had countered. "But mine will be diluted and that could mean we will eventually lose the spirit of the Dannais."

"Bah," he had argued, as if he had no Dannais blood running in his own veins.

Jenera had to suppress her anger when she thought of it. Men, even Rowan. All they ever think about is rule. She was afraid the time was near when she could no longer preserve the purer bloodlines of the *crysls*, and with that they would lose their promised miracle gift of flight.

"You cannot will worried thoughts away," came her grandmother's voice on a whisper in her mind. "You must replace them with positive ones." Jenera shook out her hair, shook her arms, and finished with a shake of her fingertips, refocusing on the wild sounds around her—the hawk's cry and the insect's buzz, the breeze playing in the leaves overhead, mycelium fungi entwined at her feet—and this time broke through, feeling herself spread wide over the countryside, flow into the trees, the rocks, the sky, touch the sun, and vibrate with it all on one resonant note. She felt the power begin to flow. She needed a gift, something of honor. A gift of…

A hawk's scream close at hand broke her concentration again.

Disappointment lodged in her breast like a stone. Had the spirit way deserted her? She hung her head, kicked at the dirt inside the triangle, then stomped out the lines altogether. Forget the traditions. She was taking this in her own hands.

It takes more than the grousing words of a man and a screaming hawk to still the heart of a Spirit Woman.

If the Dannais spirit had deserted her, her own had not. They would have their truth even if she had to climb all the way to the top of the granite cliffs in front of her. The wind picked up, forcing her to pull her cloak about her. She had better get busy.

Gathering *cots* and *pichets* from her knapsack, she placed them into her basket. And in case that wasn't enough to give the creature pleasure, she collected several yellow-spot *lilits* to add color. A few fiddle necks and a full fern frond balanced the presentation. She smiled at her creation. Rowan would have chided her, but the old man wasn't here. And what did he know anyway? She loved the old leader like a father with all her heart, but it had been a long time since he'd done any actual leading. He had left it up to her after all to prove the legend.

She swept the thought of Rowan's chiding away as she would a bothersome insect, then pinched a stem from a pale, lavender water iris and tucked it into the corner of the basket. She fitted its contoured bottom between the ridges on the top of her head and began her ascent toward the cliff nearest the spot where she had seen the great wings disappear.

When she reached the first leveling of the meadow where she thought the creature had landed, she removed the basket, crouched low, and crawled forward cautiously. The butterfly wings—rich, rusty-orange and black side up—were spread not more than a hundred steps away, but there was no body! How could it be? A pair of wings and nothing more? She moved closer and found her first impression to be true. A pair of massive Monarch butterfly wings lay abandoned! Her heart suddenly felt abandoned as well. Had the messenger met with an accident? A fall? Had the threads broken after all? She peered about, her heart refusing to believe the evidence, and then she saw them. Footprints, very like her own, leading through a space between two hulking boulders. Someone had been here before her, but who? And what had they done to the Messenger?

She passed through the boulders and found no one, only the footprints in the soft dirt, then muddy outlines on the granite fading into the mouth of a cave. Jenera carefully fit her foot into one of the prints; nearly a perfect match. She caught her breath. Something stirred in the cave. She leapt for cover behind the boulder, realizing too late as she turned to peer from behind the rock, that she had left the basket of fruit on the ledge.

The opening to the cave was completely dark, she could see nothing, but she could hear that someone, or something, was moving about. Most likely one of the big cats known to live in the highest caves of the mountain. She pressed herself further back against the rock, scarcely daring to breathe. She could see the basket right out on the open ledge. *By the Legends, I am a clumsy fool!*

And then something—someone—emerged from the shadows of the cave entrance into the light. Her heart drummed its beat into her throat as the creature stepped out, dazzled opalescent in the full rays of the sun. Not an insect, and yet not quite human, it walked upright, unmistakably female. A tall, slender goddess––a woman, bathed head-to-toe in dusty iridescence like the inside of a bay oyster—movement flowing and graceful—wide-set, intelligent eyes above high, sculptured cheekbones like the granite cliffs that surrounded them. Above her forehead, which seemed all the higher since the creature had no hair, two nodules protruded like the tips of a living crown. It was the most incredibly beautiful being Jenera had ever seen or imagined, and Jenera knew this moment would live in her memory for as long as she walked the Earth.

The creature stepped cautiously out onto the ledge and looked about, eyes sliding left and right, head turning slow and graceful on a long neck. The nodules on top of her head probed the air like delicate fingers, and then her gaze shifted straight to the basket of fruit.

She stood so near Jenera now, she could hear her slowly draw in a breath. Jenera took a step back, rattling the dry pods of a nearby buckeye.

The creature froze, retreated a step, and called out timidly. "Who is it? Who's there?" The voice piped melodically, pleasing to the ear, yet Jenera's own tiny nodules, invisible to others because of her thick, springy hair, sensed fear and confusion.

Had she caused such anxiety in the creature? What would be the outcome? She had made a mistake. She should have waited, approached more cautiously, but then she had no idea—

"Whoever it is, please," the creature went on. "Come out here where I can see you. I'm not going to hurt you." Then she stole across the ledge nearly to the place where Jenera hid.

Jenera shivered. The moment had come. The one she'd been waiting for since she tried on the ancient seer's robe from her grandmother's storage chest. She pulled herself up to her full five -oot height and stepped out from between the two boulders to face the creature.

"I am Jenera, of the *Dannais*," she said in a voice that came out much more bravely than she felt inside. "Keeper of the legends, Spirit Leader of our people."

Their eyes met, and for one terrifying moment, Jenera thought she would bolt for the trees. The creature's eyes, though gentle in expression, were large and piercingly blue. In the telling of legends, creatures seemed strange and wondrous, almost poetic. But in real life, a legend could be most astonishing. In that instant of hesitation, Jenera was shocked into recognition. This creature was not a part of a legend or a sign, not a mere clue to the future. This creature was the very one her grandmother and then her mother had told her about and for whom all the Spirit Leaders had waited. A human blessed with the gift of true flight! Jenera's heart swelled. *The great Journey will happen in my lifetime!*

CHAPTER 10 – THE SILVER SWAN

Lara had sensed the twin rock sentries held some magical power, but she could not have imagined they would conjure up a vision such as the being who stood before her now. The young woman embodied everything she'd hoped for and everything she feared at the same time. Though her first instinct was to retreat into the cave, Lara's feet were riveted to the rock. Thoughts raced through her mind faster than she could grab them and analyze. The offer of food, the proclamation of allegiance, the young woman appearing out of nowhere, face painted like a character from an exotic dance troupe, yet unlike anyone Lara had ever seen.

Seconds vibrated between them holding both promise and mystery as Lara tried to make sense of what she saw. Jenera was, at least to outward appearances, one hundred percent real and human. But like the San Joaquin filled with water, and the very apparent clarity of a sky unblemished by pollution, this woman's appearance very simply and vividly underlined the profound changes that had taken place in humans while Lara… slept.

A peaceful admiration radiated from the young woman's face and filled the distance between them with a tangible expectation. Yet, along with the tranquility she perceived in Jenera's eyes, Lara sensed a hint of power, as though this young girl—no older than the girls she had housed at Alternatives—was in the habit of commanding more than her youthful share of authority.

Jenera's body was slender and attractively healthy. Sable hair spun away from her face, its curling wisps backlit by the sun, were touched with red highlights that created a shimmering aura about her head. She was hauntingly beautiful, a well-blended mixture of several racial groups. Her eyes, alluring yet without guile, were green, flecked with gold, oddly light in contrast to the rich walnut pigment of her skin. Her eyelids, though not set in a full epicanthal fold, stretched taught over round eyes. Her lips arched smooth and full, above and below, her skeletal features—nose, cheekbones, jaw, and chin—were as finely honed.

A wedge of iridescent green shadow filled the hollows above her eyelids and extended in feathery strokes to her temples. Her brows, enhanced with a gold shimmer, slashed up and out to meet her hairline. The lower lids were lined in what could have been ancient kohl. A smear of bronze under her cheekbones emphasized their height.

From her study of world cultures, Lara understood this was not the superficial make up of vanity, but a dramatic, almost tribal creation.

The girl wore a loose tunic over trousers woven of natural fiber. A hooded cape of the same material flowed off her shoulder, held in place by a silver clasp stylized to suggest a bird or… no, a butterfly. Bracelets of hammered copper and silver circled each of her wrists.

She was amazing to look at but having had nothing but stale dried fruit and nuts for three days, Lara's eyes slid to the basket of fresh fruit a moment and then back to the young woman.

As if reading her mind, the girl lifted one of her slender arms, gestured toward the basket of fruit and nodded. She had known hunger, Lara thought, and she respected it. Without another moment's hesitation, Lara fell to her knees on the ground before the basket, her mouth watering, and took her first bite of fresh food.

As Lara sucked juicy, red meat from a plum, savoring its sweetness, a sudden stillness enveloped them, as though the mountains themselves leaned in to listen for what would transpire between the two women.

When at last Lara slipped the plum pit from her mouth and tossed it off the cliff, Jenera smiled. Her hair lifted gently away from her face in the light breeze. She knelt before her and lowered her head. "I have waited for you for many seasons, lived with the vision of your arrival since I was very young."

Startled, Lara rocked back on her heels.

"Oh, please," she said, struggling to control her vocal cords grown weak from disuse. "Just sit here beside me." She crossed her legs beneath her on the granite ledge. "Have some of this fruit. Where did it come from? I've had nothing but the nuts and raisins—" but her words trailed off unfinished. Jenera stared back at Lara as if she'd just seen an apparition.

Lara's insides quivered in apprehension. She wanted answers but was also afraid to hear them, to face the obvious conclusion that there was no going back. If they could just talk about food and ordinary things, just for a little longer, she might not have to answer the inevitable question of who or… or *what* she was.

"The fruit? Oh." Jenera faltered as if drawn from deep thought. "From the groves, below." Her young brow furrowed. "We have our own, near our valley, better tended. These are a little smaller, but good for wild grown." She smiled, swept her cape into her lap and folded her legs under her as Lara had done.

She took an apricot from the basket, held it tentatively to her mouth, and cocked her head to the side. "Forgive me, but when I saw you from below, I thought you were an omen, a good sign for my people."

Lara swallowed hard. "Your people?"

"We are the *Dannais*." Her voice grew stronger, touched with emotion. "We've lived in this valley many, many generations, abiding by the Legends. Waiting. My grandmother said there would be others, that there would be signs. Now I see that you are not just a sign, but a piece of the Legend itself."

"The Legends." Lara narrowed her gaze to Jenera's remarkable eyes. It was difficult to think when all she wanted to do was devour every piece of fruit in the basket. She had to admit that she half expected this entire episode to vanish into thin air and leave her alone and starving, the victim of another fantasy. Yet Jenera looked so intently into her eyes now, that Lara lowered an apricot to her lap. This girl thought she was part of some legend? That was preposterous. She needed to head this delusion off and now, before it got out of hand.

"Listen to me, Jenera. I can't possibly be a piece of your legend."

"Oh, I know," the girl insisted. "It's a strange story that's hard to believe. Some of our own people have turned away. They mean no disrespect to you, they've just grown impatient."

She gazed off across the horizon to the faraway granite cliffs, then breathed a long, slow sigh. Her eyes narrowed, almost closed. "It has been many years since we have observed Fiera's Fire. Not since before I was born, in fact."

"Fiera's Fire?" The notion that she could be part of this legend was absurd at best. But it was so wonderful to hear another person's voice, she didn't want to drive the poor girl away. "Tell me about it."

"The legend of Fiera and Jhan is one of my favorites. If none of the young ones ask for the song around the night braziers, I always volunteer it. Its plaintive melody, a canticle of minor notes and subtle key changes, are the most fun to sing."

Young ones? Braziers? Her curiosity piqued, Lara just smiled at her and waited to hear the story, licking peach juice off her fingers like a child at a library story hour.

"The story goes that Fiera and Jhan arrived in the valley barely alive. They were part of a colony that eventually failed because the *milkiweed* died off. That is why we cultivate it. Save the seeds."

"Anyway, our people nursed them back to health, gave them a bag of seeds to take home with them. On the day they left on their journey, the people built a fire on High Point Ledge and pushed the coals over the side as a sign of their love."

"That's a beautiful story."

Jenera's eyes glittered with tears. "That's what many think. That it's just a story to entertain the young ones. I was hoping your arrival might bring some believers back into the fold."

Lara's heart pinched a little for the young woman. It was clear her arrival could be nothing but a chance event, the unintended consequences of the reckless ego of a deranged researcher. But by the expectant look in Jenera's eyes, she doubted telling her own story in more detail would dispel Jenera's misunderstanding. If she had learned anything in her former life it was that most people—especially those bound to legend and myth-- believed what they wanted to believe regardless of facts. And it was clear that Jenera's belief, that she was some kind of long-awaited miracle, was deeply held and formed the basis of a culture. Fascinating.

One might expect the sight of such an extraordinary being as herself would instill a sense of awe; however, Jenera's attitude of reverence and humility was a bit disturbing. Lara was certainly no part of these legends, and she didn't want to let the girl go down that road, but she didn't want to trample on her beliefs either. After all, this young woman was the only representative of humanity she'd seen. For all Lara knew, she and her *Dannais* were the only ones. Just the knowledge of their existence had already dispelled much of the cloud of loneliness that had hung over her since her arrival in this remote existence. She didn't want the encounter to end.

"You know what's amazing?"

Jenera's eyes brightened and she sat forward expectantly. "Please. Tell me."

"When I was a young girl, my grandfather and I traveled to the mountains where they told of a firefall ceremony from a peak like you describe.

Jenera stood up, suddenly animated. "Yes, once you pass through the tunnel at Gate Compound, you will see it, and a whole bunch of other formations you couldn't help but recognize if you had ever been there before."

The shockwave hit deep in Lara's gut as another vivid memory rushed in. *El Capitan.* She had soared off that cliff after much preparation and red tape along with a select group of gliders the year she graduated UCSF.

Suddenly, it all made sense. The cave had to be near the south entrance of Yosemite, possibly near the Mariposa Grove. If you followed the road in, you went through the tunnel to the famous overlook, bringing El Capitan, Glacier Point, The Three Sisters, and Half Dome into view. Like a veil being lifted, the memory gave her an even more solid foothold on her geographic location. And that thought slammed into her with a fleeting sense of hope: If she knew where she was in this new reality, she could find her way home.

The next thought deflated her. If the San Joaquin was an inland sea, what chance was there she had a home, let alone a family to go back to? She let go a ragged sigh as the absurdity of her hope hit home.

"Tell me more of your Legends, Jenera," she said, resigned. This lovely young girl was most likely the only contact she would have with anything human again. She reached out and touched her hand. Their eyes met, and without words there passed an understanding, a trust born of an instant bond. "Tell me of your family."

Jenera drew her hand away slowly. Her eyes lit up in wonder when she saw that a smudge of iridescent dust had transferred to the surface of her own skin.

"O... kay." She stood and paced across the ledge then made a dramatic turn, as though she were accustomed to speaking in front of people.

"My grandmother was a seer—a Spirit Leader, a direct descendent of Cira. She taught me well—all of the legends—her lifeline was truncated—she knew we would only have a short time together. Among the items given to Cira when she emerged in this world was an amulet she was instructed to pass down through our family women, eventually to my grandmother who was Spirit Leader after her, then to my mother."

"In the long ago, Dax, one of the young men who came up from the south with a group of wanderers and spent time in our valley, was on his journey to manhood. As he climbed to the heights one day, seeking his spirit family, a magical bird-like creature circled over his head, then landed next to him on a high rock ledge.

"In fact," Jenera continued, indicating the granite ledge about them, "The place must have been a lot like where we are now." She leaned forward, snapped up the lily from the fruit basket and tucked it behind her ear. She looked about her, thoughtfully, then pulled herself back to the story. "Anyway, to Dax's surprise, it was not a bird at all, but a woman who possessed the gift of flight. She was the most beautiful creature he had ever seen, with lacy parchment wings like those of the golden butterflies that flourished in his home. Her skin was silken soft and shone like nacre pearl, her hair was the whitest silver like swan's down.

Jenera's story swept Lara along, not simply by the narrative, but by the lyrical cadence of her voice and the intensity in her eyes, almost as though in the telling, Jenera became the story itself. She closed her eyes and began to sway gently as the words rose and fell like a song...

"She enfolded him in her arms and showed him the pleasures of life. Day after day, they lived in their private paradise, Dax and his Silver Swan. Dax knew that he must return to his people to claim leadership of his tribe, for he was the son of his colony's leader. But when his group had refreshed their supplies and strength and were ready to continue their journey, he could not bear to leave her. On he stayed, rapt in ecstasy, until in late summer, the lady fell ill. Soon they realized she was with child. Dax swelled with pride but alas, when the child came forth, the lady expired. Filled with sorrow, Dax wrapped his baby daughter up in a piece of her mother's parchment wing, placed the amulet around her neck, and took her to the women of Lillit Compound." Jenera got up and paced slowly around the ledge.

The pain of loss piqued in Lara's chest. "What happened to Dax?"

"Dax? Oh. He was heartsick and broken and couldn't bear to stay with the *Dannais* without his Silver lady, so he set out to reunite with his own people and our people never saw him again."

"That's so sad." More than sad. The thought that there could have been others like her set her mind reeling. How many of Patrick's experiments were out there? Come before her?

"Yes, but not all so sad," Jenera continued as she slipped the lily out from behind her ear and twirled it thoughtfully between her fingers. "The child survived and was raised in the ways of our people and eventually grew to be a strong young woman and produced many offspring of her own."

"We don't have good records of how many *Dannais* were created in those days. Many of us have the gene passed down from the Silver Swan, the *Dannais* gene, we call it, but none of us has ever had the full gift of flight." Then she stopped, came around to face Lara, and knelt before her. "Until *you*, that is."

Until me. Lara gaped at Jenera, speechless. She gestured weakly with her hands and finally, covered her mouth with them. How long ago had all this happened?

The image of Mrs. Kelly fleeted through her mind, her fragile body curled inside her amber shell, her white hair soft about her parchment skin, the little amulet necklace... My God, what if...?

"Yes, of course, you would already know all this." Jenera's eyes gleamed with admiration.

"No, no. Actually, I...I don't." She squeezed her eyes shut and made herself breathe. It was just too, too much. What she really wanted was to run back to her cave, crawl into her sarcophagus, and pull her blanket up over her head.

Coward. This could be your only chance to find out the truth of what happened.

True. She drew in a deep breath and blew it out, then steeled herself against the urge to run. "No," she said. "I want to hear your family history from your point of view. There's more, right?"

"Well, yes. There's a lot more," Jenera said, her eyes glittering again. "There's the Legend of Kirin and Auru."

Of course there were more. Lara pulled her arms around her knees and sat quietly with her hand over her mouth so she would not cry out in panic and frighten the young girl. The entire surface of her skin prickled with goose bumps, ruffling the tiny scales on her skin. The nodules on the top of her head contracted like the tentacles of a sea anemone when they were disturbed. "Yes. Please, go on," she said, her heart breaking for all the people whose lives Patrick had drawn in, manipulated, destroyed.

Jenera returned her gaze like she could read her mind, and after a moment continued cautiously. "Kirin was a young woman of our colony, one of the descendants of Dax, a healer. She often journeyed far into the mountains searching for herbs and mushrooms known to have healing properties. On one of these trips, she came across a young man. He had apparently been wandering for days and it was apparent he was alone and hungry. Kirin shared her food with him and helped him regain his strength. He could not remember his own name. He was confused, like someone who had hit his head. Kirin called him Auru, for the color of his golden eyes. Many of the women believed him to be a god for he was much taller than anyone they had ever seen and was wrapped in a velvet cape of black and gold. The oldest of the old warned her: 'You cannot love a god, Kirin. You need to find a real man who will bear us sons.' They had much to fear, since their numbers had dwindled, and few men were left to help carry on their line, for it seemed that the women were better equipped to survive in the harsh environment at the time."

Kirin and Auru couldn't move about in the community without someone raising a brow or making a thinly veiled remark behind their backs. Kirin paid no attention. She told them they were just jealous that he did not come to love them. And, oh, how Kirin loved him. It wasn't long before they conceived and Auru moved her to the high mountains so the people would stop bothering them.

"There, Auru told her of a place where men and women lived together and raised their children in happiness, where life was hard, but the people were free, and made music and laughter together. Throughout Kirin's pregnancy, they visited the *Dannais* whose acceptance grew in proportion to the size of Kirin's belly and the promise of a child to add to the population. Her pregnancy progressed amazingly fast, faster than anyone could remember before. When it was clear she would deliver soon, she came down from the mountain and the women of Lillit Compound cared for her throughout her labor, which proved to be long and difficult. But when the baby was born, they ran away in terror, leaving Kirin alone with a hideous creature that looked more like a locust than a child. Mercifully, perhaps, there was no life in it. Cira wrapped it in a blanket soaked in pitch and sent it out across the sea in a small canoe, set aflame."

Lara's throat twisted around a rising outcry. She reflexively covered her belly with her hands.

Jenera's eyes met hers, the gesture had not been missed, and by the expression on her face and the way her gaze shifted from Lara's stomach back to her eyes, neither had its meaning.

Lara straightened her back, and her hands lifted to smooth back her hair, but, of course, she hadn't any. Jenera's brows knit in confusion. Lara simply felt foolish now, the original fear pushed down behind a warm flush.

"I'm all right. I—go ahead with your story." She was not all right. Fear squirmed in her mind like a maggot. The faint flutter in her belly became an insect scratching at her insides trying to get out.

Jenera eyed her carefully a moment longer, as if to see for herself whether Lara was indeed all right. At a nod from Lara, she fell back into her narration.

"Back on the mountain Kirin told Auru only that the child was stillborn, and the loss changed him. He became despondent, longing for the life he had lived before, and often wandered down into the valley where the ruins of abandoned cities were buried under the sea and rubble. Sometimes Kirin would go with him, listen to his ravings, make love to him in the mountains. She conceived again, but even this could not bring back his happiness. He would stare off to the South, inconsolable.

"Then, when Auru failed to return after many days from one of his journeys, Kirin climbed to their favorite vista point and found a hollow statue, liquid amber, hardened like glass, an empty shell in the likeness of the god she had loved as a man. The elder *Dannais* were convinced of his death, but Kirin wouldn't listen. They were superstitious and ignorant, she insisted. 'He has gone the same way he came. He won't be coming back.'"

Lara sat stunned. The implications of Jenera's story were too much for her to fully absorb at once. "How long has it been? Since Auru came to your people?"

"Many generations. And, of course, some say it was only a legend," Jenera said with some bitterness. "Oh, our colony was infused here and there with the blood of wanderers, and we survived. But we're not strong, and only a few have the vision of the crystal white strobe. And every now and then, a union will produce a *crysl*."

"A crysl?"

"A young one, alive, yet not fully developed, still inside a capsule, but definitely alive—genetically connected through the bloodline to Cira—the purest of the line." Her eyes glowed with pride when she spoke of young ones.

More mysteries than Lara could fathom. Some of them touching closer to home than she wanted to admit. So many questions and not a one of them would bring the answer that would take her there.

Don't despair. Haven't you discovered someone to talk to at least?

"What happened to Kirin and Auru's second child?" Lara asked, holding on to the words, not really wanting to hear the answer.

Jenera straightened, a smile came to her lips.

"Oh, that's the good part. Kirin's child was born, Anya, a beautiful little girl, strong and vital, darkly beautiful like her mother, yet with her father's golden eyes, and some of his vision and knowledge. She became the first in a long line of seers who have done their best to keep the legends alive. Her songs are still sung among the faithful, and all of her offspring have produced at least one crysl." She began to sway again and sang softly into the increasing wind:

Turn away from the burning,
turn away from the spark,
Turn away from the fire.
and honor the land.
Cherish the seed in all its turnings,
season upon season, replenish the Earth.
Do not corrupt what Mother has given,
In all things, honor the land.

Hold to the legends and honor the seed,
Preserve until the crystal light's strobe.
Time will bring us all together
at Journey's end beside the sea.

She closed her eyes and breathed deeply, a smile came to her lips. Her sigh brought with it a lightness, as though a weight had been lifted from her shoulders. She turned to Lara and took both her hands. "And now you've come! When the great alignment draws near, the crysls will come forth, and the messenger will lead the Great Migration. It's like everything my grandmother taught us come alive at once! I can't wait to tell Rowan that my efforts have not been in vain."

CHAPTER 11 - THE LEGEND SPEAKS

Jenera's voice thinly penetrated the static in Lara's head. "...but you must come back with me, don't you see? If you don't, they'll never believe me."

Lara was simply stunned. How many of them were there? Was Michael one of them? His image flooded her mind, so fresh and vivid and alive, she almost vibrated with it. She closed her eyes, clinging to the memory of his face, his touch, his clear blue eyes, as though they were the last toehold on the edge of a looming abyss.

"Don't leave me here alone," she whispered. But at Jenera's soft touch on her hand, the image faded.

Lara opened her eyes to see the girl with the startling face paint staring back at her. "Today was to be my last day, or they're going to abandon them," she said.

"What? Abandon who?" Lara grasped for the present moment.

"The crysls! They'll vote to abandon them if I don't bring proof. If we leave now, we could make it before midnight." Jenera pulled at her arm. "We must hurry."

Lara balked at her own resistance. It wasn't like her to turn her back on someone in need. In Jenera's face, she saw all the exuberance and hope of the young girls she once had cared for, desperate in their personal quests, whatever they might be, clinging to her for the only true support they'd probably ever had. Lara had given them all her resources, given them love when their own families had abandoned them, done everything she could to give them a fair chance at life in spite of their circumstances. And now, it was clear, her girls had vanished from the Earth, she thought with regret--and their children and theirs--so long ago that to grieve their passing was as useless as mourning a leaf fallen at the end of summer.

Jenera was here. Now. A sliver of hope that there could be a life here.

But what resources had she to offer Jenera and her people? It seemed that the human race was destined for extinction all along, their presence on the Earth a mere ripple in time, not worth the trouble. Thousands of years of marauding and raping, conquering and being conquered, using and throwing away. What special power had Lara against all that? What possible help could she be to these *Dannais*?

Jenera's elders were right. They could no longer live their lives by legends. Maybe that would be her gift. A lesson in reality. Lara took Jenera's hands in her own and looked into her eyes, searching for that depth of maturity she had glimpsed when they first met. "Jenera, I can't come with you."

Jenera broke away, her youthful emotion overruling reason. "But you *must!*" The wind whipped at her cape, adding urgency to her pleas. "The Legend. You're obviously the one."

"There is no possible way I could be anything to you or your people. I hardly know what I'm doing here myself." Lara gazed across the ledge, challenging the half-familiar mountains to disprove her existence in this world. If they were really there, and she was standing on granite proof that they were, then she must be real too. Granite and sky, tree and leaf, they were the solid backbone of her new existence. The reality was that she was here. But there was nothing legendary or mystical about how she arrived. She would simply have tell the truth.

"Jenera, I'm so sorry to disappoint you, but my presence here is the result of a terrible mistake. An accident," she said, appealing to the girl's reason.

Jenera knelt beside her, touched her arm. "Did you fall? Your wings are broken then? I wondered when I saw—"

"They're not my wings, Jenera," she said, more forcefully than she intended. "My wings are a glider. Anybody can fly a glider, even you." The wind carried her words away as it whipped up strong and chilly on its way to evening. Soon the night would creep stiffly into her joints. She needed to get warm.

Jenera stared back at her, eyes wide. "But I'm not a god--"

"Neither am I, Jenera."

"Well," said Jenera, on a soft laugh. "Look at yourself. You're certainly not human." Her face went immediately red. "I mean—that was—I'm sorry. That didn't come out the way I planned. You're the most beautiful—"

The words hit hard, but Lara couldn't blame the girl. "No worries, Jenera. You're absolutely right. I'm not human. Not anymore."

They blinked at each other a moment, taking it in. Then Lara smoothed the rise over her belly and let out a deep sigh. "It's cold, I need to stoke up the fire."

Jenera studied Lara a moment, then picked up a burnt-tipped stick and poked at smoldering coals banked into a pile in the middle. She tossed in a handful of dry pine needles and the flames leapt up, releasing their heat. The two women drew together in a comfortable silence near the little fire, their faces glowing in the warm light. Lara took refuge in the quiet, gathering her thoughts.

"Did you make this ring of rocks here?" Jenera asked, breaking the spell. She craned her neck to look at the ceiling. "This cave has hosted more than a few days' fires."

"The ring was here, and those canisters, and who knows what else." Lara gestured vaguely toward the dark, still uneasy. "I haven't looked too far. It's been difficult enough to—"

Jenera's eyes once again lit up with excitement.

"What?"

"I know what I will do. I will bring Rowan here! At least that might delay—"

"No!" Lara said with finality. The fire leapt as if to her defense, crackling as she inadvertently kicked duff into the flames. "You can't bring *anyone* here."

"But, if we don't prove the legend is real, that I'm not dreaming, they'll throw the crysls away."

"The fact of my existence doesn't prove anything." Lara reached for her Mylar blanket and pulled it around her shoulders. "I know nothing about any crysls. I am an anomaly. A mistake. Nothing more."

Even as she said the words, the possibilities formed in her mind at some deeper level. A little seed of dread took root. Stranger things had happened. Lara was living proof. Mrs. Kelly received a much weaker dose of the UV serum. Had she emerged years before Lara? Decades? Centuries? Had she created her own life in this place? Spawned a legend? Because that's how legends grew. Fantasy out of fact. Explanations for the unexplainable.

Jenera stared at her, some of the excitement had gone out of her eyes. She turned back to the fire and began to rock, slowly, her shoulders hunched over her knees in a way that tore at Lara's heart. "You think I'm crazy, too."

Lara put her hand on Jenera's back. "I believe in your belief, okay."

"They thought my grandmother was the One. They say Rowan, my grandfather, found *her* in a cave." Jenera looked back over her shoulder at Lara, her eyes wet, then she turned back to the fire. "Like this one."

Lara shook her head. How could she argue against beliefs internalized over a lifetime? To Jenera, the legend was real, part of her psyche as much as the paint on her face. She would fit every event into the context of that reality, including Lara.

Yet young as she was, Lara sensed that Jenera had the spark of intuitive wisdom that all great women possessed. What did her existence in this world matter if she couldn't share her truth with possibly the only person who would listen?

She leaned into the fire, scooping its warmth into her chest, then stood up and focused her eyes directly on Jenera's. She could feel the nodules on her head stretch to their limits. Jenera's eyes widened, but her gaze did not waver.

Lara pulled herself up to her full height and folded her arms across her breasts. The fire light reflected in the angular facets of the blanket draped over her like a cape. The girl in front of her sat riveted, barely breathing.

"Jenera, you must listen to me. What I am about to tell you will be shocking. It may fill you with despair. But you must hear me out and don't argue. This is for your own good as well as for the good of your people and the… crysls. Do you understand?"

Jenera acquiesced, folded her hands in her lap.

Lara closed her eyes a moment gathering her thoughts. Best to give some background first.

"Many cultures throughout time have lived their lives based on legends. Legends made up by people when they maybe didn't understand the physics… the details about how something happened. Many legends are made up by people who wanted to control others, promise them something in order to get something they wanted. Long after the original intent is forgotten, the people believed in the legends and because of that, they missed things that were real and important." *Geez. Get to the point Lara.*

"I think someone--maybe the even your own elders--could have planted this legend to keep your people under some kind of control. It's what humans do. There is no special one coming and there never was, don't you see? Just a story to keep you all waiting to take action on your own to better your lives.

Jenera's back stiffened, her lips pressed together in rigid denial.

"Now I know you don't believe this, but there's more," Lara continued. She wrapped the blanket around her and paced before the fire, trying to keep the blood pumping through her limbs. "My being here is just a stupid mistake. Not part of a legend or anyone's plan. No basis to form a whole people's belief system. I was a human, just like you. Now I am… what I *am*. A hideous monster. Unintended consequences. A mistake. A scientific blunder, an accident, not some plan for your people's survival. An accident, do you hear me?"

Jenera squeezed her eyes shut, turned away. Lara grabbed her by the shoulders, turned her back. "Look at me, Jenera."

Jenera's eyes locked on hers, lit with a crackle of fear. Lara stared until they began to fill with tears. Feeling miserable at having to tell the truth, she released the young girl.

"I'm sorry," she said at last. Sorry that she had been so gruff, and sorry for herself. "The truth is, I'm not supposed to be here," Lara moaned, losing confidence. "I don't know how to live in a cave. I'm used to electricity and television and music and cars and airplanes and traffic jams and cell phones and—I'm just an ordinary person." Was an ordinary person.

She looked out through the opening of the cave. The valley was losing its color to the dark, the first few stars had appeared on the horizon, and the air was unbearably cold only a few steps from the fire. She looked back at Jenera and couldn't remember the thrust of her speech. She pulled in a long slow breath and let it out. Jenera still watched her, wide-eyed and expectant.

Lara let go a deep sigh as she poked the fire with a stick. "If I don't cover up and get into my bed, I may freeze into a statue myself." She sat on the edge of her canister and wrapped her solar blanket high about her ears.

Jenera stared at her compassionately. "May I speak now?"

Lara cocked her head. The fact that the girl had listened the entire time without interrupting finally broke through. Humbled, she nodded. "Yes. Of... of course. Please."

"First of all, you are not a monster. You are the most beautiful creature I have ever seen." She sat beside Lara on her canister bed and hugged her shoulders. "Second, was there no God in your world of cars and electricity?"

Only men who thought themselves gods. "Maybe, Jenera." She let go a sigh. "Maybe my people looked for God in the wrong places."

"Just because you yourself are not aware of your part in the plan, doesn't mean one doesn't exist. A plan. That's why we're still here. Why we have been able to survive all this time while the world healed itself of ancient wounds. It's part of the Plan."

Lara shook her head.

"You would have survived anyway, Jenera." She touched the girl's face, her hair. The nodules on top of Lara's head twisted and stretched; softened, and shrank. "Your intelligence is built into your DNA along with your skin type and eyes, hair color. These have always been the physical qualities most impervious to the sun. It's a well-known fact that—"

But she could see it was no use. Jenera smiled at her as though she were the older experienced one and Lara were a beloved child. Wisdom, compassion, and yes, indulgence shone through her youthful expression. All Lara could do was shake her head. She could not undo in an hour what Jenera's people had believed for generations. "What has already happened is the Plan, Jenera. You don't need me."

"Then you won't come." It was more an affirmation than a question.

"It has been a lie, Jenera. It's time you stood on your own. You already have everything you need."

Jenera hugged Lara close, then looked into her eyes thoughtfully, still holding her fingertips lightly. "What you say may be true, but when your own young one arrives, you may think otherwise. It may be that I am too late to save our crysls, in which case yours will be unique in all the land."

The words chilled Lara's bones. She opened her mouth to protest: *The father was human!* She wanted to wail, but no words formed. Jenera had made up her mind. Any further argument might damage the fragile relationship that they had formed. Better not to burn her bridges, this was after all the only living person she had seen since becoming marooned in this fever dream. And then, as it did each evening once the heat of the day was lost, exhaustion bore down on her shoulders and she sank into her bed.

"I'm sorry, Jenera. This is all..." incredible, amazing, and overwhelming. She covered her belly once more with her hand. "My body demands rest now."

Jenera stood, pulled the blanket up over Lara with a mother's concern. "I'll leave you here in peace, as you wish it for now. Then, as soon as I can, I'll return and bring more food—some comforts." She squeezed Lara's fingers lightly. "My aunt is a healer. I'll consult with her about your... condition."

Lara no longer had the energy to protest. She closed her eyes, let her head fall back, and sank into a heavy sigh. When she opened her eyes again, Jenera was gone.

CHaPTer 12 – Fear OF Frass

Despite her physical exhaustion, Lara's mind was wide awake, struggling to assimilate this new development. Just as she had begun to accept her existence in a solitary world, now she had to get used to the idea that not far away, there existed an entire people with a culture as different from twenty-first century California as that of the Incas of Peru. With the exception of the inland sea, the landscape was not so changed. Warmer, perhaps, and drier. If she knew anything about anthropology, Jenera's remarkable appearance was not a product of evolution, but simply a mixing of races. The melting pot in its advanced stages—a society greatly simplified and reduced in numbers—not advanced as we were all expected future civilizations might be, but reduced to... to... what? Near primitives? And so quickly. Even if she had slept two thousand years…

" *…and so, as you can see, if the polar ice caps continue to deteriorate at the existing rate . . . rising sea levels, climate change…* ""

Words from the past. She remembered brushing them away, but if they were right back then...

"Turn away from the burning,
Turn away from the spark..."

Jenera's song. A simpler life. Had Jenera's ancestors deliberately pulled the plug? Or had they no choice in the matter? Hadn't she herself wished for a simpler life?

The old saying "Be careful what you wish for" took on a whole new meaning. Having accepted this ledge-bound existence, she had fallen into the rhythm of that very simple life almost with a kind of relief. Paring down to the basic elements of survival had a way of eliminating the trivial and often annoying details. It took her most of a day to prepare for evening, and that kept her busy enough to ignore the lurking panic she knew would destroy her if she let it.

As each day passed, she had begun to welcome the night and unconsciousness like an old friend. She postponed rising each day as long as she could, filtering out conscious thoughts she didn't want to think—the ones that led her to the conclusion she might spend the rest of her life, however long or short that might be, alone.

Now, the last of the day's heat escaped from the granite. Lara lay down on her back and stared up at the ultra-blue sky, thinking about Jenera and her people. Her hand came to rest on the rise in her belly. Jenera was certainly going to be an ally, but from what she had told Lara, her "elders" weren't going to be happy to hear the news of Lara's arrival. For them, it signified change and they would fear change as most established leaders would. Change could mean loss of control.

Lara was afraid of the change herself. Despite her predicament, over the last few days, her solitary life had become comfortable, controllable. More controllable now than her frenzied life in San Francisco had ever been, if she were to tell the truth. Her realities were frightening, but her needs were simple. Food, shelter. No complications.

But now there was Jenera.

As much as Jenera represented friendship, she also represented complications. The cave had taken on the comfortable proportions of home. The ledge, once frightening, had become her evening perch and made her feel uncannily like she had when she had watched the sea from the old Rubicon tower. Like the hidden fungal mesh that supported the forest and everything else around her, she had already built from the mountains and streams, the meadow and the cave, a framework of sanity—artificial perhaps, but effective in maintaining some sort of order in her present personal universe. Jenera's appearance, her very existence, threatened that order. Not necessarily in a bad way, but a threat, none the less. Jenera had come in peace and out of an inner conviction to serve her people, not intentionally to upset the balance of Lara's life.

The biggest question, the one that she wasn't sure she wanted answered, was the one she was afraid to think about. If there was a group of Jenera's people, then she could not rule out the possibility that there were other groups. People who were not so benevolent. Surely, man hadn't messed-up so badly that he now lived only in these isolated mountain realms. She puffed out a laugh.

Of course they had. That's what men did.

Jenera didn't give off that kind of vibe. In fact, from the moment their eyes had met, Lara sensed compassion and patience. She was safe for now, at least. Of that, she was sure. And in the silent knowing women share, Jenera had forced Lara to admit what she had been hiding from herself, that she was going to bring a child into this uncertain future.

The smell of salt sea wafting up from the water reminded her of home, of summer days so long they seemed to last forever, of the touch of Michael's hands over her soapy skin in the bath, of two Adirondack chairs on a cliff overlooking the ocean. She covered the unmistakable rise on her tummy with both hands and her loneliness grew. Where would the child fit in this strange world? Or would it be something entirely different… a chrysl?

She pulled the thermal blanket about her and willed her mind to settle. In the morning she would haul the glider back to her ledge, launch again and look for the wild fruit orchards Jenera had told her about. For now, she let the sounds of evening carry her to the sanctuary of sleep.

It took most of the morning to dismantle the glider pieces and haul them up, one-by-one, to the ledge. By the time she had it reassembled, her energy was nearly spent. The flight would have to wait until tomorrow.

She stood facing the mouth of the cave, out of excuses. She was too weak to fly, but she had many hours before the cold would slow her down.

"If you're going to stay here alone," she mused aloud, "you can't have something coming in on you from behind." She needed to explore the rest of her cave. It was a good idea. No sense putting it off any longer.

She brought two sturdy pine branches to the fire ring, dug two flares from her pile, and lashed one on each with some nylon twine from her glider canister. One for now, one for later.

For as long as she had carried flares around in her little car, she'd never had to use one. Bracing herself for the unknown, she pointed the stick away from her, arm extended, and pulled the tab. When nothing happened but a bad smell, she boldly stuck the end into the dying coals of the fire.

"Whoa!" Her unexpected shout echoed back from the cave as the reddish glow sprang up bright as a shooting star. She grabbed the other stick and began to move, holding the burning torch at a safe distance in front of her.

The cave walls were speckled granite, like the entrance, but not blackened like the ceiling over the fire ring. She shuffled slowly, further into the dark. Every few steps revealed more of a dry, meandering corridor. A thin flow of cool air told her there must be an opening somewhere in the dark cavern, enough to supply oxygen.

She called out again: "Jen-er-a." The echo came back, repeating many times over. How far did it go? A chill seized the back of her neck, flowed down her arms and through her knees. She sensed great age and long use. Generations must have used this cave at one time or another. She imagined ancient spirits lurking, hunched up in a corner somewhere above, deciding her fate.

She shook off another set of chills. "Don't be silly," she said aloud. Her echo came back alone.

No sooner had she convinced herself there was nothing there, than something flickered back at her from the deepening shadows to challenge her resolve.

She held the flame higher and took another step inside the circle of light. What she saw took her breath away. There was a pile of canisters like the ones she had found near her own chrysalis, destroyed except for one the shape and size of a large shoebox. This she scooped up and tucked under her arm. Beyond that, another larger object took on dimension and color as she moved closer. Could it be another solar blanket crumpled against the cave wall? No. This was darker, less reflective.

Her heartbeat quickened, responding to a heady mixture of fear and excitement, a physical state she had come to experience more intimately with each day in this new world. Fight or flight, she was subject to the built-in mechanisms of her animal self, but unlike the lower creatures, she could choose whether or not to react. She must go forward after all, the alternative was to shrivel up and die, alone.

She checked the torch, worried that it might go out before she could light up the second one. It was more than half burned. It was difficult to judge the passage of time in this confined space with only her immediate area lit. She turned slightly to look over her shoulder toward the mouth of the cave. Was it getting dark outside, or had she simply made a turn that blocked out most of the light?

"Stop making excuses, Lara." There was at least enough torch time to investigate this one more thing, then she would turn back and save the second torch for another day.

With renewed courage, she crept forward, clamping her bottom lip between her teeth as she used the fire poker to test the surface of what now looked more like a large abandoned, "chrysalis," she said aloud.

The echo agreed. Indeed, it was of the shape and size of the one from which she herself had emerged, only this one was tragically fragile—one end intact, the other, partially buried under a fall of rock, frail and weightless and spotted with insect frass like autumn leaves buried in last year's compost pile. Covering her mouth, she fought the urge to run, instead kneeling near the end most intact. Closer inspection distinctly revealed the embossed shape of a human foot.

Lara crouched over the time-ravaged chrysalis, poked at the pieces. Which one of Patrick's patients had it held? Mrs. Kelley? Michael? Or some other victim she had never met? The possibilities balled up in her stomach and sent her lurching, haphazard over the cave floor and scrabbling back to the entrance, in dire need of relief.

She dropped the box near her fire ring and staggered the few more steps through the cave opening to find the night was beginning to gather pinpoint stars, but thankfully, the rock held the remains of the day's warmth. She stopped, bent at the waist, palms resting on her thighs as she caught her breath, then sat down, knees drawn up under her chin. A scrape on her shin oozed tiny drops of blood.

She had succumbed to her animal instinct after all. Using her fingertips, she wiped the blood on her thumb and closed her eyes. At least she still bled red.

Deep-breathing away the adrenaline, she slowed her racing heart and fought to empty her mind. The possibility that Michael might be out there somewhere was too much to hope for, the thought that his chrysalis may have been destroyed before it was ready to release him was too much to bear.

When at last she had recovered her reasonable self, she lay flat out on her back to absorb the last warmth of the day. Others. Of course there had been others. The absurdity was that, until now, she hadn't thought much about what had happened to them. Who knew how many others Patrick had lured into his experiment? She rested her hand on her belly. Some by choice and some inadvertently. How many versions of his UV serum had he concocted? Maybe the greatest miracle was that she survived at all.

As she stared into the vast, empty sky, the existence of the *Dannais* took on a whole new dimension. Jenera, the crysls, the legends. Humans, with the essence of monarch DNA … the UV project's unintended consequences.

What if they had hatched out eons ago? Lived a lifetime alone, then perished? Had they mingled their blood with the *Dannais*? What if some were out there still, waiting to open?

What if? What if? What if?

The possibilities crowded in, running circles in her mind, clamoring for attention, then giving way to the next and the next until she slammed her hands against her ears and shouted "Stop!"

She didn't realize she was crying until the tears turned cold on her cheeks. It was time to come in from the cold and revive her fire for the night. Just go into the cave and do that one thing. Build a fire. Stay warm. Build a fire. Stay warm.

She continued to chant to herself, not allowing any other words to enter her mind while she fanned and poked at her little life-giving pile of coals, coaxing them to small flames and then to larger ones. At last, she settled into her bed, warmed by the fire and numbed by the chant until she achieved a level of calm. Nothing had really changed, after all, had it? Regardless of what may or not be possible, she was still faced with the daily task of keeping warm, keeping fed, and keeping sane, until… that was the hard part.

Until what?

Beyond the possibility of finding some fresh fruit somewhere down the hillsides, what future was there?

What point could there actually be in carrying on with the imitation of purpose in this place? It was one thing to stay focused on the basics, but seriously. How long could she carry on that charade? Especially now, knowing there was some form of humanity out there. Ha. And how would they react to her? Anxiety clawed at her, filling her with dread, threatening to rob her of sleep.

No.

Just stop right now.

She closed her eyes, calling to the surface of her mind a treasured moment with Michael. They lay in the back of his van, still salty and wet from a romp in the surf, Lara worried someone might see, Michael assuring the window tint was foolproof, pulling her closer, kissing her silent, into deepening pleasure.

She wasn't sure how much time had passed, but when she woke, her eyes focused on the canister she'd found deeper inside the cave. She sniffed, drawing herself back from the reality of her dreams to the fantasy of her present surroundings.

Did the shoebox hold some surviving morsels of food. Chocolate maybe? It might be worth the effort of breaking into. She retrieved it from near the fire, and turned it over on her lap, her sharp rock and lever at the ready. Once she had made the initial slit along the lid, it popped open as if it had been under pressure, releasing an oddly familiar scent. Old books and pipe tobacco? She breathed it in a moment before she pushed open the lid. A leather-bound book fell heavily into her lap. No chocolate. Damn. She was a bit disappointed but turned the book over in her hands with some excitement.

Food for thought was better than no food at all.

What great classic had her benefactor thought important to pass along to his misfit? Shakespere? Annie Proux? Dante Alighieri? A riveting Baldacci thriller? But there was no title on the cover or the spine, just a plain, leather-bound book. A journal. She flipped through pages messy with a spiky, uneven hand, nearly unreadable like the scrawl of a doctor's prescription. She couldn't eat it, but it would certainly provide some entertainment while the fire burned.

"First things first," she mumbled quietly to avoid the disturbing echoes of cave dwelling.

Tossing the book on her makeshift bed, she added two good sized pine logs to the fire and banked the coals beneath. Adding pine needles, the flames exploded up, casting light enough to see. She retrieved the journal, and read the opening lines.

My Dear Lara,

If you are reading these pages, then at least a small part of my plan has succeeded. You have survived the horror that I inadvertently inflicted upon you. Considering the fate of the world since your encapsulation, I can only hope that this state has given you some degree of protection from the climatic disaster and ensuing economic, political, and social calamity that has befallen our beautiful country, and I assume, the entire world.

I had hoped to witness your emergence, as you will read in the following pages. However, at this writing, I have little hope I will survive to see it. It seems that otherwise law-abiding citizens lose their humanity when faced with starvation.

All I can offer you is my apology for the damage I have caused, and in the following pages, the location of a possible island of survival. Knowing how you so selflessly cared for the young people you sheltered, I ask a favor: that if you have the ability, go to Terra City and find my son, Sloan who has hopefully survived as you have.

Yours in trust,
Patrick Allen

Lara let the words sink in. It took her a few moments sorting through the canyons of her memory to recognize the name. Had the unthinkably amoral lunatic injected his own son, already afflicted with autism, with the UV serum? What was he thinking? But she knew the answer. Patrick was controlled by his self-obsessed compulsion to have his UV Serum recognized as the genetic answer to skin cancer, adding his name to a venerated list of Nobel prize winners. As if experimenting on humans was somehow an accepted methodology. Apparently, the dramatic results of his UV experiments only sent him off in another more horrific direction. How did a parent justify risking their child's life by sending them off into some unknown future not knowing whether they would survive, let alone what that survival would look like?

Lara smoothed her hands over her own downy stomach. How indeed? She tried to imagine Patrick's anguish at discovering his child was so neurodivergent, he might never fit into society, could be bound to institutional life. Where had Sloan fit on the Autism spectrum? Profoundly impaired, nonverbal? High functioning savant? or somewhere in between? She had never met the boy, so she had no way of knowing. She couldn't imagine how it would feel to be a brilliant researcher and learn your child might never reach his human potential. There would be self-blame and torture, to be sure. She felt a pang of sympathy for the two of them. How would she feel if her baby were… impaired? Could she send it off into some uncertain future hoping for a better outcome? Lara bit her bottom lip, recalling Jenera's tale of some *Dannais* giving birth to… to… Crysls?

Lara began to rock slowly, cradling her swiftly growing belly. Would her baby be pink and rosy and blonde, like its daddy. She closed her eyes and could almost see the laughing eyes and chubby arms. The two of them would live here together. They wouldn't be the first humans to live life in a cave.

A dark cloud of worry descended over her. What were the chances the baby had been genetically transformed in her womb into something else entirely? A stranger growing inside her own skin. A scaly, bald, antenna-headed freak.

She pressed her hands against the pages of the journal, maybe a hundred of them. She was both excited and afraid to read the words they contained. A history of what came in the period between her encapsulation and Patrick's demise. Disaster? Calamity? Terra City? She recalled one of Michael's surfer pals, an Iraqi Vet, saying "We should have bombed them to the stone age when we had the chance." Is that what happened? She was having enough trouble coming to grips with what had happened to her, she hadn't given the rest of the country—the world—much thought at all. Had she survived a modern holocaust because of a madman's folly?

The book grew heavy in her hands, like an anchor dragging her down. She dropped it back in its box and wiped her hands down her thighs. Whatever had happened, she wasn't ready to read about it. Not now. Maybe not ever.

Then the absurdity of it all drove her back to the box. Was she that much of a coward? No. Of course not. She retrieved the journal and held it to her chest. She would use it for entertainment. Read a little bit each night. Something to keep her company. She crawled back into her bed, lay the book in her lap, and fanned the pages in preparation.

A stab of loneliness hit her so sharp and raw, she dropped the journal in the dirt. The pages were entirely empty. In disbelief, she picked it up and fanned them again, backward and forward, shaking the book to see if anything would fall out.

Nothing.

Except for the note in the beginning, the pages were completely, unbelievably blank. Was it some kind of joke? Or, worse, maybe something happened to him before he could finish…

Loneliness assaulted her from a place deep inside. "Screw Patrick McCormick-Allen!"

She threw the book against the stone wall, screaming at the top of her lungs. The tortured echo reverberated into the far reaches of the cave and back. "Screw the UV serum," she said quietly, then fell back in her makeshift bed, pulled the sterile, crackly blanket up over her head, and wished to god she'd never emerged into this world.

Chapter 13 – Homefront

Jenera strode silently to her place at the council, and as though she had never been away, the elders carried on business as usual without looking up. The only one who acknowledged her arrival was her Grandfather, Rowan, and that was nothing more than a simple nod of his head. She smiled when she saw that he had captured his luxuriant dreadlocks at the back of his massive neck in the leather thong she had decorated with clam shells for him as a young child.

During the winter, the council met at the Great Hall at Spring Compound, redwood doors sealed tightly against what could by early autumn be bitter cold. Summertime, however, councils were held in the ancient amphitheater at Lillit Compound, the elders sitting on granite blocks arranged in a wide half circle that faced a podium, before the central brazier.

Jenera's stomach clenched as she slipped into her seat. Esteban was at the podium.

His eyes narrowed on her as he gave the tally, an overt threat to everything he knew she held dear. "The valley fields have produced a good crop this year, the granaries are full, and will provide plenty of bread over the coming winter. With grain left over from last year, we will have a substantial surplus to sell to traders who venture up from The Owen."

Pah! From what Jenera had seen of the crops this year, a year of drought, they would be lucky to get by on what they produced, let alone supply travelers on what had been named the Lost Highway. Wanderers at best, these "traders" were primarily descendants of those unfortunates who had escaped from the southern cities with virtually nothing in their pockets but what they had stolen from someone else.

She shot a glance at Rowan, whom she knew was well aware of the truth. He must have felt her glance, for he returned it sharply, then immediately returned his gaze to Esteban, as stone-faced as ever. Jenera looked back to the podium, a growing discomfort building in that part of her she kept hidden from others. She spun the silver ring on her right hand, a constant reminder of the arrangement her grandfather had made with Esteban's father long before she was old enough to walk. When she reached her eighteenth birthday, she would belong to him. It went against everything her mother had promised her about living in freedom. But Rowan was honor bound to Esteban's father, and there was nothing she could do about it. At least not now. She had two years to learn to deal with it. For now, she avoided him as much as she could.

As a young boy, he'd been incorrigible. As a young man, he was trouble of a different kind. What had he been up to in her absence? Would Rowan challenge him? Would anyone? She could only hope.

She paid little attention to the reports of Upper and Lower River Compounds, who were concerned primarily with supplies like cloth and rope, the arts and music, and security of their northern boarders, necessities all. Yet full as she was with her own news, she found it difficult to concentrate on the statistics of whose child has entered the master ranks, what concert was being held over the next report period, and the growing population of marmots at High Meadows Pass. As protocol demanded, she would deliver her report in the proper order, after Lilit Compound, no matter how pressing or important her message might be.

Jenera's aunt Helena, Lilit's leader since the loss of Jenera's mother, Grace, gave her usual lengthy report which included announcements of births and passings, the supply of medicinal herbs in the infirmary, and the humidity at the seed depository.

But today, Helena's reporting could not penetrate Jenera's anxious mood. She fidgeted, distracted only when Helena's young daughter, Ekiria, leaned forward in her place and waved at Jenera timidly, eyes alight. Jenera could count on that one to instigate an adolescent riot if she did not begin a round of stories the moment council adjourned. She winked back at Ekiria and gave her the "shush" sign, her finger touching her lips.

Jenera did her best to hold patient, drawing on the strength of the redwoods that circled the amphitheater, more majestic than any stone column or granite dome man could ever claim to have constructed. She was comforted to know that the legends also recorded the giant trees, for she would sorely miss them if ever she must travel far and not find them close about her.

Rowan's rumbling "eh-hem," pulled her from her muse. "Jenera of Lillit Compound has a special report for us," he announced as he took his place at the stone podium. He held his open palm up to the assembly, then clenched his fist to his bosom, her signal to approach. A soft murmur built to a gaggling crescendo as some among the crowd gave up their seats at the back of the circle and moved forward to fill the space just below the podium. Rowan once again raised his palm to demand silence before Jenera took the stand.

In spite of what she knew would be inevitable opposition, Jenera admired the stately men and women circled about her. What would these people have been like in a different world? The one Lara had known? Would they be the leaders of a great nation instead of simple farmers and artisans who gleaned what little they needed from the land and satisfied themselves with sunsets and river music for their entertainment? For the difficult life they led, and the amount of time they spent working just for food and shelter, they were a regal group, attired in fine flowing robes in the winter, and cool, cotton tunics during the hot months. No one in the valley was without at least one gold or silver circlet about their neck, and many were elaborately made, a labor of love more valuable given away than kept. In a way, she envied them for being the ones who would be left behind in this beautiful valley. She and the crysls were bound for other things. They were a people divided by a genetic rift that could never be breached, nor could any one of them predict who would wind up on which side of the bloodline.

Those of the *Dannais* blood would eventually return to crysls with the new world emblazoned in their genetic codes and revealed in the beacon's strobe that called them. Those of the mixed blood would stay, a race unto their own. Who could tell which would more abundantly populate the returning habitable areas of the planet? Or if they would one day challenge one another for a place in the sun?

Jenera's gaze lingered on the familiar faces nearest her as she thought these thoughts, struggling to calm herself before she spoke. Her mission was not to conclude the right or wrong of it, only to tell them of the coming change as it was revealed to her.

She closed her eyes, drawing on her spirit power, her inner strength in the face of those who would stand against her, then opened her eyes and began.

"Four days ago, this council challenged the vigilance of many generations of Spirit Leaders by demanding that I make good my claim or forever relinquish my support for the crysls in Lillit Compound."

A low murmur rolled across the crowd and was silenced by a stern look from Rowan. Jenera raised her chin in advanced defiance of those who would outwardly mock her. She smiled at the group just at her feet who could not hide their excitement, their antenna straining to maximum extension in anticipation.

"I have come to report that our years of caring for the crysls are about to be rewarded." She addressed the crowd with dignity, waiting in silence for the meaning of her message to sink in, and just as the murmurs rose again in earnest, she began to speak in the metered chant familiar to the children who listened to her stories.

"In the caves above the valley, I have seen the one for whom we have all waited; the Leader of our coming Journey, the Messenger of whom the legends speak."

Now some of the elders talked openly among themselves, while others sat at attention according Jenera the respect her office deserved. Jenera's gaze went to Rowan, hoping to measure his reaction to the news. But he sat silently, his eyes deep set and bear-like, veiled, fixed and impossible to read. Jenera pushed a nagging hurt down and out of reach. She had so hoped for her grandfather's outward support, but obviously, it was not to be forthcoming. At least not yet.

"I have seen her; a great winged creature, more beautiful than any you have ever seen; in the image of Auru, her body shimmers like the backs of the great Monarchs, and she flies over the heights without so much as flapping her wings." She left out that the wings were mechanical; a detail they didn't need to know right now.

Esteban stood up in his place. "Where is this creature, if this is so? I see no great winged bird! What are you trying to put over on us, *Spirit Leader*?" He spat the title as if it were a slur. "Meanwhile, we keep stockpiles of life support for those things in Lillit Compound as if we had the supplies to spare?" Two others stood, lending their agreement with Esteban.

Those at her feet turned to face him, their antenna shrinking to hide in their hair.

"Yes! Where is the proof?" another one of his cronies shouted from the last row of seats and the murmurs broke out again.

Jenera seethed. Had they not just heard him report of plenty? Was there no one to oppose Esteban? Knowing that some in her council grew tired of the demands of maintaining Crysl Tower, and that some had seriously begun to doubt the legends, she had never feared their opposition would lead to all out rebellion or violence, except in the case of Esteban. He was the self-appointed leader of a small, but vociferous group who had begun to stir unrest among the humans in their midst, spreading the opinion that life in Terra City, where they could eventually reclaim the comforts of the electric, private apartments and the theater, would be much preferable to living in the Valley "like cavemen." So far, they had only his word for its viability. For all anyone else in the colony knew, they would need massive resources to restore the city, let alone, create a source of income to sustain it.

Jenera bristled. She was trapped in the middle. Destined to lead the *Dannais*, but with Rowan still alive, she had no power at all. Unless Rowan stepped in, Esteban could get away with anything he wished. As far as she was concerned, Esteban and his followers could leave anytime they pleased, though some would argue they needed all the men they had to guard their gates. But as long as she had breath in her body, they would not do so with one ounce of grain needed for the survival of the Crysls. Regardless of Esteban's ego and Rowan's damned pact, she was determined to defend the crysls to the death.

She pulled herself erect and held her palm up to the assembly, waiting for their return to order, then continued: "I promised The Messenger her privacy would not be violated. She will show herself when she is ready."

More shouting, more dissent. Helena bowed her head and Ekiria--frightened by the uncharacteristic jeering of what were usually calm, reasonable people-- buried her head in her mother's lap. At last, it was Rowan who stood, silencing the crowd as he walked to the podium.

"Jenera has given her report. As with all members of this council, we will take her at her word unless someone can give reason to prove otherwise. Does anyone here officially challenge? For if it is so, I would make the same request of you—" He shifted his gaze directly to Esteban— "Prove her false in three days or keep quiet."

Esteban stood his ground while others slowly retook their seats. He glared back at Rowan in defiance; but after a moment, seeing that he was the only one left standing, he reluctantly sat. Rowan looked around to challenge anyone who would begin another outbreak of disorder, and satisfied that he had quelled the problem, nodded for Jenera to continue.

She swallowed over a hard lump in her throat. "Her name is Lara. She is a gentle soul who speaks of land to the north near the great ocean, though she has not been there in... a long time. According to Lara, this land was once the breeding ground of Danaus Plexippus, the DNA line of our species: Monarchs. And as you all know, where there are monarchs, there is milkiweed, the lifeblood of the crysls.

"Her full story has not been revealed to me, but she can be none other than the one of whom the legend speaks: 'the winged creature who will lead the young ones across the sea to their ancestral home.'"

All eyes were fixed upon Jenera, and the elders waited, whether in true belief or respect for Rowan, for her final words. She gripped the sides of the granite podium, and fixed her most convincing gaze on the five elders who occupied the honored front row.

"Can any of you star watchers deny that the predicted alignment of the planets is only a few weeks off?" Jenera knew the answer and so did not wait for their reply. "So I say, wait and see! What have we to lose by watching this miracle happen? And what if the Journey is successful and opens up a whole new territory where those among us who have the gene can live full productive lives? Away from the cold? A journey that leads the young ones to fertile ground and a better life?"

"Begging your indulgence, Jenera." It was Helena who now stood, with Ekiria tangled in her skirts.

Jenera raised her palm. "I recognize Helena of Lilit Compound."

"I do not challenge your discovery, Jenera. I ask only what will happen to those of us who do not feel the pull of the beacon? Our loved ones will leave us for this new life. What life are we to have then here without them?"

Jenera's heart went out to Helena. She knew very well that Helena was speaking of her own situation: she did not possess the gene, but clearly, Ekiria did.

"Dear Helena," Jenera said after a moment's thought. "Do not the tiny Monarchs return to the valley every year, sometimes even to the very hillside where they were born?"

Helena's eyes filled with tears and she hugged Ekiria to her as she sat back down. Again, Jenera could hear low rumblings in the back of the crowd. She looked to Rowan and found his head bowed. She would have to go on in spite of the interruption.

"All I am asking is that we preserve the crysls for yet a few more weeks," Jenera continued, raising her voice over the noise. "At least until the planet alignment takes place. Then, if the legend remains unproven... " Jenera's voice dropped low and full of emotion, "...I will concede that we have been fools, and myself the biggest fool of all." Her chest deflated as the fatal words escaped her.

She cast her eyes upon the rest of those who occupied the front seats, whose faces she could see clearly, and addressed them as if they were representatives of the entire council. "I will step down of my own accord, if this revelation proves false," she vowed. Her eyes brimmed with tears. Who among them had sacrificed more than she?

Jenera left the podium wondering what their reaction might have been had Lara glided down into the amphitheater at that very moment. But she had not, and Jenera had little hope that she ever would. Outside the ring of trees, she turned and waited as Rowan announced the next speaker to take the podium. For the second time since she had first seen The Messenger, Jenera doubted herself. What if Lara had been right and the legend was nothing but a cruel hoax? Some mad man, long ago, had made an atrocious presumption—that he could mix monarch and human genes and come up with something that would help prevent a devastating disease; and long after he was dead, gone, and relieved of responsibility, a race of people, neither human nor *insecta*, were left on a depleted earth to battle over what resources remained.

These were chilling, grim thoughts, and Jenera was relieved when Ekiria burst upon her from behind and circled her knees with loving arms. "Jenera! Jenera! Stories! Stories!"

Jenera scooped Ekiria into her arms and shifted her to her hip. "Where is your mama, 'r-r-r-ia?" She trilled the "r" in the special way that always brought giggles bubbling from the child.

"She went home, but she said I could come. Oh please! We've had no stories while you've been away." Jenera felt her own spirits brighten. Although Ekiria was only her niece, they had a special bond born of their *Dannais* blood connection, yet deeper than that, they loved one another as near a mother-daughter bond as one could come without actually giving birth.

"All right, but back to Lillit Compound and your mother for now, and call in some of your friends. I have a special story tonight."

Jenera entered Lillit Compound alone. She did not enter the Crysl Tower, only checked the security of the lock as she passed by on the way down the polished granite corridor to her private quarters. She opened the pipeline from the low-burning brazier-heated water reservoir, filled her bath and slipped in, washing the fatigue of her journey away with the sand and grit. Relaxed for the first time in days, her mind wandered to memories of her mother. How she missed her tender touch, the sound of her voice. It didn't seem right that she would not be here now to witness what was about to happen. Indeed, Jenera worried that the lack of her mother's presence and that of the amulet she had intended to pass down would somehow lead to failure. She closed her eyes, picturing it in her mind, a tiny emerald-like vessel that had hung around her mother's neck as long as she could remember. "One day you will be its keeper," she'd promised. "…and with it a heavy responsibility."

"What responsibility, mama?" she'd asked.

"I will tell you when the time comes, my love."

But the time never came. Her mother had been lost along with her father before she could pass the amulet to her or tell her of its purpose. Now her mother and father were both gone forever. Would the missing amulet interfere with the Great Migration? Jenera had no way of knowing. But quitting now would definitely ruin it.

She thought of Bryn and the pain it would bring her to leave him behind when the time came, then pushed the thought away into the darkest corner of her mind where she could forget it for a while.

The last direct rays of sun left her skylight. Soon it would be dark and the only lights in the valley would be around the low-burning summer braziers in the centers of the compounds.

She purged her loneliness with a sigh and plunged below the surface of the water, washing the weariness of the road and day's events from her face, her hair and, as best she could, from her mind.

Refreshed and cleansed, she donned a full-length, flaxen gown of white, overlaid with a cape of black and gold filigree. She caught her mass of hair up in a tight-fitting cap of copper mesh and set out the paint pots she used to transform herself for the children's entertainment. Beginning with a whitened base, she added two upswept brows, and filled in the "v" from the corners of her forehead to the tip of her nose with an iridescent green. She rouged her mouth into a tiny bow that left most of her wide, flowing lips uncolored. Finally, she added a fragile tiara woven of copper wire to create the illusion of tall, delicate antenna, then pulled herself erect to check the result in her bed chamber mirror.

She cocked her head, recalling Lara's startling eyes. They were bright blue, larger than life. Supported by deeply sculptured cheekbones, they were the most prominent feature of her face. Jenera returned to her chrism jars, and added shadows at her cheeks, then deepened the liner around her eyes. The effect was startling. A reasonable recreation of The Messenger blinked back at her. The image made her heartbeat thump a little faster, she straightened her shoulders and let herself slip into the character.

At word of her arrival, the children at the Lillit Compound brazier hushed their excited buzzing and waited in rapt anticipation to see into what mystical character Jenera had been transformed.

Even Helena gasped as, appearing on the stage in the midst of a puff of smoke, a figure stood before them, still and silent in a wrapping of black and gold. It stood motionless for several seconds, pulling the children to the edge of their seats, until, pushing the moment near to unbearable, it began to unfold, turned its back to the gathering, then stretching out its arms to spread iridescent wings.

All at once, the face turned upon them, both frightening and beautiful. Then as if in accompaniment to one of their evening summer concerts, the figure sprang from the stage and swooped about the crowd, dipping and swirling in pantomimed flight, until, having brushed nearly every child in the room with its outstretched wings, it alighted back at the center of the stage and there stood, arms outstretched and addressed them, focusing on each little face in turn with its large, bright eyes.

"I am Lara, The Messenger of which the legend speaks."

CHAPTER 14 - ROWAN'S STORY

Rowan rested his backside against a tree and watched from the shadows as Jenera wove her story deftly into the minds of the children. His own mind reeled. Like the ancient trees for which he was named, Rowan had grown a hardwood hide to protect himself from his own memories--life events that would otherwise sneak up and bite him when he least expected. A hardwood hide so thick and strong he thought he was safe inside it. A hide so old and solid he had allowed himself to believe the legends were only just that: stories made up to entertain children. But Jenera's revelation drenched him in the truth, leaving him raw and exposed. The cherished memory of his beautiful, amazing wife soaked into him like the first rain after a long, long drought, filling every aching crevice of his mind with her smile.

Once the cracks were open, other images poured in. Young man's memories, burning and sweet, nearly unbearable. He closed his eyes against them, only to see hers, piercing and bold, daring him to deny that this day—the day he both welcomed and feared—had finally come.

He had allowed himself to deny the possibility that Jenera might actually find what she went looking for: proof that the legends were true. He had hidden that truth so far inside him that he fully expected she would return defeated, and perhaps settle into a more realistic life, pair with the partner of her own kind he'd chosen for her and produce children. Human children. He wanted her happiness, had watched long enough her restless searching for what he hoped would never be revealed.

But Jenera had found something. She was a dreamer and a weaver of fantastical tales to entertain children, but she was no liar. She had seen something. Of that he could be sure.

Now as he watched his granddaughter swoop and dance amid the crowd, his hand, white-knuckled and nicked from his latest clumsy mishap, gripped more tightly the wooden staff he used to support his ancient knees. If she had in fact uncovered the truth, his world was about to take what might be for him an intolerable shift, rending it in two. He, the patriarch of his people, would be forced to stand on one side or the other. Was he ready? He wasn't sure. Perhaps it was time someone else bore the burden of truth. Perhaps it was Jenera's time, after all.

Rowan let go a deep sigh, deflating like a worn-out bellows. He left the dance as stealthily as an old man could, picked his way among the rocks and pine needles back to his home beyond the amphitheater, and took up a position near the stairway. Hunched against a chill, eyelids half mast, but watchful, he would wait for Jenera's return.

"Come out here now where I can see you."

Rowan startled at the sound of her voice; he had not heard her approach.

While his eyesight was still keen, he had to admit his hearing suffered in the same way his joints complained when he got up in the morning and his feet hurt at the end of the day. He had already outlived two brothers and a wife. Were it not for Jenera—the sound of her voice, her energy, her spirit—he sometimes thought he would not get up at all.

"I can smell you out there hiding, old man," she called out, and he smiled to himself. He lived for the teasing lilt in her words. A granddaughter was beautiful thing. He stepped out to reveal himself and she ran to him.

"Greetings, grandfather," she said as she knelt before him. It was the first private moment they had shared since her return. His heart swelled as it always did when she was near, the girl he had raised as his own since her parents' disappearance. Her words reflected the respect and gratitude she held for what he had done.

Rowan cleared his throat and stepped back. The loss of his daughter and son-in-law while on expedition was not only a blow to his heart, but to the entire community. He had poured all of his love and energy into raising their little girl. "You are the image of your grandmother in that costume," he admitted, his voice cracking.

Jenera cocked her head and cut her eyes away. "How so?"

Embarrassed, Rowan growled at himself. "Your bearing, I suppose, and I, ah…" How could he explain? She bore a hint of a world long lost and a future promise. It was as much a presence as a resemblance. A presence which had always disarmed him. But today, she had done something different about the eyes.

Responding to his unease, as she always seemed to do, Jenera popped up and took his hands. "Come inside. I need to talk to you."

He cringed at the displeasure in her voice. He was still reeling from his earlier memories. Couldn't he just savor them for a while longer? He knew what she wanted, and he wasn't ready to hear it.

"Fine. We'll talk here then." Jenera flounced down on the step. Throwing her silken "wings" behind her, she pulled off the tiara and unleashed her springy black hair from the copper mesh. "I can't believe that Esteban. One minute he talks of plenty and the next, not enough for the crysls."

It was clear he would not be able to escape the discussion. Rowan sat beside her with a grunt. "Not everyone has as compelling a purpose as you, my dear. Esteban sees his purpose beyond our valley."

"Because *he* has no motivation to preserve *our* kind." She popped up again, this time pacing and flailing her arms. There was an edge to her tone he hadn't detected in the past. Her budding maturity, no doubt. Another sign his world was about to change.

That reality hit hard in his gut. His best friend's son could be pig headed and intractable, but he couldn't blame the young man for wanting to make something of himself outside this valley. He was full human, after all. "The world is changing, Jenera."

"But the elders just stood there like fools while he threatened our very livelihood! Do they really want to sell our bounty to wandering traders instead of take care of our own?"

Rowan leaned forward resting his elbows on his large, knobbed knees. "You know, I'm not sure, but I think I just heard you call the elders *fools?*"

Jenera slumped her shoulders and swirled back to sit next to him once again. "The legend is true, grandfather. The Messenger has come. I saw her with my own eyes."

"I don't doubt you, my child." He placed a hand on each of her shoulders and stared long into her eyes. Indeed, despite her darker skin, coming from his blood, she looked incredibly like her grandmother. He realized now this truth had haunted him for most of his life. He had good reason to believe the legend was true. He simply never considered that it would come to fruition in his lifetime. Perhaps that's why his old bones dragged him out of bed each day. Why he had stood against the rest of the elders in defense of the crysls. Why he had allowed Jenera to go on her quest. It was time he took responsibility for what he knew and for what it meant to her people.

"I will see this Messenger for myself."

Jenera lunged at him and circled her arms around his neck. "Oh, I knew you would believe me! I will lead you to her. If we hurry, we can be there by dawn."

The old man allowed the intimacy of her excited embrace and then removed her arms gently. He held her hands in his and looked sternly into her eyes. "No, Jenera. The crysls need you near. Besides, I know where to find her."

Rowan folded a few precious items into his backpack, then pulled a heavy cloak across his broad shoulders and cinched the hood close around the ropy dreadlocks that would identify him if anyone saw him pass. He slipped out the back door of his chamber in Lillit Compound and hesitated in the deep recess of his private alcove. The evening braziers had burned low, casting only the sheerest of shadows as he made his way over the stone bridge, crossing the river under the watchful eye of the great split dome and headed for the granite tunnel leading out of the valley.

He loped along at a pace that would make an elder proud, his feet familiar with this path since childhood. One of his earliest memories was of a trip through Valley Overlook Gate at sunrise, yellow light kissing granite cliffs as they tipped their heads into the first rays of the sun, three perfectly matched rising peaks gilded each morning with crowns of glory. He knew every rise and fall and turn, every boulder and crevice, every access to fresh water, every hillside rich in Fiddleneck fern, wild hyacinth, onion, and mushrooms; the stone wall erected by his ancestors, a tunnel blasted through solid rock, the *Merce* river winding through it all, oblivious, carving its way to the great inland sea.

He was deep in reverie when he heard footfalls coming from outside the gate. Was it the sound of the river below or his own footfalls that pulled him to awareness? He hadn't thought about encountering anyone on the road this early. "No fool like an old fool," he growled to himself as he scrambled his bones over the low wall at a point hidden by a stand of Buckeye.

He should have been paying more attention. Branch whips scratched at his back as he crouched low and pressed himself against the stone wall, listening. Then he heard it again. Voices ahead on the trail.

"Where have you been?" asked a voice he didn't recognize. "I was starting to think you'd forgotten me."

"There was a council meeting. Some nonsense about legends and crysls."

"Crysls?"

"Superstitious nonsense is all. Jenera thinks she's found another one of her freaks. Got nothing to do with our business. Get up off of your duff and get moving before the sun starts to beat down on our heads."

Rowan focused his attention. He didn't recognize the first voice, but the second was all too familiar.

"This Jenera. She's the one protecting the crysls?"

There was some grunting, some shuffling, then footsteps grew louder then stopped only a few feet away from where Rowan hid. His old heart pumped uncomfortably fast.

"She's their so-called Spirit Leader. Some want to believe her, but I say she's the last of a flock of half-breeds dying out." The larger man picked up his pace as they passed. "Trouble is, she's my betrothed, thanks to a deal my father made a long time ago. But that's none of your—"

"What about this 'freak'?" the stranger interrupted. He was struggling to keep up, a slight form from what Rowan could see through the branches, with a tight-fitting cap pulled down over his ears; sculptured cheekbones, a sharp, straight nose, and a tight-stretched mouth. His frame was mostly covered in a large, heavy coat which must have been someone else's, because it hung off his shoulders, and there were no hands showing at the end of its sleeves.

Using his staff to steady himself, Rowan raised up just enough to see over the rock wall. They were headed toward the Y in the trail, the right side leading into the valley from where he'd just come. The left would cross the river and continue to granite walls, the High Meadow, and if they kept going, eventually lead over Craggy Pass, a dangerous route from which few returned.

"Wait," the larger one hissed and turned half 'round.

Rowan gasped. Esteban. He ducked his head down out of sight, cursing under his breath as dried buckeye pods clattered around him.

"You. In the bushes. Stand up," Esteban ordered in a tone reminiscent of his father.

Rowan cursed himself. How could he have been so foolish to give away his presence? The only thing for it now was to try to get the upper hand. He scrabbled over the rock wall, then pulled himself up to stand before them at his greatest height. He raked his cloak down off his head, shook out his dreadlocks, and gave them one of his infamous, flame-eyed stares.

"So, Esteban," Rowan said, using his lungs like bellows to project his personal power. "Leaving your post while on duty at Gate Compound, are you?"

Esteban stood his ground, pulling himself up to his full six-foot height. "I might say the same thing of you, *old* man."

Rowan knew Esteban wouldn't back down easily. He cleared his throat. "As the leader of our people, it is my job to ensure our main gate is protected, especially when I find that you are not protecting yours. You've had plenty of time to get there since the council meeting ended." Rowan held his gaze for a beat before Esteban cut his eyes away. Seniority had won the stare down once again, but Rowan knew, it would not be long before that would change. Esteban had grown into a strong young man, bolstered by the brazenness of youth. He shifted his gaze to the stranger, taking in his steely blue eyes, his smooth forehead and small stature. He might be a small man, or even a boy. It was difficult to tell with the large coat concealing most of his body. But one thing was sure: He knew every soul in *Dannais* Valley and this boy wasn't one of them.

Esteban lifted his chin and flicked a nod at his companion. "This is… Rafael, a trader, from The Owen." The stranger allowed himself a quick glance at Rowan, before he lowered his eyes.

Rowan decided to reserve judgment on the stranger's origin. He looked like he'd have trouble reaching the first peaks of his own valley, let alone the stamina to make it over Craggy Pass. Yet here he was, and something about the boy pricked his curiosity. But it was best to get the upper hand here and now. He would consider this new arrival's purpose later.

"He's… interested in our surplus," Esteban went on, shifting his feet. "… So I escorted him here myself."

"In the middle of the night, Esteban?" It was a statement more than a question, in the style of Esteban's own father. Rowan relished the flicker of recognition in the younger man's eyes. As in all cultures dependent on security, there is little quarter given a sentry who leaves his post.

As if caught between the two wills, the stranger took a sidestep. Rowan saw flight in his eyes. Esteban stayed the younger man with a hand at his elbow.

"I'll be guiding him out of the valley after we visit the grain silos." He turned, his charge in tow, and they continued down the trail.

Rowan snorted, folded his arms over his chest, flicked his dreds back over his shoulder, and watched, lips together in a grim smile, as they headed to the trail leading to the valley floor. The son of his late partner and friend had been a problem ever since his father had died.

Their alliance had been mutually beneficial. The *Dannais* had long-standing roots in the valley, reclaiming a healthy society from the remains of what had once been a thriving civilization in the valleys below. Humans had only recently begun to re-emerge in the open, their skin highly vulnerable to the ravages of a sun grown so intense, they still wore heavy covering against it. Inbreeding had added strength to both bloodlines, sun resistance to human skin, and a hearty resilience to *Dannais* bloodlines. Which was why Rowan had pledged his granddaughter to his friend's son.

Now, as he watched Esteban and his visitor make their way down the trail, regret twisted in his gut. Most young men, Rowan knew, challenged authority at this age, but Esteban's challenge was more than youthful exuberance. Esteban longed for power, and not the kind awarded in a peaceful society. It was Jenera's rightful place—a loyal mate by her side--to step up into leadership once Rowan was too old, but Esteban's ego would chafe at the thought. With his father out of the picture, he had grown resentful, bored, and bold. A bad combination in a full-human. For this reason, Rowan kept an eye on him. He could see now; he had been too easy on the boy. But at this moment, he was more interested in getting out of the valley than dealing with Esteban. He hiked his backpack higher on his shoulders and lumbered out the gate toward more pressing matters.

The eastern sky was lightening by degrees of warm ultraviolet when at last he reached the base of the canyon overlooked by the Mariposa Grove near what he had fondly named Cora's Cave. He stopped to catch his breath. It had been many years since he'd come this way; seeking to ease what felt like an eternity of pain, he'd blocked the cave, and everything associated with it out of his memory. Standing here now, his foot at the base of several rocky switchbacks, he could not help but remember the first time he'd followed this granite stair.

CHAPTER 15 - THE GRANITE STAIR

Drawn by a natural curiosity about the caves in his valley and a mysterious pull on some deeper level, Rowan had labored an hour up the steep steps chiseled out of black and white speckled granite to reach the first of several alluring cave entrances, when hairs on the back of his neck stood up. Had someone followed him? He snapped his head around to look below. No one there. When he turned back, he was so surprised by what he saw, he nearly lost his grip on a stabilizing outcrop.

A woman had appeared as if from nowhere and stood like a statue between two boulders, thin and fragile yet glowing with a sunlit vitality and an inviting smile. Her long, silver hair lifted off her shoulders in a warm updraft, briefly revealing a body a-shimmer with luminous nudity. His mouth worked but no words came.

"Are you coming up or are you going to hang off of that outcrop until your arms fall off?"

Rowan was riveted to the spot. He could not drag his gaze away from her. Unusually large, her eyes held him in thrall for another breathless moment before they softened and her whole countenance broke into warming rays like the sun.

"Well come on, then," she called, and backed away through the opening.

Rowan smiled to himself as he took the first step. He had stayed with her on the mountain for more than a week, barely taking time out from their lovemaking to find food and water.

Back then, the climb took under an hour. Today, he thought, stretching into a nagging pain in his back, it would take much longer.

He paused a moment as he reached the very spot he remembered first seeing her. The two boulders were there, but there was no one beckoning to him. He pulled himself up, made the last switch of direction and came up on the side of the remembered landing, a flat ledge with a view of the great sea below.

The early morning slant of the sun cast a sharp angle of light across the mouth of the cave; beyond that was blackness. He saw no one, though he smelled the remains of a smoldering fire.

"Ola?" he called, falling back into his native language. He looked around, moved closer to the cave opening. "Ola?"

"What do you want?"

The strident voice startled him; he hadn't sensed anyone near. He spun around and gasped before falling to his knees, the backpack sliding to the ground. A woman stepped from between the standing stones. She held a burning torch in front of her with two hands, emphasizing the taut muscles of her shoulders and neck. She took a step toward him, jabbed the torch closer.

He shot his hands in the air. "I... I... " he stammered, but he could not speak. He had imagined

Jenera's Messenger would look similar to his Cora, but as soon as the woman stepped out into the open, the image of frail Cora fled his mind. This woman was as tall as he was. The parts of her body not hidden behind a shining short tunic were indeed iridescent like his Cora's, but where Cora had been fragile, this woman was strong. Where Cora's thighs had been thin as willow wisps, this woman's thighs were cut long and lean like a stone statue he had seen in a precious book. Her legs seemed to go on forever. Her jaw was square and regal. Her chest heaved with mounting challenge. Her eyes, large and set wide apart, raked him from head to toe, taking his measure. On top of her head was a mantle of iridescent green pierced by a pair of antennae stretched sinuously, alert to every movement of his gaze.

"Stand up," she commanded. Taking another step toward him. She steadied herself as if to fend off an attack. He could feel the heat of the torch on his face.

Rowan stood slowly, his hand blocking the heat, his loosened dreads spilled haphazardly out of their fastening. He swallowed hard.

"Jenera t-t-told me…" were the only words he could think to say, unsure if they would be his last. The space between them crackled with the heat of the torch and a mounting tension.

Rowan held his breath, transfixed, awaiting his fate, but the moment passed into the next until her countenance changed, faltered, and she lowered the torch slowly until he could see tiny beads of sweat across her brow. He started to move, she recovered briefly, but ultimately, she let the torch fall from her hand and took a staggering step toward him just before her eyes rolled up to reveal their whites and she fell forward into his arms.

Lara opened her eyes and tried to focus. The figure kneeling by her side seemed to morph from a man to a bear and back to a man again. Overcome by weakness and waves of nausea, she could barely lift her head. She looked around her, half expecting to be back in her own lighthouse bed, but the nightmare persisted. She was lying on her back inside the cave, on a warm, heavy material, something soft and supportive tucked under her knees. A silky robe was draped over her body, and the fire beside her had been stoked.

She felt detached, as if watching the scene from behind a screen. Bear-man unrolled a rectangle of woven cloth near the fire, setting out various implements: metal cups and bowls, eating utensils, and a squat ceramic pot with an acorn-shaped knob on the lid. She blinked in slow motion, let her head roll back, and followed Bear-man with her eyes. He poured a bowlful of water from her own supply and dipped a handful of moss into it, then turned back to her and used it to mop her burning forehead. She could not keep her eyes open.

"Don't worry now. You're going to be all right soon. This is perfectly natural."

His voice was deep and rumbling, like unseen rocks rolling along a river bottom. She opened her eyes again. The look in his eyes and his tender touch gave her a sense of wellbeing. She covered his huge hand with hers as he lifted the cup to her lips. She tasted metallic silver, then sweetness.

"It's a mixture of nectar and honey. It will give you strength."

She sipped the thick cool liquid, swallowed, and lay her head back. He was right; it gave her instant relief.

But then, without any warning or apparent reason, the pain that rendered her unconscious the first time ripped through her back again. She started up, gripping the sides of her bed. A firm, warm hand pressed down on her forehead.

"Hold, hold." Bear-man moved his hand to her stomach and made her look into his eyes again. "Let it work through, work through, there, there…" His words were gentle and soothing, enough for her reason to take over.

Finally, it hit her, what was happening and who he was. For a woman who had been present at more than fifty births, you'd think she'd recognize her own labor when it started. Never mind that this baby seemed to have come to term almost overnight. And the old man? He had to be Jenera's grandfather. What was his name?

"Rowan, you're Rowan, aren't you?" Her voice rasped.

He simply smiled and refilled the cup. "And not a moment too soon, apparently."

"Jenera told me… about you… loves you." Lara panted the words and caught her breath again. She felt the rise in her stomach with tentative fingers. It had hardened and moved down low toward her groin. This time, when the pressure began to build, she was ready for it. *My baby*, she thought, extracting a moment of joy from the scene. She closed her eyes, conjuring Michael's face. In another reality, it would be his hand on her forehead, his encouraging words, his baby soon in her arms. A girl maybe, squalling and hungry for her breast. She held on to those thoughts, pink and rosy, as long as she could before the fearful thought crowded in. She sought Rowan's hand and held tight. "Rowan. What if it's…"

He rested his hand on her belly and looked into her eyes. "Prepare yourself, woman. It's likely."

"You've seen this before?"

He nodded. "How long was the gestation?"

Pregnant before the chrysalis. Lara stared at him a moment, shaking her head, then closed her eyes and let her chin drop to her chest. "Only a few days," *plus a few thousand years, probably*. "I thought I was just bloated, but then I felt the quickening, then almost overnight… " She smoothed her hand over her bulging belly.

He closed his eyes and nodded.

Her throat closed around words unspeakable. She squeezed her eyes shut, held to the sides of her canister bed, and nodded her readiness to finish the job.

The wrack of pain grabbed her again from behind and twisted, pulling her down. "Arrrg-g-ghhhh," she groaned.

Jenera's grandfather quickly removed the padding behind her knees and lifted the silken gown to her hips, never taking his eyes from hers.

"Just push and let me do the rest." Rowan mopped his own brow in the crook of his arm.

"I can't," she yelled, challenging his ability to control the scene.

"You can and you will; you have no choice. Now hold, hold… " he waited a beat, then met her eyes again. "All right, this is it. Push!"

Lara pushed until she thought her heart would break and then her head fell back on the matting, her energy spent, the pressure gone. Another painless slither of warmth and she was more empty than she had ever felt in her life. There was no cry, no movement. Only the scree of a hawk in the distance and the ancient silence of the cave. She squeezed her eyes tight shut against the thoughts that assailed her. Was it still born, then? A crysl? A human? What?

She lay still, holding back her fears as Rowan cleansed the burning in her perineum and packed the area with fresh-rinsed moss.

"So," he said, uneasily. "It is as I suspected." He pulled his knife from the fire and carefully released the crysl from the after birth. "My Cora gave me two beautiful girls, and then, one of these." He found a clean cloth in his kit and began to wrap the tiny creature. "This is not the end of it all," he said gently. "The crysl she bore is one of those Jenera protects at Crysl Tower." He stood and started to turn away. "I'll take care of it, then. I'll take care of everything."

"No!" she said, and with a renewed surge of strength she lunged forward and gripped his wrist. "No, wait." She slowly released him. "I want to see. I have to... "

Rowan searched her eyes. In them she saw the question: Was she ready to face the truth? He had already said the words: she had no choice in the matter. With an unspoken understanding, he released the cloth and backed away a step as he slowly transferred the weight of the creature into her arms.

Lara caught her breath. The child floated in liquid, eyes closed, still inside a clear amber sac, every finger and toe intact, its body swaddled in its own lacy quilt—asleep—still waiting to be born. Her heart warmed and felt as though it would melt. Her fingers on the outside, tracing the little chin, the tiny nodules on top of its head, the knees folded up against its tummy, perfect feet crisscrossed above female genitalia. Lara looked to Rowan, her heart starting up again.

"We have to get her out, don't we?" She held the baby up to him. "She can't breathe, she... " But even as she said the words, the amber sac was beginning to crystallize.

"She's not ready, my dear," Rowan said, moving to her side. "She belongs with the others. Then we'll see."

Lara hugged the tiny creature once more to her breast, then handed her over to Rowan. No baby's cry, no tug at her breasts, no mother's tears of joy. It was done.

Rowan scooped the hardened crysl up into his pack and set it aside, away from the fire and her view. She rested now, awake but drowsy, her eyes cut away from where the backpack and its contents lay.

Shaking uncontrollably now, her body's energy spent, she let Rowan replace the cushion behind her knees and tuck a downy robe close around her, feeling as though she'd been torn in two. One part of her was awash with relief. The uncertainty was over. The question was answered. All that was left of Michael had been transformed along with herself into something not quite human. What possible purpose could she have to continue living?

The other part of her held to a feeble hope that she would one day hold in her arms the tiny soul that had just been born. Her child. Her's and Michael's.

Rowan stirred, she looked up.

"Sleep now," he said low, old memories crowding in. His throat squeezed with emotion. "You are going to be all right."

He wasn't sure of that at all, not after what had happened to Cora. But this woman was ten times stronger and obviously much younger than Cora had been when she'd conceived. If anyone had a chance to survive what had just happened, this woman did.

He placed a rolled bundle at the foot of her bed. "These belonged to my Cora. Some comforts, some bread, and well... you will see what else, when you are ready. I must leave you now if I'm to get home before I'm missed." He slipped the weighted backpack onto one shoulder. "Jenera will be back. I promise you that."

The woman touched his hand, and closed her eyes as sleep mercifully overtook her.

CHAPTER 16 - THE BEACON'S CALL

Sometime during the night Lara stopped shaking and fell into a warm drowse. The fire Rowan had stroked before he'd gone had grown low, but not before heating the rocks around its ring. The ambient heat dried her eyes. If only she could sleep, forget where she was, what she had become. Forget everything that had happened and go back. She used to be able to do it. Slide back into a fantasy of the way it should have been, could have been, if only.

She blinked once, slowly, the events of the day fading behind a red veil of fatigue and disbelief.

Just let it happen. Let me be home, back in Michael's arms...

She reclined in an oversized tub, cradled in a human armchair. His heartbeat boomed into her back, deep and slow, the relaxed rhythm of a consummate waterman with a swimmer's heart. She luxuriated in the warmth of his hands sliding over her shoulders, her breasts, down over her stomach and into the V between her legs.

She rose to meet his fingers as they dipped into her, teased.

"Relax." His warm breath at her ear tickled and tantalized. Obediently, she let her hips relax back down into the water as his fingers slipped over her folds, back up over her stomach, to her breasts to her shoulders, to start all over again. She closed her eyes and rode waves of pleasure like a floater in warm, tropical water.

A cooling rock snapped, pulling her out of the pleasure zone. Lara rubbed at a sudden burning sensation along her neck and upper spine. No. Not yet. The bath, the hands, the fragrance of lavender soap… the bath, the hands, the fragrance… She chanted out loud the magic words that could erase the present moment of pain and grief and return her to the timelessness of the fantasy. Eventually, the chant took her down into sleep, but the fantasy took its own direction…

She stood on an outcrop. A warm breeze ruffled the surface of the water. After a moment, a point of light appeared on the horizon, widened, an iridescent beacon sweeping the seascape. When it reached her, it picked her up along the way. Like a groundswell, it carried her along at a breathtaking speed, then slowed and released her as gently as a loving hand. She had only begun to absorb the impact of the first pass, when the beacon appeared again, swept toward her at a mind-bending pace, until at the apex of the sweep, it sliced a path to the horizon, then flashed as it continued past her and disappeared again, reminiscent of… what?

Before she could fully form the thought, the light appeared again, this time taking her fully into its spell. Breathless, she rode the swell, without thought or reason, diffused into the timeless, benevolent void, along with the infinitesimal particles of light. Then just as suddenly as it had come, the beam passed through her and reorganized, leaving her breathless, tingling, and wrapped in a sense of wellbeing.

Lara gasped, as if she had been holding her breath for years, an image of a lighthouse beacon floated momentarily then faded as she came fully awake. Except for a curious burning sensation at the base of her spine, she felt a little better, a little more in control.

On a deep breath she released slowly through her mouth, she became aware of a weight on her feet at the end of her bed. She sat up on one elbow and considered the object, a bundle…

Oh. Yes. The man, Rowan, had been here, and…

She fell back on the bed, the weight of knowledge flooding back. It expanded to fill the entire cave. Her hands went to her stomach. It had lost its fullness, but it was still somewhat swollen and tender.

And empty.

Not back to what she had been. She could never go there again, but empty in a way she could never have imagined. It was one thing to have aborted a fetus at 16, after a brutal rape. Quite another to lose what she and Michael had made, even if it wasn't quite what she'd expected. The loss was less a relief than a responsibility. She would have to face that soon, but not yet…

Just take me home. The thought came with an echo of the beacon's sweep. She blinked it away, her mind ached with yearning for something familiar, something known. Her arm went limp, dangled on the edge of the canister. *Please, take me home.* Once again, fatigue overtook her. She slept a blank, empty sleep.

On her next waking, the cold compelled her to action. She had to stoke up the fire or at least, get outside to the sun. She tried to move, but again found that her feet were weighted down. Pushing with all her strength, she sat up and tried to make sense of the shape at the end of her bed.

A satchel, no. A backpack, she realized, lifting the straps. She pulled it into her lap and opened the top. Some bread, she remembered Rowan saying, and swiftly she recovered three hard loaves from a roll of fabric inside. She sniffed one of them, and her stomach responded with a deep growl. Punching her thumbs through the crust, she broke it open. The outside was crisp and hard, but the inside was tender and fragrant in her mouth. Not San Francisco sourdough, but just as welcome to her empty stomach.

A few more bites and she was beginning to believe there was life after UV. She had devoured nearly half a loaf before she took notice of the unfurled fabric. Not just a wrapping, it was a garment and a beautiful one.

In addition to the robe he had wrapped around her before he left, Rowan had left her a gown, soft to the touch, worn but supple, pliant, and luxuriant. She stood up on legs still a little wobbly and shook off the breadcrumbs. She held the dress close to her body. It could work. Excited like she might have been at finding the perfect dress at a consignment shop, she stepped through a long slit opening at the back, shot her arms through tapered sleeves, and let it fall over her body. A perfect fit, clinging only as a bias-cut sheath could. An embroidered wreath of butterfly wings decorated the hemline which came all the way to her ankles and kicked out with every step. A quick turn spun it out in a trumpet swirl.

For the first time since awakening in this godawful place, Lara felt like the woman she once was. The woman she could be. How cliché is that? How apropos? How ridiculous.

How perfect.

Except that it was morning in the cave and freezing cold. She returned to the bed and pulled the robe around her, only then realizing that it matched the garment, right down to the filigree wings around the hem.

Rowan had talked about his Cora. These must have been hers. Cora had been like her, she remembered him saying somewhere during the long night of sweat, toil, and utter and complete exhaustion. Her mind reeled off for a moment. What had he said? Cora had been like her? She wasn't really sure of anything that night except for the outcome, and she dared not dwell on that right now. She was stiff and cold and she had to do something about it. As in every day since she emerged into this foreign place, there had to be first things first.

Fire. Water. Food.

She poked at the tiny bed of coals at the center of the fire ring. Not much activity. Had she slept that late? She poked again. Nothing. Panicked, she fanned the ashes, until she was rewarded with a tiny lick of a flame. How could she have been so foolish to let the fire almost die? She kicked at the collection of duff and small twigs gathered about the edges of her fire ring. She hardly noticed the folded sheet of parchment paper before it flipped into the fire and ignited. She watched it glow around the edges with satisfaction a moment until she realized she had no idea where it had come from. Why, it must have come from... the pack! There were written words, lines...

"Oh crap!" She used the poker to flip it out of the fire then slapped out the flames before they destroyed the entire thing.

With one eye on the discovery and the other on the fire, she flipped a few more pieces of bark and duff into the tiny licking flames until she could feel heat building. At last, she felt confident the fire would take care of itself, then picked up what was left of the paper and held it to the light.

It was a drawing. Rowan's words drifted back to her: *These belonged to my Cora. Some comforts, and well... you will see what else, when you are ready*. This must be the *what else*.

She turned the drawing this way and that until the hastily scratched figures started to make some sense. Some of the words had been burned away, but she could recognize a few: Granite Canyon, Cora's Cave, Great Sea. Though primitive and quickly drawn, some of the features of Rowan's map corresponded to her immediate surroundings. The ledge, the two rock towers, the trail down to the meadow. But as she studied it further, she began to see that it was more than a representation of her surroundings, it was a map of the greater area and a specific place marked with a star.

CHAPTER 17 - ON THE HIGH MEADOW

Esteban gestured impatiently from halfway down the hillside. The boy knew he should leave now, follow the powerful man down to the river, but he couldn't pull himself away from the vision. When Esteban scowled at him and barreled out of sight, the boy turned back for one more lingering look. The young woman who kept watch over the girls playing in the meadow stood now at full alert and he could not take his eyes off her. Each time one of the girls ran to her arms, they were greeted in a warm embrace. Her smile was a gentle gift to each wild heart that danced her way. His own heart ached as she framed their young faces in her hands, smoothed their hair, and cooed approval or encouragement.

The man in him knew he should leave before they discovered what Esteban had done. But the boy in him, lonely and afraid, longed to run to those welcoming arms, press his face to that breast, confess all, feel the assuring hand of forgiveness on the back of his head. He wished he was eleven again. He'd be back at home, back in his own skin, locked safely inside his whirling, relentless, jagged mind. A mind that had been a confusing and often exhausting place before, but at least it had been familiar. And although his mother had often held him at arm's length, at least she had been there.

Tears seared down his cheeks. None of this was his fault. He hadn't chosen this path, but now it seemed he was stuck on it. He ground his fists into his eyes and turned, scaring a bevy of quail into flight, then took off noisily under the sound of their beating wings and the clamor of the battle going on inside his head.

Jenera scanned the edges of the meadow, keeping watch over her charges. She closed her eyes and listened to the rasp of late summer grasses on the hillside below. A warm breeze caressed the meadow and titillated the tiny hairs on her arms. She breathed deeply and opened her eyes once again, measuring every footstep of every child racing the meadow around her, ready to run if one small foot should fall too far from the boundaries she'd set.

All around her, the young girls of Lillit Compound ran through head-high milkiweed, competing to see who could collect the most summer-dried seed pods in their baskets. Their sweet laughter filtered through a static of worry in Jenera's mind. Rowan had missed breakfast with her for the third morning. Only last evening, she had checked his quarters. Nothing was out of place, there had been no trace of heat in his private brazier, and that made her more nervous than ever.

And then her antennae went on full alert at a flurry of soft, percussive sound. Was that footsteps running just outside the meadow? The hackles rose on the back of her neck. She ducked instinctively and spun around, her heartbeat notching up. Off to her right, a bevy of quail lifted in unison and flickered noisily into the air just as Ekiria rushed to her side. Her senses settled a little.

"Ekiria! You snuck up on me!"

Ekiria jumped up and down, nearly spilling the contents of her basket. "Did I win?" She held the brimming basket up for inspection.

They had been on the meadow only a few minutes and the child's basket was nearly full. Of all the young girls in the compound, Ekiria was the most energetic. She pushed the boundaries of every limit, which could be wonderful, but for Jenera, it could be a challenge.

"Well, let's see." She took the child by the hand and together they sat on a low rock at the edge of the meadow where she could give her the attention she craved without losing sight of the perimeter. "If we stop the contest too soon," she whispered close to Ekiria's ear, "we won't have much of a harvest, will we?"

She took the moment to scan the nearby tree branches. The quail had once again settled in the low brush around the tree trunks, the only sounds other than the children's laughter their soft, bubbly coos.

When she refocused on Ekiria, the young one's lower lip quivered. "But I wanted to be the dancer, like you said. If I win."

"You'd like Alta to dance with you, no?" Ekiria continued to stick out her lower lip. Jenera let herself relax into the child's world for a moment. "And if everyone fills their basket, by next week, we can all dance and we'll have enough milkiweed seeds for our seed deposit—"

Before she could remind Ekiria why they collected the seeds, giggly laughter across the meadow turned to shrill screams. Jenera stood erect, her body tingling with alarm. Three little girls ran toward her while several stayed behind, crouching down around a slumped figure in the tall grass.

"What is it? What's happened?" She started off at a run. The frightened girls came at her all at once, legs pumping, arms pointing, seed pods flying out of baskets getting trampled under running foot.

"It's grandfather Rowan!"

"He's down there!"

"Hurry!"

By the time Jenera made her way through the tall milkiweed plants, most of the girls had surrounded the limp form of her grandfather's body.

"Ekiria, get the water jug from my basket." Ekria ran off as Jenera dropped to her knees and gently scooped Rowan's head into her lap.

His breathing was too shallow. He looked as though he'd fallen down a rocky bank, face first. "They took it," he moaned, his eyes fluttering open. "I tried to stop them, followed them as far as I could, but… "

Jenera daubed a corner of her tunic against his bloody lip. "Shhhhh. You're all right now. Just breathe."

Ekiria returned with her basket and the jug of water. Jenera tipped it to his lips, then wet a corner of her garment and washed his face.

Rowan winced under her attempts to clean blood from his brow, then tried to sit up long enough to get her to look seriously at him. "They took it, Jenera. I've failed you all…" His head dropped back.

"Took what, grandfather? Who took what?" But Rowan said nothing more.

"Ekiria! Take Alta with you and run straight to Lillit Compound."

Ekiria ignored the order and threw herself on Rowan, grabbing one of his arms. "Grandfather!" She pulled at him with no response. "Don't be dead. You have to watch me dance."

Jenera pulled her gently away. "He's not dead, Eki, he's sleeping. But you can help."

Ekiria got up reluctantly.

"Go tell Helena to come fast and bring a litter. Hurry!"

Ekiria scrambled across the meadow and down the switchback trail, surefooted like a fawn following its mother. She was used to running. She ran everywhere. She couldn't help herself. But her friend Alta was already tired and lagged behind. Now she bent over to catch her breath. "Ekiria. Wait."

Ekiria turned and went back to her friend.

"Sit here." She guided her to a flat rock where they could sit next to each other. "We're just like two deer in the forest, running from a wolf. We have to keep going or he'll catch us."

"There's no wolves." Alta's face had already turned from bright red to pink and she breathed easier.

"Maybe there is. You don't know." Ekiria rolled her eyes. "Wolves and trolls, and..." She trailed off, listening. "Wait. Something's right there," she said, pointing to a switchback below them.

Alta's expression told her she hadn't seen a thing. "Let's just go," she whined, and pulled on Ekiria's arm.

"No. You go. I'm going to go see what that is."

"Eki, no! You'll get in trouble. Helena--"

"You get Helena. I'll meet you later. At the counting."

Alta stood, hands on her hips. "Ekiria, you just told me we were running from wolves, now you want to go after them?"

It was the first time her friend had ever resisted her, and she had to admit going off alone was a bad idea. "Shhhh. Just wait here a minute. I have to at least see what that was."

Alta sat down, shivering. Ekiria crept forward, listening as she went. There was a furtive movement behind her, just off the trail, then silence. She crouched low, barely breathing, imagining what or whomever was doing exactly the same thing. She stood slowly, keeping her back turned. "Okay, I don't see anything," she called out dramatically. "Let's go."

She took a couple of steps in place, but she didn't go. She waited, and sure enough, a small figure darted from behind a big rock, stumbled a little, then rolled down the hill and out of sight. One of the boys from the colony? Maybe. But why would he hide from her?

"Ekiria," Alta's frightened voice broke her thoughts. "Are you coming?"

"Yes," she said making her way back to the trail. She wasn't sure what she had just seen, but for now, Rowan needed help, and she was wasting time. "Let's go."

CHAPTER 18 - AN EMPTY SHELL

Lara straightened and stretched her back to relieve aching muscles, her gaze landing on the granite wedge stretching out into the water. There was no mistaking it. It had to be the formation Rowan had marked on the map, a great slab of flat rock that created a promontory from which to view the valley. Lifting her damp skirts, she ventured a few steps forward, knelt to touch the ancient stone with her fingertips. Rusty lichens prized the cracks with leafy fingers, slowly decomposing granite to piles of sparkling sand at its base.

The ruin struck a lonely chord in Lara's memory, one of many that played melancholy in the background of her days in this place. Her lighthouse had been made of wood and stone. What would it look like today? Was it there at all?

Giving in to exhaustion, she lay down and pressed her back flat on the stone surface, absorbing what little heat radiated from it. Her back ached and her feet throbbed. If that weren't enough, she'd been plagued with an annoying itch around her torso, something she assumed was a symptom of her body returning to normal after the rapid growth and conclusion of her pregnancy.

After a moment, revived and hungry, she sat up again, pulled half a loaf of bread out of the backpack, took a bite and gazed out over the stone ledge, understanding once and for all, the vast expanse before her could be none other than California's San Joaquin Valley under an inland sea that wasn't there in 2023. If the National Geographic had been correct in forecasting the effects of climate change on the planet, including the flooding of the San Joaquin, at least a thousand years had passed since she last walked the Earth—maybe more, depending on how long it had been this way.

She kicked at a pile of loose granite with her toe. None of that made any difference now. There was nothing she could do about it but find a way to live through another moment, another day, another hundred yards down the trail, which would take her into shreds of foggy mist.

She studied the map again. She had to be in the right place. Three rivers converged, the dam, the spillway, a stream leading to the sea. And the words:

Here you will find your treasure.
'Til we meet again,
R

If this was indeed the dam, she was at or very near one of the circled Xs on the map. As far as she could see there was nothing here, but after two days' travel, she wasn't about to turn back. Down switchbacks and through fern-shaded glades, through wild orchards of peach and walnut, she'd been close enough to a brown bear to smell the juniper berries on his breath, and far enough from anything human to feel the weight of loneliness in her heart.

No. She wasn't about to turn back. If nothing else, the exercise would do her some good.

The sun worked its magic, her limbs grew supple. She was ready to tackle the last leg of Rowan's "treasure" map. If the scale was correct, and the map assured her it was close, she couldn't be more than an hour's walk to the spot circled on the edge of the sea.

Rowan had thought seeing the place for herself was important. She owed him that much. He had literally saved her life and taken charge of… of… she didn't want to think about the bundle he'd wrapped up and taken away with him. Not now. Maybe not ever. But she was alive, and he had been the one to save her, so, she'd go. She'd see. She'd think no further than that.

Gathering the hem of her gown along with her courage, she climbed down from the crumbling structure to the path below.

Most of the going was easy, a gradual descent down a game trail marked by coyote scat and deer tracks, and now her tracks in the soft dirt. She crabbed over a block of granite split in half by tree roots and emerged from a stand of cottonwood unexpectedly into the open.

The fog, though it had lifted from the ground to form a high ceiling overhead, had sucked the color out of everything. A wide, flat river bottom, sandy and damp, stretched out ahead, a silver ribbon of water dividing the valley down the middle.

She studied the map again. The X was definitely on this side of the river. There was the rock outcrop. If she were any judge, the location was maybe five hundred yards ahead. It was much bigger than she had expected compared to the marks on the map. But it did resemble an old shipwreck as Rowan had noted. Gentle wind pushed low, lapping waves up against the *hull* of it, which jutted out into the water.

Lara stood a moment longer, the nodules on top of her head tingling--a new, intrusive sensation that gave her no comfort.

Maybe that's what it's for. Don't get comfortable here, there's something you need to pay attention to.

A physical link to those gut feelings she so easily brushed aside in her former life. Was she missing something here? Or was she simply afraid?

What was it Michael always said when asked in an interview if he was afraid out there in the giant waves? "I'd be lying if I said I wasn't afraid facing down a forty-foot wave. But letting fear rule is always a fatal mistake."

Words to live by.

She took a moment to gather her wits about her and calm her pounding heart. She was standing on solid ground. Nothing to be afraid of. Wiping a thin veneer of perspiration off her forehead, she surveyed the open space before her. The only apparent danger was ruining the shoes that had protected her feet from the rocky trail she had followed. What she would give for her trusty old Reboks right now. The trail ahead was wet sand, which might actually soothe her aching feet. Thinking rationally again, she removed the shoes and arranged them on a flat rock near the trail where she couldn't miss them on the way back.

The nodules on top of her head tingled again. There was something out there. Something Rowan wanted her to find. What had she to lose, really?

On a last, fortifying breath, she stepped out into the wet sand and followed the trail in the direction of the outcrop.

The rock formation loomed sheer and unapproachable, but the back side wedged out gradually, providing easy access to the top. Using her hands and feet like a crab, she climbed to a higher, flat surface and sat, then splashed water on her face from a shallow pool collected there. The mild salt taste surprised her, but it made sense. Saltwater intrusion was predicted.

A fragment of memory teased her senses. She had so missed the scent of the ocean. But, before she could close her eyes and indulge the sensation, a movement in her peripheral vision drew her attention. But, then a trio of concentric rings disappearing in the water's surface, there was nothing. A bird or a fish, most likely. But just as she turned away, her antenna picked up a scintillating signal, sensed rather than seen, and then… A form, surfacing and dipping out of sight like a dolphin in a gentle wave.

She climbed another level higher and stared at a central point in the near distance for as long as she could without blinking. But whatever it was she had seen was gone and the nodules on top of her head settled.

Of all the changes that had taken place in her body, the nodules were the most alarming because they seemed to have a mind of their own. She resisted the urge to feel up there. The prospect of them being something like snail antenna poking out of her head came close to triggering her gag reflex. Instead, she distracted herself by picking her way across a shallow pool, its rocky edges lined with a colorful collection of shiny, succulent moss. Maybe they were the treasure. Something other than fruits and nuts to eat.

Stretching her hand up to a crevice for leverage, she pulled herself to the highest ledge, bent over, and dragged in her breath in deep draughts until her heart rate slowed.

She didn't notice the figure standing only a few feet away until she stood upright and met it head on. A shriek tore out of her throat, unexpected and raw. She yelped and backed a few steps away, until she realized the figure was simply that: A transparent mold of a person, poised with arms at its sides, as though watching the horizon.

Remembering to breathe, she stepped close again to get a better look. The hands were rendered in minute detail right down to fingernails and wrinkles and joints, all delicately embossed on the inside of the shell. Lara reached out a finger and touched the surface of an arm at first timidly, then with more confidence.

"My god." She couldn't help tracing her hands over the hips and up the sides of the perfectly formed torso. Well-developed latissimus dorsi veed out to formidable shoulders. Sinewy trapezius thickened at the base of the neck, leading to a smooth head.

Like her own.

The material reminded her of the shell she had peeled off her own body, but thicker and stronger, more distinctly formed, and perfectly intact. It was split in two from the top of the forehead, bisecting the torso, and down the front of each leg, as if a person had just unzipped it like a wetsuit, stepped out of the mold, and walked away.

Under her former circumstances, she would have been shocked. But after what had happened to her the last few days, nothing about this world surprised her anymore.

"If these were just a little closer..." She placed a hand on each side of the torso and pushed gently to see if she could move the halves together without breaking them. The material was resistant but surprisingly plyable.

"Yes."

She slid her hands up to the shoulders to do the same but pulled them back suddenly as a chill zinged up her spine. A fleeting image flickered in her memory. Michael's shoulders, strong and hard, hunched over her. She stepped back a moment, her hand at her throat, heart thudding out of rhythm. She shook the image away. Just a memory. This is nothing but an empty shell. Still, she drew back a step, folded her arms, and continued to study the statue.

Whomever—or whatever—had been inside, had strong pectorals and plated abdominals, bare and smooth to the hip bones, larger than life, but human.

From the hips down, there was a different story. Starting there, the body left impressions of an intricately detailed texture, segmented, spreading down over the well-muscled legs, like a fine armor. Curiosity overcoming fear, she continued to press the two halves together, the thighs merging at an impressive bulge at their junction.

My, my.

Unless the artist had an overactive appreciation for the masculine physique, the model was better endowed than any real man Lara had ever heard of, much less seen.

Taking a step back to admire her efforts, her eyes traveled up the front of the figure. All that remained was to push the two halves of the face together. She sucked in a couple of deep breaths to steady herself, and hesitated, her hands suspended near the ears of the statue as if about to bestow a blessing. Except for the eyes, which were curiously large, the face was… familiar. A strong chin, the planes of the cheekbones high and smooth, a generous mouth. Her breath caught, her fingers quivered. The first sting of tears blurred her vision. There was only one face like it in the world.

It had to be a trick, an aberration, or maybe she simply saw what she wanted to see.

She wiped her forehead in the crook of her elbow then carefully placed her hands on the sides of the face. Her thumbs pressed gently against the cheekbones, and she pushed the pieces all the way together. The reality of it struck a blow to her middle. It was Michael's face, fixed in solidified amber, staring through her as though she didn't exist.

"Michael," she whispered, and it sounded like a prayer.

She could scarcely breathe as she absorbed the impact of its presence. There was no denying it. He had been here, whole and living, like herself. A little larger than life, maybe. And wearing some kind of alien body armor, but there was no mistaking his features.

Lara raised up and pressed her lips to those of the empty shell, knowing they would be cold and brittle, but she could not stop herself.

Loneliness broke over her like an oncoming wave, fed by a grief more consuming than any she had experienced since arriving in this place. Maybe, if she just stopped breathing, she would simply expire and have done with this entire nightmare.

She slumped down against the legs of the statue and stared listlessly across the sea until stinging tears blurred her vision.

The crushing weight of it overtook her soul as wave after wave of grief surged over her. Michael had been here, but when? Yesterday? Last year? A thousand years ago? She stared off across the water, salt tears drying on her cheeks, until, once again, a movement near the river mouth grabbed her attention. Wiping her eyes clear, she watched, holding her breath, as a tall, powerful figure stalked slowly out of the water.

CHAPTER 19 - LIFE REVISITED

He stood alone now, watching her increase the distance between them, until she disappeared into the fog, her small footprints in the sandy river bottom the only proof that she had been there at all. The footprints and a lingering warmth in his center stimulated something in his memory that cranked his heartbeat up a notch. Something Rowan had told him about that he didn't believe could be true. But maybe it was.

Now, his heart beat as though it would pound right out of his chest, driven by the excitement of finally knowing that another being very like himself, actually existed right now, in this lifetime. He longed to run after her, to see that face again, that body, but he held himself in check. It was obvious she had been terrified at the sight of him. No sense in making it worse. Besides, he considered, she had only one option for escape without crossing the river. She would have to climb back up the spillway to the old dam. Not only would it slow her down, it would take her right to his grotto's front door.

He took a deep breath and exhaled slowly to control his heart rate and settle his loins. He'd spent the entire morning collecting his dinner. It would be foolish to run off without it, especially if he expected company.

He returned to the rocks to retrieve his catch, a decent batch of mussels and clams. Some freshwater crawfish from the river and a few wild onions gathered along the way would make a meal that would be hard to refuse.

Slinging a knotted bag over his shoulder, he headed off, keeping close to the outcrops so he would have cover once the path emerged from the fog. His mind reeled with possibilities as he made his way, and end to his ever-present loneliness, top on the list. He wondered now if the woman had already discovered the entrance to his grotto, for surely, she must have come down that way if she were on this side of the river. So why then had she been so surprised to find him there by the water?

Doubt filled his chest with a desperate, inconsolable ache. The physical changes brought about by his second transformation were alarming, even to himself. It should not have been a surprise that the first being to see him in his new state went running away in panic. He might have done the same under similar circum-stances even if he had been looking for someone.

A gull screed overhead, and he looked up to see them circling, the flat disc of the sun straining through the fog. He was nearing the end of cover. Cutting away from the bank, he quickly found her footprint trail; she was likely thinking like he was, keeping near the rocks and out of sight once she lost the cover of fog.

As expected, he emerged suddenly, the riverbank drenched in sunlight, her small footprints the only sign of her. He tipped his face to the warming sun, standing still for a few long moments. On another day he might climb to the top of the old dam, bask in the sun, and allow his system to pump fluids into his deflated wings. He would master them one day. Today, he had other things on his mind.

With the base of the spillway not a hundred yards away, he stepped back into the shadows and scoured the landscape. He was still getting used to input overload that came with his new heightened senses. Ultraviolet auras blurred the edges of objects and his brain had to stitch together dozens of repeated images to create one that he could discern. Thanks to the human brain's miraculous ability to make sense out of chaotic input, the process was getting easier, more automatic. It was compelling and distracting at the same time.

He was focused on the flowing play of light at the top of the spillway when the striking image before him began to take shape. His breath caught; he balanced himself against a rock, captivated by the image as it sorted out in his mind.

It was her.

The folds of her dress fluttered and caught on her legs in the light breeze as she tipped her head back and let the sun warm her face.

Compelled to get a better look, he took a step forward, clumsily knocking loose some decomposed granite with his foot. *Damn!*

She straightened, cocked her head, listening, waiting. He held his breath, and crouched low, waiting to see what she would do. After a moment, she relaxed her shoulders, sat down, and tipped her face once more to the light.

More careful this time, he climbed a few feet higher to get a better look.

At the rustle of a squirrel skittering in the duff, she tensed, watched it go, then lowered her head again.

It would be warm up there on the ledge, their kind needed that, he'd learned. Once again, she raised her head. Apparently satisfied that he hadn't followed, she unfolded herself onto her back; arms stretched out over her head, eyes closed, iridescent skin glowing, breasts full and supple pushed at the fabric of her gown. His mouth went instantly dry.

When at last she arched her back and stretched to get up, a surge of desire possessed him, buoying him up on a swell of exquisite pain. He gasped out loud, then ducked out of sight as she shot up and spun to look in his direction. When he peeked up over the rocks again, she had scrambled over the spillway and into the alcove below.

His alcove.

Taking the higher, more difficult route over the rocks, he made his way there from the top, then dropped down to within a few yards of the alcove and listened.

There was nothing, not a sound. Surely by now she had found his grotto, his furnishings, his tools, his simple attempts to make a life alone bearable. Surely, she would see that he was nothing to fear, even if he looked a bit... *different.* Breathless seconds dragged on to minutes as he shifted his weight, trying to get comfortable without making a sound.

That! Right there! Lara thought, bolting upright. That was definitely not a squirrel. She knew better than to ignore her heightened senses. Too many times in this new life she had let her limited human awareness override her new natural instincts. She quickly gathered her gown and scrambled out of the light and down a crude stair to a ledge at the base of the spillway. Again she alerted on sounds and vibrations. Had he seen her? Was he creeping closer?

She pressed herself against the rocks and quickly assessed her options, realizing too late she had dropped onto a ledge that formed a dead end. The only way out, unless she wanted to climb straight down a ragged cliff, was back the way she'd come.

Toward *him*.

She knew she had rested too soon, but she had exhausted her strength. It was not enough that she'd found evidence of Michael, but that thing, that... *monster* was like something out of a Ridely Scott Alien movie. She'd run at top speed for more than a mile, something she hadn't done since she was twenty. And how long ago was that, really?

Her breath came in short gasps now. She was in deep doo doo. If he had followed her, had seen her scramble down, she had run herself into a trap.

"Dammit," she hissed, spinning around, but it was too late. She was pretty sure she could hear him breathing. The creature had caught up to her, and she sensed he was near enough to block the only way out. Unless...

She backed away as quietly as she could and pushed deeper into the narrow alcove until her eyes adjusted to the shadow and she saw a pair of carved wooden doors, one of which stood open. Drawn by curiosity that belied her fears, she took a step closer and peered inside.

Dust motes spun in a series of light shafts beaming in from evenly spaced sources in the alcove wall, illuminating shelves, pots, and wooden utensils. To her immediate right, there was a rocking chair made of colored woods inlaid in intricate patterns of mother of pearl. Fascinated, she ran her fingers over the design. This was not some creepy giant insect lair, but what looked to be a comfortable living space, artfully planned, taking advantage of the water from the spillway to create a source indoors.

She took another step, captivated by what she saw. Cupboards and shelves were fitted into crevices, adorned with beautiful objects, obviously crafted by someone of great skill and vision. A clever kitchen, well used, boasted a deep sink that looked like it had been salvaged from an old farmhouse. There was a polished redwood bar, a tall stool, and a substantial stove created from a pairing of metal drums. Heat radiated from coals resting in a bin below the drums; still warm, she imagined, from a morning meal. At the far end of the enclosure, some twenty feet away, an enormous bed with a carved wooden head and footboards, was covered in furs. The sleeping area was intricately assembled with symmetry and grace and was partially lit through a series of openings in a smooth stone wall. She drew closer to the bed and smoothed her fingers over one of the spiral-carved finials on the footpost.

Whoever had created this was a master craftsman, with the love of the wood in his hands.

Memory chewed at her as she stroked the fine redwood and then a flicker of light caught on something at the headboard post. She stepped forward, fingers quivering as she reached for what appeared to be a sturdy gold chain. She slipped it off the post.

On the chain was a round medallion, a man carrying a child out of the sea on his shoulder. St. Christopher. Lara's stomach went queasy, she steadied herself with a hand at the bedpost. She held the medallion in her fingers, its meaning searing into them. She knew what had to be on the other side before she turned it over, and when she did, her hand began to tremble:

LYFE

"Love you forever," she whispered, rubbing her fingers over the engraved letters. She had given the medal on the gold chain to Michael for his twenty-ninth birthday, just weeks before this nightmare began.

Life. It was what he had given her on the day they met, and what she had taken away from him.

Her knees weakened, wobbled, and she stumbled back, knocking a large wooden plank from its position leaning against the wall. It banged and bounced, sending up an echoing racket over which she had no control. She yelped and hopped out of its way.

Then there was a shout, footsteps clamoring through the alcove, and... he was there, a dark silhouette against the light streaming in from the spillway windows.

His tall, muscular body filled the doorway, large ice blue eyes, oddly faceted, an angular jaw. Sinewy arms, shoulders, and pecs under darkly iridescent skin. Below that iridescence gave way to a tapered torso, abs defined in layered segments smooth as black satin. Her eyes traveled down over the sculpted six pack, past narrow hips to the place where smaller segments, that looked supple as kidskin, emphasized a generous bulge. She swallowed hard as her gaze lingered where his thighs converged.

He stood still, barely breathing, as non-threatening as a six foot plus creature not quite fitting the description of a human could be. Probing antenna on top of his head surged toward her as if they could span the barrier between them.

The two of them froze, eyes locked on each other, each waiting for the other to make a move. It made sense that this could be Michael's work, that he had been here, lived here. In fact, as she thought about it, this is exactly what he *would* do. Make the best of his situation, make a life for himself, surrounded by the things he loved. Pour his creativity and soul into it. But this creature, this—insect-man. She couldn't put the pieces together in any way that made sense. Unless you took in the color of the blue in the eyes that blinked at her, the set of the jaw... *No.* It was... impossible, wasn't it?

At last, Lara broke the spell and took a breath. She cast her gaze around the room trying to make sense of it. Of anything. If he were going to pinch her head off and eat it, it would be her last. She'd best make good use of it. She had nothing to lose.

She shoved out her fist, dangling the medallion close to his face, for surely this token and this entire space had belonged to her Michael at one time. "What have you done with Michael?"

Her voice echoed against the walls of the grotto, and then faded along with her resolve. The creature took a step closer, she stood her ground.

His grip was surprisingly gentle as his hand closed around her fist and pulled her into the light. He looked directly into her eyes now, and as if sensing her underlying fear, his features softened. With his free hand, he tilted her face to his with an iridescent fingertip under her chin. "Michael?"

His voice was deep, layered with reverberation. Lara couldn't breathe. Something about the face, the tone... Her heart thumped faster, pushing her on.

"Let go of me." She struggled free of his grip, backing up a pace, leaving only the necklace behind.

It was his expression that held her, more pain than menace. He held the necklace reverently, as if it were a precious thing. "This belongs to me."

Lara stepped back and found herself leaning against the bed.

"No. It isn't. What have you done with him?" she pleaded again, the words twisting tight in her throat as they came out.

He looked at her more intensely now, his startling eyes taking in every inch of her. Shocked at the surging response of her body, she pressed herself back against the bed under his unrelenting gaze.

He took a step forward, the satiny segments at his hips shuffling like cards in a deck. Fear and longing fought a battle in her stomach, each emotion straining against the other. Jenera's grandfather, Rowan, a man she trusted and revered, the man who helped her deliver the crysl from her body and in doing so had saved her life, had sent her to this place, to this... man. Would he have sent her into danger? She didn't think so.

Her eyes fixed on the necklace dangling in the creature's fingers, then to his incredible eyes, then traveled down his torso and her face flushed with heat until she had to squeeze her eyes shut at the manic arousal building inside her.

He leaned in, touched her chin with a knuckle. "Look at me," he ordered.

She squeezed her eyes shut tighter, turning her head away. Increasing the pressure on her chin, he turned her face back to his. "Look... at... me..." he said again, his tone firm but not aggressive.

She could feel the heat of his breath on her face and her own breath quickened. Slowly, she opened her eyes to see that his expression was guarded, as if he could read her thoughts. "Am I that different from you?"

She gazed at his face, his shoulders, his pecs, his hips, and then she was stunned to silence. He tipped her face up to his, holding her gaze for another long, excruciating moment before he let go of her chin and leaned away. All she could do was blink and brace herself for his next move. But he simply slipped the gold chain back over the bed post.

She tensed, holding her breath as he reached over her head. He froze a moment, waiting until she saw that he was only pulling a length of cloth from a cubby hole over the bed, then he wrapped the cloth low on his hips and tucked it in, covering his loins.

Heat rose in her cheeks as she watched him turn and move slowly back to the alcove and out of sight. She allowed herself to breathe a little, considering his words. For the last few moments, terrified in his presence, she had forgotten how she had changed. From the inside out, she was herself, not some half insect freak with feather scales and, what were they? Antenne? Whatever. She was like him, but different. More human, less insect. Female, frightened, and most definitely, aroused.

She flinched and the heat returned to her cheeks when he suddenly reappeared in the doorway. He emptied a sack of items onto the wooden counter next to the stove, then sorted and separated, discarding some pieces, reserving others. Stepping aside, he pulled a bowl from a wooden shelf and thrust it out an opening in the stone wall, capturing a trickle of water that had been conveniently directed away from the spillway.

The immediate threat of his closeness eased, not without, she realized, a touch of disappointment. If he'd wanted to hurt her, he could have done it already. Instead, he was preparing food with the ease and rhythm of someone who had designed and built his own kitchen. Her comfort increased as she watched his muscles respond with precision and grace, as though unaware of the curious folds of black and marigold pleated down the middle of his back. Her heart went to quick-step again. If she was alive and transformed in this world, a half human, half insect being, then it stood to reason the same thing could have… probably had… happened to Michael. And now that probability stood before her preparing a meal in a hand-crafted kitchen that reminded her of home.

Her chin quivered. She pressed her lips together. Dare she believe? Was it too good to be true?

If he was disturbed by her presence, he didn't show it. Instead, he stooped to a basket of wood kindling and stoked up flames under the metal drums, then returned to his work, splitting green onions, never looking around, as if she did not exist. She breathed easier. Curiosity was beginning to overtake her fear. Without taking her eyes off him, she pulled herself up onto the furs and rubbed some heat into her feet.

He thrust a misshapen pot out the window to fill and placed it on the stove, then scooped something from a small container and sprinkled it into the pot, all the while humming softly to himself. *What was that? Goodbye Yellow Brick Road?*

Once again, he went outside taking the familiar tune with him. She felt suddenly abandoned. Why? His gestures, the rhythm of his moves, the tilt of his head, his voice, the way he stood--all this--stirred her in a way that watching Michael had always done—standing in her kitchen, a bath towel wrapped around his hips, cooking breakfast. How could she be so sure it wasn't him? He looked different. Frighteningly so, but he was right. She looked different, too. Not so different from him.

He came back once more, this time carrying something that looked like small potatoes in a hand-tied bag. He shoved a handful of the potatoes out the window, rinsing the vegetables, then dropped them into the steaming pot. A handy garden. Running water. Lara smiled. It was so Michael. And he seemed so unaware of the fact.

The tingle returned to her center.

Her body knew.

She slipped the gold chain off the post and lifted it over her head, arranging the medallion between her breasts.

Her heart knew.

She let herself slip into the furry softness of the bed and ran her hands over the smooth contour of the bed post, feeling oddly more safe than she had since emerging into this new world. She was so tired. If only she could convince her mind, she might be able to fall asleep. Instead, she watched the amazing creature before her with a grain of gratitude sprouting inside her.

Rowan had sent her back to life.

She sat up, pinching the medal between her fingers. "Michael?" she said, tentatively. He glanced over his shoulder a moment, confusion knitting his brow, then went back to stirring the pot on the stove. "I have a story to tell you."

CHAPTER 20 - LEAP OF FAITH

He awoke with a start, stiff and cold, confused at first, as always. The intensity of the light and input from multiple images still challenged his focus in the morning. The chair was not a good choice for sleeping, but once his vision coalesced to focus on one image, he remembered the reason why. The woman was in his bed.

Ah, yes, the woman. Pulling a fur around his shoulders, he stood, flexing and stretching the muscles in his legs. Last night, his humble offering of fish stew had opened the floodgates of words. She talked into the night. Her story was fantastic, unfathomable. If one was practical, if one took it at face value, one had to believe it was true.

The two of them were unintended consequences of an experiment gone wrong. She believed he was once a man named Michael. A man she loved. He'd given her permission to use the name. She could call him anything she wanted, as long as he could listen to the sound of her voice. He could see why this Michael had been in love with her. Her eyes, her mouth, the way she moved her shoulders. Even the antenna on top of her head moved gracefully in tune with her body, as if it were perfectly natural for a human to possess them.

Everything about her pulled at his heart and some unnamed place deep inside him. Why? Because she was the first woman of his kind he'd seen? No. It was something deeper. Something engrained in every cell of his body.

At first sight of her, down by the water, he'd felt a sudden tug in his groin. Men, or whatever he'd become in this reality, weren't meant to be alone. But wrapped in his rabbit fur blanket at his kitchen bar, her eyes flashed emotion as she told her tale and it triggered a different kind of longing. Her words painted vivid visions of sunlit sand, distant horizons, giant ocean waves. The words and the mesmerizing cadence of her voice sent unseen, sensual tendrils to find that place inside him where dreams were born.

He had no actual recall of any of the things she told him, any of the things she sacrificed trying to save her Michael. There was only the reality of her existence, and the soft fullness of her lips as she formed the words. The man in him wanted more than the taste of her lips. But when he reached for her, his excitement ruffling the natural armor at this groin, she'd backed away.

How could he blame her? Not more than a week earlier he'd more closely resembled her. Since his second transformation, even he was frightened by the changes that had occurred in his body. How could he expect her not to be afraid? Besides, what did they have in this world but time? Just the fact of her existence was enough for him now. More than enough. He pushed his desire down deep and simply listened to her talk. And talk, and talk…

Sometime after midnight, sated by another bowl of soup and fresh squeezed orange juice, she'd drifted into exhaustion. He'd scooped her up and carried her to his bed, tucked the fur around her, then settled in his oversized chair. At one point during the wee hours between midnight and dawn, she'd cried out, terrorized by a dream. He'd stroked her forehead, held her close, until she'd settled back into a deep sleep.

She was showing signs of what Rowan had seen in him, weeks before his *transition*. Blue veins close to the surface of the iridescent skin at her temples, an orange tinted pattern near the area at the base of her long neck and continuing down her spine. He longed to comfort her, tell her it would be all right, but he knew from experience, he could make her more comfortable, but the actual second transformation was something she'd have to endure on her own. It had been more than a week since it had happened to him and he was still dealing with the changes.

He watched this Lara's even breathing a moment longer, still in disbelief. She wasn't a figment of his imagination. She was real.

Lifting the redwood plank that had been knocked over earlier, he stood it up against the alcove wall. The rough-hewn surface called to him, ready for shaping. Into what, he wasn't sure, but when he'd first seen the downed tree, it spoke to him from a distant memory. He'd spent the most of two weeks figuring out how to split off a plank-sized piece, scrape it flat, then hauled it back to his home. Lara's story had given him insight into the soul of the wood and something missing in his own.

He stoked the evening's coals into energetic flames and set a pot of water to boil, then watched her sleep until it steamed. Wild spearmint tea to warm the soul and revive the spirit.

Crushing the leaves into two small wooden bowls, he poured the water over them, then carried one to her bedside. She had not stirred since her dream.

With a last look from the alcove doorway, he took his bowl of steaming tea outside.

The sun was just lighting the western mountaintops, the air still crisp and cool. He finished the tea and climbed to the spillway to perform his warming ritual, more vital now than before his transformation. The warmth of the morning and the thought of her sleeping nearby filled him with a building optimism. There was no basis for it, other than the thought—the hope—that he might not have to spend the rest of his days alone.

Oh, he was thankful for his friend, Rowan, whom he'd had the good fortune to encounter on one of his foraging missions down into the valley. Together they'd unearthed many useful items abandoned by humans who had once populated the area; the trip he'd found the deep sink he'd installed in his grotto kitchen. But he had resisted coming into the *Dannais* valley.

"It's not enough to simply make a home, son. You need companionship," Rowan had advised him. Then Rowan told him his own story, how he'd found Cora. "Losing her had broken my heart," he'd told him, "But I wouldn't have traded the moments we shared for anything in the world. Never doubt that there will be someone for you, I promise."

He had written it off to an old man's sentimental memories. But he was wrong. Rowan had kept his promise. And if she gave him the chance, he would do his best to make sure she was safe and loved.

A noble cause, one he would set about, in time. For now, he had enough on his plate trying to master the new configuration of his body, and these wretched wings. He turned his back to the sun and flexed his rhomboids, preparing his shoulders for wing expansion.

That was the key, he'd learned so far.

Preparation.

At least the physical activity would keep his mind off the woman sleeping sleek and warm, back in his own bed. Still uncomfortable with his physical changes, he concentrated, willing his stored body fluids to flow from his core to the thready veins that, when filled, supported his new wing structure. Winged insects made it look easy. They acted on instinct. With one purpose. To migrate, lay their eggs, propagate their kind. And for that they had to fly, so they just did it. His wings were more supple and muscular, like the wings of a bat. He was strong and intelligent. He could master this thing.

But it hadn't been that easy. At least not so far. *Think it through*, he told himself, rubbing the elbow he'd scraped and bruised the day before. *You might not survive another crash landing.*

And get your mind off *her*.

That, he realized now, was going to be the toughest part. Because, from the moment he'd first laid eyes on her, he could think of nothing else. Those sculptured cheek bones, the wide set eyes... It wasn't attraction he felt. Well, yes, there was that, but he knew deep inside a place he could not clearly identify that she was right. What he felt when he looked into those eyes wasn't so much attraction as it was recognition. Whatever he was now; whatever he had been before this transformation, she saw it in him. This body, this brain, this Michael, lived inside him somewhere, and seeing that recognition in her eyes had opened a tiny crack to his interior. Everything that had been true and real for him all that time ago must still be there.

A tiny spark of energy surged inside him now, awakened by those eyes, that mouth, the sound of her voice. If only he knew how to bridge that gap between who he had been and who—what—he was now…

"First things first," he reprimanded himself aloud. Concentrate.

He set his feet shoulder-width apart as he had already learned, to adjust his center of gravity. Then he squared his shoulders and focused his energy on the task of expanding his wings until he began to feel the flow racing through his veins, gaining momentum, strength, surging through the ever-expanding network of the wing structure between his shoulder blades until his wings stretched another full body height above his head, poised together like hands in prayer. The tightly segmented area of his rhomboids from which the wings emerged expanded to support the weight transfer from his body.

Focusing his energy there, he slowly opened the massive structure, taking care to keep the left wing level with the right. He took a few steps, testing his balance, and closed the wings again, breathing in through his nose as he did so to purge his mind of the pain and frustration of his first attempt the day before.

He had simply stepped off the edge, which sent him plummeting down the hill. The bulk of his weight may have been transferred to his wings, but he still had a heavy man's body suspended between them. He would need to get a bit of a running start. That much he'd learned. In time his muscles would grow strong enough for spontaneous takeoffs. Hopefully. But for now, he needed to use the laws of physics to launch himself.

Rolling his shoulders one more time, he backed up several paces, flexed his rhomboids, pecks, and abs, folded the giant wings against his body, and knowing he would involuntarily hold his breath, he packed his lungs with oxygen, crouched in a runner's start, then charged for the edge.

After a sip of tea and a bite of bread in his kitchen, Lara ambled out to the rock ledge to find the spot of sun she needed to get herself fully awake and shake the sensation of the visceral dream that woke her:

She arched her back, her left hand gripped the bed post over her head, her right pressed firmly against his chest. He straddled her, every muscle taught, expectant, faceted blue eyes searching, waiting for permission. The moment stretched on. Yes, let it be. They were in his bed, floating on furs and desire, as though all the differences between them, and more than a thousand lifetimes, had melted away. Every cell of her being longed for him, needed his touch, and nothing… not fear of the present, or the future… was worth denying him, least of all his strange skin, not so different from her own. She circled her arm around his neck, pulling him closer, "Michael," she whispered...

The aroma of spearmint penetrated her dream. Inhaling deeply, she pushed herself up on an elbow, a warm pulse of longing lingered in her chest. She gazed around the enclosure. She was alone. She hadn't realized how much she missed being with a man. The question of whether or not he was Michael no longer mattered. In her dream, she had been a breath away from knowing just what was under that living body armor. Her cheeks burned at the thought.

Once warm and pliable again, she had wandered back down toward the water's edge, weaving her way among the ghostly outcrops hidden by the fog when she last came this way. When she first spotted him, she thought he was just a butterfly, a large monarch perched on a nearby tree branch. But as she moved closer she realized it had been a trick of perception. The winged creature *was* far away, which meant it was man-sized, and the wings towered over its head. She scrambled closer, gripping the St. Christopher medal at her throat, holding her breath as she watched him fold his wings back against his body and charge off the spillway like there was some kind of safety net below!

"Oh my God!" she yelled and broke into a run. She knew he was in trouble the moment his feet left the ground, the spillway was too low, his angle too straight, and there wasn't even the slightest breeze.

An uncontrollable scream tore from her throat as one of his wings collapsed and wrapped across his body, blinding his fall. By the time she reached him, his wings had sagged back to their original coxcomb size, thin and gauzy. He blinked at her through drops of blood, his forearms scraped raw.

"Are you crazy?" Lara kneeled beside him using the hem of her gown to stop the flow of blood at his brow. It ran red like hers, after all.

He recoiled at first, then relaxed into her touch. A smile teased the corners of his mouth. "So, you're not afraid of me anymore?"

Her eyes flicked uncontrollably to the convergence of his thighs. Except for the unusual pattern to the surface of his skin, there was no evidence of arousal.

She cleared her throat. "Not… at the moment. I could give you some pointers on how to fly, though."

He teased one of her antenna with the tip of his finger. "I figured you'd be gone when I got back."

The heat of his touch traveled from the antenna on top of her head right through to her center. Her heart raced in response, the memory of the dream still vivid in her mind. She raised her palm tentatively to his cheek, brushed his lips with her thumb, moved closer until she could feel his breath on her lips, see the longing in his eyes. It was as if she had been transported back to her dream. She'd been given a second chance. A chance that could change everything.

She pressed her lips softly to his, tasted. He breathed, but waited, as if he didn't understand. Michael would have been all over it, devour her.

"Who are you?" she asked again, not really needing an answer. She touched her finger to his bruised chin. The skin was smooth, like her own. She touched his cheeks, his forehead. "What are we?"

He winced as she examined his head wound, then reapplied pressure. "We just are. Why question? The everyday things, they come to me like breathing. I work with my hands. I sleep, I eat, I fish. I built a home to live in. That's who I am. If there's something else, I don't know what it is." He slipped an arm around her shoulder and pulled her closer. "Your Michael, he was a human?"

Lara trembled. It was unsettling that he kept referring to Michael as if he no longer existed. He had Michael's hands, that certain way he half smiled when he was teasing. The sudden image of Michael enclosed in the chrysalis assaulted her for a moment before she willed it away.

"Not… in the end. No." She continued the pressure on the cut at his brow. "But not so different than you." It was true. The longer she held him, the more closely they seemed to fit.

He fingered the medal at her neck. "You gave this to him."

"I did."

He touched the ring on her finger. "And this?"

She nodded. "He had it made for me."

"And you were human then, too."

"Yes." Lara touched his chest, let her fingers play down the front of him to the soft plates of his abdomen. "But not anymore."

His body responded, he pulled her closer, tasted her shoulders, her neck, her lips. "Rowan told me about his Cora. That we had probably come from the same place. Said there would be someone for me someday."

"Rowan…" Her hand slipped to her stomach, remembering the moment the crysl emerged from her body. She looked into the eyes of its father. It wasn't yet time to share that moment with him. "He helped me, too."

"I didn't believe him until I saw you," he answered, and for a few magical moments, they rocked in each other's arms, each taking the other in, testing the boundaries of what they dared, until Lara, breathless and weak, pushed her hand firmly against his chest. It was as though the ground shifted beneath them and set her floating in a euphoric giddiness, except that in the next moment, a painfully high-pitched whine pierced her ears.

"Lara. What's happening?" he asked, and the noise whine grew louder. She could see his lips move but all she could hear was that shrill, piercing buzz, just like in Patrick's lab, right before she blacked out.

He stroked his fingers down her arms, allowing her some space. Again, he was speaking to her, but she couldn't hear his words.

Maybe the strain of the last few days had finally caught up with her. She was simply exhausted. The incident with the crysl, the endless walking, the shock of finding him. Maybe her time had finally run out. She was fading, the energy draining out of her moment-by-moment. Like Rowan's Cora. She couldn't stay here.

She had to get back to her cave, her bed, but she couldn't muster the energy to move.

He stroked her cheek. "Lara." Her name felt familiar on his tongue like he had called it in his sleep. "Lara," he said again, stretching the syllables out like a prayer.

Her eyes were closed, her arms hung limp at her sides. He shook her gently. "Stay with me. Hold on."

Her body was on fire, the back of her neck blistering in red blotches.

He knew this.

Knew it well.

She was going into second stage metamorphosis. The fever had nearly killed him when it happened to him and would have were it not for Rowan who had come upon him in his last moments and dragged him into the water.

If she didn't cool down, or at least slow the process, she would meet her end in a swirling a pile of ash before he ever got to know her. That wasn't going to happen. Getting to his feet, he lifted her up and raced toward the sea.

It is my firm belief that the effects of climate change as the result of our addiction to fossil fuels will take centuries to repair—If we stop every damaging act today, humans will still require protection from UV into the next century if they are to remain on the planet's surface. Without exception, future generations, worldwide, will live with a greater UV problem than we face today, having a more profound effect on civilization perhaps even than the industrial revolution.

-- Patrick Allen, International Conference on Genetic Research,
Geneva Switzerland, 2030.

CHAPTER 21 - SLOAN'S DILEMMA

The sun disappeared behind the eastern peaks of the Sierra, dragging the heat of the day away with it. Sloan pulled the oversized jacket about his ears and sat between two gnarled tree roots twisted across the narrow trail. His deformed feet were a burden in the best of conditions and the shoes he'd appropriated must have belonged to a bear. They flopped up and down on his ankles, wearing blisters on his heels. After a full day on the rocky trail, scrambling in shoes that didn't fit, he lagged yards behind the man. Now, he watched the man called Esteban clump away down the trail ahead of him, his longer legs making short work of stepping over roots and rocks and muddy places. *Maybe he'll just keep going, never look back.*

Then the *Neanderthal* stopped, listened, and turned around.

Maybe not.

Esteban stood, hands cocked on hips and glared at Sloan as if he were an annoying rock stuck in his shoe. "What's your problem?"

"No problem," he said, his chin puckering into a hard knot. There was no point in complaining. Sloan bristled with angsty resentment. In his old life, his feet were smooth, and pink, and rarely made it outside--the feet of a pampered, over-protected child. Now they were so arched, they met the ground only at the heel and toes. His ankle cocked back with an extra joint, making it hard to walk for long distances.

Nice work, dad. Fixed the brain but trashed the body.

"Well, get up then. We're almost there." Esteban pointed his walking stick toward the distant passage.

Sloan ignored the command. He had come on this journey of his own volition, and he had no problem leaving it if the mood struck him. He owed nothing to Esteban, despite the man's belief otherwise. He slipped off an offending shoe and rubbed his misshapen foot. For a grown up, Esteban could be as dumb as a rock. It was true. His followers had scavenged enough parts of the rusted and fallen wind turbines to cobble together one that generated enough energy to leave the equivalent of a porch light on at the proposed trading post.

But without the ability to manufacture any new parts, it wasn't likely they'd get much more accomplished. The materials and equipment inventoried in his father's diary had long since succumbed to the ravages of weather, time, and scavengers from cities long dead and devastated.

"It will be pitch dark in an hour," Sloan pointed out, then pulled off the other shoe and examined his heel.

"So, we'll walk by moonlight," Esteban argued.

"It will be barely a quarter moon."

"And you know this because… "

Sloan just shook his head. As he'd read in literature from his birth century, it was clear this man Esteban's elevator not only failed to go all the way to the top, it was missing a few floors between.

Esteban adjusted the pack on his shoulder. "You afraid of the dark, Bug Boy?"

"Only if I can't see where I'm going." Sloan tucked a handful of Monkey Flower leaves around his heel and into the toes of the shoes, ignoring the taunt. The only reason he'd allowed himself to get hooked up with this moron was to lead him to the *Dannais* colony. But then, almost all of the men Esteban brought to Terra City were morons who thought they were going to revitalize something that had never met its original potential to begin with. They were nothing but a gaggle of wind-up toys with only a couple of cranks left.

"It's five miles to the gate, at least," Sloan speculated. "You want to march 'til midnight, go for it." He scooted further into the tangle of tree roots and leaned back against his pack. If Esteban wanted him to keep going, he'd have to carry him.

The only promise his father's diary fulfilled was that the underground chamber where his chrysalis had been sealed off from the effects of climate change had done exactly that. But his father hadn't accounted for the world going berserk and unleashing atomic doomsday. Nor had he considered the survivors would be so lacking in gray matter they would never bother to search the Vault for anything useful.

He gazed out at dim light in the valley below, like an old lantern with dying batteries. It was the first time in his young life he'd been far enough away from Terra City to see it for what it was: Just another failed experiment of Dr. Patrick McCormick-Allen.

Despite the pain in his feet and the promise of rest, Terra City was the last place on the planet he wanted to be.

Esteban stared at him for a beat, then pulled the pack off his back and cursed the weight of the crysl as he rummaged past it for his water bottle. He drank the last of it and tossed it down. "Actually, I don't care if you come or not. What do I need your scrawny ass for? The diary tells it all, right?"

Right. Like he'd leave it out where someone could get to it. Sure there was a treasure trove of technical information about Terra City in his father's diary, there was also a very detailed description of Sloan's Autism and his father's hopes that in some imaginary future he would emerge into a world with advanced medicine that could help him communicate with the world outside his own mind. Funny how that played out. His mind was doing great. It was that advanced world thing that had failed.

Sloan had emerged into this existence all on his own with nothing but memories of a family he couldn't reach, a mother who was afraid of him, and a demented father obsessed with the idea he could change the structure of his DNA. Well, at least that part was true. For the first time in his life, there was a pathway between what he saw and heard inside his head and the ability to express himself in any intelligible way. He now had a different view of the world, more organized, less pointy and disturbing, more three dimensional.

And then there were his hands and feet.

Sometimes he wished he'd never read the diary; never learned about the limitations he'd experienced in the past. Those facts were now stuffed in his head as vivid as permanent ink like Mark Twain and history, biology and chemistry and global science, Shakespeare and Salinger and Schlesinger and every other body of knowledge he'd devoured when he'd discovered the Vault. But now, at twelve years old, with his new ability to actually communicate with the outside world, he had mostly hidden away from the morons who showed up at Terra City. What did they care that Socrates had it all figured out centuries before they were born, that religion dragged the next batch of morons through the dark ages, and by the time people were actually beginning to take the pulse of the planet, the morons had found a way to nearly destroy it.

Was it the promise of a better life for him that compelled his father to do what he did? Then why do it to all those others? And why not do it to himself, too, while he was at it? What kind of father would shoot his kid up with some kind of serum, not knowing how or when he would end up and then not do it to himself?

He slumped against the tree trunk, he pulled his hands inside his sleeves against the cold. His kind of father. That's what kind. It was all in the diary. His father's hope for a better future, better medical care, better options for a profoundly autistic boy.

In other words, a nutcase.

He leaned his head back against the tree and closed his eyes. An image of Jenera circling her arms around that young girl gave his heart a squeeze.

"It's just a stupid fantasy," he mumbled.

"What?" Esteban, asked, lazily.

"The diary," Sloan said more forcefully, covering his reverie, the truth of his circumstance coming vividly clear. He would have been there in the meadow with the *Dannais*, with *her*, if his father had put him in the cave with the others. But no. He'd built a whole city and put his chrysalis inside it. In a gold-plated case, no less, like young King Tut, a treasure to be discovered in some future life. He pushed his resentment down. "The diary," he said again, letting his resentment out "It's nothing but the journal of a failed scientist hoping for absolution."

"Abso-what?"

Sloan sighed, and prodded the roots with his shoulder, trying to find a comfortable position, wishing he'd never mentioned the diary. The promise of it kept him in some sort of good standing with Esteban, but he had no intention of ever handing it over. "Forget it. You you'll never need to know."

Esteban stared at him and scratched his head. "Arrright," he growled, dropping down to sit. "We'll rest 'til morning, then we're on our way first thing." He rolled over, poked Sloan with his walking stick. "We'll lock this crysl away and by this time next week, I'll have everything I need from the *Dannais* supplies to stock up my outpost."

Everything but a brain, Sloan thought. He tugged his jacket closer around his ears and pulled his cap down hard. He'd made up his mind; he'd had enough. He was never, ever, going back to Terra City. Especially if this fool and his band of miscreants thought they were in charge. After what he seen on the meadow, he figured he'd take his chances with the *Dannais.*

Listening to Esteban breathe, he stared at the sky until the growing darkness revealed millions of bright stars. His perception shifted to embrace a persistent fantasy: the earth was inside a shiny black dome, pierced like a sieve with millions of tiny holes, an unimaginably bright light filling all time and space just outside... He started to smile, then shook himself free. *Don't go there. Not now. Pay attention.*

Sloan slid his eyes over to see that Esteban had finally slumped into a loose mound.

Time to go.

He quietly put on the tortuous shoes, lifted his pack, and stepped away from the snoring moron.

The mountains changed character under a quarter moon. A large rock on the trail became a bear, a meandering tree root became a snake, and the stars shown bright enough to light a path to the edge of time. The sheer freedom of being alone on the trail at last pumped his heart a little faster and let him forget how cold he was.

The Great Bear strode across the sky, a constellation his father had shown him, back when he could barely acknowledge his own excitement. Had his father known he'd loved him? Loved their time together? Hard to say. Sloan had trouble expressing himself back then. The autism was like having his mind in prison, constantly bombarded with scintillating input that he could neither control nor break through. Now he was free to explore and express himself, which was better, he supposed, but only seemed to magnify his loneliness. Tonight the solitude felt bigger than the night sky. Bigger than the universe. And there wasn't a sigh deep enough to make it go away.

The diary was all he had left of his family. It gave him glimpses of his former life and what had happened to his father after… Sometimes he wished he'd never read it. Words and pictures circled like specters through his thoughts, even when he didn't want them to. Especially the ones about Lara Paine. There were heaps of them. According to a news clipping preserved in the diary, she had been the one hundredth missing person in San Francisco in 2023.

Sloan couldn't help wondering what number he had been. And of those, how many had actually survived? He put himself to sleep most nights, trying to fit all the pieces together. The words in the diary were engraved in his memory like a code that must be solved before his thoughts would settle. Hyperthymesia, it had been called in the studies he'd read in the Vault's library. The ability to remember every detail of every image ever seen. The studies said the condition could likely be triggered by an event, such as being struck by lightning, that could temporarily or permanently alter pathways in the brain. In his case, however, Sloan knew, he had been that way since he was an infant. The condition could be a blessing or a curse. The jury was still out as far as he was concerned.

Having perfect memory was like having perfect pitch, it was always trying to tune up the flat notes. His was a gift of autism which many would treasure. But Sloan knew he was prone to obsession, something he must have inherited from his father. He could not turn it off. Since reading the diary, he often found himself standing alone or looking out over a rock cliff, lost in his father's words, not remembering how he got where he was. It was good fortune if nothing else that the metamorphosis had "rebooted" his brain to think in more linear, tangible directions. But sometimes he just wanted his own thoughts without his father's echoing through them.

...Biosphere III... Terra City... Lara Paine... UV-invaded atmosphere... chrysalis... global warming... one hundredth missing person... Hera's Vault...

Sometimes, he just wanted peace. "Enough!" he cried out loud, his mind fell silent, and the sounds of the forest rushed in—wind in the pines, an owl hooting to a mate, water tumbling over stone somewhere in the near distance.

He'd walked through the night, and a breathless dawn awaited. Off to the east the mountains were faintly outlined in purple, the sun would soon follow. To the west, the lopsided moon that had followed him through the night had slipped down and nearly out of sight. And just like that, his legs gave in to fatigue, and he sat down where he was in the middle of the trail, pulled his knees up to his chin, wrapped his arms around them, and let his head drop to rest on them.

Esteban would wake soon to find him gone, but he had been careful to leave plenty of tracks leading down toward Terra City, before turning back, covering his tracks, and shadowing the trail in the opposite direction. Esteban would soldier on to the Vault with his precious cargo, happy to be rid of him, he supposed. Regret that he'd been part of what had happened on the meadow tugged as his conscience. He pushed it down where he could concentrate on his present moment.

If his memory was right, the *Dannais* village lay behind the next saddleback. He could be there by late afternoon if he kept his pace. But for now, his feet needed attention. Again.

He crawled off the trail behind a brake of fern and gingerly untied his boots. His feet hurt, but the Monkey flower padding had helped a lot. He quickly replaced the packing with fresh wads of grass, then replaced the foul shoes and stood up, testing the fit. It would do for a few more miles.

Rolling his shoulders, he set off again and the litany started up like a playlist in his brain.

...Biosphere III... Terra City... Lara Paine... UV-invaded atmosphere... chrysalis... geothermal energy... Hera's Vault...

Sloan kicked at loose stones in the trail. *Chrysalis.* He still had nightmares about the day he awoke to find himself in an alien skin with an empty belly and a shout bursting from his lungs in a new, terrifying reality. A chamber not unlike his old bedroom. Profoundly and irrevocably alone.

He pushed the memory of that terror deep down inside and kept going. He would never return to that place again. Ever.

Purple Milkweed makes Doomsday Vault
San Francisco Chronicle, July 2024
*Seeds from North American Purple Milkweed
(asclepias cordifolia) were recently delivered
to the Santa Barbara Gardens Conservation
Seed bank, as well as the Svalbard Global
Seed Vault where they will be preserved
against a potential terrestrial catastrophe
which could render them extinct.*
*These hardy perennials are native to
California, Oregon, and Washington and are
essential to the survival of Monarch
butterflies.*

--Patrick Allen, Report on UV resistance
properties in Monarch butterflies.

CHAPTER 22 - ROWAN RETURNS

Rowan rolled over in his bed, the muscles in his back complaining bitterly. He closed his eyes, willing his aching bones back to sleep, but a furtive movement caught his attention. His eyes fluttered open again.

"Grandfather!"

The voice was sweet and ringing, but painful inside his aching head. He tried to prop himself up on one elbow but failed miserably. "Oohf."

Ekiria jumped from the bedside and hollered out the door. "Jenera, he's awake!"

"Quiet, child, you'll wake the dead." He tried again to prop himself up, this time successfully.

Jenera slipped into the room. "I think she just did."

"What?"

"Wake the dead."

Jenera came to his side and smoothed gnarled and twisted locks from his forehead. "Looks like she did a good job."

"By the God of Joaquin, I feel like I've been buried at the bottom of a boulder slide."

"You're safe, now, grandfather." Jenera reached for the pitcher next to the bed and filled a stoneware cup. "Some cold tea and honey. Drink up."

Rowan drank the cup dry and put it out for more. There was something he needed to tell her, something that made him feel anxious and unsettled; but he couldn't for the life of him organize his thoughts. "How long have I been here? In bed, I mean?"

Jenera topped off his cup. "Three days. We found you unconscious, up on the high meadow. What happened to you?"

Rowan flexed his hands, rolled his gaze around the room and then back to Jenera. He wasn't sure exactly what happened. And he wasn't sure he was ready to tell what he did remember. He splayed his fingers over his chest. "I think my ribs are cracked," he croaked.

Jenera propped a pillow behind his back, tried to comfort him. He drank the cool liquid, the room coming at last into focus, and he breathed into the soreness. Jenera motioned to someone in the doorway.

"Bryn." Rowan nodded to the full human who had become a loyal supporter of the *Dannais*.

Jenera turned away to catch an exuberant Ekiria streaking through the doorway and circled her back the way she had come. "You can see grandfather later. Bryn and Rowan have business now."

Rowan closed his eyes and listened as the sounds of their laughter faded into the trees. He opened his eyes again to find Bryn studying him with very serious, slate blue eyes. He was a formidable figure, despite his youth. One he could trust not play games with serious matters. "What happened, Rowan?" he asked?

"I don't know," Rowan answered. It was a half-truth. He sat back on the pillows and pushed heavy twists of hair behind him. He didn't know exactly what had happened, but he knew who, and he didn't know quite what to make of it. "I feel a pressing dread, that's all," he admitted.

He cut his gaze toward the doorway, the window, then lowered his voice. "There's something. *Something*. But I can't see it, can't get to it right now." He pounded his fist on the mattress, then winced, and glanced at the window again.

Bryn scooted one of Rowan's carved stump stools closer to the bed and sat. His eyes narrowed on the old man's, clearly seeing through his denial. He glanced over his shoulder to make sure the door was firmly shut. "Don't waste my time, Rowan."

Rowan relaxed a little. "I don't want to cause alarm."

"That rock has already rolled down the mountain, old man!" His words were hard to hear, but Rowan listened. Bryn was right. He'd taken off alone, without telling anyone where or what he was doing. Rowan cut his eyes back to the window.

Bryn lowered his voice and kept after him. "When we first brought you here, you were in and out of it.

You ranted, then slept. You talked about the crysls, called for Esteban, said you were falling... "

Rowan growled to himself and spit the name out as if it were a bitter taste. "Esteban."

Bryn inched closer. Rowan searched the face of the young man by his side. There was no doubt in his mind that Bryn was completely trustworthy. Although he had come from far away, he and his family were loyal to the colony. He had stood alongside Jenera as she protected the *crysls*, joined the other men of the *Dannais* in planting and harvest, helped to fortify the west gate against intruders from The Owen. There was no doubt in his mind that Jenera had already confided in Bryn everything she knew about her quest and the legend. Not even a blindman would deny their bond was stronger than any pact he had made years ago. It was going to be a problem sooner than he was willing to admit. Alas, there was nothing to be done about it now.

He closed his eyes, forcing himself to concentrate on what had happened on the ridge.

The first face before him was, as always, his Cora. He smiled and let her image pass. The next was of the tall woman with the flaming branch. He took another drink of tea and began to tell Bryn of the encounter, working his way to the end.

"And so, the last thing I remember is..." Rowan looked into the highest corner of his mind and crushed his eyes closed. " ...the crysl."

He put his gnarled fingers to his chin. "It was in my backpack and... "

Bryn clamped his hand on Rowan's wrist, his gaze intensifying. "Esteban. You called for Esteban..." he prompted.

Rowan shook his head, emotion gushing forth. He couldn't hold it in any longer. "No, I didn't call *for* him,

I… " He covered his mouth as the visions came tumbling into his mind accompanied by a rush of bile up his throat. "*I cursed him!* By the gods! Where is he?" He came up off the bed despite the pains shooting through his body.

Bryn steadied him, offering his arm. "Hold on." He helped him sit back down on the edge of the bed. "You rest. I'll take care of Esteban."

CHAPTER 23 - MILKIWEED FESTIVAL

Ekiria squirmed under the attentive hands of her mother. Being chosen to dance on the night of the Milkiweed festival was an honor she was about to abuse. She never liked going against her mother's wishes, but this time, she couldn't help herself. Something was going on and she was going to find out what it was.

"Hold still, Eki," her mother warned. "You don't want these wings falling off in the middle of your solo, do you?" Her mother had worked through the day to complete the wings, adding flecks of mica and mother of pearl to catch the light of the fire when Ekiria danced. The whole compound had watched the process and *oohed* and *ahhed* over the beautiful creation.

"No, mama," Ekiria crooned obediently. She knew she'd be shedding them soon. Her mind was buzzing with what she had seen. A person—a boy, she thought—not from the colony. There, in the bushes, then *poof*! Gone. And right when Rowan was left in the meadow. She had to know who he was, where he'd gone. She lay awake that night thinking about him, making her plan.

There was lots of activity now, over near the braziers. She could slip away, and no one would notice; but it would be easier once the ceremonies began.

Everyone would be focused on the dancers. Who would miss one silly butterfly in a circle of twenty?

She twisted and strained to find her friend, Alta, in the confusion. Alta didn't know it yet, but she was a part of the plan.

Her mother licked her fingers and calmed a few stray hairs away from Ekiria's face. She endured it with a smile, ready to burst away the moment she got the nod of approval.

Jenera observed the scene from her doorway with detached excitement. Spring compound was alive with activity. From every household, the young girls darted and called to one another, checking their headdresses, their aprons, their homemade wings; hurrying to place their blankets and baskets as close as they could around the central brazier. The sweet fragrance of last-minute batches of honey cakes wafted through the air.

She nodded to Ekiria's mother as their eyes met across the compound. *There's one mother who's got her hands full.* Ekiria's energy and enthusiasm were contagious. Even the boys, though they did not take part in the actual harvest, were excited about the evening's festivities, if not for the dancing and music, at least for the honeyed treats and games that would inevitably bring out their competitive spirits.

Most of the adults saw the Milkiweed Festival as welcome, but frivolous entertainment. Even those who shared some of the *Dannais* trademark signs in their facial structure and their nubby head nodules tended to play them down, cover them with hats, or ignore them entirely. To them the festival was a distraction from the coming cold and the hardships it brought to the colony. The actual harvest was secondary.

Year after year, with the help of the young ones, Jenera harvested the seed, led the ritual, kept the legends. Only the elders in the colony believed in them, and they were slowly dying off.

Doubt and fear sat on Jenera's shoulders like storm clouds ready to drench her spirit. Unless Lara made a surprise appearance, nothing would change. She was beginning to feel like discovering The Messenger had been a figment of her imagination.

A warm prickling at the hairs on the back of her neck, her nodules stretching, signaled Bryn was near. She turned to find him standing right behind her. Their eyes met and held, reminding her of the bond they'd shared even as young children. Friendship, loyalty, and something more that was more difficult to define. It was clear in his expression that he felt the same connection. He had only to open his arms for her to ignore all propriety and lean into the safety, the serenity of his chest. And, because he respected her and her grandfather, she knew, he would never be the one to cross that barrier without an invitation.

"Oh, Bryn, I was so scared when I found him on the meadow. I don't know what I'd do if anything happened to him."

He leaned in close enough for her to smell the heat on his skin, yet respectfully distant, though the look in his eye said he wished it could be otherwise.

"He's resting," he said softly, before she could ask, and brushed a stray hair behind her ear. "His pride sustained the most damage. Says he can't remember anything."

His feather touch set off a vibration in her soul she could scarcely contain.

"Stubborn old bear," she said, stepping away from the temptation to lean against his chest. Best to focus on the problem at hand. Rowan was their elder, but as elders eventually do, he often indulged his child spirit. "This morning he was acting sheepish, hiding something."

Bryn's neck muscles tensed, a familiar sign of his agitation. She raised a questioning brow. "What…"

"I need to find Esteban." The color of his eyes went dark, his mouth suddenly rigid. "Have you seen him?"

"Esteban? We rarely see him here at Lillit Compound." The nodules strained on the top of her head. It wasn't hard for Jenera to cast Esteban in the role of villain. He'd challenged her at council, defied Rowan in front of the elders, and on an evening not that long ago, had made unwelcome advances toward her, tried to push his marriage claim ahead of schedule. *Best not to share* that *information with Bryn.* With Rowan out of the way, however, Esteban could become more aggressive. "You think he had something to do with whatever happened to Rowan?"

"I'm headed to Gate Compound to find out." His face said there would be hell to pay if it was true.

Bryn had long ago accepted she was promised to Esteban. It had so far stopped him from acting on what clearly was in his heart, but it had never stopped him from going full on big-brother protection mode. As much as she wanted to see Esteban account for his behavior, she worried what might happen if Bryn truly went after him. Bryn had a peaceful spirit for a full human. It was one of the reasons she allowed him in her life. But the children didn't call him The Rock for nothing.

He was a physical powerhouse that generations of living in the catacombs of the southern cities and the desert heat of The Owen had not diminished.

Esteban was strong, but in a fair fight, he'd be no match for Bryn. Trouble was, Esteban wasn't known for fighting fair.

"I was hoping you would help me supervise some of the preparations," she ventured. It was a feeble ploy, she knew. If it was true that Esteban had harmed Rowan in any way, distracting Bryn would only delay the inevitable.

He sent her an apologetic look that lasted longer than a mere excuse to miss the festival. "This can't wait. But with luck, I'll be back here before things get started."

Jenera watched him stride purposefully across the commons toward Gate Compound. She pushed her annoyance down. His single-minded intensity was another reason she loved him. Yes. It may not be proper. She was promised to Esteban, but she knew deep in her soul Bryn was the owner of her heart. She may be lying to everyone else. But she could not lie to herself.

"Alta! Wait!" Ekiria caught up with her friend before she rounded the corner of the common kitchen. She had to hurry. Already the braziers were being lit and some of the elders were making their way to the fires.

Alta's face opened into her familiar glowing smile. "Oh, Eki, you look…"

Ekiria grabbed her friend's arm and pulled her back to the edge the kitchen, away from the festivities.

"Wait! What are you doing? We have to…" Alta watched with wide eyes as Ekiria yanked at the straps of her new Monarch wings.

"Help me with these."

"But Eki, it's almost time to go!"

"Shhhhh." Ekiria cut her off with a finger to her lips. "Listen. You have to help me." She squirmed out of the wings and pushed them at her friend. "Here. Put these on. I want you to dance my solo tonight."

Alta's eyes grew even larger as she pushed back. "*Nooooo!* What are you doing?"

"Alta, please. I can't do this without you." She pushed the wings back at her, looking over her shoulder to make sure no one saw.

Alta held on to the wings, shaking her head. "To help you do… do what?"

Ekiria swallowed hard. Alta was her best friend and would follow her anywhere. But when she got that worried look in her eye, Ekiria knew she was going to have to push. Before Alta could voice her fear, Ekiria pulled off Alta's wings and made her case while she replaced them with her own. "Remember the other day on the meadow? When we went to get Helena? I thought I saw someone?"

Alta nodded as Ekiria turned her around roughly, tightening the wings with an extra knot to take up the slack on her smaller shoulders. "Well, I did. See someone, I mean." She flipped her friend back around and gave her a pleading look. "That someone had to be there when Rowan got hurt. I'm going to find out who he is. Tonight. No one will miss me. You'll do my dance and— "

"But why don't you just *tell?*"

"No," Ekiria hissed. "Not yet. There's something about him. I have to find out." Ekiria pulled a bag of chrism jars from her belt and quickly smeared iridescent green above Alta's eyes, spreading it up and out to her temples just like her own. A quick smudge of fire orange under her cheekbones completed the image.

Alta started to cry and breathe faster. "No-wah!"

Ekiria smudged again, blotting out the tear streak with a fresh swipe of color. "Don't do that, you'll mess up my face."

Alta sniffed and tried to pull herself together.

Ekiria knew she was crossing the line. Making Alta do something she didn't really want to do. She didn't want to hurt her, but she had to stick to the plan. She had to make it to the high meadow before dark if she were to pick up the boy's trail. She had to leave *now*.

"I'm sorry. If there was any other way..." She pushed Alta's shoulders back against the wall as she sneaked another look around the edge of the building. No one was near. "Stay here until the dancing starts. It won't be long. Otherwise they'll see it's not me and..."

"What if something happens to you?" Alta slumped down to sit on the ground, her back to the wall. "They'll make me tell."

Ekiria squatted down, put her hands on Alta's skinny knees, a little pang of remorse flitted through her heart before she pushed it down. "He's only a boy. Nothing will happen to me."

Alta dropped her forehead to her knees, her shoulders quaking. "But I can't dance like you. They'll *kno-wah!*" Remembering the makeup, she pushed tears away from her eyes. When she looked up, Ekiria was gone.

Sloan was standing in the meadow a moment before he realized he had arrived at the place he was looking for. His mind had been preoccupied as usual with passages from his father's diary. The sun slanted low, running long shadows across the grasses, blurring the details and softening the spaces between dark and light. The shadows made it look different than the last time he was here, but this was definitely the place. He remembered *her*, sitting on that log over there at the edge of the clearing.

His feet screamed to get out of his shoes and his mouth was dry as summer grass. He sloughed off his backpack and slumped to the ground right where he was, found his water bottle and tipped it up to let the last drops plop onto his tongue. He carefully untied his shoes and rubbed his feet. The soft green grass he'd used for packing had saved him from blisters, but his feet ached from miles of walking. He couldn't take another step.

That was okay. From where he sat, he could see across the valley to the chiseled cliffs beyond. From the ledges of Terra City, he could see far down the dry side of the mountains, but nothing—not the wide vistas or the thermal pools, or even the deep caverns outside the Vault—nothing on that side of Craggy Pass compared to the granite formations that rose nearly vertical from the floor of this valley. The silhouettes were familiar. He had read about this place. A valley, carved and polished by ancient glaciers. Nobel names marched through his memory: El Capitan, Glacier Point, Half Dome, Three Sisters. Sacred before civilized men named them, sacred still now that men were scarce.

Sloan breathed deeply, exhaling fatigue, closing his eyes. He lay back in the weeds, arms sprawled, shoeless. The only sounds on the meadow were the first chirrs of crickets before nightfall and the rustling of grass. A hawk screed somewhere in the distance. He allowed himself to rest, savoring the quiet, the peace…

"Do they hurt?"

Sloan nearly jumped out of his skin. The voice came from behind him without so much as a foot fall or a twig snap as warning. He jumped up and spun around, the pain in his feet stabbing him to his core. "Aghhh! What?"

"Your hands, they're like…" A girl reached toward him. Sloan reared back, still in shock over her unexpected appearance, and the sight of her. A tiny thing, yet bold and fearless, face blazed with color. She continued forward as Sloan scrabbled away. "…hooks," she said, finally, pointing. "Your hands are like hooks."

Sloan shoved the offending body parts deep into his pockets.

"Wait, stop!" The girl reached out again. But it was too late. He backed straight into the log at the edge of the meadow and flipped over backward, landing with a groan and a crunch on the other side. She rushed to the log, vaulted up using both hands, and peeked over.

Sloan rubbed his head and glared up at her. This isn't what he expected. He hadn't planned… *damn*, she was staring, expecting an answer.

"No." He dusted himself off. "My hands don't hurt. But my head does now, thanks to you."

She slid the rest of the way over the log and smoothed out her tunic. She was younger than the other one—flat-chested, narrow in the hip. She wore a headband of shiny wire, sprouting tiny, twisted spikes. She reached out a hand to help him up, her eyes on fire with purpose.

"I'm sorry. I tried to warn you," she said, pulling a piece of her tunic from where it was stuck in her underwear without the least tick of embarrassment.

Sloan could not take his eyes from hers. She waited a beat, then pulled him up with an energy larger than her stature suggested she could possible possess. Holding tight, she took the opportunity to give his misshapen hand a thorough inspection, then shrugged her shoulders, dropped it, and twirled away back into the milkweed.

"Why did you come back?" Her gaze dropped to his feet and grew wide before she shifted her eyes away.

"What do you mean?" Sloan brushed himself off, picking his way through the weeds to grab his shoes.

She turned on him now, closing the distance between them. "I *saw* you." She poked a finger into his chest and drilled those firey eyes into his. "I saw you here; right here. Three days ago. You ran away. Now you're back. Why?"

Sloan pushed past her and moved to the edge of the meadow where he could see down to the valley. Smoke spiraled up like shredded ghosts in the fading light. He could faintly hear voices echoing up from below. They were singing down there and laughing. Three days ago? A sizzle of anxiety zipped through his arms and down into the pit of his stomach. *What had she seen?* "I… don't know what you're talking about."

The girl slipped up behind him now, peeked out over the valley, and let out a big sigh. "It's the Milkiweed Festival. I'm supposed to be there. But I wanted to find you. And you came back."

Sloan tried to swallow back a gobble of guilt but succeeded only in making it worse. His knees loosened under him and he sank down, squeezed his eyes shut. He would not cry in front of this girl. When she dropped down in front of him and touched his shoulder, the guilt turned to grief, squeezing wet sobs out of him anyway until he had lost all resistance. When he looked up, he saw that her eyes had welled up too. She dragged a skinny finger through the color on her cheek and smeared it on his face. His heart thumped against his ribs. What was it about these people that made him melt? Even one so young. His own mother hadn't shown him an ounce of care and now this little girl had shown him compassion and sympathy that was so much bigger than herself. He swallowed a hard lump in his throat. He was tired of all his pent-up anger and resentment. Worn thin by fear and doubt. The girl with the painted face rocked back on her toes, hands on her knees, and stared expectantly into his eyes until the layers of doubt and fear slipped away like petals falling from wild roses.

"It's okay. I'm not going to tell anybody." She smudged another patch of color on his other cheek and gave him the kind of smile that could soothe a broken heart. Then she reached out and took his hooked hands gently in hers and held on. That was the final straw. The one that broke the dam, letting the tears spill over.

He let them come, wracking his body, emptying his soul while she sat patiently in front of him, holding his hands until he quieted.

And then, in the fading sunlight, he told. Told her everything, even the part about Esteban taking the crysl away from Rowan.

She listened without a word until, exhausted, he dropped his head onto his knees and the first stars began to creep up into the sky.

Ekiria waited a beat, then jumped up. "We have to go get it back!"

Sloan blinked at her. "What? Get what back?"

The crysl. You said Esteban took the crysl. We have to get it back!"

Sloan shook his head. "Oh, no. I'm not going back there. Ever!"

"But we have to. It's the legend. The crysl. It's *hers*."

Sloan looked at her and scratched his head. There was nothing about a legend or a crysl in his father's diary. Nothing. He shook his head. "I'm not going."

"But we *have* to. Don't you see? It's what Jenera's been waiting for."

"Jenera?"

"You know, Jenera. The one you *wanted?*" Ekiria pulled away and ran to the middle of the meadow. She began to sway and turn, humming a slow melody, and then she began to tell the story. She could never tell it as well as Jenera, but she did her best.

"Long time ago, when the world was old, the *Dannais* were born. They were willowy tall, and fragile, with wings of black and gold. They flew from the cliffs and drifted on the wind. Most men had gone underground to escape the heat of bad light from the sun and the Terrible Destruction. But the *Dannais* survived inside their caves, inside their protective shields.

"Later when men began to venture out, explore, some returned to this valley and fell in love with the *Dannais*. They made babies and the babies grew up and were stronger. Their human offspring began to populate the land, some look more like the *Dannais* than others. But every now and then, instead of a human baby, a crysl was made. They didn't grow, they didn't open, they just got hard and shiny.

"The people didn't want them, but the legend said they would keep, so the *Dannais* stored them away. In Crysl Tower. Meanwhile, the men's bloodline prevailed. Very few of us are left who possess the original gene. The legend says there were more though.

And one is coming that has all of the original gene, and the coming of her offspring will signal the time of the Great Migration, when the *Dannais* will emerge to once again cover the earth."

Sloan pinched a seed pod from a milkweed plant and twirled it between his fingers. One of the fires in the valley below burned bright enough to catch it in the light. "*Danaus Plexippus*," he said.

"What?"

"Monarchs. They *are* in the diary."

CHAPTER 24 - EKIRIA'S ADVENTURE

Jenera slipped quietly into the tower, smoke rising from the small smudge of white sage she held aloft. She had been here earlier, in the full light of day, but she felt compelled to check on her charges one more time. Something was out of kilter, she sensed it in her pores. With the planet alignment only a week away, she couldn't afford to miss anything. To make a mistake. She was the Spirit Leader. It was up to her to ensure the crysls were ready. Her face paint was applied, her costume ready, she had just enough time to take a quick peek, if for no other reason than to ease her mind in preparation for the evening.

She lit a small brazier near the entrance, then circled the tower floor, passing her fingertips over milkiweed plants as she went. Seedlings on the first level, young plants on the next, and mature plants on the third, where they stretched their heads toward the spiral of crysls they would someday feed. Since she was a young girl under the tutelage of her mother, it had been her duty to rotate the flats each day to enduce even exposure to the sun, ensuring there was always a supply of milkiweed at the ready.

Since her mother's disappearance, care of the next generation fell entirely on her shoulders. She had added the ancient smudge ritual on her own. Better to be safe than sorry, her mother used to say, for all the good it did her.

She scanned up to the latticed opening at the top of the tower. One hundred and twenty crysls spiraled around the stone walls, each in its own woven hammock, waiting as they had done since the first Spirit Leader took on the job of caring for them, all those generations ago. For now, at least, everything seemed peaceful and in order.

She rested her hand on a crysl nearest the entrance, one of the most recent added to the nursery. "The day is coming soon, sister, when we shall finally meet."

If the legend is true.

It wasn't the first time today doubt crept into her thoughts. Rowan had been attacked, there was no sign of Lara. And Esteban? Who knew what he was up to? Whatever it was, Jenera had a bad feeling about it. At the door, she gave the smudge one last pass, watching the fragrant smoke spiral up toward the opening in the top of the tower. The crysls were real. There was no doubt about that. And if one day, she turned out to be the last one standing, she would preserve them with her life.

She stepped out of the doorway and secured the heavy cross bar behind her.

Holding the smudge high over her head, she moved quickly out to the central area of Spring Compound where the crowd had grown to include nearly everyone in the colony. She flicked her gaze around the circle of faces, noting the elders, her aunt, most of the women from Gate Compound. The Gate men would use the protection of the community as an excuse to stay behind. The way she felt right now, perhaps that was a good thing.

The people from Lillit Compound were putting the finishing touches on tables laid with corn and squashes, nuts and dried fruits and breads; and of course, the honey cakes the young boys craved.

The little girls would be fluttering around behind the main building, anxious to make their entrance. Jenera smiled, happy for Ekiria. The thought of her dancing around the fire sent her a tickle of joy. Her niece had been bursting like a cottonwood pod in anticipation of the dance. Ekiria would no doubt someday succeed her as Spirit Leader.

Remembering Rowan, Jenera's shoulders sagged once again under a growing dread. She was happy to see Maude from Lillit Compound heading her way with a tray of food balanced in her arms. "Rowan up to eating?" she called out.

Jenera smiled and nodded her head. "He's weak, but I've never seen him turn down food." Not much escaped notice in her village, even in the middle of Festival. Maude's lighthearted laughter lifted Jenera's spirit. A beautiful, capable woman, she was half *Dannais*, healthy and strong. A survivor. Her husband, a human refugee from Terra City, had given her three children: Ekiria's friend, Alta who was in the ceremony, and a young son on the sidelines, pushing his way to the front. The oldest, Peck, inherited the *Dannais* gene, and was a close friend to Bryn.

She worked her way closer to the central brazier, scanning faces in the crowd. Bryn and Peck were not yet among them. She slipped her wrists through handcrafted silks that formed her Monarch's wings, nodded to the drum leader, and took her position at the center of the circle.

A single drummer silenced the crowd after a few slow beats and was soon joined by another and another until a lively rhythm had them clapping to join in. The rhythm slowed again until the single drum tapped out a soft heartbeat that grew louder as it went.

Ta-dum, ta-dum, ta-dum.

Jenera unfolded herself slowly, in time with the beat, first one arm and then the other, transforming herself from a tightly held crouch to an upright figure standing at full height. The other drummers joined in again. She danced around the brazier, the embodiment of a full *Dannais* adult, swirling and dipping as she had done so many times before, silky wings catching the firelight, sometimes spreading out to simulate flight and sometimes concealing her body from view. She let the drum beats move her, giving herself up to the rhythm. Worry and fear could wait until the dance was over, but for now, she was caught up in the drama of the life cycle of the *Dannais*.

Now, the throbbing rhythm grew faster. Jenera spun and danced through the crowd and through the outer ring of revelers. Then, right on cue, the drumming stopped abruptly, then started again with three healthy beats, a change of rhythm signaled the young "monarchs" to begin their dance.

Jenera glided to the sideline, near Maude's table of food and sampled from a tray of fresh figs. The little ones flitted in, reproducing her dance as best they could, each with her own unique set of monarch wings. Jenera couldn't help but smile at their faces, all made up with paint and laughing. She raised up on tiptoe to spot Ekiria's wings among the others. There she was, spinning and spinning. *Not her usual approach, but…*

Someone grabbed Jenera's hand from behind. "Oh," she yelped, half expecting one of the young boys to be grinning up at her when she turned around.

Instead, it was Bryn. He clamped his hand firmly around her wrist and pulled her away to the sidelines.

He leveled his gaze at her. "Esteban wasn't there." His voice carried a shot of urgency. "Not for the past three days that anyone can recall." He was distracted by the sounds of the dance for a moment, then turned back to Jenera. "Festival or no, we've got to… "

At a commotion near the brazier, he snapped his head around.

Jenera pressed her hand to his chest. "Something's wrong."

The music had stopped. Several mothers rushed toward the center of the circle. Jenera took off at a run with Bryn on her heels. Concerned people pushed aside to let her get to the center of the disturbance.

Maude held little Alta in her arms. Her knees were bleeding, and she had a goose egg growing on her forehead. Jenera recognized Ekiria's wings crushed on the ground beneath Alta's feet. She knelt down beside the quaking child. "Alta? What's going on?"

She sobbed out the words. "I got dizzy… and… I fell… and…"

Jenera put her hand against Alta's cheek. "You're okay, sweetie. It's just a few scratches… but you know that's not what I mean."

Alta's face streamed with tears. "I *told* her I couldn't do it. *Told* her not to go."

Someone pushed a wet cloth into Maude's hand, and she wiped dirt off her daughter's face. "Told who, honey? What are you talking about?"

Jenera's stomach lurched. She had known something wasn't right. But she never thought it would involve Alta and Ekiria. She picked up the ruined wings and looked into the eyes of the worried child. "Where, Alta. Where did she go?"

Alta's sobs deepened; her shoulders convulsed. Everyone was staring at her now. She buried her face in her mother's lap and pointed in no particular direction.

Jenera stroked Alta's hair. The child must be terrified. "Alta, you're not in trouble. Just tell me. Whisper it in my ear. No one else will hear you."

Slowly, the child sat up and did as she was told.

Jenera turned to Bryn. "She went to find who hurt Rowan."

Bryn fixed serious eyes on Alta. "How long ago?"

His voice was a little more demanding than Jenera's had been. Alta's mouth opened and closed, looking back and forth between the two adults. Jenera stepped in. "She could be in danger, Alta. We need your help to find her."

Alta stood now, rigid, face paint smudged down the front of her dress. "We had lunch, and then we practiced our dance, and then she... she said she was going back to the meadow." She looked plaintively at Jenera, pulled her lower lip through her teeth, and then looked at the ground. "... she... told me to stay there, behind the kitchen, until the dance started."

Jenera rested her hand on Alta's head a moment, then looked up at Bryn. "She's got, maybe, a couple of hours head start?"

❀

Sloan dropped the milkiweed pod at his feet. Ekiria took a few spirally steps closer to him. "Put your shoes on. We have to go." She pulled on his arm, trying get him up.

Sloan just stared off into the distance. "I told you, I'm not going back there."

"But why?"

Sloan got up and moved away from her to look back down on the valley. His mind burned with the memories of deep loneliness, despair, and years of fending for himself. He never wanted to go back to that. Ever. She was just a kid. She wouldn't understand.

He pulled his cap off his head, rubbed his hands over the smooth surface of his head and down to his neck. Huh. He was only a kid too, really. It wasn't fair. None of it.

"Jenera says sometimes telling somebody else about a problem, makes the problem seem smaller."

Sloan pulled his cap back down over his ears and folded his arms, tucking his deformed hands into his arm pits. He bit back a nasty remark. He shouldn't be angry at her. None of this was her fault. He puffed out a burst of air, deflating his ego along with it. "What's your name?"

The girl moved in until she stood even with him, and shot her chin up to a proud angle. "I'm Ekiria, daughter of Helena." She slid her eyes over to look at him. "I will be a Spirit Leader one day."

"How old are you?"

"Twelve. Well, eleven. Almost."

Sloan rolled his eyes. Ten. A child. What could she know about loneliness? Deprived of the sun and its light? Would telling her make any of those memories go away? He took a few more steps to the end of the meadow where he could see increased activity down in the valley.

Again, she moved in beside him. "That's okay. If you're afraid? I won't tell anyone. I'm good like that. You can trust me."

Sloan straightened to alert. "Yeah? What about them?" He pointed down into the valley. Torchlights danced around the central brazier like tiny fireflies.

Ekiria observed the scene under furrowed brows for a long moment. "Uh oh."

For the first time since she'd appeared, he recognized fear and uncertainty in her eyes. He followed her gaze to the valley below. The lights that had been moving rhythmically around a central fire had broken away, formed a ragged line that streamed all in one direction. The look on her face turned from fear to guilt.

Sloan turned on her now. "Whadaya mean, 'uh oh'? What did you do?"

"They're coming this way. Alta must've told." She grabbed him by his sleeves and pulled away from the edge. "C'mon. We've got to go *now*. They'll catch up to us if we don't."

Sloan twisted out of her grip, scooped up his shoes and scrambled back over to the downed log where he could see better what was going on. More torches were being lit from the central fire where people gathered for a moment, then headed off in the opposite direction from the first. He was so exhausted and aching, he doubted he could make it down into the compound below without collapsing, let alone back to Terra City.

Panic gripped his chest. Every cell in his body felt the squeeze of a trap. Overwhelmed, he slumped to sit on the log, dropped his shoes on the mossy ground at his feet and rested his head on his hands. He had made up his mind. "I'm staying right here."

"No. We *have* to go after the crysl."

Sloan stared up at her and shook his head. "Trust me, Ekiria. You and I can't get to the crysl by ourselves. It's too dangerous."

She pushed her face close to his, eyes blazing challenge. "Come back with me, then. You need to tell them what happened. Even if they put you in jail, they're nice. I promise."

Sloan let go a laugh. She was relentless. But he could not go another step.

"Go and meet them. Let them see that you're okay. They'll be relieved. They can do what they want with me. I'll be right here waiting."

She scowled at him another moment, and then, she leaned in and planted a kiss sharply on his cheek, snatched the cap off his head, and dashed off to the trail down.

Ekiria had only made two switchbacks out of the meadow when she ran headfirst into Jenera, Bryn, and Peck. "By the stars in the universe, Ekiria, what *are* you doing up here?" Jenera cried. The child seemed to defy every attempt to keep her under control.

"I know what happened to Rowan!"

"Well that's just fine young lady, and how did you think we'd feel when we discovered that you were missing?"

"It was Esteban. He hurt Rowan, and he took the crysl." She pulled Jenera's arm. "You've got to come with me. I'll show you."

Jenera easily resisted her pull. "It's okay, Eki. This isn't your problem. Bryn and Peck will get it sorted. I promise you. But right now, we have to get you back to your mother. She's worried sick."

"But the crysl. It's *hers*, I thought I saw something in the meadow and I thought I could find—"

Jenera pulled the cloak from her own shoulders, wrapped it around the girl and turned her in the direction of home. "You thought wrong, young lady, and no wild stories are going to keep me from seeing that you stay in your room for a good long time. Your mother is beside herself with worry."

"But I know—"

"Not another word out of you." Jenera handed her over to one of the Gate Compound men who had come along on the search. "Zeke, please see that she gets to Helena. We'll be along shortly." Ekiria clamped her lips tight shut and shoved Sloan's cap deep into her tunic pocket.

Jenera pulled Bryn and Peck aside and waited until the rest of the search party had filed back down the switchback and out of sight.

"Well that went better than I thought," Bryn said, wiping sweat from his brow.

Jenera stood motionless, the nodules on her head flexing. "There's something to it, though. I can feel it. She wanted me to see something up on the meadow."

Ten minutes later, Jenera found herself staring into the eyes of a young man so frail and frightened, it pained her to watch Bryn bind his tortured hands with rope.

CHAPTER 25 - BEAR MAN RISES

Sloan recognized the bear of a man the moment he stood up from the fire. He was thankful to see that the old man had survived Esteban's attack, but it was clear by the sharpening of his gaze, he had recognized him from their first encounter on the trail. The man, Bryn, who had led him down the trail with his hands tied behind his back pressed his big hands down on his shoulders as he presented him.

"Let him go, Bryn," Bear Man bellowed.

Sloan's captor only tightened his grip. "He had Ekiria up in the meadow, he—"

Bearman scowled at him long enough for Sloan to wonder if maybe he'd made a colossal mistake. Maybe he should not have taken Ekiria at her word. These people could very well be worse than Esteban . Since surrendering himself in the meadow, his hands had been lashed behind his back; he had been pushed down the trail without regard for his injured feet, and the first person he faced among the colony was the old man Esteban had robbed and then beaten unconscious on the trail.

While the woman he'd seen at the meadow had been gentle and compassionate with her charges, it seemed this man, a human, was just like the ones he'd learned to avoid in Terra City.

But just as he was beginning to lose hope, Bear Man took a step forward, using a staff for support. "I said let him go."

The man's grip loosened. Sloan slumped to the ground. Then the man, Bryn, untied his hands and slipped the circle of rope from around his neck. Sloan let out a sigh of relief.

"Who are you?" Rowan demanded.

Sloan blanched, steadied himself with his hands on the ground. A crowd of people had gathered close. All eyes were on him. He rubbed raw skin around his wrists where the bindings had chaffed and shifted his gaze from Rowan to Bryn. His mind raced. He cast his gaze around frantically. Where was the woman, Jenera? She was the one Ekiria promised to take him to, not this old man leaning on a staff.

"What's wrong with you boy? Can't you speak?" Rowan's voice prodded him again.

He rubbed one of his feet against his calf, trying to relieve the ache. If he stalled, maybe she would come. It was all he could think about. He swallowed hard, struggling to find his voice.

"My... my feet hurt."

Rowan stepped forward again, inspected the boy's feet. Concern pinched his burly brow as he noted they were raw and bleeding. If he noticed they weren't like any human feet he had seen, his expression didn't show it. The elders closest to the scene gasped as they saw what he saw. Then, his eyes slid to Sloan's and held his gaze.

"One of you, get Helena." Then he moved closer still, and knelt low so that his lips were close enough Sloan could feel his hot breath on his ear. "Where is the crysl?"

Sloan's eyes grew wide. So much for stalling. He took in the faces of those who surrounded him. Many of them looked like the men who brought him here. But others bore characteristics he recognized. Chiseled faces, iridescent skin, smooth heads with antennae nodules prodding the air. He may have an advantage here, if he was brave enough to make use of it. If he could offer something, maybe he would find what he longed for.

Bear man poked his shoulder. "Answer me quick if you know what's good for you." The old man was obviously recovered from the merciless attack he'd witnessed. But Sloan had come all this way. He wasn't going to roll over. Not yet. This human was the leader, that was for sure. Sloan saw no traits of the *Dannais* in him, but he saw wisdom, and looking past the blazing fury in Rowan's eyes, he had seen, had felt, some compassion.

The woman they called Helena rushed to his side. She opened a bag of small pots and pouches, inspected his feet. The moment she saw their condition, she stood up to Rowan. "This boy belongs in the infirmary, not this impromptu tribunal."

Sloan could see that her words stung the old man. Rowan addressed her sternly, but with respect. "In a moment, Helena. They boy will keep." He returned his burning gaze to Sloan.

"Who are you and where is the crysl?" His voice grew louder, as if he'd forgotten himself. Sloan felt his heart sink to the pit of his stomach. He tried to pull himself up to stand, feeling every bit on the brink of caving into hysteria, when a commotion at the doorway of a nearby dwelling caught everyone's attention.

"Sloan!" Ekiria ran at them, with the woman he'd seen in the meadow in rapid pursuit.

"Quiet, girl." Rowan roared at the child, holding his staff high in the air. A shiver prickled up Sloan's spine. The entire crowd was now focused on him like he was some animal in a circus. He pulled his cloak around him, wishing he could disappear.

"What crysl?" Meadow woman demanded. "What are you talking about?" She stood toe-to-toe with Bear man now, challenging his silence. "What… crysl?"

He stood his ground a few heartbeats longer and then, without taking his eyes from Jenera's, he gave his command. "Helena, take the prisoner to the infirmary."

Sloan shifted his gaze between Jenera and the old man, who seemed to be in their own private battle of wills. But when Helena began to gather her implements, it was clear who the leader was.

"Wait." Jenera stepped over to the prisoner who now looked into her eyes as if he had seen an apparition. She stooped to examine his bleeding feet. "The first time in our history we take a prisoner, and this is how we treat him?" She leveled a scornful glare at the two men. "He looks to me like he can barely stand, let alone walk on those injured feet."

Bryn looked at his own feet and then back to her, then with a brief nod to Rowan, he scooped the boy up in his arms and carried him off toward Lillit Compound.

Jenera followed them with her eyes until they were out of sight, then turned back to Rowan who was leaning heavily on his staff. She stepped in close to support his elbow. "Let's go back to my chamber."

They turned and moved slowly through the murmuring crowd. She saw out of the corner of her eye that Ekiria followed at a respectful distance.

Jenera helped Rowan into the chair near the window of her chamber and lifted his feet to a stool. She poured a cup of water from her earthen jug and handed it to him. The redness faded from his cheeks and his breathing began to settle. "I'm glad to see you're feeling better," she said.

Rowan grunted, let his head roll back against the chair, and released a long sigh. Ekiria crept into the room, pushed up against Jenera's side and pulled her arm in close around her. Jenera let her be. "Ekiria has told me most of the story already, Rowan. You might as well tell me the rest of it."

One of his eyes opened and cut back and forth between them. "You are both carriers of the gene," he said quietly. "I suppose you have a right to know. At least, I have no right to deny you."

His words sent a spike of dread through Jenera's heart. What had he been hiding from her and for how long?

He shifted his feet off the stool and planted them firmly on the ground, his hands gripping his knees as if to ground himself. "So, it is exactly as you foretold, exactly as the legend says," he began, then proceeded to tell them about meeting Lara and sending her off to find the creature he'd befriended many years before and because the creature forbid it, never told anyone of his existence.

"And you let me go on my quest, knowing this? Let me be challenged by the colony when you knew all along the legend was true?"

Rowan squirmed uncomfortably in the chair. "Don't you have any brew? Some bitter ale, maybe?"

"The *crysl*, grandfather. Then we'll see about ale." Jenera's voice was stern, but her touch was soft as she smoothed the twisted strands of hair off his forehead.

She was angry that he had kept this story from her but understanding of his plight. Everything she had prepared for had been preserved in the caves above the colony for longer than any of them could say. The very existence of these new generations of *Dannais* spelled the end of the era to which Rowan belonged. If the legend was true, then some of them would leave, never to return, driven by a larger purpose than survival in this valley. Jenera knew, had always known, that she was destined to respond to the signs. And she also knew that Rowan would not. Nor would Bryn. Her heart squeezed at the thought.

She pulled Ekiria closer in her arms. She was just a child, but she bore the gene and had already learned more than Jenera knew from the boy, Sloan. Jenera saw herself in her young niece. Passionate, empathetic, powerful. She would someday be a person to recon with. There was no denying that she, too, would respond to the beacon call, and because of that, despite her young age, Jenera wanted her to know everything for no other reason than to keep her from running head-long into dangerous situations she hadn't yet the power to control.

Rowan rested his forearms on his thighs and wrung his hands as he spoke. "A few years back, I came upon a creature near the old dam. He was heartsick and near death, but showed the signs of what we know to be *Dannais*, only far advanced. Like your Messenger. He was skilled at survival, and I helped him as much as I could. He'd made a life for himself, encouraged by the fact that, as I told him, another like himself may soon appear. I told him of the legends and of the chrysalises I'd found up in the caves that were still intact.

Jenera startled, the first signs of anger furrowing her brow. Rowan held up his hands to fend off a reprisal.

"I know, I didn't tell you." He went back to wringing his hands. "Maybe I should have."

"Maybe?" She'd guessed he was holding a secret, but the magnatude was beyond her imagination.

Ekiria jumped up, grabbed her grandfather's hands. "Sloan's one too, isn't he?" She turned to Jenera. "Isn't he?"

Rowan lifted his head and looked at her as if he had just realized she was in the room. "What did he do to you?"

Ekiria spun away, exasperated. "He didn't do anything to me." She fisted her hands at her waist and looked to Jenera for support. "He's not bad, he's just scared." Ekiria looked from Rowan to Jenera and back again. "Esteban's the one. *He's* got the crysl. At the outpost." Ekiria's antennae shot to their limits.

Outrage creased Rowan's forehead. "Outpost! What outpost?"

Jenera stood up now, turning on them. Esteban had once again proved he wasn't worthy of respect. She was going to have to speak with Rowan about that later. Right now, there was a more pressing issue. "Forget Esteban . Tell me about this crysl!"

Ekiria blinked at Jenera, mouth agape. "I thought you knew."

Rowan stood now, limped across the room, and turned back to face Jenera. "It's hers. Lara's. I was there when she gave birth. She was afraid. She…" His face folded into a grimace that could only mean deep pain, as he grabbed his side. He limped back to the chair and slumped down, dropped his head into his hands. "When I found her in the cave she was nearly passed out from the labor. A crysl. I helped her deliver it. Told her I'd take care of it; bring it to you. To the tower, but…"

"Esteban hurt him on the way back… He took it," Ekiria interrupted. She flew to the window and pointed off toward the infirmary. "Sloan knows where he's going. He's not bad. He wants to help us. We can get it back! We can—"

Jenera held her hand up to hush the excited child. She leveled her gaze back on Rowan. "You took her crysl child and sent her away? Knowing I was waiting for her to come?"

Rowan raised his head and looked at her, his eyes brimming wet. "You don't understand." He took another long draught of water, his mouth suddenly dry. "My Cora," he managed, before his throat closed around the words.

Jenera focused on the ropy veins in his old hands. He was trembling. She waited a beat, then prompted him. "Go on."

Rowan exhaled a ragged breath. "Three days after Cora bore her crysl, the one that's up in your tower now, she began to change. A second metamorphosis, which it is said is a normal progression. But something went wrong." He dropped his head in his hands again, his mind repelling the sight of her crumbling form, eventually turning to liquid and then nothing more than an unrecognizable mass of debris, like decomposing leaves on the forest floor. He swallowed and raised his head to look at Jenera, unable to speak the words. "Cora didn't make it. But the other one did. Only a week ago. A strong male. The one I told you about."

Jenera rose and went to the window. "And you believe now Lara will go through this second metamorphoses?"

"*Is* going through. I saw the signs of it when I was with her. It's probably what brought on the labor." Rowan squeezed his eyes shut again. "If it goes the way it went for Cora, she would have had three days before going back into chrysalis form. That's why I sent her to *him*. I hoped maybe one of her own kind, one who has been through the change and survived, would be able to help her through."

Jenera paced the room, anger and frustration ratcheting up her heart rate. She glared at the men in the room landing finally on Rowan. How he could have let this happen was beyond her. She'd had her own run ins with Esteban, and she hadn't told Rowan about it. They would only have dismissed his behavior and advised her to be more careful. That was on her. But losing the crysl was intolerable. She would not be ignored or placated. And she would not let Ekiria be subjected to the same treatment.

She scooped the ten-year-old under her arm. "Ekiria is absolutely right. I'm going after the crysl."

CHAPTER 26 – WORLDS COLLIDE

He gripped the tow rope tightly in gloved hands, feet planted firmly on the slip-check deck of his favorite gun, a sleek, narrow surfboard he'd designed and fabricated himself. His buddy hit the jet ski throttle, heading into the building swell that could easily grow to more than fifty feet before it broke. The commentators would later say he was lucky, catching the biggest wave of the day, but he knew, as did all Mavericks surfers, catching a giant wave at Mav's and making it back on shore to surf another day had nothing to do with luck. It took perfect coordination between the surfer and his tow partner, perfect timing to whiplash him into the swell at just the right place. Then in that last breathless second before he let go of that rope and the sound of the jet ski faded away, he was the embodiment of life itself, not just a rider of the waves, but a rider of the big blue lonely planet itself. That jubilant, powerful rush was better than any drug, almost better than sex. That high that easily blocked out thoughts about the world-famous surfer, Mark Foo who had died on this very break in 1994 (that would come later when he saw the video). In that moment, just before he released his grip, time stood still as he made his choice: Back off the lip of the wave and slide away into safety or let go and drop into the sheer adrenaline-pumping rush of riding a giant wave. For him, there really wasn't a choice. He lived for that adrenaline rush, that race against a mountain of blue-green water, the pure exultation of carving into the face of it while his heart beat in suspended animation…

He woke with a start at the soft *plish* of something near his elbow in the water. He straightened, the familiar dream slipping away like the tide, ending the way it always did just before he let go, leaving him empty and wanting. It was the one thing he'd recognized from a former life that he must have lived before finding himself here in this virgin landscape, the one thing he could not make sense of, until now. He shifted his weight, ensuring with care the woman cradled in his arms was still breathing.

Only a fool would continue to deny what he knew deep in his bones. That dream, those memories belonged to Michael. Belonged to *him*. He had shoved the memories away, so deep inside he'd forgotten the name. But it came to him now, rolling back from a long-lost past.

His mother calling him in from the beach for dinner: *Michael…*

His father, a loving reprimand, pulling him back from the brink of disaster: *Michael!*

Lara, gasping in his ear, breathless and hungry: *Michael!*

Now, he pressed the back of his hand against her cheek. The water had done its work. Her skin, though still flushed under its iridescent coating, was cool, closer to normal. Blistery red blotches near the back of her neck had coalesced into the beginnings of a distinct stained-glass pattern, iridescent white and soft orange framed in filigree. He traced the outlines with his fingertips, remembering what Rowan had told him before he'd slipped into his own transition. Soon the pattern would draw into two parallel ridges, like an embryonic spine between her shoulder blades. For the next few days, she would exist in a suspended state, and if all went as it should she would emerge once again, a whole new creature. But before that happened, she would be completely encased in amber, trapped as it were with her senses fully intact. He had been terrified when it happened, to him. He could not move, didn't need to breathe, but every molecule of his senses prickled on high alert. He had stood rigid, trapped during a heart-pounding lightning storm, frozen when he was sniffed by a pair of curious bear cubs until their mother balked at his presence and hurried them away. He'd witnessed sunrises and sunsets, and the ocean dream, over and over. Always ending the same.

Now, his heart went out to the precious soul he held in his arms. He couldn't stop what was happening, but he could protect her. He needed to get her back to his grotto to ensure her safety from predators while she was in this vulnerable state.

He adjusted his feet under his body and stood. She was feather light in his arms. He pulled in a long breath, a familiar ache squeezing at his chest. Overwhelmed by the compelling need to protect her at all cost, he climbed the shallow bank at the water's edge and headed toward his home next to the ancient dam.

By the time he reached his ledge, the night was filled with stars, the great circle crowned the night sky overhead. How many nights had he stared up at that formation, aching for something he could not name. And now, he knew beyond all doubt that he held that something in his arms, and her name was Lara.

Lara floated in a silent amber sea, heat receding from her limbs, her chest, her face. A moment ago she thought she had found a reason to hope again, to dream again, to love again. Rowan had led her to

Michael. He was different. Alarmingly so. But so was she, right? They were freaks but they had found one another, and it was something to hold on to, something to set this world right again. And then, in a wave of blinding heat, a chirring screech grabbed a hold of her senses, so loud in her head she thought she might die. She'd clamped her hands over her ears and squeezed her eyes shut under the pain of it until she thought it would consume her completely.

And then, like the gush of relief after releasing the crysl from her body, there was profound silence, peace. Was it over then? The struggle? Her life? Just when everything she had longed for was in view? Her heartbeat slowed to a dull tap high in her chest. God had a terrible sense of humor after all. If there was a God, because, surely the God she had been taught to love in her youth would never let the world come to this.

PART THREE

SLOAN

CHAPTER 27 – A NEW PAIR OF SHOES

Sloan basked in the comfort of the infirmary in the compound they called Lillit, surrounded by light and warmth and care. It was even better than he had imagined that day on the meadow when he'd first seen the way Jenera had cared for the young ones. He'd spent the first hour with Ekiria by his side while her mother, Helena, measured him for a set of clothes that fit and, her biggest challenge, a pair of shoes that wouldn't assault his feet.

Once Jenera had convinced Rowan that he should accompany them on their mission to Terra City rather than keep him here as a prisoner, she insisted they wait to go until his feet were healed and had decent protection so that he wouldn't lose the use of them for his effort.

"We can wait a little," she'd told them. A few more days one way or the other aren't going to make a whole lot of difference to the crysls, but that time can mean all the difference to this young man."

"But what about the planets?" Ekiria chimed in, jumping to her feet. "They're supposed to line up in seven days. We've got to get the crysl back before that happens!"

Bryn and Peck, the ones likely to take on the mission, nodded their like minds while Rowan coughed an unintelligible word behind his gnarled hand.

Sloan rolled his eyes. He hadn't challenged his new friend when they were up on the meadow; she'd almost been in a trance, chanting out the words. And his newly acquired manners told him it wasn't a good idea to contradict the people you were counting on to accept you into their fold. On the other hand, there wasn't a book in the library at Terra City he hadn't devoured, and astronomy was one of his favorite subjects. He had climbed every branch of that particular tree of knowledge and despite the fact that their legends were based on the story, he could not let this pass. The earth revolved around the sun, contrary to the beliefs of some of the ancients and no amount of fantasy or wishful thinking could change that.

But what was the point of starting a new life if he didn't speak his own truth? He exhaled a raggedy breath and for the first time he felt safe enough to express himself naturally, without holding back.

"In about seven days, the moon, Mercury, Venus, Earth, and Saturn will definitely appear to be aligned in the sky. But in fact, they only look that way from our point of view, and in very general terms that can mean simply being on the same side of the sun at the same time." Any junior high school kid in 2023 knew that. His left brain picked up the thread and pushed him forward. "In all the scientific records—and I've had practically nothing else to do for the last year but memorize scientific records—there has never been any physical impact on Earth as a result of this alignment."

He took in the various expressions of the souls in the room—Bryn and Peck folded their arms across their chests and didn't venture a blink, they would withhold their judgement; Rowan nodded in agreement as Sloan expected he would. The old man knew way more than he let on and held his opinions close to his chest. Ekiria scowled in disbelief and would have blurted her disappointment if Jenera hadn't put her hand firmly on the young girl's shoulder. But it was Jenera's reaction he sought most. Would she reject his knowledge like all the others, or would she, as he'd imagined with all his heart, listen to him?

But when he lifted his eyes to her, she was staring at Rowan as if a great truth had just been revealed to her; one that Sloan had not yet learned. He had no choice but to make his final point, then he would see. "What surprises me is that primitives, such as yourselves—by that I mean not ignorance, but without the technology to discover—know of the dates that such an alignment will next occur."

Rowan bristled, breaking the connection between he and Jenera and fixed his gaze intently on Sloan.

"It's true," Jenera said, stepping forward. "Our existence appears primitive to anyone who has experienced the world that went before." She placed her hand gently on Ekiria's head. "To those who are too young to understand why we chose to isolate ourselves from the cities. But we are not ignorant of science. Nor do we reject it." She looked pointedly at Rowan a moment before she went on. "However, Sloan. What you may or may not already know is that the *Dannais*—those of us with enough of the gene to call ourselves *Dannais*—have a set of instincts that full humans do not. I don't need to look to the stars to know that the day approaches. The coming and going of the equinox and solstice are written in our DNA along with all the other nuances of the natural earth. In seven days, aligning with the Spring Equinox, the mature crysls will begin to awaken, they will break free of their confinement and feed, and if all goes according to legend, the Messenger will return and lead a migration that is unprecedented in our history. It is not because of the planet alignment, it is because of the arrival of the leader in that season that is most beneficial to a successful migration."

Rowan scuffed the wooden floor, his gaze fixed on his feet.

"You can call it a legend," she went on, "Or you can simply call it the natural order of Life preserving itself. It is the same thing."

She relaxed into the chair next to his bed and took one of his hands in hers. His heart swelled at first with a profound longing, then as the heat of her hands seeped into his, that longing was replaced by a sense of calm and contentment he'd never known. That care was what he'd seen on the meadow, what he needed to move forward.

"As I said, it has nothing to do with the planets." He avoided Ekiria's eyes, knowing she would be upset to hear this."But I do need to ask you some things," Jenera said, her tone going serious. "Are you feeling up to it?"

Anything. I'm up to anything you ask at all as long as you hold my hand. "Yes ma'am."

"How long will it take you to lead us to Terra City?"

"Return to Terra City?" His voice held a coward's squeak. His heart shrank a little. Did she have to ask the one thing he'd sworn he would never do?

Seeming to recognize his reluctance, she said. "Not alone, of course. You, me, Bryn, and Peck, maybe a few others? We know generally how to get there. In fact, some of our colony have ventured there in the past." At this confession, her eyes cut away, and he sensed this was a difficult admission. Something she wasn't ready to share, so he didn't interrupt her to ask.

"I understand there are... certain risks. But, our chances of being successful, of finding the crysl and getting it out safely, would be a lot better with you as a guide."

Sloan took this all in. He couldn't stand to see the pain in her expression from what appeared to be a deep scar on her heart. "It is a tough journey. The trail isn't maintained. And, there have been geological, that is, geothermal changes over time."

"We're aware of this," she said, shooting a wary look at Rowan. "We've lost some of our people attempting to go there."

Rowan studied his feet and drew in a loud, low breath.

"But this crysl—The Messengers Crysl —s precious to us."

Sloan rolled his lip in and closed his eyes. He could hardly breathe thinking about it. Those chambers, his room, the Vault, the library, the unbearable loneliness, were haunted by painful memories of his parents, of his former self, and of the humans who had died there. Sloan could feel them all around him. "I... wasn't planning on ever going back there," he heard himself say, covering her hand with his misshapen one. "It's why I agreed to come with Esteban. Not to join in his scheme, but to lead me here, away from all the ghosts."

"Ghosts?"

Sloan stared at her wide eyed, realizing what he'd just said. "You don't know?"

Jenera shook her head as she once again cast a glance at Rowan. He pushed away from the wall where he'd been hulking and sat down in the chair on the other side of Sloan's bed. "Tell us about the ghosts, young man, and don't leave anything out. We've had people go to explore the city and never return."

Sloan's mouth went dry. He realized now that a chamber of bones he'd discovered in one of the catacombs could likely be the people Rowan spoke of. By the fearful look he saw on Jenera's expression, he guessed they were important to her. He began to shake his head, but she squeezed his hand. "It's all right, Sloan. It's better to know the truth so we can face it head on."

"It's a long story," he stalled, his throat closing on the dryness.

Rowan passed him a glass of orange juice he'd only half finished. "We're not going anywhere until your feet are ready for the journey." He sent Jenera a patient look. "We've got plenty of time, so why don't you start from the beginning?"

CHAPTER 28 - HERA'S VAULT

"It won't be easy," Sloan said. He sipped the juice, soothing his dry throat. Five sets of eyes focused on him now and it made him nervous. "Good juice," he said, stalling again. "Best I've tasted."

"It's just orange juice," Ekiria said, calling him out. "They don't have any juice in Terra City?"

"Let him talk, Eki," Jenera scolded, and guided her to sit in a chair by the foot of the bed. "Why. What's the issue?"

Sloan lifted a shoulder, the prospect of going back made him cower. "It's… dangerous."

"How so," Jenera asked. "Tell us the truth. Everything you remember."

He sipped more juice. "It's kind of a long story."

"The more we know," Jenera prodded, "the better chance of success. I need to understand what we're dealing with."

Sloan pressed his lips together a moment. He didn't really want to think about it, but this was Jenera asking and he couldn't deny her.

He huffed in a breath and let it out. "The first thing I remember was peeling the chrysalis off my skin, and finding the food and water. At first I thought I was in my room at home. My bed, my games, a few books. But once I was fully aware, it was clear, I was somewhere else. Once I was able to move, to stand upright, to take a few steps, I opened the door of my chamber to find the ones around it had not survived in the way I would later learn my father and his engineers had intended."

Rowan mumbled something unintelligible that sounded like a curse. "Explain. If you can, that is."

Sloan gritted his teeth. Did they think he was stupid because he was deformed? He'd spent the last year studying the plans to understand what went wrong. He straightened against the headboard, sorting his feelings. Was he mad because these people treated him like a kid, or mad at his father for screwing everything up? Or just plain mad? He glanced around him at the faces of the souls intensely focused on him and saw only good intentions.

"Of course I can," he said at last, pushing down the need to lash out. These people were not the enemy.

Ekiria left her chair and crawled up in Jenera's lap. "So, what happened?"

"There was a geothermal event inside the facility." Sloan rolled his eyes. "They should have known. I mean, geothermal energy was part of the plan. That whole area was—is—an active site. Heat and energy in inexhaustible supply. But something went terribly wrong, and judging by the rockfall and open shafts in the catacombs in and around the Vault, it happened more than once, mostly before I... hatched."

Ekiria perked up. "Wait. Hatched?"

Sloan sent Jenera a scrunchy brow. "You know what I mean, right?"

Jenera stroked Ekiria's head and explained. "Sloan was preserved in a chrysalis shell inside his chamber like the Messenger I told you about. When the chrysalis broke open, he could move and breathe like we do now."

"Right," Sloan went on. "I was protected inside my shell, until it started to peel away. My chamber protected me, too. It was mostly dry and undamaged. The fresh air system still worked, and the door to my chamber was unblocked. But other areas of The Vault were completely blocked by rocks, and others remain to this day filled with bubbling hot water.

Jenera fixed him with a pained look. "What about the others?"

"Others?"

"Surely there were others living in the facility. You weren't alone for—"

"There were bodies," Sloan went on. "Who knows how long they'd been there. They were just dried skin and bones. But others, near the entrance to the Vault..." he looked up to fix his gaze on Rowan. "Others were obviously killed more recently. It looked like they were caught by surprise."

His gaze slipped to Jenera a moment as he sifted through a conversation he had had the first time he'd met up with Esteban. *Fools*, he had called the pair when Sloan described the bodies. *Snooping around where they didn't belong.*

Ekiria turned her face into Jenera's chest. She rocked her in her arms. "How long would you say, you were there alone before Esteban showed up?"

Sloan shrugged. "A long time. Maybe a year? Maybe more? I mean, I wasn't completely alone. There were people—humans—living in the chambers on and off. There's a travel route in what they call The Owens."

Bryn stepped forward now, his eyes intense. "Travelers? Who are they? Where did they come from?"

Sloan shrugged again. "I'm not sure. I mostly stayed out of sight when a group showed up. I don't look, you know, exactly human, and I was afraid they would—"

"It's all right, Sloan," Jenera said. "You were right not to put yourself in harm's way. You have good instincts."

Sloan's heart warmed at her encouragement. "I did eavesdrop on them. Sometimes I stole stuff from their backpacks. Some food. A knife. Things they might not miss right away. From what I could gather, there are a few populated areas in the south, but supplies are scarce, and bands of people explore up the valleys looking for resources, safety.

Most of them aren't bad people. Not really. Just hungry. And tired. Desperate for food and shelter. They only stayed long enough to rest and discover there were no resources at The Vault. Well, none they could access easily. Boiling hot water is a pretty tough obstacle if you don't know how to get around it. Everything of value that was easily accessible had either been destroyed by the eruptions or looted by others long before them."

"Sloan tells much the same story as Lara," Jenera said. "She was left in her cave with cannisters of food and survival gear."

Sloan sipped again from his juice, then put down the cup. "My dad wrote about her in his diary. He worried the cave wasn't secure enough to preserve her from what was coming. He had planned to move her to Terra City, maybe as a way to help me. But obviously, that... didn't happen."

Jenera cocked her head and her antennae stretched toward him. "Help you?"

322

Sloan sighed. It wasn't easy to put into words without feeling completely unloved and unwanted. "He thought future doctors could fix my brain."

"Your brain?" Jenera's brow pinched over her nose.

"It's… complicated. Let's just say my brain is a sponge you can't wring out. They call it hyperthymesia. I remember every detail of everything I've ever seen."

"From the day you were born?" Ekiria asked, astonished.

Sloan nodded, glanced around the room. "From the day I was born. Except, I couldn't talk about it. I remember holding a pillow over my head so I wouldn't hear or see any more. It was exhausting. I screamed a lot. I knew the words I wanted to say. Knew way more than I wanted to know, but I had no access to them. My father was patient, but my mother didn't know what to make of me, was actually kind of afraid of my responses, so she basically stayed away."

The rejection.

The abandonment.

He lifted his eyes to Jenera's and read compassion in her eyes.

"Anyway, my father injected me with the UV serum, and more than a thousand years later, here I am. I've still got a brain full of information, but at least now I can talk about it."

Five pairs of eyes blinked at him.

"Maybe too much." He shrugged.

Jenera smiled at him, "So, ironically, it was his own UV serum that helped you."

"I guess so. Except, I look like a cockroach." He held up his claw-like hands.

Ekiria jumped off Jenera's lap and scooped his hands up in hers like she'd done out on the meadow. "You don't look like a cockroach, to me."

He gave her a half grin, loving her simple innocence, mourning the loss of his own.

Rowan cleared his deep throat, drawing his attention back to the moment. "Who is this Hera?"

Sloan sucked his teeth a moment. "She was a sort of background character in the Iliad. She had lot of power, not all benevolent, if you go by the story. But what my father picked up on, I suppose, was her protective power."

Bryn narrowed his eyes at him. "And you know this because... "

Sloan cleared his throat and shifted his gaze to the broad-shouldered man who towering over him. He swallowed hard on a dry throat. It wasn't that long ago that Bryn had bound his hands and drove him down the mountain. His tone said he still wasn't ready to accept his word for anything.

"Like I said before. I spent two years alone in The Vault. There's a library. It's full of... well... you know... books." He cleared his throat. "The Greek myths, right?"

Jenera stared into his eyes a moment. "I know nothing of this Illiad, but I know something about myths and legends. There's usually a grain of truth to them."

Then, she put her arm across his shoulders and pulled him close like he'd seen her do on the meadow with the young ones, and his heart completely melted. None of all that ancient mythology mattered to him now. He would do anything to stay in this world, in this time, with her.

"So, how long will it take you to lead us there?" she asked again. "A day, a week?"

With Jenera's arm around him, there was no denying her. "Would you be going with me?"

"Of course," she answered over Rowan's immed-iate "No."

He let out a long breath. It was the last thing he wanted to do, but he couldn't say no to her. "We could likely make it in two days, maybe three."

"Does Esteban have other men with him?" Bryn asked.

Sloan nodded. "He has a chamber filled with grain and other supplies that he sells and trades with travelers. There are usually two men stationed there."

Jenera huffed a laugh, nodding to Rowan. "That would be our grain and supplies."

Bryn asked, "Did he say what he plans to do with the crysl?"

"He said the crysl would be worth its weight in grain."

Rowan growled under his breath. "I should have known it would come to this." He lifted his gaze to Jenera a moment before he gave his order. "Bryn, Peck, escort Sloan over Craggy Pass and get that crysl back."

Jenera sprang to her feet. "Not without me, they don't."

Bear Man stood and raised his hand, but before he could resist, Bryn stood by Jenera's side. "She's coming with us."

"But she's—"

Bryn stood his ground. "She spent three days in the wilderness by herself to prove the legend. And she's put up with enough of Esteban's nonsense already."

"It's too dangerous. Her parents never came back."

"Which is why I need to go," Jenera returned. "I have a right to see what happened to them. Besides that crysl should have come to me in the first place."

Her accusing words hit Bear Man visibly in the gut. He stood speechless a moment, catching his breath, then glared at the group a long beat, the silence stretching around them, until at last he sat down heavily. "All right. You all go. I'll take care of Esteban. But by the gods if anything happens to Jenera, I'll—"

Bryn rose to his full stature, a formidable foe that made Sloan shrink a little just looking at him. "I'll protect her with my life," he said, and the look in Jenera's eyes when they connected made Sloan's heart squeeze. It was clear, Bryn would do anything for her, too.

CHAPTER 29 – METAMORPHOSIS

Michael laid her fast-hardening form gently on his bed, her back curved and her arms and legs tucked up close to her body like a child inside the womb. It might have been better to lay her down on the mossy ledge outside his home, the night temperatures would ensure she didn't overheat again, but he was exhausted after staying for hours with her in the water. Inside his alcove home, he could be sure she was safe from predators if he fell asleep, which was likely in his present state. For now, the thick amber coating over her body was still cool to the touch. He could monitor that and take measures to cool her if needed, though he suspected the crisis had passed.

If her transition mirrored his, the entire process would take five days, give or take. All he knew for sure was that when she became cognizant, when she opened her eyes for the first time in her new body, he wanted to be nearby to tell her she was safe. That she was going to be okay. Eventually.

He spent the night in his chair, dozed when he could, awakened at any sound. No sound came from the figure on the bed. He'd pressed his ear to her back several times and couldn't hear even the faintest heartbeat. The only proof of life inside her amber shell were the orange and black patterns developing on the ridge line between her shoulder blades.

He left her side only to collect more potatoes, onions, and asparagus from his garden. It also occurred to him after hearing her story, that it might have eased his own transition to have had an infusion of milkweed leaves and blossoms during the first confusing days afterward. Combined with the chamomile and honey he kept on hand, he could make her a tea that could be helpful settling into her new existence.

Once he had laid in supplies, checking on her several times during the process, he made himself some fortifying mushroom and spearmint tea and sank into the chair he had made with his own hands as if preparing for this day.

The process itself was fascinating. Having only experienced it from the inside out, he was amazed at how tiny details in her skin changed over the next two days. While her upper body—head and breast—retained their downy white iridescence, her torso from below her ribcage past her navel to her hips was quickly turning a silky gold with small white dots distributed evenly over the top. The darker pattern was developing over her lower extremities, as layer upon layer of velvet scales spread.

By the third day, subtle ridges developed above her occipital lobes as the mounds under her closed lids expanded. It would be the most startling and unsettling change she would need to learn to negotiate. Her eyes would be larger, multifaceted, and deliver information to her brain in a way she had never experienced before.

On the fourth day, he had just sat down to sip his mushroom tea when he noticed the skin of her eyelids had effaced and retracted, leaving her new eye structure wide open. He put down his mug, leaned forward, and cocked his head. He had the distinct sense that she was conscious and looking straight at him from inside her amber shell.

Lara soared above her lighthouse home drawing in a slow, expanding breath as she circled higher and higher on the updraft. She was in her happy place, her own, private Nirvana. Everything in her life was coming into alignment. She was living in her ancestral lighthouse home, a place that felt magical and solid at the same time. A place that had been a beacon to all who were lost over the years. She had a career that gave her the same feeling. She was helping young women who might not otherwise have a good chance at life. She had a man who loved and cared for her. A celebrity in his own right, yet grounded and talented in so many ways. A man who had left that celebrity world behind for the moment and would be waiting for her when she landed. A man she adored who was willing to accept her as an equal. A man who...

Wait. What is this?

She wasn't soaring, she was lying on her side, and she wasn't breathing. How could that be? She thought about sitting up but couldn't move her arms. Then reality pushed its way in. Soaring over her lighthouse was the dream. She was back in her cave. Dreaming. But why couldn't she move. Now what's happened?

The last thing she remembered was... Oh my god! The last thing she remembered was the creature— Michael—leaping off a cliff! She had rushed to his side and...

Light hit her eyes like a river of spears and the room shattered into a thousand pieces.

Every ounce of her being wanted to thrust her arms up to deflect the glare, but she could... not... move.

She was a captor, assailed by images edged in multicolored auras. They shifted, overlapped, and resettled, over and over again, dicing her world into tiny pieces until she thought she would not survive. And then the optical carnival ride began to slow, and finally, like the brain eventually sorts out the image seen through a new pair of prescription glasses, one solid scene coalesced: She was not in her cave, but on the bed in Michael's grotto. She shifted her gaze slightly to see that he was there, sitting in his hand-carved chair, sipping from a handmade mug, his entire image edged in the bright purplish glow of ultraviolet light.

Her heart thumped hard in her chest; once, twice, three times, and then fell into a soft, even rhythm. He was looking at his mug, rocking slowly, and the sight of his torso, his shoulders, his remarkable new features, sent her a hit of memory. She'd seen him jump, she'd run to see what happened, they'd connected on an almost human level and then, the world began to spin, her legs had turned to noodles, and he was taking her into the water…

Suddenly, he put down his mug, stepped to the bedside and knelt beside her.

"Lara!"

Michael! She wanted desperately to reach out to him. It no longer mattered that his head was bare and his eyes were so big, or that his body was covered in feathered scales. She wanted to touch him like coming home, but she couldn't move a muscle or make a sound. She could only look at him in desperation like a person with a spine severed at the neck being kept alive by machines.

He pressed his ear against her back a moment, then drew away, placed big hands on either side of her face, then gazed deeply into her eyes. "Your heart is beating again. I know you can hear me, because that is how it was for me."

She thought to blink, shift her pupils, anything to let him know she heard him. But her body didn't respond.

He kept talking in that deep, low voice that somehow quelled the fear building inside her. "You are in the last stages of a second transition. Your heart is starting to pump. I know it's frightening, but you will be released soon, probably by noon tomorrow, if this goes like it did for me."

Tomorrow? She couldn't possibly exist in this personal prison another minute. And then it hit her. *Transition? To what?* Was she going to break out of this confinement and look like him?

The image before her started to shift again, as if her brain could only handle one concept at a time. She wanted to squeeze her eyes shut against the dizzying scene, but she could not. And then his voice came again, soft and rhythmic, an almost hypnotic cadence and smooth timbre more soothing than the actual words.

"You are going to be all right. The amber will release you soon. First, you will be able to blink your eyes. Then you will be able to move your arms. It will happen soon. You are going to be all right."

Assailed by images she could not unsee, she made herself focus on the beat of her heart growing stronger by the moment. Or, if it was possible, the more she focused on her heartbeat, the stronger it seemed to get. Okay. Maybe she did have some control. She closed her eyes and concentrated, feeling the blood pulse all the way to the tips of her fingers, and in the tiny valves in the arteries of her legs.

Wait! She closed her eyes? She opened and closed them again, saw the tiny featherlike scales around Michael's eyes arrange themselves into smile lines that were almost familiar.

"All right," he said, standing up and moving a few steps away. "It's happening."

Her body responded, her eyes rapidly blinking, her fingers twitching, until, in her great enthusiasm, her elbow jerked sideways and broke a slit in the amber coating. And then the entire capsule expanded, like breaking the vacuum seal on a package of nuts. The pressure release popped open her lungs and she gasped in her first breath since this ordeal began.

Images spun again. But she was breathing. She concentrated on one of the images until it settled and cleared. He was at the sink breaking leaves into a crock of boiling water. She moved her shoulders back and forth until the amber shell split more and she was able to move her neck, brace her arms on the bed and push into a sitting position. She dragged in a ragged breath, her lungs expanding more each time she did it.

By the time she'd bent her knees to split the lower part of the shell, he was sitting beside her again. This creature with Michael's DNA, his smile, looking like a god from some ancient myth, offered her a steaming mug of tea.

CHAPTER 30 - CRAGGY PASS

Jenera cinched up Sloane's backpack and turned him around. "How does that feel?"

The young man straightened and smiled. "Not bad. But these boots are the best."

He tightened laces all the way up to his knees on the pair of boots Helena had fashioned for him from a pair in the castoff pile at Lillit Compound. Felted inserts filled his high arches to relieve the pressure on his calves and made it possible for him to keep up with the others all day.

They had spent their first night well off the trail, Bryn and Peck taking turns on watch to make sure they weren't seen by Esteban or any of his men. Unarmed and slow moving, the only thing they had going for them was Sloan's knowledge of the facility and the element of surprise.

Jenera pulled her cape around her, wishing they could have had a fire, but they couldn't take that chance. Sending Peck out ahead to make sure the coast was clear, she, Bryn, and Sloan packed up their gear and were ready to make the next leg of the journey which, according to Sloan, would bring them to within sight of the high caverns of Terra City. Jenera was excited not only at the prospect of rescuing a crysl that belonged to the Messenger, Lara, but secretly, Sloan's words while he was still in the infirmary had lit a fire in her gut she had never felt before. What secrets lay hidden in The Vault?

She hefted her backpack over her shoulder, slipped her arms through the straps, and cinched it down. At Bryn's nod, she climbed up over the embankment where they'd spent the night and followed him back to the trail. Her body felt stiff and tired, but her mind flowed with possibilities.

This place, The Vault, contained a storehouse of information that had been preserved since the before the *Dannais* time. Could this be the treasure her mother and father had made it their mission to find? One foot in front of the other the trail disappeared under her feet as she let her mind wander, a good way to ignore the fatigue building in her calves.

She had been fourteen when her mother told her she and her father were leading the expedition to find the place Bryn's parents had passed through when venturing into the *Dannais* valley. Her people had heard of things in the wider world from other travelers passing through. There was supposed to be a great storehouse of riches, and, according to Bryn's family, a site of great historical significance. This is what sparked her parents' interest.

Her mother had always retold her grandmother's stories, but she was by far the more practical of the Spirit Leaders. Legends were one thing, but they had to survive in the real world. If this news was true—that there was a great treasure trove of knowledge not that far from their valley—they might for the first time have access to information about the world before the Great Destruction. Information that could change the course of their lives.

"This place—Terra City—is not that far away, according to Bryn's family," her mother had told her. "Just a few days' travel."

Jenera had clung to her mother when they said their goodbyes. "But what if something happens to you? How can I go on?"

"Don't worry about us. We're just going to go have a look and see for ourselves if there's anything of value to be gained. If there's something to it, we'll come back and organize a team to do a proper exploration." Her mother had gripped the amulet around her neck, a bright emerald gem of a vessel her grandmother had passed down to her. "Take care of your grandfather and the crysls, and when we get back, I'll pass this amulet along to you, all right? Soon, you will be Spirit Leader and take over where I leave off."

"But what if you don't come back?" Jenera couldn't explain the fear building in her gut. It was the first time they would be separated, and she was overcome with the strongest foreboding she had ever felt in her young life.

Her mother smiled and smoothed her hand over Jenera's hair. "We'll do the ceremony as soon as I return, and then you'll know all. I promise."

It was the last time she'd seen her parents. A team of men from Gate Compound set out to find them, but an early winter storm had blocked the high pass, and they returned without completing the journey. Jenera had vowed to go and search for them herself, but her grandfather had forbid her to leave. "You are all we have left of the line of Spirit Leaders, Jenera." He had promised they'd send another search party at the spring thaw. But when spring came, they'd had a really long, cold winter and the upper passes never cleared of deep, impenetrable snow. That had been two years ago.

At the sound of footfalls ahead, Bryn signaled for them to get off the trail. They climbed over a massive fallen pine and crouched behind a huge granite boulder. Peck joined them with his finger to his lips, then when they had moved where there was no chance of being seen or heard from the trail, he whispered: "Esteban is coming this way. He's alone."

Jenera and Bryn exchanged glances. To Sloan he hissed: "How much further?"

Sloan dug in his backpack, pulled out his water container, took a drink. "We're still climbing, but once we start downhill, maybe half a day?"

Jenera closed her eyes and slumped against the rock, remembering Sloan's words. The bodies he'd seen just as he'd come out of his chrysalis—that would have been about two years ago...

"Jenera? You alright?" Bryn whispered. "Do you want me to carry your pack?"

She looked at him blankly, and realized she'd been tromping blindly over the trail, her thoughts deep inside her head. She smiled at him now, grateful for his concern. "I'll be fine," she lied. If what she suspected was true, she might never be fine again.

The footsteps drew nearer. They hunkered down, fell silent as the lone traveler made his way back toward the *Dannais* Valley. When they could no longer hear his footfalls, Sloan stood up. "He'll be heading for Rowan. To make his ransom bid."

"Good," Bryn said, hefting his pack. "Rowan will keep him occupied while we secure the crysl."

CHAPTER 31 – THE BEACON CALLS

Michael and Lara stood a short distance apart on the top of Ship Rock, their wings fully expanded, testing the wind. "Either we wait for the wind to pick up, or we start from higher ground," Lara said, the latter probably the best idea. While she had marveled at how quickly she'd adapted to balancing with the great spread of wings from between her shoulders, the balance wasn't the same as that of her glider. The wings were heavier, more supple, and capable of flapping, so they didn't need as much of an updraft. But that was the rub. She had never had to pump a glider wing to fly, and after witnessing Michael's disastrous first flights, she was a bit afraid to try.

She'd spent two days at his cavern home, letting him feed and care for her until she was able to stand and move around without crashing into things because of her strange new visual input. But once under control, that vision gave her incredible new insights into the full color spectrum of the natural world. Plants that had been just beautiful flowers to her former senses, now were highlighted by intense hues that beckoned to her like the smell of a really good meal. Everything was edged in color like the one and only time she'd taken a microdose of psilocybin. It was beautiful, intense, and distracting. If it wasn't for Michael right there beside her, she might find her way back to her cave and hide.

They had stood on "Ship Rock" a couple of times, letting their wings expand and deflate, "Just to feel what it's like," Michael had coached. But she knew he hadn't lifted up to fly on his own again yet for a reason. He had taken a terrible fall his first and second time out and he wasn't ready to try again any time soon.

Instead, they had spent their time getting to know one another. Again. The new Michael looked more like The Alien except for his very recognizable face. But she relaxed a little when he gently reminded her, she had changed a bit herself.

To say that she was a woman with a pair of wings stuck on her back like a Halloween costume was a massive understatement. The wings, gauzy and supple when not in use, were a bit cumbersome. It was a reality she had to learn to live with, along with psychedelic vision. But once they lay together in his bed, their bodies entwined, it didn't take long to forget all that strangeness and give themselves over to the incredible sensation of their new and surprisingly sensitive "naughty bits".

Their new bodies were designed to ensure there would be no question of reproduction. The moment his hands moved down her shoulders, over her breasts, and down to the feathered layers between her legs, all thoughts of segments and scales and antenna and wings dissolved into pure, unquenchable, heat. If this is what it was like for the actual Monarchs, she understood why there were so many of them.

Again and again, they tested the limits of their new bodies, found new ways to please, to experience, to let go. A thousand years of lost time fell away. And at the same time it felt like only yesterday, he'd proposed to her on the cliffs, sliding the beautiful gold and aquamarine ring on her finger. The ring she still wore and a sign of his promise to her. They erased the years and the distance between them one embrace, one kiss at a time.

Now they stood on the precipice of what could be the greatest adventure of their lives, or the end of everything. Sooner or later, they had to try it and as far as she was concerned, it was better to get it over with. "I say we go today. Now. From right here."

Michael stood tall, like the empty husk of himself that stood nearby on the rock, his eyes flashing with courage and determination. "All right," he said. "We're in this thing—whatever this thing is—together."

"On three," she said, filling her lungs with a huge gulp of air. "One… two… "

They jumped together, their eyes locked on each other for the first moment, then Lara shifted her attention to giving her wings a powerful pump, gaining altitude almost immediately. Another good surge, then a right bank using her arms to guide her direction, and she was soaring over the water. She looked around for Michael and her heart cringed when she didn't see him, until suddenly there he was swooping in a wide arc just below her, correcting, then pumping, then sailing up into the sun. My god, it was amazing, exhilarating, magical.

They circled higher and higher, then swooped back over land. Every now and then, she caught a glimpse of Michael's face, his smile lighting up his eyes, ultraviolet light reflecting off his wings. On and on they flew, picking up nuances in tactics, maneuvers, dives, and climbs, making several more passes until she signed him to head toward her Eyre.

She arrived first at her ledge, amazed at her ability to control her landing. Michael's landing was more like sliding into home plate, but he made it in one piece without damaging anything but his pride.

Breathless and elated, they waited impatiently for their wings to soften and settle before falling into each other's arms.

"That was epic!" he cried, releasing her to shoot his arms over his head. "Better than Mavericks!"

Lara laughed until tears ran down her cheeks. This Michael was so close to the Michael she had fallen in love with in another world. "You remember! Mavericks!"

He blinked at her with those big eyes for a moment. "I did, didn't I?"

She beamed at him, hope filling her all the way up. "Yes you did."

She had just circled an arm around his waist, and stood by his side, gazing out over the view of the valley below when the strobe found them. "Oh my gosh. There it is again! Did you see it?"

She gasped in a breath as it swept over them and then away like an ebbing wave. It happened every time they stepped outside together.

Whether they were at her Eyre or his grotto, the strobe found her, overtook all thought, sweeping across her vision in an ever-increasing arc, demanding her attention. Each time it swept over a point far on the horizon, there pulsed an ultraviolet light that seemed to strike out across the distance and connect directly to her soul. She stood transfixed, as the strobe hit once, twice, three times, always with the same, lightning-strike intensity, until she could scarcely breathe. She turned away before the fourth strobe could hit, and looked straight into Michael's eyes, which were even wider than her own, if that were possible.

"You saw it then?"

His expression told her he had, though he stood speechless a moment longer before he answered, nearly breathless with awe. "I think it's showing us the way home."

Up on the meadow, Ekiria and Alta lay on their backs in the sun, on break from morning lessons. Ekiria shot a finger at billowing clouds in the sky. "A bear, see? There's it's big legs, fat belly and tiny tail."

Alta bunched up her nose. "I don't see it. Where?"

"Come on, Allie. Look, it's holding a fish in it's paws. Don't you see it?"

"I don't know, maybe," Alta whined.

Helena called out to them to come under the tall pines to continue their lessons in the shade.

"Oh, darn, the wind is blowing away his head, now he's… "

"A big butterfly," Alta said, shading her eyes.

"No, not a butterfly, silly…"

"No. Really," Alta cried. She jumped to her feet and pointed into the distance. "A great big butterfly. See?"

Ekiria squinted her eyes and got up.

"Girls, come on. We've got a lot to cover," her mother called.

Ekiria angled her head toward her mother a moment, but she couldn't take her eyes off what she saw, watching with her mouth wide open. Not one, but two butterflies, circling and dipping, coming closer and closer. They weren't just big, they were…

Alta came over and grabbed her hand. "Those can't be real."

"Mother!" Ekiria cried. "Come here. Look!"

Helena headed off across the meadow toward the girls. "Now ladies, I don't have time for this today, I…" Then looking up to see what Ekiria was squinting at, she dropped her basket full of treats. "What in the wide world?"

A moment later, two giant monarchs swept over the open space, their shifting shadows circling one another over the meadow, before they fluttered up in higher and higher arcs, then slid away beyond the granite cliffs.

CHAPTER 32 - TERRA CITY

When Jenera stepped to the top of the craggy overlook next to Sloan, she was stunned into silence. She had expected to see the vast valley Sloan had told them about along the way—high, sharp peaks, pumice dunes, hot springs, and volcanic domes. She had lived her entire life under towering rock formations and the roar of water carving its way through ancient stone. The landscape he described sounded like it could be on another planet.

Instead, when she reached the top, tired and out of breath because of the altitude, there was nothing but polished granite and more mountain peaks as far as she could see. Her legs and feet ached with the miles they'd endured, and she couldn't imagine what it was like for Sloan. Disappointment sank into her bones. "I thought you said it was downhill from the summit?"

Sloan's bony shoulders drooped and he puckered his lips a moment before he spoke. "It is. Mostly. By nightfall, if we keep moving at our current pace, we should be able to see Terra City off that way." He pointed toward the highest peaks in the distance. Jenera blew out a tired breath, then glanced at each of them in turn.

Peck took a couple of steps forward, hands on hips, and scanned the horizon. "If we want to be back ahead of the alignment, we have to keep going." Despite his pragmatic tone, Jenera had to respect his opinion. There was no point in complaining. Bryn's friend, Peck was nothing if not committed to the success of his assigned mission, whatever it was. She didn't know him well, but Bryn trusted him and that was good enough for her.

She let her pack slide off her back and flexed some of the fatigue from her shoulders.

Bryn stepped beside her, sending her a sympathetic look. He lowered his head and rubbed the back of his neck a moment before he spoke. "So, march hard the rest of the day, one more night on the trail, and arrive about mid-day next? That would still get us back during the alignment event," he said, his gaze touching Jenera's a moment before he continued. "without so much hardship on Jenera and Sloan."

His steady gaze held a silent pledge to stay by her side no matter what, and something more. They hadn't had a real private moment since Esteban's treachery had been revealed. That fact hung between them like a rock in the shoe, growing sharper with every step. Did his actions nullify their agreement? Or simply make it that much more of a threat? The answer remained to be seen, but she was grateful Bryn was here with her now. The rest would have to wait until they had the crysl back in their possession.

"Sounds about right," Sloan said. His tone suggested he'd read questions between them. He glanced at Jenera briefly before he turned away.

He had agreed it would take two days when she'd asked, and she realized now as the miles piled up, he'd probably left off the additional day to please her. She would have to be more careful in the future not to put that kind of pressure on him. He was just a boy, after all.

"Well," she said, hitching her pack up higher on her shoulder. "We'd better get started then."

Eight hours and four pairs of aching feet later, they were looking down a switchback trail to what travelers had called The Owens as the last rays of a setting sun turned distant peaks orange.

Sloan stopped and let his pack slide down to rest against a granite outcrop, then dug in the pack and came out with an object Jenera could not identify. He handed it to Bryn.

"There," he said, pointing in the distance. "Take a look while there's still enough light. Follow that ridge down. There's an obvious man-made structure. You should be able to see a light burning at the main arch."

Bryn sent the boy a puzzled look a moment before lifting the narrow cones to his eyes, the way he'd seen him do it. "Where did you get these?" he asked.

Sloan kicked at the dirt. "Like I said. When travelers came to the City, I sometimes, took stuff. These are binoculars. Pretty handy, right?"

Jenera folded her arms over her chest while Bryn acknowledged seeing the light, then proceeded to scan the entire area. "Why didn't you bring these out before? They're amazing."

"Been around for centuries," Sloan said without the slightest hint of disdain.

Jenera laughed softly and closed her eyes a moment. His confidence relieved a nagging tension that had been building over the last part of the day. The closer they got to finding the truth about her parents, the harder it was to take the next step. Her eyes popped open when Bryn pushed the binoculars into her hands.

"Oh!" she said, turning the dials to focus as Sloan instructed her. The distant valley looked so close through the lenses she felt she could step right into it. She scanned the zig-zag trail down the ridge, followed it to the bottom and suddenly there it was. A wide, natural stone cave faced eastward. It was evident there had at one time been many structures marching up the hill, although now they were mostly crumbled to ruins. At the top level a massive structure had survived, perhaps because it was tucked inside the giant maw of the cave. Its sides swept up and came together in an arch like praying hands. At the base of the structure, there were a pair of massive doors, a light did indeed cast a faint glow over the top of them. On either side of the structure, stone walls spread out and up, and would have sealed the cave from top to bottom, except that it had crumbled apart in places, leaving gaping holes.

"One could hardly call it a city," Jenera said, handing the binoculars to Peck. "I thought there would be more to it."

Sloan set his shoulders, excitement creeping into his eyes. "There is, actually. The bulk of it extends into the cave. It looks a lot more impressive when you're standing at the base of it." He lowered himself to lean against a fallen pine, showing the same fatigue Jenera felt. "It is actually downhill from here now, I promise, but it's still a few hours' march to get there, so it's best we rest here for the night, get a fresh start in the morning."

Assembled around a small fire, they heard in the distance what Sloan speculated were wolves, and later, after their fire burned low and they had bedded down, he identified the sharp chirps of a mountain lion mother calling her young all too close to their camp.

Jenera shivered and wrapped her arms around her knees. She buried her face in her arms. She couldn't remember ever feeling any lonelier. A moment later, Bryn's arm came around her shoulders and pulled her into his side. Without a word, she let herself sink into his warmth. If they were back in *Dannais* Valley, that closeness would be questioned. She was, after all, betrothed to Esteban. But here at what felt like the top of the world, Bryn had shown her what freedom from Esteban could be. Her heart warmed to the thought, and she let it sink in. Morning found her curled inside his cape beside the remaining coals of the fire.

Bryn offered a chunk of honey cake from his pack. "You sleep okay?"

She propped herself up on an elbow and looked around. Sloan was packing up his gear, Peck was nowhere in sight.

"Where's Peck?" she asked, taking the offered cake.

Bryn cleaned crumbs off his hands on his pants. "He's scouting ahead."

She sat up and took a bite of the sticky cake, thinking about what this day could hold in store. Finding and bringing home the Messenger's crysl was their first objective, one which could not fail. But the prospect of discovering what had happened to her parents—possibly finding their remains—made her want to curl inside herself. Every step she took on the trail took her closer to that possibility and the thought of it was paralyzing. How had she let her fears—her grief—pull her so far off track? Her responsibility was to the crysls. She couldn't be weak or paralyzed in this moment. She was the Spirit Leader. Everyone was counting on her.

She pulled Bryn's cloak tighter around her shoulders as she watched him finish packing up his things. He picked up a stick to spread the coals of the fire, but when he lifted his eyes to hers, he stopped and sat beside her.

"Are you alright?"

"I'm good. I've been distracted, though, thinking about my parents."

He gave her a thin-lipped smile. "Understandable."

"I'm ready for whatever comes next. But there's something I have to do before we go any further. Something I should have done before we left the valley." She pulled a leather bag from her backpack and laid the contents out on a rock near her feet, then glanced around their camp to find Sloan. He was curled up against a pine tree just outside the fire ring.

"Sloan?"

He raised his head quickly as if he'd been feigning sleep and sent her a questioning look.

"I need your help."

He stood, brushing pine needles off his bottom where he'd been sitting in the dirt. "Whatever you need."

"I'm going to perform a quick ceremony before we make the last march to the Vault. I want you to do this with me." She selected two chrism jars from the items.

He cocked his head. "Me?"

"You have the gene, don't you? Who else is going to do it?"

"Well, I… guess so."

"Just stand still a moment." He did as he was asked and let her paint his face with the green and gold colors from the jars, then did the same for herself. "We are going to ask for the strength of our ancestors as we go forward today."

His eyebrows arched a moment, and when understanding dawned, he took a deep breath and bowed his head to her. "As you wish," he said, almost in a whisper, and she knew he would take the gravity of this moment seriously.

She picked up a piece of pine duff and drew a large enough circle on the ground for both of them, then stepped inside and motioned for him to step in with her.

Chin held high, she faced him and took both of his hands in hers, then lifted her gaze to the farthest Western horizon. "Not for us, but for the true *Dannais*, we ask your strength and guidance for the journey ahead, wherever it takes us."

Without being prompted, he repeated, "Wherever it takes us."

She gave him a smile and a nod, then used her sleeve to wipe the paint from their faces. She was brushing away the remains of the circle in the dirt when Peck returned to the camp.

He squinted his eyes at the three of them a moment as if he sensed he had interrupted a private moment, but instead of acknowledging or asking questions, he shifted straight into Peck mode. "I'd say we've got a good four hours march to get to Terra City. Best we get started."

Bryn cleared his throat, spread the coals and doused them with water.

"Right you are. Best get started." He stood, offered a hand to Jenera, and levered her up.

Jenera had to admire the way Sloan took the lead and forged ahead on his misshaped legs without complaint. She kept her own aches and pains to herself. Her feet were screaming for some relief when at last he held up his hand for them to stop.

"Come here and have a look," Sloan said. "But stay in the shadows."

They closed ranks, moved in beside him, and followed his pointing finger down the trail to a massive structure at the bottom of the narrow canyon they were about to descend.

"That's the primary entrance to the Vault. It was designed after the Chapel of the Holy Cross in Sedona… " he said, turning back to them, then realized, having had no access to anything outside their valley but stories passed down from travelers, they had no idea about the famous architecture he was talking about. "You'll, um, see when we get closer.

With new energy, and yes, the fact that they were finally going downhill, Sloan took each switch back with new enthusiasm.

"The whole area sits on a complex of lava domes formed by massive volcanic action fifty or sixty thousand years ago," he said, waving his arms to take in the view before them.

"So, I'm assuming the lava is inactive?" Peck asked.

Sloan slipped but caught himself on some loose pumice rock. "Oh, it's active alright. Not a day goes by when you're in The Vault you don't feel a few tremors. That was the whole basis of power for the complex. Geothermal energy. The lava sits under the domes even today, that explains some of the more recent incidents, and unfortunately, compromised the power plant and The Vault."

Jenera caught up with him, matching his pace. "So, tell me about this vault. People say there's a treasure? At least, that's what my parents went looking for."

Sloan slowed as the switchback shifted to a steep place where they needed to climb over rocks.

"According to his diary, The Vault was my dad's pride and joy. There were a bank of computers and power generators to keep the city connected to the rest of the world. But he predicted a cataclysmic event that could easily knock out power and the ability to communicate, so he created and fortified a massive, old-school library filled with books on every subject possible. His diary told all about it. And he was right. Long before I emerged, there was a catastrophic failure that took out the internal power plant, some of the structure failed, and many chambers within the main complex were filled—and are still filled—with steaming water fed by the natural geothermal heat under the caves. Few if any from the original colony survived.

"But you did," Jenera corrected.

"Because I was still in my chrysalis, I didn't need oxygen or water. And, I was inside a hardened chamber and the door lock was uncompromised. My air source to the surface wasn't damaged. But there are many places where a cave-in could seal a person off in a small area. The oxygen would get depleted pretty fast, unless there was someone around to dig them out. I suspect that's what happened to the people I told you about that came here a couple of years ago. A cave in that trapped them without enough air to survive."

"My parents," Jenera said, the familiar ache squeezed her heart. "You're probably talking about them."

Sloan fell silent. Of course. He'd figured that out. "I can show you… if you want."

Bryn moved up beside them. "How did you find them if they were sealed in a cave in?"

"Because in the same way they were instantly blocked off, another event could shift, reopening the chamber. It is the basic flaw of construction in this place. The underlying volcanic and geothermal structures of this area means seismic events are common and there's no way to predict where or when. The only certainty is that they will occur, and often."

As if speaking up to confirm the danger, the ground beneath them rumbled, then shifted beneath Jenera's feet. She half squatted to maintain her balance, and shot a wary glance back to Sloan.

"Like I said. It's common. The good news is, that same phenomena is the reason we can still get into The Vault. The Main entrance is blocked off, but an incident further up tumbled in a massive wall. That's how we'll get in."

Jenera fell silent and concentrated on putting one foot in front of the other. Finding her parents' remains was not something she was looking forward to, especially if they had been crushed and mangled, but it would provide some sense of peace knowing exactly what had happened to them.

They had traversed a wide, dried-up mud flat, dropped down another set of steep switchbacks, and had just rounded the shoulder of a towering stone cliff when Sloan stopped in front of Jenera so quickly, she almost crashed into him.

"Sorry," he said low, "There it is." His voice held a note of reverence.

The massive structure that looked like a pair of praying hands from a distance now stood before them ten times taller than anything the *Dannais* had ever built.

The doors that had looked so substantial at its base from afar were set askew, one side standing open enough to drive one of their grain wagons through.

"The main entrance?" she asked.

"Yeah. Like I said, it's blocked." Sloan pointed to the area to the right of the entrance. "We'll circle around to the side, head up the stone stairway, and come in through that upper chamber."

Peck stepped in front of the group. "If Esteban's men have posted a lookout, they'll probably be right by the doors."

"Makes sense," Bryn agreed.

"Right," Sloan said. "Travelers often use that area for shelter when they come this way. As long as they don't go too deep inside, it's safe."

"And if they go deeper?" Bryn asked.

"Like I said, that area is unstable. A party could very easily get trapped in a seismic event."

Sloan hooked his thumbs in the straps of his pack and continued. "I think you guys should stay back here inside the tree line for now and let me go in and check it out. If they see me, well, they know I've been with their boss, so I could probably talk my way past them."

Sloan pursed his lips, took the binoculars out of his pack. He scanned the doorway. "I don't' see any activity, but they'll have the advantage if they're inside the vault doors. We wouldn't see them until it was too late."

He handed the binoculars to Peck and pointed to the far side of the massive structure. "You can see a section of the stairway, just there. Now follow it up to the right, and there's an opening. That will drop you into the cavern outside my old chamber. It's one of the most secure areas left in the complex, outside the actual library vault."

Peck handed the binoculars to Bryn. He looked through them a moment, then nodded.

Sloan looked at each one in turn, ending with Jenera. "Stay back here inside the shadows and watch.

If I don't signal you at least ten minutes after I pass through the doors, you guys skirt through the trees and get up those stairs. I'll meet you there."

"And what if his men don't let you go?" Peck asked.

Sloan drew in a long breath and blew it out. "I have a plan for that."

Jenera's stomach lurched. "I think we should stay together. He's just a boy, I—"

Bryn pressed his hand on her shoulder and nodded to Sloan. "A boy who lived practically alone in this place for two years. He knows what he's doing, Jenera. Let him go."

Sloan gave her a confident smile. "I've done this many times when people camped inside the doors. I'll be all right."

Jenera couldn't help scooping him into her arms and giving him a long hug. "You better. That's an order."

Sloan pressed his lips together and watched them retreat into the tree line, then he marched straight up to the front door in his knee high, laced up boots like he owned the place.

CHAPTER 33 – CONVICTION

Lara and Michael woke in each other's arms inside her cave, the remains of a fire glowing softly in the early morning light. Their flight testing, and subsequent love making on the stone floor had drained nearly all of Lara's energy so that she could barely move.

She rolled to face him and smoothed her hand over his chest, feeling it rise and fall, until at last, he turned to face her.

"Good morning," he said sleepily.

"Would have been a little more comfortable to wind up at your grotto rather than my cave."

He rolled on his back and pulled her over on top of him. "I'll keep that in mind next time I follow you off a cliff."

She smiled into his eyes, getting used to seeing her reflections in the sky-blue facets. They were strange. They were different, but his expression held the same intensity, the same conviction, the same devotion she had always seen in his eyes when he looked at her.

"So, where do we go from here?" she asked, not really expecting an answer. Whatever expectations they'd had in the past no longer applied.

Michael considered a moment, then rolled his gaze around the roof of the cave. "Well, isn't it obvious?"

Lara surveyed the scattered cannisters, the sarcophagus bed, the metallic blanket, the cold stone floor. "What? That I need to move my operation to your place? That's a given."

A soft laugh rumbled up through his chest into hers. "A given. For sure. But I was thinking about the beacon. I can't get it out of my mind."

"Me either. Mostly." Laying in his arms was a pretty good buffer, but she saw it in her own mind now as though she were replaying the moment. "It's growing stronger, and I'm afraid there will soon come a moment when we won't be able to resist."

"I agree. We don't have much time." He stared at her a long moment, letting his words sink in. "It appears to be lining up just as Jenera predicted. Everything is falling into place."

"So, you believe Jenera is right. That this isn't just a horrific mistake? That we were destined to come here and lead the first migration of the *Dannais*?"

"It's not what I believe, Lara. It's what *is*. That doctor, Patrick, never had any of this in mind when he developed the UV serum. But it did happen. The world is obviously not what it was before we got sucked into this thing, but we're here now, and we have to deal with *this* reality. Jenera and her people have been planning this for their entire lives."

She drew in a long breath and let it out slowly. Like the old Michael, he looked at the world through logic and reason. And he was absolutely right. It did no good to try to fit things in the framework of the past. That was gone. All gone. He had resigned himself to that fact and it was time she joined him in this new reality.

She rolled off of him and stood, adjusting the weight of the gauzy wings at her back, a sensation she doubted she would ever get used to. The silken robe

Rowan had given her lay over her makeshift bed. She slipped it over her head, realizing now the reason for the slit in the back of the gown from the nape of the neck to the waistband. Rowan's Cora had already made the second transition. Interesting. And also frightening, considering she had died in childbirth soon after.

Lara forced her thoughts back to the present. She had a lot to be thankful for. They had the will and the means to survive. There were changed, but they were stronger, and they had some mad skills. They were learning more every day. And soon, they would go on another journey into the unknown. Together.

The segments of his back muscles shifted as he stood and donned the sheath he wore around his hips. She couldn't take her eyes off him. "You seem so settled. Your beautiful home on the dam, your furniture, your garden. You have created a sense of balance for yourself in this place. Are you willing to leave it for a place that is entirely unknown?"

"Are you?"

Lara thought about Jenera and her commitment to the crysls. How generations of *Dannais* were counting on her to organize a migration. How, as a person so young, had she seen her path so clearly before her? She was ready to sacrifice everything and follow it to the end.

However fantastic and unbelievable the events leading to this moment, Jenera had foreseen the entire thing. There was no doubt in the young woman's mind that Lara had been sent here to lead the first migration of her people into the wider world. What would they find on this journey? Lara didn't want to guess. But the one thing she knew for sure was—to her surprise and relief—there was no doubt she and Michael were in this thing—whatever this thing was—together, and nothing would ever have the power to separate them again.

"Yes," she said, and she believed it. "With you by my side, I can do anything."

He fixed her with his fantastic eyes and lifted a brow. "So, the next step is?"

Lara strode to the edge of the granite ledge and scanned the horizon. "Fulfilling Jenera's request."

Michael crossed the ledge and stood next to her, then slipped his arm around the small of her back. "Which is?"

"Present ourselves before her people. Prove that we exist. Rowan already knows of both of us, but according to Jenera, the *Dannais* won't believe it until they see it."

"And how do you propose to do that?"

She closed her eyes, drew in a long, slow breath through her nose, and let it out slowly, remembering a time in another life when she'd taken a leap from a granite cliff in this very valley. The thought of it triggered an adrenalin rush that prickled the base of the wings in her back. "I have a plan."

CHAPTER 34 – ALL THINGS GO

Jenera stared down at what appeared to be a deep sink hole just inside the broken walls. Sloan had been right about one thing. The damage to the side of the cavern was so extensive, the noonday sun shown inside like a beacon, illuminating columns of steam rising from the massive pool of water at the bottom. Whatever protections the builders had put into place had been devastatingly defeated by Mother Nature. What remained looked like a soaring cathedral with the light shining through straight from Heaven.

On the walls opposite the water there were another set of doors, which Jenera assumed by Sloan's description, was the interior air lock passage to the actual vault living quarters and library.

"We're certainly not going to go down there," Peck announced, taking a step back. "You can feel the heat from here."

"But it's the only way in," Jenera argued. "There has to be a way."

Bryn fixed his gaze on Jenera. He'd seen how she'd suffered when her parents went missing, and she knew he would do anything to help her deal with that loss.

Peck picked up a rock, threw it into the abyss, and dusted off his hands, then raised his arm to indicate the steaming body of water before them. "This is obviously a dead end," he said on a laugh. "No one, including Esteban could have crossed that."

"He could and he did."

They turned at the sound of Sloan's voice as it echoed in the cathedral-like chamber.

"Sloan!" Jenera rushed toward him and wrapped him in a welcoming hug. "Did you see anyone? Esteban's men?"

He dropped his pack, sat down, and started unlacing his boots. "Yeah, I saw them."

"So, what happened? I was beginning to worry they'd stopped you."

He loosened each boot, thrust out his legs, and leaned back on his elbows. "They let me pass because they were dead."

Jenera gasped. "Dead?"

Sloan slid off his boots and wiggled his toes, then let out a sigh of relief. "That tremor we felt back up the mountain just before we came down? I'm guessing it was centered here, near the front gate. It's happened there before. A larger quake weakened that structure a long time ago, and every new one takes down a little more. I saw the remains of a fire just inside the opening, and when I went further in, I saw a boot attached to a foot sticking out from under a pile of rubble."

"So you think they were crushed?"

Sloan shrugged. "At least one person was. Esteban typically left two men here. But, I only saw the one foot."

Jenera sat down beside him, taking the opportunity to rest as it was clear that despite the special boots Helena had made him, his feet were suffering fatigue. "How far are we from where you discovered the other bodies?"

Sloan sent her an understanding look. "Not far from here. We have to pass the location to get to The Vault."

Jenera looked at Bryn. "I want to rest a bit and then keep going." The ground below answered with a mild vibration. Her gaze shot to Sloan.

"An aftershock," he said, pulling a canteen from his pack. "You can expect to feel them throughout the rest of the time we're here. Comes with the territory."

Peck's face was visibly pale. He backed a few steps away. "Shouldn't we, you know, go back outside?"

She lowered her eyes a moment, then met Bryn's and then Sloan's. The tremors were unsettling. She didn't blame Peck for being hesitant. But she'd come all this way and she wasn't going back. "I came here to get the crysl and that's exactly what I'm going to do. By myself if I have to."

"You won't have to." Bryn knelt beside her, dug a jug of water out of his pack and offered it to her. "Peck, why don't you keep watch at the entrance, signal us if there's a problem."

Jenera stood at the edge of the sinkhole next to Bryn and Sloan; a musty, sulfur odor assaulted her nostrils. The sinkhole was about a hundred meters across; one half the circumference was a sheer wall of the type of granite Jenera had traversed her entire life. Without climbing gear, there was no way they could get around to the doors from that side. The other side was asymmetrical, with rock falls just as forbidding. She glanced over her shoulder to see Peck's silhouette in the sunlit space at the tumbled wreck opening to the cavern.

"So, I know it doesn't look like it from here," Sloan said, "but once we get over those boulders, we can walk along that ledge. It's narrow, but safe, I promise. My chamber—the place where I came out of my chrysalis—is to the right of those doors. The original cave-in is just outside there."

He leveled his gaze at Jenera, and she understood that he was warning her of what they would find. Bryn touched his hand to her low back. "You sure you want to do this?"

"Do I have a choice?"

He pressed his lips together. "I suppose not."

"Then, let's get to it. We've already spent more time than we planned, and I don't expect the journey back to go any faster. Rowan is probably wearing a groove in his floor pacing with worry."

Getting over the boulders proved to be a little more of a challenge than Sloan had let on, but once she had climbed over the last one, the going got easier.

When they came to the area about fifty feet in front of Sloan's chamber, he put his hand on her shoulder. "Off to your right, near that rock fall." He indicated the place with a nod.

Jenera dragged her upper lip through her teeth. Bryn's eyes asked the question. "Okay," she said. "I'm okay." She took a few steps in the direction. Bryn shadowed her closely.

There were indeed two separate locations, about six feet apart, where what looked like human remains lay in various stages of decomposition. One skull was crushed, the skeletal bones scattered out of place; the other was completely intact, almost perfect, as if the person had been trapped in a protected space. She inched closer, squatted down, and glanced up at Bryn. "What do you think happened here?"

He moved in by her side and squatted next to her. "I don't have a lot of experience with caving, but I do know that if a person is trapped in a small space, they will eventually use up all the oxygen." He shifted his gaze to the crushed remains. "That person was maybe luckier. Death came quickly."

Jenera bowed her head and let the tears flow. "Judging by the size of the remains, the crushed skeleton is much larger than the one left intact. If these are my parents, the larger one was likely my father, though I don't see anything I could identify."

Bryn pressed his lips together and nodded. "Makes sense."

Drawing on the strength he lent her by his touch, she crawled closer to the other remains and gazed at the torso, taking in the structure of the perfectly formed skull. There was still a scrap of cloth partially covering its neck. Holding her breath, she extended shaking fingers, lifted it away and gasped when she found what she was looking for. There, under the shredded fabric was a leather thong that seemed to be weighted down behind the neck. With a quick glance at Bryn, she lifted the strap and pulled, until, tumbling two of the neck vertebrae apart, a heavy pendant swung free.

Her mother's amulet.

CHAPTER 35 - LET THE FIRE FALL

Rowan tossed in his bed, an image of his Cora slowly slipping away from him haunted his dreams. She suffered on the other side of an impenetrable wall against which he beat his fists to no avail. And then, his eyes fluttering open, he realized he wasn't pounding on a wall, someone was pounding on his door.

"All right, all right, I'm coming. Stop that racket!" He stabbed a foot through his trousers and hobbled to the door.

It was barely open a crack when Ekiria rushed him, Alta not far behind. "Grandfather!" She nearly knocked him off his feet.

"Whoa, there. Just a minute!"

"We *saw* her. We saw The Messenger!"

"What? No. Where were you?" If he was to get any peace he would have to go along with her, then send her on her way.

"Alta and I were up on the meadow. There were two of them. Circling way high up. You have to come see." She pulled on his arm.

"Hold on." He was shirtless and shoeless and his back was still stiff from sleep. "Give me a minute to get dressed. Their appearance was a bit of a rude awakening, but he had no business sleeping the day away when his granddaughter, Bryn, Peck, and the strange young man, Sloan were depending on him to watch for that troublemaker, Esteban.

"Two of them you say?" he said, shuffling back to his sleeping quarters. And then it hit him. Two? Had it been long enough for Lara to have found her way to Bryn, and made the transition? That thought was enough to get him moving faster.

"Two! We came straight here to tell you. We need to tell everyone," Ekiria called out, and he heard his front door shut with a bang. He poked his head out of his room, buttoning his shirt, and sure enough they were gone.

Twenty minutes later when he came out onto his porch fully dressed with his beard freshly groomed, there was a crowd gathering near the compound gate. He could see Ekiria and Alta jumping up and down, pointing up at the high cliff. People were shading their eyes scanning the sky over the valley.

"What's happening?" he asked, finding Helena among the crowd.

"There's smoke up on High Point, see it?" She pointed to the high dome that towered over the valley at the midpoint.

Rowan strained to see what they were all looking at. His eyesight wasn't great, and his stiff neck wouldn't let him look up without leaning practically over backward. But if he squinted his eyes just so, he did see a whisper of smoke.

"It looks like a small, controlled fire. Do you know of anyone planning a trip up there?"

Helena shook her head. "No. At least, no one registered with the guard. The girls say they saw Jenera's Messenger. Do you know anything about that?"

"They woke me up a few minutes ago with that story."

"They have pretty vivid imaginations, I know. But I did want them to tell Jenera about it. Have you any idea where she is?"

Rowan's ears heated. He shifted his gaze back to the heights away from Helena's discerning eyes. When he'd agreed to let Jenera go with Sloan, Peck, and Bryn to retrieve the crysl, he'd kept that mission to himself. He saw no need to alert the whole community before they knew exactly what had happened. It had been four days, and if they had been able to stick to their plan, it would be two more before he heard from them. No need yet to sound an alarm. But he didn't like the idea of keeping secrets from the woman who, with Jenera away from the valley, was technically second in command at this moment, should a crisis of leadership occur. If he were truly honest with himself, that crisis had likely already happened.

He glanced up to the peak to see that the whisper of smoke had widened to a ribbon. His heart gave a little kick. Valley lore told of fires built on that spot to signify an important event. When enough coals accumulated, they would push them over the cliff, creating a fall of fire.

All the pieces of Jenera's story were coming together. If Lara had in fact found her mate using the map he'd given her; if she'd completed the transition he'd seen coming and Michael was able to save her; if Jenera and her team were able to rescue Lara's crysl; if the planet alignment truly did coincide with the hatching of the oldest crysls; then the *Dannais* were indeed about to witness the first flight migration in their history.

Guilt gathered, burning and heavy in his gut. He had carried this story alone too long. And Helena needed to know before Jenera returned. "Actually, I wouldn't be surprised if there was something to Ekiria's claim."

Her eyes went wide. "What do you mean?"

Rowan took her arm and gently pulled her away from the others where they couldn't be overheard. "We need to talk."

They sat together in two woven chairs on Rowan's porch and watched the smoke ribbon on the ridge waver in the dusk as Rowan told her of all the events since Jenera had returned from her journey to find The Messenger, how he came to know Michael, how he'd delivered the crysl in Lara's cave, how it had been wrenched from his arms outside Gate Compound.

Helena sat back and blinked at him a few moments. "And you suspect Sloan of this treachery?"

"No. Not Sloan. It is clear that he did not go along with what Esteban was doing, but at the time of the abduction hadn't full knowledge of what was happening."

At that moment, one of the young boys stalked up to the porch and handed Rowan a folded piece of the crude paper they made at Gate Compound. He stepped back a safe distance before he spoke. "That man, Esteban told me to give this only to you, Grandfather."

Rowan shot a glance at Helena, unfolded the paper and read, then folded it back up. The boy looked like he expected trouble. "Did you read this young man?"

He shook his head vigorously. "No sir."

"Okay then. Run along to be with your friends."

The boy took off as fast as his little legs would carry him.

Helena arched a brow at him.

Rowan let out a tired sigh. "He's asking a ransome. For Lara's crysl."

CHAPTER 36 - THE AMULET

Jenera's limbs turned liquid. Bryn scooped her up before she melted into the ground. He curled her into his chest and absorbed her grief until she hadn't the energy to shed another tear, the amulet gripped tightly in her fist.

"I'm sorry," he said finally, gently stroking her back. "I'm so sorry."

Jenera wiped her face on her sleeve, feeling spent, thankful for his constant patience. She had dealt with her parents' loss many years ago, and although finding their actual remains left her raw, it also closed a door that had been left ajar in her heart, a crack that let in the cold. It would take a little more time, but whatever else happened in her future, she knew now she would eventually be able to say goodbye to them.

She leaned away from him, handed him the thong with the amulet, turned her back to him and looked over her shoulder. "Will you put it on for me?"

"Of course."

The pendant felt foreign and heavy at first, but the moment it warmed to her skin, the weight lifted. The amulet was finally where it belonged. She only hoped she would one day discover the significance. Until then, she would keep it safe.

She turned to see the concern in his eyes. "I'm okay. Really." She looked at Sloan. "You have no idea what you have done for me. Thank you."

He nodded and lowered his head.

Then, with her fingers gripping the amulet, she said: "Let's go get that crysl."

They followed Sloan into his chamber, which as he had described, was still entirely intact. Jenera stared at the surroundings. She had never seen anything like it. Compared to the main hall that had been flooded with water, his chamber was small and completely dry. She picked up what looked like a lizard made entirely of tiny colored bricks of a material she couldn't identify. She held it up to Sloan.

"It's Legos," he said with a smile. "Everything here is from my room before my father gave me the serum." He dug in a container of the bricks with his fingers, grabbed a couple and snapped them together. "See, you can make things with them."

Jenera snapped the tail off the lizard and snapped it back on again, glancing around the chamber. There was so much she longed to know about the world before. But now was not the time. "So, the crysl?"

Sloan moved to the center of the room to a pedestal made of a hard, white material that looked like a man-made nest. Cradled in the nest was an object wrapped in one of the shiny metallic blankets like the one she'd seen in Lara's cave. She hesitated, shooting a look at Sloan. "Is this where you emerged?"

Sloan stared at the shape under the blanket a moment as if remembering. "Mine was more—full blown I guess you would say." He shivered. "But yes. This is where I was when I broke out of my chrysalis. Would have been better to have someone like you

372

there, when it happened." He rested a hand on the shiny package. "This one will be lucky."

Jenera stared at the package another moment, then slowly stepped forward. She pulled back a piece of the blanket, revealing a perfectly formed crysl, just like the ones she'd watched over most of her life. She lifted her gaze to Bryn. "It's beautiful."

He nodded, slipped off his pack, and held it open while she folded the blanket back over the crysl and slid it inside, her breast expanding with a sense of accomplishment. The ground set off a rumble, and although this chamber was wholly intact, they could hear rocks tumbling outside the door.

Sloan went to the door and peeked out. "It's clear, but we need to get out of here now. The earth is restless today."

Chapter 37 - Fiera's Fire

Michael dumped another armload of boughs on the smoldering coals, stepped back, and dusted debris off his hands, bombarding his hyper-sensitive antennae with the piquant scent of pine. It had taken most of the day to accumulate the small mountain of glowing embers on top of the ledge. He surveyed the horizon then turned to Lara. "I'd say we have another hour before it's dark enough."

Lara moved closer to where the cliff began to curve toward the edge, memories crowding in. She had made the leap off the legendary Glacier Point a half a dozen times with her glider, each time overcoming a deep surge of fear before she took her running start. It had always been worth it once her feet left the ground. There was no view like it anywhere else on earth. But taking this leap with her own set of wings set her fear threshold at a whole new level.

They'd practiced at least ten times in the last three days. Each time she felt stronger, more in control. But this jump came with risks they hadn't faced before. The fact that it was many times higher wasn't really the issue, though it was giving her a little queasy rush right now, looking over the edge. What bothered her was the footing. You had to take a running start down a curving granite dome. Once on that downward slope, one slip of the foot and there was nothing to stop you tumbling over the edge to your death. She had never been worried about her footing with the glider. She had run herself off a cliff hundreds of times. But her own wings, though larger and lighter, had more moving parts. And her body mass was many times that of the monarch's by comparison.

She turned back to the glowing coals and watched Michael arrange the logs they would use to push the coals over the edge; one lay horizontally behind the pile, the other two would be used to push that one along. Would it actually work?

He looked up at her now, reading the question in her eyes, and closed the distance between them. "It will work, Lara," he said, placing his hands on her shoulders. "It's going to be spectacular, just like you wanted. We can do this."

She forced a smile. "Says the forty-foot-wave rider."

"Oh, and how tall would you say is this peak you're about to jump off?"

She lifted a shoulder. "From the valley floor, about three thousand feet."

"It doesn't get any more badass than that."

And just like that, Michael came into full focus. They had gone through their own metamorphosis unlike any other humans on earth and they had come out the other side, changed but still who they were on the inside. She gazed at him now, the antennae on her head and every other cell in her body quivering with desire and a strength she had never experienced before.

Ellen Ripley, move over. Lara was about to do something no human had ever done before. Well, part human, anyway.

"Right," she said, swallowing the annoying lump of fear. It had given her the necessary dose of adrenaline;

now it was time to use it. "Let's go over it one more time."

Michael stepped to the other side of the pile of coals. "Okay, we get pumped up, and when we're both fully expanded, we each take one of those poles and push against the log until all the coals spill over the edge. It will be slow, a little bit at a time. But it will achieve the effect you want. Once all but coals to light our path have cleared the slope, we drop the poles, make the run, and launch."

Jenera was first to see the smoke. She stopped at the crook of a switchback that afforded a view into the Valley and slid her pack off her shoulders. They started hiking before dawn and had come within sight of their valley without a break since they'd passed the summit. Jenera was exhausted, the only thing keeping her going was knowing Lara's crysl was safe in Bryn's backpack as he marched in front of her, and the promise that they would be on the valley floor by dark.

"That better not be anywhere near the grain silos," Peck said from his position behind Jenera.

Jenera's brow crinkled, and she glanced at Bryn. If he'd noticed Peck had been in a foul mood ever since they'd emerged from Sloan's chamber, he didn't let on. He was a friend to Bryn, another full human who had seemed loyal enough, but she didn't know the man well. The fact that Bryn had allowed him to come had been enough for her. Now she wasn't so sure. It was as though he'd never believed they'd find what they were looking for, and now that they had, his demeanor had changed.

"And why would that be of concern to you?" Jenera challenged, unable to let her feeling pass. He was beginning to not only annoy her, but remind her of Esteban. She wondered now if Rowan or Bryn had seen this side of the man, because if he had, surely, he would not have sent him along on this mission.

"You're not concerned about what this crysl means for our people?" he prodded. "It will just encourage them to believe in fairy tales."

Jenera bristled. It was true that many *Dannais* had begun to doubt the legends; she was surprised, however that Peck seemed to be among them. She couldn't let that deter her now, but she filed it away for a future discussion with Rowan.

"I'm concerned about whatever that fire means," she said. "There's not a whole lot of fuel on the highest peaks, so it is curious to say the least."

Bryn's brow crunched a moment as he considered the exchange between Jenera and Peck. With a telling glance at Jenera—*so he had, noticed, she thought*—he hitched up his pack and scanned the horizon. "It looks like it's coming from High Point Ridge." They would compare notes later.

"Fiera's Fire," she said, softly, recalling a story her mother had told her when she was very young.

"Fiera's Fire?" Bryn asked.

Jenera picked her way down the rocky trail, checking the column of smoke at each turn that brought it into view. "It's one of the legends. The story goes that to celebrate his union with Fiera, Jahn built a fire on top of High Point Ridge and spilled the coals down the cliff in a fiery fall. It was said that his vows to love her for eternity could be heard like a song all over the valley as the embers created a spectacular display."

"I read a book in the library about that. Well, sort of," Sloan said, catching up to keep pace behind her. "Your valley has more or less been protected as a sacred place throughout time, though the firefall practice was actually started as more of a commercial venture."

Jenera glanced over her shoulder at him. The boy was a mystery to her. One moment he was comforting her over the discovery of her parents' remains, then next he was spouting facts from some ancient storehouse of knowledge. "Interesting, but not very romantic."

Sloan kept putting one foot in front of the other, his cheeks noticeably red. "Actually, I... like your version better."

Jenera had to let go a laugh. It was a relief to make small talk along the trail after all they had discovered back in the cave.

Then her thoughts took a switchback of their own that made her shiver. Was her version of reality so different from others'? So many of the legends were focused on their valley, so much of her education was limited to the confines of her home. Her purpose was wrapped completely up in preserving the crysls and the ways of her people. The mere existence of this library of Sloan's created a tiny crack in her world that threatened to let in a different light. After meeting Lara and now Sloan, it was pretty clear the world was much bigger than she knew and that thought left her feeling a bit uneasy.

Her thoughts spun round and round in her head so relentlessly, she barely noticed the trail under her feet.

When they arrived at Lillit Compound, dusty and exhausted, the first stars were already appearing in the sky. The central brazier was lit, banked low; but oddly, there was no one around, not even the night watch.

Jenera shot a worried glance at Bryn. "I expected Rowan would be so desperate for news he would have met us at the north gate." But there was no sign of him. Worry tickled the tips of her antennae.

Bryn slid off his backpack. "Wait here. I'll go check his bungalow."

Sloan stepped up close behind them. "Where is everybody?"

"I don't know, Sloan. Rowan would be very upset that a fire in the brazier was left unattended." She lifted her eyes to High Point Ridge where dark smoke was invisible against the night sky. There was a faint orange glow at the top. Her antennae expanded to their full length, sending prickles down her neck to the tip of her tailbone. Her senses had been on high alert ever since they'd first seen the smoke over the valley. Now she fairly buzzed with anxiety.

Bryn hustled back to the group. "Rowan's not there, and there's no one at the Infirmary either."

"That's not right," Jenera answered.

She turned to see Peck stalking away without a word. "What's go into him? He's been jumpy ever since we left Terra City."

Bryn frowned as he watched Peck stalk away. "I suppose we'll find out soon enough."

Jenera was so exhausted, she didn't care anymore. All she wanted to do was go to her bungalow and drop into her own bed. But she couldn't do that until she had placed the crysl safely inside the tower. She let go a deep sigh and opened Bryn's pack "I've got to get this crysl to safety before I collapse right here."

She saw no one as they approached the tower, fatigue dragging at every step. Anticipating her need, Bryn removed the security brace and pushed open the thick, redwood door. A rush of cool air from the tower's high vent caressed Jenera's face like a cool breath, bringing with it the shushing sound of the crysls rustled by the draft and the familiar scent that bathed her in calm whenever she visited here. She paused at the threshold, removed the metallic blanket from the crysl, and held the precious being close to her chest. It was larger than the others, and clearly in the early stages of development. While she could identify various body parts through the amber shell, there were no apparent color changes in them.

Lately, when she climbed the stairs spiraling to the top of the tower, the crysls at the highest level clearly showed signs of marigold and black in the burgeoning wing structures at their backs, and their lower extremities had developed small white spots over a black background.

Lara's crysl would go in a special place at the lowest level, separated from the rest so they could differentiate it from the others. If the legends were true, this creature would indeed become something she never dreamed she would witness in her lifetime. The child of The Messenger would be the purest of the pure and carry the strongest *Danaus* gene into the future.

She placed the crysl carefully in one of the woven hammocks, stepped back, and let out her breath. At least part of her world had been set to rights.

When she glanced at Bryn, he was focused on her, took her hands in his. "What is it?"

She stared at him along moment, resolve hardening in her heart. As far as she was concerned Esteban's despicable act cancelled any loyalty or repsonsibility she had to Rowan's promise to his old friend. They only loyalty she would honor was the unspoken bond between her and the man who stood before her now. If Rowan didn't renounce him, Jenera would. Because she would damn well leave the colony before she would fulfil the betrothal to that scoundrel. Relief flooded her.

Bryn was human and she was *Dannais*, and if the legends were true, she would one day lead her own migration. Which meant that their parting would be inevitable one day. But with the threat of Esteban gone, they could spend what time they had left together.

She squeezed his hands and turned away before tears could fall. "We need to talk. Soon."

She returned her gaze to the highest point of the tower. Better to focus on the task at hand. "But right now, I need to check those top level crysls. We're close to the alignment. If they're ready for the migration, they should be showing signs."

Bryn held her eyes for another beat, then stepped dutifully away.

Sloan stepped up behind them. "Can I come with you?"

"Come with me?" No one beside her had been up this staircase for as long as she could remember. It was expected that someday, Ekiria would learn to tend the crysls, but Sloan's interest was encouraging. He had shown himself to be intelligent, caring, and very obviously in possession of the gene, though in a different manifestation than any she had seen. When her time came to lead a colony north, Ekiria would need someone to help her with the third wave. "Of course," she told him. "Watch your step."

When Jenera reached the top tier, Sloan at her heels, her suspicions were confirmed. "See these markings," she pointed out. "The last time I was up here, only last Spring, they were vague and pale. Now, they are vivid and startling: You can see their bodies tucked inside yellow, marigold, black and white folds. The topmost crysls' amber coating is completely transparent. See these cracks and veins along the top and sides?" she went on, pointing out the details. "That can only mean they'll be breaking out soon."

Sloan squinted his eyes, drew close, and traced a finger along the cracks in the crysl closest to him. "Fascinating. Like when I emerged from my chrysalis."

"Yes, and no. These crysls are the result of an actual biological mating of male and female *Dannais*, which are at least half Monarch, half human."

Sloan blinked at her. "So, like, second Gen. Something my father never imagined."

She considered a moment. "You are probably right about that. As Lara explained to me, it was never your father's intent to create a new species."

Sloan traced the outline of what looked like a wing inside the crysl near his shoulder. "Think they'll have wings like monarchs?"

Jenera smiled at him. "Well, that would be a given, considering they are expected to migrate like the monarchs. At least, those described in our legends have wings."

His eyes drifted to the amulet around her neck. "There is a whole section in my father's diary about the serum, the dosages, and his predicted outcomes. It was one of the last studies he made."

"Serum?"

He nodded. "There's some in that amulet, and there's more in the Vault, though I've never seen it."

Jenera felt her legs weaken. "Where is this diary?" she asked, tightening her grip on the stair railing.

"It's all right here," he said proudly, then backed his way down the steps toward the stairway. When she gave him a worried look he relented. "Well, it's in the Vault, too. Somewhere."

"Somewhere?"

"I took it out of the library. To keep it safe from… intruders…. Um. There was an event. The chamber where I hid it has since been blocked. But I know where it is."

She began to follow him down, less concerned about the actual diary than what it contained. "Is that right," she said, trying to keep the discussion light. The fact that some of the original serum existed—that she could actually have some of it hanging around her neck right at this moment—was a shocking revelation.

Serum.

Dosages.

Transformations.

The possibilities spun in her head.

"The whole process," she said, cautiously. "How long do you think it would take?"

Sloan stopped and looked up at her. "You're thinking about Bryn."

"No, I just…" But he was absolutely right. She *was* thinking about Bryn.

He raised a brow at her. "It's pretty obvious, you'll never allow yourself to be mated to Esteban. Bryn is your true soulmate, right?"

She pressed her lips together. "A boy who's spent years alone and hasn't yet achieved puberty, what do you know about soulmates?"

"Um… the Vault. I mean, everything you ever wanted to know about the human race is, um, in that vault." Those high boned cheeks pinked again. He pulled his cap down hard over his ears and they started to slowly to ascend the rest of the stairs before he attempted to explain.

"The results of the first inoculation were of course unpredictable. My father had no idea what was happening or how. But, throughout the rest of his lifetime, he conducted many experiments, studied formulations, dosing, and outcomes. He documented everything in his journals."

Jenera, stopped as they neared the bottom of the stairs. She wanted to keep this conversation completely confidential at this point. "Go on."

"I'm… sorry. I wasn't as interested in the details of his studies as I was in some of the the history of the American West, astronomy, and Marvel comics, you know."

Jenera deflated. No. She did not know. But the possibility the serum represented sparked new energy in her. "But, you'll take me back, right? Show me this diary? This library? Surely you don't consider me an intruder?"

Sloan's forehead scrunched together. "No. Of course not. It's just that. I'm not sure it's a good idea to open that Pandora's Box."

"Who's Pandora?"

Sloan huffed out a sigh. "Another myth. Some say Pandora's box held gifts, others say she released evil into the world. People use it as a metaphor."

Pandora's box. Metaphors. Jenera had to give Sloan a lot of credit for immersing himself if the knowledge in the Vault. What she did know was as Lara had once told her: there is always a grain of truth in a legend, and it made sense that it also applied to this myth. Whatever it was, they had more important matters to attend to. Sloan's Vault would have to wait. She gripped the amulet at her neck, snagged her backpack from the ground, and slung it over her shoulder.

"Let's go," she said, heading away from her home.

Bryn snagged her by the elbow. "I… thought you said you were exhausted. Needed sleep."

Sloan nodded his agreement. "I could sleep for a week right on this spot."

She shook her head at the young man, then smiled at Bryn. He was looking after her welfare as always. "I know. I do. But I need to go to Lara. Tell her we retrieved her crysl. Maybe persuade her to come one more time. We need her."

"You are talking about another two-day hike into the mountains. Are you sure you're up for that?"

Jenera blinked at him a moment, mouth agape. "Of course I'm up for that. I have to be. The crysls are about to—"

He sat on a stone bench outside the tower and pulled her down next to him. "You are absolutely right. The crysls are nearing their emergence, which means they need you more than ever right here. If Lara is who you say she is, she will not abandon the *Dannais*."

"But the alignment—"

"Is supposed to be tonight. I know. If Lara doesn't come, I promise you, I'll go find her myself. In the meantime, you need to get at least a few hours rest and some food in you or you'll be no good to anyone."

CHAPTER 38 – ESTEBAN'S FOLLY

Rowan crushed the handwritten message in his fist, anger building as he paced back and forth in front of his bungalow. He had been expecting a demand from Esteban since he'd sent the search party for the stolen crysl. The fact that it had finally come was a good sign their plan was still in play. What Rowan hadn't expected was the man to use one of the young ones to deliver it, rather than stand before him face-to-face like a man. But he should have expected it. Esteban had shown himself to be a coward in the past. Rowan had the young man, Sloan, to thank for giving him a heads up. One thing for sure was he was not going to hand over half the colony's winter supplies to one man's folly no matter how good a friend his father had been. He tossed the message in his woodstove and stepped outside.

Helena was hurrying the little ones out of Lillit gate, and he fell into step behind them to see that every soul in the village was on their way to the meadow to witness what was happening at High Point Ledge.

When he arrived near the river crossing, he stopped to look up. The glow, though still confined on the ledge, had indeed grown larger and brighter.

"Times are changing, old man."

Startled, Rowan turned to find Esteban standing behind him, arms crossed over his chest, a smug expression on his face. Ironically, the younger man's words confirmed his own thoughts. But he wasn't about to let on that it worried him. "Sending a child to do your business, Esteban?"

"Tomas will make a strong gatekeeper one day."

"I'm sure that's not what you had in mind when you sent a boy rather than coming to me yourself."

Esteban shrugged off the rebuke. "The world outside this valley is awakening after a long sleep. It's time you let go of fairytales," Esteban said, channeling his father. "Men are on the move up and down The Owen and there's riches to be gained. The *Dannais* are in a position to reap the benefits if they have the courage to accept the challenge."

"The *Dannais*?" Rowan questioned. He planted his feet firmly in place like his namesake tree. "The *Dannais* have taken great pains to remove themselves from all that and have survived many generations in peace by doing so. I'm not about to set the back door wide open to strangers now."

"It's happening whether you want it or not."

"You threaten to take what does not belong to you?"

"If you don't see reason."

Rowan leveled his gaze at the defiance he saw in Esteban's eyes. "We can't eat riches, son."

"But I'm not just talking about gold or silver. We can trade for tools, weapons, transports. You can't live in this isolated valley forever."

"Your human genes are showing," Rowan said, standing his ground.

"What's that supposed to mean?"

"It means you are starting to sound greedy, boy."

"Greedy?"

Rowan raised a brow which made Esteban soften his belligerent stance. "You couldn't get the council to agree to supply your personal outpost with our winter's provisions, so you took the matter into your own hands and stole a crysl to hold for ransom."

"You gave me no choice!"

"The *Dannais* have given you and your family safe harbor for three generations, yet you have always been free to leave the valley and strike out on your own if you wished. There was no need to resort to treachery. All I've got to say is, that crysl had better not be in any danger."

Esteban brushed Rowan's concern aside, throwing his arms up in the air. "What's one more crysl? Your granddaughter's got, I don't know, dozens, up in that useless tower."

"Useless? Jenera has been caring for those crysls since she was a young girl, and her mother before her, each one carries a precious gene that could repopulate our kind. *That* crysl—the one you nearly killed me to take away—is the offspring of The Messenger herself, destined by the legends to be a great future leader."

"The legends," Esteban said, derisively. He closed the distance between them, his full arrogance on display. "And what do you suppose will happen to *you* old man, when your precious crysls are borne away on a Great Migration?"

Rowan stared at him a moment, anger boiling in his veins. He had been lucky to have lived out his life in this valley. But he would never deny the *Dannais* their destiny to fend off loneliness. How many years did he have left after all? The thought sent a new ache in his old man's back. He willed himself to ignore Esteban's venom. If the rescuers had indeed gotten past him on their mission, this discussion was moot anyway. He let out a long sigh and looked down his nose at the young man who reminded him so much of his father, in every way but wisdom. "Exactly what do you want, Esteban?"

Esteban rolled his shoulders and lifted his chin, a move that said he expected to get what he wanted. "Give me one half of what's in the silo now and I will bring you the crysl, unharmed. Next season, I'll return and with traded goods that will change all of our lives for the better. It's a win-win. You and your people will continue to survive in the valley, and I'll have a successful outpost on the most travelled passageway of our age. I'll need a wagon, and several men for starters. Peck has already agreed to—"

"Peck has agreed?" That notion hit Rowan like a blow to the stomach. What had he missed about this young man?

Esteban scuffed the dirt. "Well, I'm sure he will, once he learns of my success. He'll be my right hand man once I take over the colony."

Rowan seethed. This had gone way too far. "Take over the colony?"

Esteban shrugged. "Well. Once Jenera and I are joined in—"

Rowan wanted to roar. Instead he thrust his face into Esteban's and spoke in a low growl. "After kidnapping the crysl and holding it for ransom, you think I'd honor my vow to your father?"

At that moment, Peck strode out of the shadows. "What's happened? What's going on?" His voice was shrill and excited as he pointed to the ridge. "We could see it from the meadow. There wasn't a soul in Lillit Compound!" He turned back, his eyes widened when he saw the man he had fairly pushed aside was Esteban. He shot his gaze between the two men.

"I take it, you are all back, safe and sound," Rowan said, clenching his fists.

"I... Yes. All is..." His gaze shifted again to Esteban. "Uh, as it should be." He finished with an emphatic nod.

"Go ahead and say it, Peck," Rowan demanded, watching the man's face carefully.

Peck lifted his chin, sent a quick glance to Esteban, then took his sentry's stance. "The crysl is secure, uh, as you requested. By now, Bryn and Jenera should have placed it in the tower."

Esteban's face blanched. "The crysl? *You* brought it back here?"

Rowan grasped Peck's hand, shook it, then slapped him on the back. "Good work, son."

Peck kicked the dirt, avoiding Esteban's glare. "I promised I would get the job done. It wasn't easy, but I kept everyone safe and returned with the prize," he said. "They sent me ahead to find out where everyone was."

Now Rowan crossed his arms. It was time to end this farce. "In due time, son. Right now, I have another job for you."

"But Jenera and Bryn. They're worried about the fire, I came to find out—"

"We're all fine. I'll catch up with them soon." Peck relaxed, glanced up at the glow, his brow furrowed. "As you wish."

Rowan stood silently a long moment, considering his next move. It pained his soul to do it but the incorrigible young Esteban gave him no choice.

"Provide Esteban with his six month's *personal* share of what's in the granary, and one of the smaller carts, then escort him to his bungalow so he can load up his belongings."

"What?" Esteban croaked.

"Then go with him all the way to Craggy Pass," Rowan went on, shifting his gaze to Esteban. "You are no longer welcome among the *Dannais*. Sell your own supplies if you wish, or travel The Owen on your own. But you are never to set foot in this valley again."

Esteban's huffed out a laugh. "You can't be serious! Six months personal supply? I can't survive on that. You made a promise to my father! I was to be mated to Jenera. The leader of—"

Rowan held up his hand. "Your father and I were friends and when he died, I vowed to raise you as my own. I kept that promise. Now you repay me with treachery." He shook his head and turned his back on the man. "My job is done. I have nothing more to say to you."

Peck's lips set in a pale, grimm line. He stepped away from Esteban. Rowan fixed him with his fire stare, sensing tension between the two younger men. "Is there something you want to tell me?"

Peck shook his head. "No… I…" He avoided looking at Esteban. "I've just returned from a six-day journey. Isn't there someone else who can—"

Rowan banged his staff on the ground. "The sooner you leave, the sooner you will get back for rest. Unless of course, you wish to leave the colony and join Esteban."

"*Uh, no!* No sir. I'll go, I… " he stammered.

Rowan could see going with Esteban at this moment was the last thing the young man wanted to do. But he had no choice. "Then off with you, now, before I change my mind."

This was a teaching moment, and it would be interesting to see what lesson the young Peck was going to learn.

Rowan stepped across the threshold of the ancient stone bridge where many of his people had gathered. Some carried torches, others were empty handed, all of them had their heads cranked back on their necks, mouths agape. The air crackled with excitement.

When the first glowing embers began to spill over the high ledge, shouts echoed all over the valley. What was going on? Certainly, it was no accident. And if it was planned, Rowan should have been first to know. He should find out and have the hides of those behind this! Instead, he stood transfixed just like the rest of them, holding his twisted tendrils away from his face so they didn't obstruct his view. Never in his long life had he seen such a thing. Like the massive waterfalls of spring, the cascading fire lit up the entire valley, casting everything in an eerie glow.

"Grandfather!" A thin voice rose above the rest. Jenera? Was she back safe? He dragged his gaze away from the spectacle, looking for the source of the cry. And then he saw her. A small figure breaking away from the shadows and running toward him.

"Grandfather!" she called again, Bryn taking long strides behind her.

Rowan scooped her in an embrace and pointed to the fire fall. She laughed out loud. He had never seen her so joyous.

"We saw the smoke early this morning, and after a while, I remembered. It's Fiera's Fire."

He blinked at her a moment. There were so many legends, to him they all ran together into a litany of fantasy, one pretty much the same as the next. Having one actually play out before his eyes gave him a new perspective. And now that Jenera was back safe, he was ready to listen to anything she said. "Refresh my memory, child. What does this one foretell?"

CHAPTER 39 – THE MESSENGER'S FLIGHT

Jenera watched in awe as red-hot coals flowed over the cliff and down the granite face. Like a river of fire. It was one thing to tell the story of Fiera's Fire to a group of excited children, quite another to actually witness the event: a torrent of fire plunging down the side of a sacred cliff. Her mouth went dry watching it.

She spoke to Rowan without taking her eyes off the spectacle. "It's got to be related to the alignment and the migration. I just checked on the crysls and they're thinning, cracking down the sides. I saw the face of one of them and I swear, its eyes were open and focused on me."

Bryn stepped forward, leaned in to her, and pointed to the ledge. "By the legends, I swear I just saw two figures jump off that ledge."

Jenera strained to see. It was high and too far away, but, indeed, there appeared to be two figures plummeting from the high ledge. "Oh my god!" she gasped, resisting the overwhelming urge to cover her eyes. "They're plunging to their death!"

"No." Rowan said. "Not plunging. Diving."

The figures were momentarily out of sight, but then as they passed over the area where the fallen coals lit the valley with an eerie glow, she saw them again, soaring down from the cliff on wings spread wide from their narrow bodies. They circled ever lower, and as others began to see them too, a low murmur of awe built around them.

Jenera stepped forward, barely able to breathe. "It's Lara. It has to be!" She cupped her hand over her mouth as she watched the figures swoop and glide. She could scarcely believe her eyes. Deep inside, she knew Lara wouldn't abandon them.

But as the figures circled lower, and they could see more detail, Jenera wasn't sure. One, unmistakably female, looked similar to Lara, but not exactly as she remembered. The other, definitely male, followed the female's lead, a broad smile on his unusual, handsome face. "Who do you think they are, Grandfather?"

Rowan watched with a satisfied grin. The pair continued to circle the crowd as if they were enjoying themselves. "It's your Messenger, child. Just as you predicted. And Michael. I told you about him." He followed their moves, appreciation glowing in his eyes.

"The one who could save Lara once she went into transition?"

He nodded. "By the look of it, I'd say, they saved each other."

Then suddenly, the female gave a pump of her wings, swooped up, and soared away across the great meadow toward the amphitheater and the great hall. The male followed close behind.

Jenera swallowed a huge lump in her throat and might have melted to the ground in amazement if Bryn hadn't been there to catch her.

"Look out!" he said, pulling her close to his body. She heard them before she saw them. Dozens of people, *Dannais* and humans alike, running toward them. "We need to get off the bridge," he urged, grabbing Rowan's arm. "Get his other arm, Jen. Let's *move*."

But they were too late. The people swept around them like the river in flood, driving them along at a pace too fast for Rowan to keep up. With Bryn on one side of him and Jenera on the other, they managed to keep him upright until they were past the bridge walls, then spilled off the main road, keeping their elder from being trampled in the fray.

By the time they reached the amphitheater, both Rowan and Jenera were out of breath. The theater was packed, latecomers standing along the back and sides, gazing toward the podium. Still supporting Rowan between them, Jenera and Bryn skirted the crowd, and when they came out from under the skirts of ancient redwoods flanking the stone steps to the great hall, there they were.

Two tall, muscular creatures, not exactly lepidoptera, as Sloan had schooled her on the trail, but not human either. *Freak*, Lara had called herself, but Jenera couldn't bring herself to think of any word but *magnificent*. Their monarch wings spread up and outward behind them, their bodies shimmered under iridescent scales—his tending toward a dark, dragonfly green from the waist down, hers warm and golden.

The two striking creatures took a moment to smile at each other with unbridled admiration. Then, at her nod, his wings visibly slackened and folded behind his large, muscular shoulders. Hers draped over one shoulder, creating the effect of a layered cape of marigold, black, and white, windowpane lace.

She gazed over the crowd for a moment, acknowledging their presence with an approving nod.

When she lifted her hands, palms up over her head, excited voices fell silent. The woman's gemstone blue, faceted eyes glimmered in the torchlight as she continued to scan the crowd, her antennae in full extension.

Those closest to the podium, mostly the young ones who pushed their way forward at any event, retreated into the arms of their parents. She smiled at the little ones. "There is no need to be afraid."

Her voice was clear, but had a layered quality, as though echoing in a sphere close around her body. She indicated the row of benches in front of her. "Come sit where you can all hear what I have to say."

Jenera grabbed hold of Bryn's hand, holding her excitement in check. Rowan watched in silence, his expression giving away no emotion. Ekiria, dragging a reluctant Alta along with her, pushed her way to the front of the group and sat down squarely in front of the creature. A moment later, the rest of the little ones followed and crowded in, the smallest sitting cross legged directly under the creature's feet.

She waited until all was silent and still, then placed her hands on the podium. "I am Lara, the Messenger of which your legends speak." Again, she surveyed the crowd, making eye contact with as many souls as possible all around the amphitheater--the old, the young, the obvious *Dannais*, and the humans. "But what I am here to tell you is not exactly what you may have heard before." She craned her long, graceful neck. "Jenera? Are you out there? Please," she said, indicating the podium beside her. "Come here and stand by me."

Bryn gave her a little push from behind. "Go. This is your moment."

She hung back. "Rowan?"

Rowan nodded. "Bryn's right. You belong up there with her. This has always been your story to tell."

She pulled in a long breath but kept hold of Bryn's hand. "Come with me. Just stand nearby. Please."

Rowan nodded his approval and Bryn stepped forward. The crowd murmured as they made their way among the towering redwoods to the front of the amphitheater and finally to the podium. She could clearly see now that this magnificent creature--though her eyes were incredibly complex, her neck longer, and her entire body an intricate pattern of monarch orange and filigree--was in fact the creature she'd first seen in here eyre at Mariposa cave.

She looked down on Jenera now, a full head and shoulders taller than she remembered, then placed her hand on her shoulder. "It is good to be with you again, Spirit Leader."

Jenera's throat closed tight. Seeing multiple images of her own face reflected in those gemstone eyes, she was unable to utter a sound. Instead, she simply took a knee before this incredible being.

Lara's heart swelled in her chest as she gazed up at towering monuments that looked down on her beloved valley. How many times had she crossed that stone bridge holding her grandfather's hand? Climbed up the Mist Trail to Vernal Falls? Gazed at the sheer granite face of Half Dome? Soared off the top of El Capitan? Knowing the cataclysmic changes that must have occurred on earth to fill the San Joaquin Valley with salt water, it was comforting to learn that places like this had survived despite man's reckless stewardship. So many places in her world—crowded cities with skyscrapers blocking the sun, airports with jumbo jets lined up on the tarmac waiting to fly around the world, massive machines churning over thousands of acres of wheat, fighter jet streaking across the sky leaving contrails behind. All that would seem foreign and frightening to those young ones staring at her now. What could she possibly say to them to make them understand the value and beauty of the place they called home? She knew that she would eventually do exactly as the legend foretold. But right now, she felt the need to give them a deeper explanation. One that would soothe her own heart.

She stepped forward, placed her hands on either side of the podium, and spoke to the expectant faces of the crowd. "When I came into this world, I was alone and frightened beyond imagination. I had no idea what had happened to me or why. All I knew was that I had emerged into a new world in a different body with none of my friends or family nearby.

"Without your Spirit Leader, Jenera, I'm not sure I would have survived. But she came to me, told me of the legends, brought me food, friendship, and hope. And for that I will be eternally grateful."

She offered her hand to Jenera, then shifted her gaze to Rowan. "The fact that you and your people – the *Dannais* and the humans among you--have survived for generations in the valley after what must have been catastrophic circumstances, is a credit to your strength and resilience. It is also a testament to the life-giving power of this valley which has survived through the millennia."

"When I was a young woman, before my transformation, I feared for the earth and what the humans of that time had done to destroy it. So, it is a great relief to me to find that at least here, in this valley, there is a colony of peace-loving people living in harmony with the land."

"I visited this exact spot many times in my life before," she said, smiling at the young ones at her feet. "This is truly a sacred space. We called it Yosemite. Even then these granite walls showed signs of the ancients living in this valley. Its waterfalls and carved rock precipices were so revered by our government, they made laws to protect it and places like it so that they could never be destroyed by mining or logging, or any other commercial development. I am pleased to see that it has survived to nourish the earth and the people who live here."

She fell silent a moment, glancing around the crowd. "But it is clear, many things have been lost. The valley below your gates once fed an entire nation, and now most of it is under salt water. This does not bode well for the rest of the country. I fear what we will find on our journey. But if the crysls contain beings with the strength and wisdom of Jenera and her grandfather Rowan, then I have no doubt that whatever we find, we will not only survive but thrive."

She drew in another deep breath and continued. "I cannot say whether my presence here was predetermined, as Jenera claims. I don't believe I am a god to be worshipped, nor do I possess any supernatural power. What I can tell you is that since emerging from our second metamorphosis, like the monarchs who live in your valley, both my soulmate and I have felt the same beacon call. No doubt, that same call has awakened in the crysls you have so lovingly preserved in Crysl Tower."

She favored Jenera with a pointed look, then she lifted her gaze to the night sky and raised her arms overhead. "Is it a coincidence that all this is happening just as the planets appear aligned? Maybe. Maybe not. As my partner reminds me," she said, meeting his eyes a moment and taking his hand, "… our old life is gone. We must respond to what is happening right now, because this is all we have." She squeezed Michael's hand; he stepped to her side, her partner, her protector, and with those towering antennae alert over his head, her prince. "We are apparently a new order of Lepidoptera I will call *Danaus Plexipus Sapiens*, a Monarch/Human hybrid. We are prepared to lead the first wave of this new line of Monarchs into the wide world beyond this valley, as your legends foretold."

She lowered her arms, turned her blue faceted gaze on Jenera. "Now, with great respect and confidence, I give you your Spirit Leader, Jenera of Lillit Compound." Lara stepped aside, gave her a bow, indicated for her to step forward.

Jenera's heart raced. She swallowed around a huge lump in her throat, anxiety pinching off her words. Lara leaned in close enough for her to inhale the dusty scent of her iridescent feathered neck. "Trust the legends, Jenera. It is clear, your time has come."

Jenera blinked at her, feeling a pulse of courage surge through her as she once again saw herself reflected in Lara's amazing eyes. She could feel her antennae stretched high above her halo of hair, sensing the excitement in the air. She turned and faced the crowd, taking time to let their cheers ebb and flow away.

"This morning, I visited Crysl Tower. The crysls in the topmost tier showed signs of effacing. Cracks are beginning to form, a signal I take to mean they are nearing their time of emergence."

A murmur went up from the crowd, and the little ones in front clapped their hands in excitement. They had grown up on the legends and knew exactly what that meant. She raised her hands to once again silence the crowd. "I don't know how long it will take, but once all have shed their shells, they will need a couple of days to gain strength from the milkiweed plants we have harvested and tended and learn how to use their wings. I don't know yet what form they will actually take, but I can say that I made eye contact with one and it was clear to me she saw and acknowledged me. I have no doubt they will be *born* with all the knowledge they need to fulfill their destiny."

Another wave of gasps and comments swept the amphitheater. She looked toward Lara and Michael. "I am both grateful and concerned about what is to take place here. None of us has ever done anything like this before." She turned back to the crowd. "But of one thing, I am sure. We have prepared well for this moment, and I have all confidence that our Messenger and her mate will be successful in leading the first wave of *Dannais* northward to our ancestral homes."

A loud cheer went up. Those who were sitting stood and the applause echoed over the valley. She cast her gaze on Rowan and Bryn standing beside her and gave herself over to a glowing feeling of accomplishment and satisfaction she had never known before.

"Now, I want you to return to your homes and I will call us all together when the crysls are ready." She watched a moment longer until she had confirmed her people were leaving the area and heading home.

Then she turned to Lara. "Thank you for coming back."

Lara put her hands on both of Jenera's shoulders. "I was a fool to doubt you. To doubt your story. You were right, after all."

Jenera bowed her head a moment, soaking up the praise. "Where will you go until the crysls are ready?"

"Michael has a grotto below the dam near Gate Compound. Rowan knows where it is. We will stay there until the beacon call commands us to come forward." She held her hand out to Michael and stepped into the center of the amphitheater where they expanded their wings and took off looking as though they had been flying like monarchs all their lives.

Jenera, Bryn, and Rowan watched them until they were out of sight and then Jenera turned to Bryn and put her hand in his the way she'd seen Lara do with Michael. "Take me home," she said, "I really do need that rest."

CHAPTER 40 - INTO THE MYSTIC

What do you miss the most about our old life?" Lara asked, watching Michael clean a handful of freshwater clams at his reclaimed sink. After their monumental dive the night before, Lara had been exhausted and slept most of the day away. At least, that's what her stomach told her.

When she'd awoken, he was gone, the late afternoon sun slanting through the small window openings along the outer wall of his bedroom. But once her antenna tuned in to her surroundings, she knew he must be nearby.

Now, he worked at his basin, preparing their meal in the generous, quiet way he'd done several times since their reunion. The way he'd done in her past life. He dropped the clams into a pot, along with wild onions, mushrooms, and fiddlenecks, then filled the pot with water and placed it on the grill. He stood with his back to her a moment before he turned to look at her, his eyes taking her in slowly from the top of her antennae to her shoulders, her breasts, and down her long body. She could almost feel the touch of his gaze on her skin.

"I wouldn't call it missing, really," he said, his head quirking to one side.

"What do you mean?"

He leaned against his redwood counter, cast his gaze around the space he'd created for himself. "I have everything I need."

"That's…" She was going to say absurd but held her tongue. Who knew the extent a person's identity remained after the extraordinary events they'd been through? She certainly didn't feel completely herself. "But you remembered us, right?"

"What I… remember… is a longing for something I couldn't describe. There was obviously something missing, something that left an aching hole in my gut. But I couldn't put it into words." He took a step toward her, cocking his head the other way. "At first, I was mostly in survival mode. Hand to mouth. But later on, once I was able to explore further, I found remnants of what used to be."

"Like what, exactly?"

He lifted the pot off the grill. "My pots, the grill. Even the sink. Scavenged from down below. Rowan told me about vast piles of tools and conveniences the old civilization had used and thrown away. They make regular trips to find useful things."

"Landfills?" Lara wondered out loud. "Thrifts? Or people's actual homes?"

Michael lifted his shoulder. "The people are gone, so, why not make use of what they left behind?"

She couldn't argue with his logic. She had noticed the *Dannais* had many "repurposed" items in their village. But the idea of the people being gone made her heart squeeze a little. What exactly had happened to them? And honestly, did she really want to know?

"I miss shopping at the local fish market, and the fancy restaurants on the bay. I miss scallops, Chilean sea bass, plated like works of art, and fancy umbrella drinks. I miss cooking with you in my lighthouse kitchen, the sound of the waves crashing against the cliffs in a winter swell—" and so much more.

A sudden rush of memory—the faces of the girls at the shelter, her grandfather's smile, the banister leading along the spiral stairway to her lighthouse bedroom—made her heart squeeze into a tiny, cold ball. She needed the comfort of something real. Something personal, something she could hold on to. She slid off the stool where she'd been sitting and went to him, her own longing pushing past the unfamiliarity of the profound physical changes in their bodies. After what they had accomplished the night before, she had to appreciate every single one of those changes. She pressed herself against him now, rested her hands on his chest a moment then ran them up and over his shoulders and clasped them behind his neck. "I missed us," she said, looking into his eyes.

He cocked his head. "Us?"

"You and me. Our life together before… Do you remember, Michael?"

He straightened, pushed away enough to look into her eyes. "The dream," he said, his brow ridges coming together.

"The dream?"

He stared at her another long moment as if arranging images in his brain. "I'm hurtling down a wall of water, a massive wave at my back, the world and everything in it vanishing against the thrill and possibility of catastrophic danger. It comes often, always the same, and I never quite reach the bottom… And then after… after… there was… *you*."

"It's a memory, Michael. Not a dream. You were a world class surfer. One of the best. You surfed Maverick's among an elite few. You traveled the world, and then yes, you came home. To me."

"Mavericks is real?"

"That break. That massive wave. Yes. That's a real place. A real memory. The beacon? Like you said. I think that's where it leads."

His breath visibly quickened as he took her words in. "Yes," he said, his voice rough with emotion, his limbs fairly shaking with realization. "We can go there. These wings, these bodies. They will take us there."

She swallowed hard, stared into his intense eyes. "I don't know what's there after all this time, but I feel it, too. The force we perceive as a beacon is the driving force behind the monarchs' migration. It takes them back to the place they started. It leads back to us," she said, her voice husky with emotion. Her body shuddered as a warm ripple raced down her back and over her hips. "Once it starts up again, I doubt it will let us go."

"Then we better take care of business, before the beacon takes over."

"Take care of business?"

He pulled her close again. Feeling his heat through the sensitive outer layers of her new skin melded her like a magnet. A magnet she couldn't have resisted if she wanted to. The realization sent shockwaves through her system.

"I've missed you, Lara," he whispered against her neck. "Even in this new skin." He ran his hand back up to her shoulders, traced his fingers over her jaw, and tilted her face to his. If she looked anything like he did—and she had to assume she did—then he'd be seeing a face familiar, but not quite human; bejeweled eyes, a smooth head with graceful antennae seeking out every nuance, a mouth open and eager. "I remember you," he said again, his voice a deep rumble in his chest. "If you're not ready for this, I can wait, but you need to tell me now because, this body seems to have an instinct all its own and I'm not sure how much control—"

And like him, her body answered, lifting to fit herself against him. It was crazy, it was irresistible, it was absolutely unreal. This new body of hers, its new contours, feathery scales, urgings, longings, could not refuse him even if her old self was afraid. And as if to back up the feeling, heat surged within her, driving her on. There was already no turning back.

"I'm... ready," she said on a gasp, and slid her hands around his neck again, bringing his mouth to hers. "I am so damn ready."

In one powerful move, he scooped his hand under her bottom, lifted her against him, and walked them slowly to his bed.

Lost in desire, they rolled together, different but the same. His mouth on hers, deepening the kiss until she could scarcely breathe, then traveling down to her breasts, giving each attention. This was Michael, all the way, his need expanding with hers, his hands sliding over her ribs, her stomach. He broke the kiss, pulled back and stared into her eyes, his desire reflected there for only her to see. Then, like he had done so many times before, he rolled her over, kissed the back of her neck, skimmed his hands down her stomach, and pulled her to her knees in one sweeping movement that was as exhilarating as it was sudden. She arched her back and pressed into him, knowing what he wanted, what pleased him, what would please her.

"Lara," he moaned, gripping her hips, "My god, Lara." He slid one hand to her hips and pinned her against him. He was hot and heavy, pressed gently but firmly against her, the other hand sliding around to find her wet heat, then plunging fingers into her, slowly at first, then faster and faster. They rocked together as the heat built between them and her legs felt as though they would melt underneath her.

"Yes!" she cried out, one hand gripping the back of his thigh, heat waves rippling through her sex. "Please," she begged, breathless, her mind crazy with desire. "Michael, now. God, please. I need you inside me now!"

With a moan that could have been an animal growl, he slipped his hand away and returned it to her hips, then thrust inside her in one slick, solid movement. Her swollen muscles clamped tight around him and they began to rock together until, like turning up the heat on the grill, they were close to boiling over. And then, with a rush she had never felt before, the heat transitioned to something entirely new. There was animal need, but there was also a sensation so raw and inexplicable she stopped trying to define it and gave herself over.

She closed her eyes, her mind exploding in a full spectrum of brilliant, pulsing light. Every other sensation gave way to the link between them—a hot, vibrating connection that radiated around them in a building wave that transcended the physical world to a separate reality without any boundaries. On and on they rode the wave together, the rest of the world, their memories—past and present—disappeared under the intensity until, weak with longing and desire, another separate pulse began to keep time with their own.

She opened her eyes and saw it barreling toward them, the rolling beacon of light racing toward them, lifting them up, carrying them along, turning them over, letting them go, again and again and again.

"Do you see it," he asked, his voice husky with desire. "Do you feel it?"

"Yes," she answered, her sex ripe with longing at the center of her being.

"Then let go," he whispered. "It's time."

"Yes," she gasped, and gave herself over to the sweeping wave as they crashed over the wave together, plunging into a turbulent foam of brilliant, ultraviolet light.

✿

Lara lay on her back, breathless, watching Michael fill a pitcher of cool water through his kitchen window. When she was at last able to speak, she said, "That was... I don't know, not our usual round of lovemaking."

He paced across the kitchen and poured her a cup of water while he drank from the pitcher. "No wonder there are so many monarchs."

Lara laughed, thinking about the thousands of golden wings draping the branches and leaves of eucalyptus trees near her lighthouse home on the coast. "I'd suggest we do it again, but I don't think I can move right now."

He sat next to her on the bed and rubbed her low back. "We've got a lot of time to make up for, but maybe not just now," he said on a low laugh, and the warm sound of it gave her hope. Hope for themselves and hope for the Dannais. She leaned into his caress and sipped from her glass.

Footsteps sounded near the entrance to the grotto, and then there was knock on the plank doors. They looked at each other, eyes wide, antenna turned toward the sound.

"Wait right here," he said, grabbing his wrap off the bedpost and wrapping it around his hips. He opened the door to find Rowan standing there, Ekiria holding his hand.

"What is it? What's happened?"

Rowan pushed his dreadlocks off his face and licked his lips. "It's the crysls. They've emerged. Dozens of them. They're all up on the high meadow."

CHAPTER 41 - THE FIRST WAVE

Jenera stood overlooking High Meadow, Bryn by her side, pride filling every corner of her heart and soul. The meadow was aflutter with golden wings; some spread wide open, reflecting the sun, others closed up tight, revealing their dusty undersides; each under wobbly control of a young, yet completely formed *Dannais*. They were there because she'd cared for them, fought for them, devoted her life to them. And, if Lara's story was true, they were never supposed to exist. Yet here they were, oblivious to their benefactor. And it was a good thing, because after the last few days, she was so exhausted, she doubted she would be much help to them if they needed it.

"They're not quite what I expected," she admitted quietly. They had more than quadrupled in size since she'd first discovered their discarded shells in shimmery flakes on the tower floor. She had climbed the winding stairs to unfurl its top and watched as they took flight one-by-one, straight to the meadow she had so lovingly cared for all her life. Now, their bodies were nearly as big as her own, and the dark spots on the lower wings of the males were larger and more distinct. The female bodies, like Lara's, were more golden in color, while the males, an iridescent green so dark it was nearly black.

Bryn just shook his head. "They look just like Michael and Lara to me."

Jenera stepped forward. "Oh, don't get me wrong. They are incredible. And yes. Human forms, adolescent versions of Michael and Lara. But there's something different about them and it has nothing to do with their appearance. Listen."

Bryn stared at her a moment. She could see fatigue in his eyes, too, but as always, he was willing to indulge her. He cocked his head and watched silently another moment, then shook his head. "I don't... hear anything."

She smiled back at him, nodding her head. "Exactly."

He sent her a confused look.

"They don't need words to communicate. Watch a moment, over there." She indicated a male and female a few yards away.

As if in a dance, their antennae bobbed gracefully over their heads, leaning toward one another, their wings dipped and swirled as they lifted off the ground together then drifted down to land on their feet.

"They remind me of the young girls dancing around the brazier at the milkiweed festival," she said.

"Yes, they do," Bryn agreed, with new interest.

Jenera continued to watch in admiration. "They're selecting mates, pairing up, all without speaking a word."

Sloan, looking for all he was worth just as exhausted as she felt, took up a place next to Bryn. "Wow. This is incredible, and you're right," he said, excitement building in his voice. "Once they form a pair, they move off to the side." He indicated the space near the far end of the meadow. "They do talk, though, see?

You can see their mouths moving. Oh, that pair just kissed."

Sloan's eyes met Jenera's with a satisfied smile. "And look at those two, over there," he said, pointing out another pair. "They've deflated their wings, and they're walking like Michael and Lara. Did you see it? He found her a sprig of milkiweed. She's eating it. See?"

Jenera's heart squeezed a little, a wave of unexpected loneliness setting in. Right now, in this moment, Bryn stood beside her, holding her hand. But there would come a day... She pushed the thought down where it couldn't take away from this moment.

"Yes, I saw." She pulled them back into the shade. "Let's let them sort themselves out without gawking. I feel like I'm intruding."

Bryn squeezed her hand, and together, they retreated to the edge of the meadow and took up seats on a granite slab near the spring where they could witness the incredible event without disturbing the participants.

"You did good Jenera," Sloan said softly, his voice full of admiration. "They look healthy and strong, and they came straight out to the meadow just like you wanted."

Jenera shook her head, her smile widening. "Oh, I can't take credit for that. By the time I realized what was happening, they had already devoured the milkiweed in the tower, their wings had inflated and dried, and they had made their way to the top and taken off. I didn't give them any guidance at all." She watched in total amazement for another long, silent moment. "What we are witnessing is next level."

"Like Michael and Lara," Sloan confirmed.

"I'm... not so sure. I haven't spoken privately with Lara at all since she and Michael found each other.

They were human before they were transformed into what they are today. Lara explained to me that her *Dannais* instincts were strong, but, at least before she connected with Michael, her human side could override them. These *Dannais* are completely new beings. Their bodies look human, but their behavior isn't learned. It's nature."

"But they could have human memories, couldn't they? I mean, they had human ancestors at some point, right?"

Bryn propped his chin up on his hands. "You mean, like they know where to go because their cells remember?"

"I mean genetic memory. My dad wrote all about it."

"These *Dannais*," she went on, indicating the activity on the meadow with a sweep her arm, "they definitely have human genes. But they have more *Dannais* than human which leads me to believe they will be governed more by instinct than memory."

Sloan sent her a doubtful look shrugging a shoulder. "It depends. According to my father's diary, Lara and Michael's doses were accidental, unplanned. Even mine was crap shoot. But later, he experimented with doses, delivery, how much, how deep."

He shifted his gaze to the tiny vessel around Jenera's neck. "That amulet you're wearing? That's an entirely different formula. Low volume, high strength, faster turnaround. It's all in my dad's journals."

Jenera stared at it now, a tiny thread of hope forming in her mind.

Bryn's eyes widened. He grabbed Sloan by the shoulders. "You're saying a human could transform in this present lifetime using that serum?"

Sloan winced at the pressure from Bryn's hands, until he eased up a bit. "So what I'm saying is we should go back to the vault, study his papers, the formulas, there could be a way to—"

Jenera grabbed Bryn's arm, pulled him away. "Guys, look."

Out on the meadow, every pair of *Dannais* stood alert, faces lifted to the sky, antennae stretched. In the distance, two figures sailed in the morning sky, growing larger as they made their way.

"It's them," a gruff voice said behind her. And she turned to see Rowan approaching, Ekiria at his heels, and what looked like nearly the entire village making their way toward the meadow.

The pair circled lower until one broke away coming toward them, while the other continued to circle.

Lara landed in front of them, her wings fully extended, her golden scales shining in the morning sun. Jenera stood speechless, marveling at the sight. The woman she had met at Cora's cave was still there, as was the woman who'd spoken at the podium a few days before. But now, there was something different, something transcendent and beyond human, both frightening and benevolent.

Her eyes connected with each one of them in turn, Rowan, Ekiria, Bryn, Sloan, and finally, Jenera. "I'm truly sorry for making you wait, Spirit Leader. But as you can see," she said, indicating her wings and faceted limbs, "I had some adjustments to make."

Then her eyes fell on Sloan. "Come here young man."

He took a deep breath and stepped forward. "My father wrote about you in his diary. He didn't mean to hurt you. Not any of you."

She rested her hands on his shoulders and her smile seemed to light the entire meadow. "I know. None of that matters now. He wanted me to find you and look after you, too. But it seems you are in good hands now," she said, smiling at Jenera.

A light flashed across the sky and those of the *Dannais* gene registered it with varying degrees of attention.

Lara stepped back. "The beacon calls, my friends. I don't know whether we—any of us--will return," she said, indicating the newly emerged *Dannais* on the meadow. Jenera felt rather than heard the words, because Lara's mouth did not move at all in the delivery. "The beacon of the First Wave of *Dannus Plexipus Sapiens* calls and we will follow as we cannot do otherwise." And then she fixed her magnificent, faceted eyes on Jenera, so penetratingly direct she could scarcely breathe. "But I do know that whatever happens, my heart and soul will never forget you, Spirit Leader. Follow the legends, learn all you can, and some day, when the next wave is ready, perhaps we will meet again."

"Wait!" Ekiria yelped and pushed past Jenera. "You have to take these with you!" She looped a woven satchel over her head and passed it reverently to Lara. "It's milkiweed seeds. If the legends are true, there might not be any where you're going. We've been collecting them for you."

Jenera gazed at her, mouth agape. In all the excitement, she'd forgotten. Now the feisty youngster had stepped up. Heart brimming with love and pride, she put her hands on Ekiria's shoulders and pulled her into her arms. "Good work, Eki. You will make a good Spirit Leader one day."

Lara gave the young girl a gentle smile. "Indeed, she will."

Lara looped the satchel over her shoulder and secured it across her body so as not to impinge her wings, then without further words, she lifted into the air, and with one last look at them, her wings spread, lifted her up and away over the other winged creatures on the meadow.

Ekiria covered her mouth and watched in awe. "Do you think they will really come back to us?"

Jenera smoothed a hand over Ekiria's head, careful not to disturb the antennae straining toward the retreating wings. "They must, little one. Like the snow comes in winter, and the flowers in spring, they are governed by instincts millions of years old."

And then, like a ray of dawn streaming down through tall trees, a bright strobe of light swept across the meadow. Lara joined Michael and hovered over the fluttering young ones below. As the next beacon of light swept through, the entire group lifted together like a fluttering golden cloud. On the next sweep, in a whoosh of flickering wings, they followed it high into the sky, above the trees, above the granite canyons.

Jenera could feel the energy of the entire village behind her as she gathered her beloved family and close friends about her. Rowan, who had carried the torch for so long, and her aunt Helena who had supported him; Ekiria, so young and full of energy and spunk, and Sloan whose canny brilliance had led them to the vault; and finally, Bryn, her lifelong friend, constant companion, the full human who had proven his loyalty beyond any shadow of doubt.

"Did you see it?" Ekiria squealed, taking Sloan's hand. "That pretty light?"

Sloan let go a laugh and spun her around, picking up her excitement. "Yes, I saw it. Who couldn't?"

Jenera pressed the amulet between her fingers and held her breath a moment. Bryn circled his arm around her shoulders and covered her hand on the amulet. "Wherever you go, I go," he said. And then, as if giving his blessing, Rowan moved forward to embrace the two of them as they watched the golden cloud rise even higher, then turn toward the great inland sea.

"Till we meet again," Jenera said, watching the last of the monarchs disappear out of sight. "Till we meet again."

Thank you for reading Monarch – The First Migration. I hope you enjoyed the reading it as much as I enjoyed the writing. Authors thrive on reviews. It would make me very happy if you'd take a moment to visit the Kat Drennan Author page on Amazon and leave a rating or review. You can also signup for my newsletter at www.katdrennanbooks.com.

ABOUT THE AUTHOR

Kat Drennan writes sensual stories set where fantasy and romance meet.

From the curling surf at the edge of the continent, to the granite sculptures of the Sierra Nevada; from San Francisco to Death Valley and all the way to the Mexican border and beyond, California's unique landscape and colorful, dramatic history step forward as characters in each of her novels.

She is an alumna of the Squaw Valley Community of Writers, and Romance Writers of America, where she was a past Secretary of the Contemporary Romance Writers Chapter of RWA.

Based in Ojai, California, Kat loves her Master's swim team girlies, cycling tours with her Hunky Boy, Fred.

She loves to hear from her readers. You can follow her at www.katdrennanbooks.com, sign up for her newsletter to find out about new releases, or follow her Facebook page: @katdrennan to leave a comment and hear about new releases, freebies, and other promotions.

www.ingramcontent.com/pod-product-compliance
Lightning Source LLC
Chambersburg PA
CBHW051057030726
47504CB00006B/1669